SOUTH OF THE RIVER

Although her mother does not approve of Fred Simpson, Mary Bates is sure her love for him is right and that things will work out in the end. When Fred is accused of cowardice, Mary's life is turned upside down. Her brother, Tom, is finding his new job full of temptations and George Taylor's brother Philip is, as usual, up to no good, threatening to plunge the family into disaster. Set in Southwark in 1903, this is the continuing saga of the Taylors and their cockney neighbours, the Clarkes, who made their first appearance in *Old Father Thames*.

SOUTH OF THE RIVER

SOUTH OF THE RIVER

by

Sally Spencer

Magna Large Print Books
Long Preston, North Yorkshire,
England.

British Library Cataloguing in Publication Data.

Spencer, Sally
South of the river.

A catalogue record for this book is
available from the British Library

ISBN 0-7505-1378-0

First published in Great Britain by Orion, an imprint of Orion
Books Ltd., 1997

Published in Large Print 1999 by arrangement with Orion Publishing
Group Ltd.

Magna Large Print is an imprint of
Library Magna Books Ltd.
Printed and bound in Great Britain by
T.J. International Ltd., Cornwall, PL28 8RW.

This book is dedicated to all the people who have helped and encouraged me in my writing, but especially to Katie Garrett, Peter Kaleta, Isabel Miller, David Morgan, Gitte Morgan, Marie Garcia Woods and Katie Pope

PROLOGUE

Spring 1903

The scissors-grinder had parked his cart on the corner of Southwark Bridge Road and was pumping furiously on his foot pedal. In his right hand he held a carving knife that a washerwoman had just given to him, and as he pressed it against his rotating grindstone, sparks flew off in all directions.

He was not the only honest street trader trying to scrape a living on that mild spring day.

The salt-seller pushed his handcart from door to door, chipping a little off his huge block here, and a little there, until he had sold a couple of pounds.

A fishmonger, standing between the handles of his cart, announced to all the world that his fish were so fresh that 'it's a wonder they ain't still floppin' about'.

A street entertainer popped a piece of broken glass into his mouth in the expectation of earning a few coppers from the small crowd which had gathered round him, while a watercress-vendor held out his basket in the hope of tempting passers-by, and a sweep, his brushes over his shoulder, examined the skyline for badly smoking chimneys.

Nettie Walnut, ignoring all these diversions, turned left by Southwark fire station, and made her way towards number thirty-six, Lant

Place, where she was certain there would be a warm welcome and a cup of tea awaiting her.

Nettie was a tramp—but no ordinary one. As she told anyone who would listen, her family had been vagrants for well over two hundred years—and if they didn't believe her, they'd only to check the records that St Saviour's Workhouse kept of its casual paupers.

Nettie had reached her destination. She knocked on the door, and waited patiently. There was the sound of footsteps coming up the passageway, then the door opened and Colleen Taylor was standing there.

'Nettie!' Colleen said. 'I didn't expect to see you round here at this time of year.'

'I's 'ere to see your babies, isn't I?'

'Then you'd better come in.'

Nettie followed Colleen down the passage to the kitchen. The twins were both there, Ted crawling around on the floor, and Cathy sitting in her highchair.

'I 'asn't seen them since the day they was born,' Nettie said. ' 'Asn't they grown?'

'They have,' Colleen agreed. 'It'll soon be their first birthday, and they're becomin' more of a handful with every day that passes.'

Nettie looked around the kitchen. 'Your 'usband at the wood yard on the 'Ibernia Wharf, is 'e?' she asked.

'That's right,' Colleen agreed.

'What's 'e want to go down there for?'

Colleen laughed. 'Because that's where he works.'

Nettie nodded her head sagely. 'Yes, I believe there is people who 'as to work for a livin'.'

Colleen picked up the kettle and headed over to the sink. 'Fancy a cup of tea?'

'I's not bothered either way,' Nettie said, 'but if you's makin' one, I supposes I might as well.'

Colleen filled the kettle and put it on the range. 'So where have you been since we last saw you, Nettie?' she asked.

' 'Ere an' there,' the old tramp said vaguely. She stuffed some evil-looking tobacco into her old clay pipe, and struck a match on the heel of her boot. 'I likes to see different places. That's why I wouldn't go into the work'ouse fulltime, even though they thinks the world of me in there.'

Colleen smiled. 'Would you like a nice piece of bread an' marge, Nettie?'

'If you's 'aving some.' The old woman looked down at Ted, and then up at Cathy in her highchair. 'Does you want me to tell your little babies' fortunes for you?'

'Is it really possible to read their fortunes when they're so young?'

' 'Course it is. Their futures is written in their palms the moment they's born.'

Colleen picked up a loaf and reached across to the Welsh dresser for the bread knife. 'Go on, then, tell me what you see,' she said. 'It might be a bit of fun.'

Nettie squatted down next to Ted, who stopped crawling around and looked up in fascination at the brown-skinned woman with the clay pipe in her mouth.

'Don't be frightened, my little one,' the old tramp crooned, gently taking his hand. 'Nettie don't want to 'urt, I just wants to see if you's goin' to be 'appy.'

Colleen cut an extra-thick slice off the loaf—Nettie always liked it that way. 'What does it say?' she asked.

'I sees a long life for him. It's in this line 'ere,' Nettie told her, tracing her finger along Ted's palm. ' 'E'll give you a lot of grandchildren, this one.'

She released Ted's hand, and walked over to the highchair where Cathy was sitting.

'And what about you, my precious?' she asked. 'Is you goin' to 'ave babies an' all?'

Cathy gurgled happily, and didn't look the least worried when Nettie took her pudgy little hand.

Nettie had read Ted's palm immediately, but she stood gazing at Cathy's for some time, as if she was searching for a different answer to the first one she'd found.

'Well?' Colleen asked.

'Daft thing, fortune tellin',' Nettie said. 'I sometimes don't know why I does it,' and then she released Cathy's hand and headed towards the back door.

'Are you goin'?' Colleen asked.

'Yes, I 'as to be on my way,' the old woman replied, in a shaky voice.

'But what about your tea?'

'It's not tea that I's wantin' right now. I's off to 'ave a glass of gin.'

PART ONE

All Change!

CHAPTER 1

Lant Place was not a big street by London standards, but the people who lived there liked it well enough. It started at the corner of Southwark Bridge Road, crossed Sturge Street and Queen's Court, and then came to a dead end. The terraced houses had been built as two-up, two-downs, but over the years, several of them had had kitchen extensions added. Many of the residents took in lodgers, giving the paying guests the front bedrooms and settling themselves in the back, from where they overlooked their own yards and the yards of Grotto Place.

The houses all had tiny front gardens. Some of them—like Lil Clarke's—were as lovingly cared for as if they'd been the grounds of stately homes. Others were treated as nothing more than dumping sites for things like broken furniture and rusty prams, which people couldn't bear to throw away, yet no longer wanted in their houses.

There were no manufactories on Lant Place, unlike the much bigger Lant Street, where there was both a patent leather factory and a corkmaker's. It was a good thing there weren't any factories, Lil Clarke often thought, because somehow it wasn't quite *respectable* to have that kind of thing going on close to your own doorstep.

Annie Bates plumped up the cushion she'd painstakingly embroidered with poppies, then looked around her front parlour. The anti-macassars were straight on both the mock-leather sofa and the matching armchairs. The rag rug in front of the tiled fireplace had been given a thorough scrubbing and was as good as new. The ornaments in the display cabinet positively gleamed, and the picture of the sailing ship, which she'd bought down at the market the day before, now hung pleasingly on the wall opposite the window.

The cushion with the poppies on it still didn't look right. Annie picked it up and rearranged it again.

'Stop yer fussin', Annie,' her husband Tom told her. 'Everyfink's fine for the party as it is.'

Annie smiled. 'It might be fine to your eyes, but it won't be to my mum's.'

Tom grinned back at her. 'I'll tell yer what I'll do for yer, then. I'll make sure that the very first person 'oo arrives parks 'is bottom on that chair, then yer mum won't even be able to *see* the cushion.'

'Very clever,' Annie said. 'And what about the rest of the room? How are you going to hide *that* from the famous Lil Clarke tour of inspection?'

'Yer worry too much.'

A slight frown came to Annie's face. 'Oh, I know I do. It's just that I feel so guilty.'

'Guilty? What 'ave *you* got to feel guilty about?'

'You work so hard on the river, and all I have to do is look after the house.'

'An' a smashin' job yer make of it.'

'I don't want it to be just smashin'. I want it to be absolutely perfect.'

Tom put his arms around her. 'It *is* perfect—as long as you're 'ere in it.'

Annie kissed his neck. 'I love you.'

'An' I love you.'

They had been married exactly a year to the day, which was the reason for the party which Annie was getting herself into such a state about.

The sound of several sets of footsteps coming down the street alerted Annie.

'That'll be the first guests,' she said, breaking away from her husband—though what she really wanted to do was to ask him to carry her upstairs and make love to her.

Annie walked over to the fireplace and checked her appearance in the engraved mirror. A pretty girl—with naturally springy hair the colour of dark chocolate, and green eyes which seemed almost to glow—stared back at her, and looking over the pretty girl's shoulder was a man with jet-black hair, brown eyes and a strong chin.

'Don't worry. You look a real picture,' Tom said.

There was a knock at the front door. 'If only I'd had another half hour to get things really straight!' Annie said.

Tom grinned again. 'Yer could 'ave 'ad another *day*, an' yer'd still not 'ave been ready,' he told her as he stepped into the passage to open the front door.

Standing on the pavement outside were all four of Tom's family: May, his widowed mother; Joey, his younger brother, who desperately wanted to be a boxer; and his two younger sisters, Mary and Doris.

' 'Ow's the 'atbox business, Mum?' Tom asked, as he led the family into the front room.

'Terrible,' his mother told him. 'There just ain't no call for 'atboxes at the moment.'

'So what are yer doin' to earn a livin' now?'

'Makin' paper flowers. An' on a Friday, I boil up beetroot an' sell it down at the New Cut market.'

Tom shook his head in admiration. When his dad had died, his mum had converted their front parlour into her own little factory, and now she made anything and everything from brushes to fly paper, according to demand.

'Yer've got the place lookin' very nice, I'll say that for yer,' May said to Annie, glancing around the front room.

Tom gave his wife a look which said that he had told her as much himself.

'I had good training,' Annie said, thinking of her mother's front room, which was crammed with far too much furniture—most of which they still owed the tallyman for.

The Taylors turned up next. George had lost part of his left leg at the Battle of Omdurman, but he managed to get around fine on the wooden one which had replaced it—even if it did look like he'd stolen it from an old-fashioned

Victorian table. Colleen had a lovely smile, despite her large nose. She had been brought up in her father's pub in Cheshire, and now worked as a part-time barmaid in the Goldsmiths' Arms.

'So how are the kids?' Annie asked Colleen.

'A real handful,' Colleen admitted. 'I love 'em dearly, but sometimes it's a pleasure to leave 'em an' go to work.'

'Who looks after them while you're out at the Goldsmiths'?'

'A girl who lives on Southwark Bridge Road. I don't pay her much, but I think her family's glad of the money.'

'Yes, with the way things are on the river, I expect they are,' Annie said.

She didn't explain—she didn't have to. Everyone in Southwark understood how much the mighty Thames could affect their lives. When the river was busy—when there was work for the dockers and watermen—then the costermongers sold all their wares and the clog dancers soon filled their caps with coppers. But when trade was in recession—as it was that summer—people lived on fish instead of meat and were always out when the rent man came round.

Another knock on the front door announced the arrival of the Clarke family, who lived at number thirty-four, and this time it was Annie who answered it.

'How are you getting on, Dad?' she asked, after she had kissed her father.

Sam Clarke's eyes flashed, like they always did when he was going to make a joke. 'Woolly 'eaded, that's 'ow I am.'

'Woolly headed?' Annie repeated, looking at her father's straight, thinning hair.

'Yer lookin' in the wrong place,' Sam said. 'It's *inside* me head I'm talkin' about.'

' 'E's been unloadin' a wool ship from New Zealand,' Lil Clarke explained.

'Goodness knows, I'm glad of the work,' Sam told his daughter, 'but so much of the wool 'as got up me nose that by now me brain must be full of it.'

Annie laughed. 'And how are you, Mum?' she asked.

Lil Clarke smiled. 'I'd be doin' fine if it wasn't for these cantankerous children of mine.'

She turned to look at the two children in question. Eddie, who had dark, tousled hair, and had just turned sixteen, was training to be an automobile mechanic. Peggy, in complete contrast, was much paler and fairer than her older sister, and had an other-worldly look about her, as if she belonged in a fairy story, rather than on the streets of Southwark.

'Just look how respectable yer sister is,' Lil said to her two younger children. 'An 'ouse of 'er own an' everyfink. That's what you should be aimin' for.'

Annie laughed again. 'They're still only kids, Mum.'

Eddie scowled at being called a kid, but it didn't seem to bother Peggy. Not much *ever* seemed to bother Peggy: as long as she had animals around her, she was quite content just to drift through the rest of life.

'It's never too early to start bein' respectable,'

Lil said firmly. 'Is it, Sam?'

Sam grinned. 'You mean like your china plate, Nettie Walnut?' he asked.

Even after nearly twenty years of marriage, Lil rarely noticed when Sam was making fun of her—and she didn't now. 'Well, Nettie *is* very respectable ... for a tramp,' she said weakly.

The front parlour was getting quite crowded, and there were still two more people to come, but nobody minded. It was nice to get together for a good rabbit every now and again. That was what families were for.

Tom Bates and Peggy Clarke were standing near the door.

' 'Ow's yer goat gettin' on?' Tom asked Peggy.

'Napoleon's doin' luverly,' Peggy said enthusiastically. 'It was ever so kind of yer to give 'im to me.'

'An' it was ever so kind of *you* to be one of the bridesmaids at my wedding.'

'Think nuffink of it,' Peggy said, but it was goats, not weddings, that she wanted to talk about. 'When Napoleon's finished growin', I'm goin' to get a cart an' charge all the kids in the street a farthin' to go for rides in it.'

'Yer should make a fortune,' Tom said, trying not to laugh. 'What are yer goin' to do with the money?'

Peggy checked around the room to make sure her mother, who was sitting near the fireplace, couldn't overhear her, then said, 'I'm startin' me own zoo.'

'An' where are yer goin' to 'ave this zoo?'

Peggy looked at him as if he'd lost his marbles. 'In our back yard, o' course.'

Tom shook his head doubtfully. 'I can't see yer mum ever allowin' that.'

'I'll only be keepin' little animals,' Peggy said. 'It's not like I want an elephant or nuffink. Mum won't mind.'

'Is that right? Then why are we whisperin'?'

'She won't mind in the *end*. I'm just givin' 'er a bit of time to get used to the idea.'

Annie was half-listening to Tom's sister Mary talk about life at Stevenson's match factory, but what she was really thinking was how much Mary had changed in the last year or so.

When they'd first met, Mary had been nothing more than a child, who still had her puppy fat and wore her short blonde hair straight. Now the fat had melted completely away, the hair was in curls which cascaded down to her shoulders, and what had once appeared to be nothing more than a cute little button nose was rapidly developing into her best feature.

'It's that Miss 'Unt, 'oo really gets me,' Mary was explaining. 'She's always pickin' on me ...'

'She always did pick on the pretty girls,' Annie said, thinking back to her own days in the factory.

'... an' some days, I get so fed up with it all. I just feel like screamin'.'

'I'm sure you do,' Annie said sympathetically. 'Why don't you leave, like I did?'

'It ain't that easy when yer've got no trainin'.'

'I hadn't got any training when I joined the telephone company,' Annie said, although that was not quite true. She'd had no training in operating switchboards, but before they'd ever agreed to take her on, she'd had to have elocution lessons from Miss Crosby, her old board school teacher.

'That was a good job yer 'ad at the exchange,' Mary said. 'It's a real shame that you 'ad to lose it.'

'It was company policy,' Annie told her. 'They just don't employ married women.'

'Well, they should 'ave more sense. Losin' a good worker like you, just 'cos yer've got an 'usband—that's plain silly.'

And a great pity, too, Annie thought. She and Tom could certainly have used the extra money she would have earned. Besides, she'd never been used to staying home all day, and, if she was honest with herself, it was starting to bore her.

'How's that young fireman of yours getting on?' she asked Mary.

Like Peggy earlier, Mary glanced quickly across the room to see if her mother was in earshot. 'Fred's doin' fine,' she said, almost in a whisper.

'So what's the problem? Doesn't your mum like you going out with him?'

Mary sighed. 'Me mum wouldn't like it if I was goin' out with the Prince of Wales.'

Annie laughed. 'Quite right, too: he's far too old for you. But what's your mum got against Fred Simpson?'

'She thinks I'm too young to start 'avin' boyfriends, but you wasn't much older than me when yer started goin' out with our Tom, was yer?'

'No, I wasn't,' Annie agreed, 'but my mum didn't like that any more than your mum likes you seeing Fred. You just have to give mums time to get used to things, Mary.'

'I'll 'ave grey 'air by the time *my* mum thinks I'm ready for a boyfriend,' Mary said wistfully.

The last two guests to arrive were Harry Roberts and Belinda Benson. Harry, a powerful figure with sandy hair, was a sergeant in the river police—or the Wet Bobs, as they were known. He had once been in love with Annie, but despite that, he had still helped prove that his rival, Tom, had not committed the murder that he'd been imprisoned for.

Belinda was an 'honourable', though she never used the title. She was what people called a 'big-boned' girl, and though no one could deny that her face was attractive, every single feature which made it up seemed larger than life. She had worked as a telephone operator with Annie and now spent a lot of time with Harry—'giving him his supper', as she liked to put it, which was a nice way of saying she was doing something nice girls didn't do, and couldn't give a hang about what anybody thought of it.

'Have you finished preparing the food yet?' Belinda asked Annie as they stood in the passageway.

'I was just getting around to it.'

'Good, then I've arrived just in time to give you a hand.' Belinda turned to Harry. 'You go through to the front room,' she said bossily. 'Annie and I have some work to do.'

'An' no doubt some gossip to exchange,' Harry said with a knowing grin.

'Possibly, but since most of it will be about you, and I know how modest you are, it's better said out of your hearing. So why don't you save yourself the blushes and go and make yourself amenable to the rest of the guests?'

'Yes ma'am,' Harry said, saluting smartly, then opening the parlour door.

Belinda and Annie walked down the passageway to the kitchen.

'I must say, you two seem to be getting on very well together,' Annie commented.

'Oh, we are,' Belinda agreed. 'I was no innocent flower when I met our Sergeant Roberts, but the things he's shown me in the last twelve months ...'

'Belinda!'

'Oh, don't come the blushing virgin with me,' Belinda said airily. 'From the looks of him, your Tom can put on a good show when he wants to.'

Annie smiled. Belinda could be simply impossible sometimes, but she was never going to change, so you just had to accept her for what she was.

The food—eel pie, oysters, cold cuts of beef and ham—was already out on the kitchen table, and all that remained to do was to arrange it tastefully on Annie's best plates.

'Have your family met Harry?' Annie asked, as she stretched up to reach the crockery on the top shelf of the Welsh dresser.

'They haven't actually met him, but I've certainly told them all about him.'

'And what did they say?'

'What did they say? What do you *think* they said when they learned that their high-bred daughter was going out with a common policeman? They were outraged.' Belinda chuckled. 'I think that's part of what makes it all so much fun.'

In the front parlour, Tom and Harry were talking about the river, where both of them felt much more comfortable than they did on dry land.

'I tell yer, it's gettin' 'arder an' 'arder to make ends meet as a waterman,' Tom said. 'Sometimes—like now, for instance—traffic on the river's so slack that yer can go for hours without pickin' up a passenger.'

'That's what I like about my job,' Harry said. 'Yer never spend any time just 'angin' around.'

'An' when yer do get to row somebody out to their ship, they usually act like they was doin' yer a favour by even gettin' in yer boat,' Tom complained.

'Well, if yer not 'appy, then maybe it's time you was lookin' for some other line o' work?' Harry suggested.

'I agree with yer. But what?'

Harry hesitated for a second. ' 'Ave yer considered joinin' the Wet Bobs?'

'Me? In the river police?'

'Why not? Yer a smart lad an' a good rower. Yer'd take to it like a fish to water.'

'Yer forgettin' me criminal record,' Tom said. 'First of all, there's the twelve-month suspended sentence for the fight I got into with Rollo Jenkins an' his gang. An' then, of course, there was the murder charge.'

'You wasn't guilty of that, so it don't count, an' as for that other matter—yer suspended sentence—I was just thinkin' that now I've got a bit of influence in the Force, we might be able to find some way of overlookin' that.'

'Yer'd be takin' a chance, puttin' my name forward. Are you willin' to do that?'

Harry shrugged awkwardly. 'Why not? If yer can't go out on a bit of a limb for the bloke 'oo asked yer to be the best man at 'is weddin', 'oo can yer go out on a limb for? So what do yer say? Do yer fancy joinin' the Wet Bobs?'

Tom thought about it. As a river policeman he would be getting regular wages instead of being at the mercy of the wharfingers and sailors he normally had to rely on. And police work might be more interesting than ferrying people to and fro.

'Well, *do* yer want to give it a try?' Harry asked.

'Do yer know, 'Arry, I rather think I do,' Tom replied.

Eddie Clarke and Joey Bates did not really know each other very well, but as the only two lads at the party, they had naturally drifted towards one corner of the parlour together. They were about the same age, but they were far from the same size. Eddie was small and wiry, with the hands of an artist. Joey, thanks to his weight training, had grown four inches since his brother's marriage, and had fists as hard as house bricks.

'I'm goin' to 'ave me first fight soon,' Joey said.

'Yer first fight?'

'Yes. I'm goin' to be a boxer.'

'I see,' Eddie said.

'Somefink wrong with that?'

Eddie shrugged his shoulders. 'Nuffink, I suppose. Leastways, not if your idea of fun is to step in a ring an' 'ave some bloke beat 'ell out of yer.'

'An what's your idea of fun?' Joey demanded. 'Tinkerin' about with motorcars all day? That's no life for a man. It ain't natural, neither. If God 'ad wanted us to 'ave motors, 'e'd 'ave put 'em in 'orses.'

The two boys glared at each other.

'Boxin',' Eddie scoffed.

'Motorcars,' Joey retaliated.

Each of them looked around, deciding where to go next. Back to their mums? That was unthinkable. Go and join Harry and Tom? From the way they were talking to each other, it didn't seem as if they would welcome the intrusion. So it looked, Joey and Eddie thought

30

simultaneously, as if they were stuck with each other.

It was Eddie who broke the silence. 'No point in fallin' out now that we're related, is there?'

Joey grinned. 'Naw. Each to 'is own, that's what I say.' He hesitated for a second. 'Will yer come an' watch me first fight? Only, I could do with a bit o' support to egg me on.'

Eddie thought about it. He didn't want to see a boxing match, but the foundations of his newfound friendship were too shaky for him to refuse. 'I'll tell yer what,' he said finally. '*I'll* come an' watch yer first fight if *you'll* come down to the garage an' let me show yer the cars.'

Joey said, 'Yer've got a deal,' and the two boys solemnly shook hands.

Belinda and Annie carried the food into the parlour and placed it on the table, while Tom dispensed the drinks—mostly beer for the men and port and lemon for the women. The children stuck to plain lemonade, but not without a certain amount of indignant protest from Joey and Eddie.

'When yer twenty-one yer'll be old enough to drink,' Lil Clarke told her son.

'But our Annie's drinking, and she's not twenty-one,' Eddie protested.

'Annie's married,' his mother said. 'It's respectable to drink when yer married, 'owever old yer are. Ain't that right, Sam?'

'Whatever you say, me old dutch,' Sam replied, winking heavily at his son.

'Looks like if I ever want a pint, I'll 'ave to get 'itched first,' Eddie mumbled.

'What was that?' Lil demanded.

'Nuffink, Mum.'

Annie had prepared enough grub to feed an army, but somehow most of it managed to disappear, and by half-past six everyone was feeling bloated.

Harry went over to the window. 'I'd like to propose a toast,' he announced.

Belinda bent down, so her mouth was level with Peggy Clarke's ear. 'Oh Lord,' she whispered. 'Now the fat really is in the fire.'

'Men are devils for makin' toasts,' Peggy whispered back, remembering her sister's wedding.

'It's 'ard to believe it's exactly a year since Tom an' Annie got married,' Harry continued. 'Some'ow, the time just seems to fly by, don't it?'

'Not when you're listening to men make speeches,' Belinda whispered to Peggy.

Peggy giggled, and from the other side of the room, her mother shot her a hard stare.

'Well, they say that the first year makes or breaks a marriage,' Harry said, 'and yer've only to see the way Tom an' Annie still look at each other to realise there's not been much breakin' goin' on in this 'ouse. I think that's about all I've got to say ...'

'Hear, hear!' Belinda said, a little more loudly than she'd intended.

'... so now I'll give yer the toast. To Annie

and Tom. May all their troubles be little ones.'

They drank the toast, then Harry stepped aside, and Tom took his place.

'I'd like to thank yer all for comin',' he said, 'an' if I can propose a toast of me own, it's this. We've all been through some rough times in the past—what with me gettin' arrested an' everyfink—but the last year's been about as quiet as it could be. So let's 'ope things stay that way.'

'Yer temptin' fate,' Sam called across the room, and though he'd meant it as a joke, he was closer to the truth than he realised.

CHAPTER 2

The narrow ledge was eighty feet above the ground. Behind it was a small sloping roof which formed the apex of the Southwark Bridge Road Fire Headquarters, and in front there was nothing but a stomach-churning drop.

Fred Simpson was perfectly at home up there. In fact, if he'd had time, he would have climbed the sloping roof, because he knew from past experience that the view from the top of it was spectacular: St Paul's in one direction, and the Kennington Oval on the other; Lambeth Palace to his right, the Tower of London to his left. However, there was no time to climb up the roof: this was a fire drill, and the stopwatch was ticking.

Moving swiftly but carefully, Fred made his way along the ledge to where Archie Tucker, one of his comrades, was lying flat out. Once there, he bent down, picked the other man up and slung him over his shoulder.

'Don't you go botherin' about breakin' no records today,' Archie grunted to him. 'I'd rather get there slow than 'ave us both go fallin' over that edge.'

Fred grinned. 'Don't worry, Archie. I ain't never lost one of me customers yet.'

He walked quickly along the ledge to where a temporary sling had been erected, and slid Archie into its leather harness. Then, after wrapping the rope securely around his arms and back, he lowered Archie over the edge of the building.

'Remember: nice and slow,' the other man said.

Fred braced himself to take the weight. Archie was a big bloke—most of the firemen were—but he himself was a strong man with bulging muscles and a broad back, and, if he'd had to, he could have handled twice the load.

Fred began to let out the rope, and Archie, instead of being suspended just by the ledge, began to move towards the ground.

'Too fast, yer eager young bugger,' Archie shouted up. 'Much too fast.'

Fred grinned again. He might complain now, but Archie knew that in a real fire, with flames lapping all around them, speed such as he was employing would be very important. Archie also knew that drills like this were the only real opportunity the firemen were given to make sure they'd got their techniques right.

The other fireman bumped gently to the ground. Now it was time for Fred to get off the roof himself. He couldn't go by the sling, as Archie had done, because there was no one to operate it, so he'd have to go another way.

He looked down into the yard, and saw a group of firemen stretching out the jumping sheet. On other occasions, he'd held the sheet himself, so he knew just how big it was, but knowing something and seeing something were two entirely different things. Down on the ground, the sheet seemed huge. From the ledge, it looked no larger than a pocket handkerchief.

Fred stepped to the edge and launched himself into the air. It does not take a man long to fall three floors, yet there was time for him to feel the air whooshing past him and to see the ground looming up in front of him. Then he hit the sheet, bounced, and was soon back on his feet.

The captain consulted his brass stopwatch. 'Not bad, Simpson. Not bad at all.'

Fred beamed with pleasure. To be told that by the captain was almost as good as getting knighted by the King.

The station's recreation room, with its big old billiard table, was a popular gathering place for men who were off duty, but when Fred entered it, the only person sitting there was an ex-fireman called Bob Doyle.

Doyle was an ancient man with a mane of grey hair and a weather-beaten face. It was years since he'd retired from active duty, but he seemed unable to keep away from the fire station where he had spent most of his working life.

'I saw the way yer conducted yerself up on the roof,' Doyle said. 'I think it's just possible yer might 'ave the makin's of a good fireman in yer.'

'The captain said I wasn't bad,' Fred said.

Bob raised a bushy grey eyebrow. 'Did 'e, indeed? Not bad! Well, yer honoured.' He took a packet of Black Cat cigarettes out of his jacket pocket, and offered one to Fred. 'Tuppence 'a'penny for ten, these things cost nowadays,' he told the young fireman. 'Ain't that outrageous?'

Fred struck a match, lit the two cigarettes, and then sat down opposite Bob. 'We spend all our time complainin' about breathin' in smoke when we're workin',' he said, 'an' when we're off duty, what's the first thing we do? Why, we light up a fag!'

Bob coughed. 'You're right, there. Did I ever tell yer about the worst fire that I ever fought?'

'No. I don't think yer did.'

'It was the great Tooley Street fire of 'sixty-one,' the old man said. 'Yer've never seen anyfink like it. *Nobody* 'oo's workin' at this station now 'as seen anyfink like it.'

Fred took another drag on his cigarette. 'Yes, I 'eard it was pretty bad.'

'Bad? That ain't the word for it. It started in

Cotton's Wharf, an' before yer knew where yer was, it 'ad spread as far as 'Ay's Wharf—which is two 'undred yards if it's an inch. The real problem was in what they'd got stored there, yer see—cotton, sugar, tallow, rice, spices, jute an' 'emp.'

'Doesn't take much to start any of them things burnin' up,' Fred said.

'Oh, an' o' course saltpetre for good measure,' Bob continued. 'Well, like yer say, all them things burn as easy as anyfink, an' on top of that, we 'ad the problem of gettin' enough water to fight the bleedin' fire with.'

'But the fire must 'ave been right by the river.'

'It was.'

'Well, then?'

'Yer not thinkin', Fred.' Bob shook his head as if to say he really couldn't imagine where they found young firemen these days. ' 'Ow much of a difference is there between 'ighest an' lowest tide, would yer guess?'

'About twenty feet,' Fred estimated.

'Twenty feet nine inches, to be precise. Well, when the fire broke out it was *low* tide, an' we couldn't reach the river, could we? The only water we could get was out of 'Ay's Dock, an' all the time there was explosions and things meltin' like billy-oh. There was so many tons of molten tallow pourin' into the river that in the end it caught fire. An' if that wasn't bad enough, we 'ad the general public to deal with.'

'Gettin' in the way, were they?'

'They were doin' more than that. They were

takin' risks even we wouldn't have taken.'

'What d'yer mean?'

'They thought it was a great show, d'yer see, so they were 'iring watermen to row them out, so they could get a better view of it. Quite a lot of 'em got so close they were burned to death. There was more people lost their lives in the Tooley Street fire than ever did durin' the Great Fire of London.'

Fred whistled softly. 'I didn't know that.'

'Then the tide turned an' a lot of the tallow was washed away. Watermen as far as Millwall were collectin' it by the boatload.' Bob chuckled. 'Sellin' it, too, the crafty buggers. Tuppence 'a'penny a pound, they got for it. Mind you, you didn't even 'ave to be a waterman to collect it. All the roads round Tooley Street were ankle deep in tallow an' grease.'

' 'Ow long did it take you to finally get it under control?' Fred asked.

'Believe it or not, it was two bloody weeks before we 'ad it all extinguished,' Bob said. 'I can still remember the amount of the damage.' He closed his eyes. 'Eighteen thousand bales of cotton were destroyed, ten thousand barrels of tallow, five thousand tons of rice, three thousand tons of sugar, a thousand tons of 'emp, another thousand of jute, an' enough tea to quench the thirst of everybody in the country for a week.'

'Could it 'appen again?' Fred asked.

'No reason why not,' the old fireman replied. 'The equipment's better these days, an' maybe the fire regulations are bein' more strictly enforced, but them ware'ouses are still dealin' in the same kind of stuff, an' it'll burn just as easy as it ever did.' Bob rose creakily to his feet. 'I'd better be gettin' back to me lodgin's. Me landlady plays 'ell with me if I'm late.'

'An' we don't want that.'

'No,' Bob agreed. 'We bloody don't.'

The Goldsmiths' Arms, at the corner of Lant Place, was considered by most of the locals to be a good boozer. The first of its three entrances led into the public bar, where men could speak as they liked without worrying about offending their womenfolk, and—if they were in the mood—have a spirited game of snooker. The second entrance led into the saloon bar, the haunt of couples—courting and married—and of men who perhaps felt themselves a little superior to the rough blokes in the public. Finally, there was the jug and bottle department, where it was possible to see children as small as six struggling with the big jugs to be filled with beer for their thirsty parents.

'We'd be lost without the Goldsmiths',' Sam Clarke often said to George Taylor. 'Well, more than lost if the truth was told. I think we'd all go doolalli,' and he was right.

From her vantage point behind the bar, Colleen Taylor looked around the saloon of the Goldsmiths'. A lot of her regulars were in that night. There was Dick Todd, the milkman—and reputedly the worst-tempered man in Southwark—grumbling away at his beer, and Maggie White, who worked at the bath house and always came in for one drink on her way home—but *only* one. And there, in their usual corner, were Mary Bates and Fred Simpson.

Courting suited Fred, Colleen decided. When he'd first starting coming into the pub, he'd had such a baby face that if it hadn't been for his broad muscular body—which could only have belonged to a fully grown man—she might have refused to serve him. Since he'd been seeing Mary, however, his face seemed to have grown more adult, and now a long straight nose and firm mouth lay beneath the thatch of dark brown hair.

Yes, Colleen thought, Fred had grown out of boyhood and turned into rather a handsome man. She herself was very happy with her George, but looking at Fred she could not help wishing—for just a second—that she was a few years younger and unattached.

Fred was telling Mary the story of the great Tooley Street fire. 'Imagine it—the river actually burnin' up with all that fat an' tallow,' he said.

'Yer lucky that *you've* never 'ad to fight a fire like that one, ain't yer?' Mary said.

'Well, I am in a way—an' then again, I'm not,' Fred replied enigmatically.

' 'Ow d'yer mean?'

'Firefightin's what I've been trained to do, an' it seems a pity to miss the big one. Not that I ever want anywhere to catch on fire, yer understand, but it's like ...' Fred waved his hands helplessly as he tried to express what was on his mind. 'It's like bein' a good footballer, an' only allowed to play against teams yer know yer could beat.'

Mary looked at him anxiously. 'But wouldn't yer be afraid of a big fire like that?'

'Yes, but not in the way you mean. I wouldn't be afraid of gettin' killed—I'd be afraid of losin' me nerve.'

The anxiety on Mary's face increased. 'Why is that more frightenin' than gettin' killed?'

'Because in the Fire Brigade, yer not one man workin' on yer own, yer part of a bigger operation. An' if yer not doin' yer job properly, then yer comrades probably can't do theirs, either. So at best, yer not makin' a proper showin' of it, an' at worst, yer could be riskin' the lives of the other firemen.'

'But surely they'd understand. Everybody gets scared at one time or another.'

'It's a luxury *we* can't afford. That's why, if a fireman once loses 'is bottle, none of the others ever want to work with 'im again.' He laughed. 'Work with 'im, did I say? It's as much as they can do to bring themselves to even *speak* to 'im.'

'It seems terribly 'ard,' Mary said.

'That's the way it 'as to be,' Fred replied, then changed the subject. ' 'Ave yer talked to yer mother yet?'

'Talked to me mother?' Mary repeated, although she knew full well what he meant. 'What about?'

'About us.'

'Well ... no.' Mary admitted. How she wished

41

that she was not so timid; that she could find the courage from somewhere inside her to tell her mum that she loved Fred and he loved her, and that was all there was to it. But she had always been timid—even at school—and it was terribly hard to try and change now.

'She'll 'ave to know sooner or later,' Fred said, 'An' I'm gettin' tired of seein' yer be'ind 'er back.'

'I will tell 'er,' Mary promised.

'When?'

'Soon.'

'Look,' Fred said, 'I'm a solid, honest bloke, an' I love yer with all my 'eart. I want to marry yer, an' the sooner the better.'

'Maybe when I'm a bit older ...'

'Yer eighteen next birthday. As far as I'm concerned, that's old enough to be thinkin' about gettin' married. I mean, it ain't as if I couldn't support yer. I've got a good steady job ...'

'I know that.'

'... an' in a couple o' years I could be promoted up to Leadin' Fireman.'

'I'm sure yer will be.'

'An' there's somefink else,' Fred said, taking Mary's two hands in his.

'What else?'

Fred looked down at the table. 'I've always shown yer the proper respect, ain't I?'

'Oh yes, yer've never been anyfink but the perfect gentleman with me.'

'Well, that's the problem,' Fred said. 'Feelin' about yer like I do, I don't want to be the perfect gentleman for much longer.'

Mary swallowed hard. 'Maybe we could ...' she began. 'I mean, if yer want to ...'

'No,' Fred said firmly. 'Not until we're married. It wouldn't be right. So yer will talk to yer mum, won't yer?'

'Yes,' Mary promised, 'but yer'll 'ave to give me a while to get used to the idea.'

'An' 'ow long's a while?'

'A week or two.'

Fred sighed. 'Well, I've waited this long. I s'ppose I'll just 'ave to force meself to wait a little bit longer.'

CHAPTER 3

Colleen looked at the clock on the kitchen mantelpiece. It was a quarter past four and Maisie Dunn—the girl from Southwark Bridge Road who looked after Ted and Cathy while Colleen was at work—was already fifteen minutes late. Which means that I'm goin' to be late gettin' to the Goldsmiths' an' all, Colleen thought, an' I don't expect Mr Wilkins is goin' to be very pleased about *that!*

She looked down at the children. Cathy was tugging on the ears of a fluffy pink rabbit, and Ted was making one of his slow, thoughtful expeditions across the kitchen floor.

'The trouble is that I just can't afford to lose me little job,' Colleen told the twins. 'Not now we've got all the expense of lookin' after you pair.'

Ted came to a halt by the leg of the kitchen table, and gazed up questioningly at his mother.

'Oh, I'm not complainin',' Colleen told him. 'I'm glad you came along as twins, instead of one at a time. Honestly I am. But do you see how I'm fixed?'

Ted nodded seriously, as if he did see. Cathy, having failed to de-ear her toy herself, held it out so her mother could have a go at the job.

A sudden, unexpected shiver ran down Colleen's back, and though she tried to fight it, the memory of Nettie Walnut's last visit invaded her mind.

It had been a lovely spring day, Colleen remembered, the kind of day when it seems that nothing can possibly go wrong—and then Nettie had told the children's fortunes.

'I sees a long life for him,' Nettie had said when she'd examined Ted's palm, and then she had looked at Cathy's—and her eyes had shown her shock.

'Daft thing, fortune tellin',' Nettie had mumbled.

'It is!' Colleen said now, to both herself and her children. She picked up Cathy and hugged the baby to her. 'Nothin's goin' to harm you,' she promised. 'I won't let it.'

It was twenty past four when Maisie Dunn finally arrived and found Colleen in the kitchen, still holding her infant daughter tightly to her bosom.

'I'm awful sorry I'm late, Mrs Taylor,' Maisie gasped, as if she had been running.

'I should think you are sorry,' Colleen told her. 'Mr Wilkins was expectin' me at four o'clock, an'—'

'Only the reason I didn't get 'ere on time was 'cos I went to see about this job, yer see?'

'A job?' Colleen repeated, a sinking feeling in her stomach. 'Another job?'

'That's right.'

'Where?'

'At the tannery.'

'An' did you get it?'

'Yeah, I did. I don't want to see yer stuck, so I'll mind the kids tonight, but as from tomorrow, yer goin' to 'ave to find somebody else to do the job.'

'If you'd rather stay with us, instead of workin' in that horrid place, I could maybe pay you a bit more than I do now,' Colleen said, though without much hope.

'Could yer afford to give me twelve an' a tanner a week?' Maisie asked.

'No,' Colleen replied heavily. 'Twelve an' six a week would be beyond me.'

'Well, it's what I could earn with overtime at the tannery,' Maisie told her. 'I'm sorry, Mrs Taylor. I like lookin' after the children, honest I do, but yer've got to be practical where money's concerned, 'aven't yer?'

'Yes,' Colleen agreed. 'I suppose you have.'

When Colleen returned from the Goldsmiths' Arms that night, she found George sitting at the kitchen table with a piece of paper in front of him and a pensive expression on his face.

'I've been talkin' to young Maisie,' he said. 'She seems set on leavin' us.'

'Yes,' Colleen agreed. 'I think she is.'

'So, we'll need to look for a new girl, won't we? Are you workin' tomorrow?'

'No. It's me day off.'

'Well, that's a blessin', at least.' George picked up a pencil. 'I'll write out the advert now, an' see it's put up in the newspaper shop window first thing in the mornin'. With any luck, we should have somebody by tomorrow night at the latest.'

'I've been doin' some thinkin' on the subject while I've been at the pub,' Colleen told her husband.

'That spells trouble,' George said, and then he smiled to show that he didn't really mean it. 'An' just what particular side of the subject have you been exercisin' your brain over?'

'We're always goin' to have trouble employin' local girls, because sooner or later they'll all find a better job in the tannery or the match factory.'

'Call workin' in the tannery a better job?' George asked. 'Ever smelled it when you were walkin' past? The stink of all them hides is enough to turn your stomach.'

'Some people'll put up with any amount of stink if the pay's good,' Colleen said. 'An' you have to admit, George, twelve an' six a week *is* good.'

'Maybe it is,' George conceded, 'but I'm still

not sure where all this is headin'. You say we'll always have trouble with local girls, and perhaps you're right, but what's the alternative?'

'We could take in a girl from St Saviour's Work'ouse.'

'From the work'ouse?'

'Yes. Why not? We couldn't pay her that much a week, but at least she'd have a room of her own here, instead of havin' to sleep in one of them dreadful dormitories.'

George frowned. 'I'm not sure I'd be happy about havin' a live-in servant,' he said.

'A servant!' Colleen repeated, giggling. 'You are gettin' ideas above your station. She'd be no more of a servant than Maisie was, 'cept that instead of goin' home to her mam an' dad every night, she'd be stayin' here with us.'

George, who had always thought things out slowly and carefully—a fact which had made him an excellent sergeant in the army—turned the matter over in his head.

'She'd have to be the *right* girl,' he said finally. 'I mean, I'm not acceptin' the first one they send us.'

'I'll make that quite clear when I go an' see 'em tomorrow,' Colleen promised.

'An' I don't want you gettin' too attached to her, because if she doesn't work out like we hope she will, she's goin' straight back to St Saviour's.'

'I won't get too friendly.'

'I know you an' your soft heart ...'

'I won't get too friendly with her,' Colleen insisted. 'I promise you I won't.'

'All right. I suppose it's worth at least givin' the idea a try,' George said.

St Saviour's Workhouse was bounded by four roads, but its main entrance was on Quilp Street, and it was to this gate that Colleen went the next morning. She gazed up at the tall brick walls which surrounded the workhouse. Even in the bright morning sunlight it looked imposing and totally unwelcoming.

Colleen knocked on the small door set inside the gate. A porter opened it. He was wearing a uniform which included a peaked military cap.

'Overnight paupers ain't admitted till six,' he snarled, then he noticed Colleen's neat appearance and his expression changed. 'Sorry, madam, but yer don't know 'ow persistent some o' these wretches can be.' He forced a smile to his face. 'What can I do for yer?'

'I'd like to see someone in charge,' Colleen told him. 'I'm looking for a gi—for a servant.'

The porter's respect for her was going up in leaps and bounds. 'Well, yer've come to the right place,' he said. 'There's loads of young women in 'ere 'oo'd jump at the chance of workin' for a respectable lady like yerself.'

Colleen, who had never been called a lady before, felt herself blushing.

The matron was a woman of around forty-five. Like the porter, she was wearing a uniform—a long white dress—and also like the gruff man on the gate, there seemed to be a hard edge lurking beneath her smile.

'We are always most pleased to see our

paupers settled in new homes,' she said, 'but we must first make sure that those homes are suitable.'

'Of course,' Colleen agreed.

'Now, you say this girl's duties would principally be to look after your two children?'

'That's right.'

'And what are your circumstances?'

'Pardon?'

'What is your husband's occupation, Mrs Taylor? And, since you want the girl as a nanny, am I to assume that you have a job of your own?'

'I'm a barmaid,' Colleen said.

The matron frowned. 'Strong drink has been the downfall of many of the poor wretches whom we shelter inside these walls,' she said severely.

'But me husband's the manager of Hibbert's wood yard,' Colleen added hastily. 'He drinks himself—but not much—an' I don't touch the stuff at all.'

The matron nodded, somewhat mollified. 'A wood yard manager. That seems most satisfactory,' she said. 'Would you like to take the girl with you now?'

'Now?' Colleen asked, surprised that it could all be accomplished so quickly.

The matron laughed, but there was not much warmth in it. 'Why not?' she asked. 'How long do you think it takes a pauper to pack her belongings?'

'Well, the thing is, me husband wants to see her first,' Colleen said. 'Interview her, like.'

'That's not the usual procedure,' the matron said, frowning again. 'Normally it is *I* who decides who's placed.'

'You don't know my George,' Colleen said. 'He was a sergeant in the army, you see, an' won't employ anybody unless he's given 'em the once over first.'

The matron gave the matter some thought. 'Very well,' she said reluctantly. 'Since you seem to be offering such a good situation, I will make an exception to my usual rule on this occasion. When will your husband be home?'

'Round about seven.'

'Then I will send one of my girls to be "interviewed" by him at seven-thirty. Will that suit you?'

'Yes,' Colleen replied.

She hoped George did approve of the girl, because the idea of having another meeting with the formidable matron was far from appealing.

It was exactly half past seven when they heard the timid knock on the front door.

'That must be the girl now,' Colleen said. 'D'you want me to answer it?'

'Please,' replied George, who was just settling down to a mug of strong tea.

Colleen walked up the passageway and opened the front door. The girl standing on the step was a thin little thing who looked about fourteen, but might have been older. She was wearing a grey, shapeless dress which had been darned in several places. Her skin was very pale, her features pinched, and the expression on her face was one of near terror.

'Are you from the work'ouse?' Colleen asked.

The girl bobbed down in a clumsy curtsy. 'Yes, ma'am. Please, ma'am, I'm Lizzie 'Odges.'

Colleen sighed. George wasn't going to take this one, which meant a second visit to St Saviour's.

'You'd better come in, Lizzie,' she said.

As they walked down the passage, Colleen listened to the frightened breathing of the girl behind her—a breathing which grew even faster when she saw George sitting at the table.

'This is my husband, Mr Taylor,' Colleen said.

Lizzie bobbed down again. ' 'Ow d'yer do, sir? Pleased to meet yer, sir.'

'Take a seat,' George said.

Lizzie did, lowering herself into it carefully, as if she expected it to collapse under her, and all the time her frightened eyes roved the kitchen, searching for unexpected dangers.

Colleen took the chair next to George's. 'Your matron told me you're one of the best workers she's got,' she said, hoping the lie would help to put the girl at her ease.

Lizzie jumped up and did a half-curtsy. 'Yes, ma'am. Thank you, ma'am.'

'Oh do sit down again,' Colleen said, 'and there's no need to go through that pantomime every time you speak.'

'No, ma'am. Sorry, ma'am,' Lizzie said, sitting down and aiming her eyes towards the scrubbed wooden table.

'Tell us a bit about yourself,' George said.

The girl looked completely bewildered. 'W ... What do yer want to know?'

'Well, how long have you been livin' at St Saviour's Work'ouse, for a start?'

'Most of me life. Me dad died when I was very little, an' me an' me mum had nowhere else to go. Then, a couple o' years ago it must 'ave been, me mum died. So I'm all alone in the world now.'

George nodded his head sympathetically. His own mam had been brought up in the workhouse, after his grandfather—a cooper—had become too ill to carry on his trade. But that's no reason for goin' soft now, he told himself. They could only rescue one girl, whoever they chose, so they had better make sure that their choice was up to the job—and he didn't think that this one, with all her nervousness, was.

'Do they treat you well in the work'ouse?' Colleen asked, trying to draw the girl out a little.

'We get porridge for breakfast, an' sometimes there's meat 'stead o' gruel for supper,' Lizzie said.

'What I really meant was, are you happy with your life there?' Colleen said.

' 'Spect so,' Lizzie replied, as if she really didn't know what Colleen was talking about.

'But do you think you'd be happier livin' somewhere else?' Colleen persisted.

'They don't let us out,' the girl said.

Now it was Colleen's turn to be confused. 'I beg your pardon?' she said.

'We ain't allowed to go outside. Leastways,

not very often. Comin' 'ere today was the first time I've set foot on the street for three or four years.'

Colleen sighed. This was turning out to be very hard work. 'An' how did you *feel* once you were outside?' she asked.

'Terrified,' Lizzie admitted. 'It's so noisy outside. There's people rushin' everywhere, an' if yer not careful crossing the road, yer'll as likely as not get run over.'

This was no good, George decided. He didn't think the girl was suitable for them, and plainly she did not think *they*—or at least the lives they led—were suitable for *her*. She would be much more at ease in the workhouse than facing the world of Lant Place.

'Well, it was nice of you to come, Lizzie,' he said kindly, 'but I don't really think—'

There was a sudden sound of loud wailing from upstairs.

'That'll be Cathy,' Colleen said, rising from her chair. 'Oh dear, once she wakes up like this, it's usually hours before I can get her to sleep again.'

'Let me go an' deal with 'er, ma'am,' Lizzie said.

'Oh, I don't really think ...' Colleen began.

'Please, ma'am,' Lizzie said. 'I'm very good with little babies. The women up at St Saviour's are always givin' me their kiddies to look after.'

Colleen looked at George, who nodded that he couldn't see any harm in it. 'All right,' she said. 'The babies' room is at the top of the stairs. First door on the left. I'll give you a couple of minutes, then I'll come up.'

Lizzie approached the stairs as if she was about to climb a steep mountain.

'Maybe they don't have stairs in the workhouse, either,' George said. He looked into his wife's eyes and read both sadness and pity there. 'It's no good, you know,' he continued. 'Whichever way you look at it, she's not the one we need.'

'Well, *I* like her,' Colleen said stubbornly.

'So do I, love, but we have to think of the kids. How can we leave a girl like her in charge of them?'

They heard Lizzie open the bedroom door and then, miraculously, the crying stopped.

'She said she was good with kids,' Colleen said, with a triumphant smile on her face.

'Probably got nothin' to do with her. Cathy must have just decided to stop cryin' on her own.'

'An' when has she ever done that before? Anyway, if we go upstairs, we'll soon see, won't we?'

Hindered by his wooden leg, it always took George a minute or so to get upstairs, but all the time he was climbing there was no sound from the bedroom.

'You don't think she's gagged our Cathy, do you?' he asked his wife worriedly.

'Don't talk daft,' Colleen said. 'She's not that kind of girl. You can tell that right away.'

'Still, I've never known Cathy to quieten down so quickly,' George said.

He pushed the bedroom door open and saw Cathy—with no sign of a gag at all—sleeping in Lizzie's arms. But it was Lizzie's eyes he really noticed. The haunted look had gone from them, and had been replaced by an expression of contentment which could almost be called bliss.

'You really like children, don't you?' he said.

'I love 'em,' Lizzie replied.

'Right,' George said decisively. 'When can you move in?'

CHAPTER 4

Sergeant Harry Roberts left the busy street behind him and marched down the narrow passageway which led to Wapping Police Station, the headquarters of the Wet Bobs.

It was a funny place, he thought fondly. The building was so narrow and old fashioned that it didn't really look much like a police station at all. In fact, if it hadn't been for the blue light hanging from the wall outside, a casual stroller could have been excused for assuming it was a counting house or the offices of a shipping company.

The young, fresh-faced constable on duty by the entrance saw Harry approaching, snapped instantly to attention and saluted with a precision which was a pleasure to see.

Harry stopped and looked him up and down. 'I'll say this for yer, yer very smartly turned out, son,' he said after he had completed his inspection.

The constable's face lit up with pleasure. 'Thank you, Sergeant,' he said.

It was nice to give the new boys a bit of encouragement, Harry told himself as he entered the building. Come to think of it, it was nice to give *anybody* a bit of a helping hand whenever you were presented with the opportunity.

Wapping Police Station smelled, as it always did, of tar and new rope. 'Luverly,' Harry said to himself. Tar and new rope. The smells of home. That was what the station was to him: not just the place where he worked, but his home. For seven years he had slept in the clean, spartan dormitory and taken most of his meals in the canteen.

He had spent countless hours in the duty room, sitting under the portraits of long-dead superintendents and reading the latest reports of bodies which had been recovered from the river and of children who'd gone missing. He had got used to the sound of gently lapping water being the last thing he heard before he fell asleep, and the first thing which greeted him when he woke up.

His thoughts shifted to Belinda Benson. He had never met anyone quite like her before—in fact, if he was being honest, he'd never met anyone even *remotely* like her. She was rich—or at least, her family were. She'd been educated, and not at a board school either.

Belinda was a lady, and she even had a title to prove it, although when they were in bed together she didn't *act* like a lady, Harry thought to himself. Not that she acted like a man, either, he added hastily. Well, not *exactly* like a man—but she certainly wasn't prepared to just lie there and have things done to her.

He checked his watch. It was ten-twenty-five, and at ten-thirty he had a meeting with the superintendent in which he would do his damnedest to try and persuade his boss to forget the past and allow Tom Bates to join the Force.

Superintendent Drummond of the Thames River Police was a large man with clipped iron-grey hair and a fine, bushy beard. When Harry entered his office, he was sitting behind his oak desk, though like many of the Wet Bobs who'd served some time in the Royal Navy, he looked as if he would have been more comfortable out at sea, riding a rolling deck.

'So what can I do for you this morning, Sergeant Roberts?' Drummond asked, taking out his pipe and stuffing it with navy-cut shag tobacco.

Harry, standing immediately in front of the desk with his legs apart and hands behind his back, shifted his weight slightly from one foot to the other. 'Er ... it's about Tom Bates, sir,' he said.

Drummond tamped down the tobacco, then struck a match and lit his pipe. Clouds of blue-grey smoke enveloped his head. 'Tom

Bates? The name sounds familiar, but I can't quite place him.'

' 'E was the bloke what got arrested for the murder of Rollo Jenkins.'

'Ah yes. Jenkins was the Newington Hooligan we found floating in the river, wasn't he?'

'Yes, sir.'

'And if my memory serves me well, that was the case which earned you your sergeant's stripes.'

'That's right, sir.'

'So what would you like to tell me about this Tom Bates? He's not in trouble again, is he?'

'No, sir. Far from it. The fact is, 'e'd like to join the river police, sir, an' I thought that you might be willin' to sort of smooth 'is way for 'im.'

The superintendent frowned. 'This isn't the first time you've stuck your neck out for this Tom Bates, is it?'

'No, sir, it ain't,' Harry admitted. 'I spoke up for 'im in the Tower Bridge police court when 'e was arrested for fightin' an' disturbin' the peace on Tooley Street.'

'That was with Jenkins again, wasn't it?'

'Yes, sir. It was about six months before the murder.'

'You almost lost your job because of speaking up for him, didn't you, Sergeant?'

'Yes, sir, I did,' Harry admitted. 'But I was right to trust 'im, wasn't I?'

'Were you?'

'I think so. 'E didn't kill Jenkins, an' 'e 'asn't

been in no trouble since then. In fact, 'e's settled down nicely.'

'Has he, indeed?'

'Yes, sir. Got 'imself married last year. A luverly girl, 'is wife is, an' all.'

Drummond smiled. 'So why exactly do you want to help Tom Bates? For his own sake? Or for the sake of the lovely girl he got married to?'

Harry grinned awkwardly. 'Well, to tell you the truth, sir, I *was* a bit in love with 'is wife meself once.'

'I thought so.'

'But I'm over that now—got a gal of me own, as a matter of fact—an' I do think Tom'd make a good bobbie.'

Drummond's smile faded and he was serious again. 'There are plenty of men without his checkered past who would make good bobbies,' he pointed out. 'Why shouldn't any vacancies that arise go to them instead?'

Harry gazed at the wall for inspiration, and found it in the cutlass which was hanging there. 'We take on so many sailors 'cos they know the water, don't we, sir?' he said.

'Yes, that's correct.'

'Well, Tom knows the water. An' 'avin' been what yer might call a minor villain as well, 'e knows somefink about the criminal element we 'ave to deal with.'

'You mean, set a thief to catch a thief?'

Harry shrugged. 'I suppose so, sir, but I wouldn't 'ave put it quite like that meself.'

The superintendent applied a new match to

his pipe. Once more, clouds of smoke billowed forth. 'Tricky,' Drummond said, and then he seemed to come to a decision. 'Very well, Sergeant Roberts, I will recommend Bates. But if it turns out to be a mistake, it will be *your* mistake, and you will have to pay the price.'

'Then it'll be just like old times, won't it, sir?' Harry said, grinning again.

Eddie Clarke and Joey Bates stood on the pavement facing the big green double gates of the Queen Street garage where Eddie worked as a mechanic.

'The place is locked up for the night, but I've got me own key,' Eddie said proudly. He opened the small door in the left-hand gate, and stepped inside the garage.

'Bit dark in there, ain't it?' he heard Joey's voice say from behind him.

'Won't be for long.' Eddie flicked the switch, and the place was bathed in light. 'See! We got electricity.'

Joey, despite himself, was impressed. He looked around the garage. It was a massive, oblong room, and had more motorcars in it than he had ever seen in one place before.

'This way,' Eddie said.

They approached a line of two-seater vehicles with large cylinders, almost like oil drums, on their fronts.

'What's them?' Joey asked.

'Serpollet steam cars,' Eddie said in disgust.

' 'Ow do they work?'

'They've got a paraffin-fired boiler. I ask yer,

'ave yer ever 'eard of anyfink so pathetic?'

'What's wrong with paraffin-fired boilers?' Joey asked.

'What's wrong with 'em is that their day's gone,' Eddie told him. 'Steam's dead, an' anybody 'oo really understands engines—like me—knows it. *They're* even worse,' he continued, pointing to a row of vehicles plugged into brass wall sockets.

'What do they run off?' Joey said.

'Ain't it obvious?' Eddie asked cuttingly. 'They're electric cars—that's why they're plugged in.' He waited for Joey to ask him what was wrong with them, but when it became plain that the other boy wasn't going to, he continued. 'The only problem is, yer can't drive very far before you 'ave to charge 'em up again. They tried electric cabs in the city a few years back. Quite a lot of 'em, there was. Now there ain't any, 'cos what's the good of a taxi cab that's only got a range of thirty miles?'

At the very end of the garage was a four-seater open-topped petrol car with brown leather seats and two enormous brass headlights at the front. Its carriagework was white, and its mudguards and wheel spokes were painted red.

'Now this is really somefink,' Eddie said. 'The Renault Sixteen. It's new this year an' it was the star attraction at the Agricultural 'All exhibition. It's got a twenty-'orse-power engine, an' it'll go like the clappers. What d'yer think of it?'

Joey still stinging at the way Eddie had spoken to him about the electric car, gave the Renault a quick, sweeping glance. 'It's all right,' he said.

'All right? It's bloody marvellous.'

Joey was determined not to show any enthusiasm. 'I s'ppose it is marvellous for them that can afford it. 'Oo owns it, anyway? Some toff, I expect.'

Eddie grinned. 'Not some toff at all. This garage owns it. We're modifyin' it.'

'Why?'

' 'Cos when we've finished workin' on it, we want to try an' break the world speed record.'

'What for?'

Eddie gave Joey a look which said that of all the stupid questions his friend could have chosen to ask, that had to be the stupidest. 'Why does anybody ever want to break records?' he said. ' 'Cos that's what they're there for.'

' 'Ow fast will it 'ave to go to do that?'

Eddie shrugged. 'Nobody's really sure, 'cos cars are improvin' all the time. Five years ago, the record was thirty-nine miles an hour ...'

'Now that is fast.'

'It's 'ardly movin',' Eddie said dismissively. 'Four years ago, the record stood at sixty-six, an' this year somebody knocked it up to seventy-eight. We're probably goin' to 'ave to aim at an 'undred if we're to 'ave any chance.'

Joey whistled softly. 'An 'undred miles an hour,' he repeated. 'Think of that! An' which silly bugger's goin' to be daft enough to try an' drive at that speed?'

'Yer lookin' at 'im.'

'Yer what!'

'I'm the best driver in the garage. Mr Rockcliffe says if anybody can do it, it's me.'

Joey shook his head slowly back and forth. 'If yer ask me, yer want yer bumps feelin'.'

Eddie glowered at him. 'An' so do you. At least I'm puttin' *my* faith in science.'

'So am I. The science of boxin'.'

'Science of boxin',' Eddie sneered. 'It's nuffink more than brute force an'—' He stopped, suddenly. 'We're about to 'ave a row again, ain't we?' he asked.

'Looks like it.'

'Let's not.'

'No, let's not,' Joey agreed. He examined the Renault again. 'Now I come to look at it proper, I 'ave to admit it's quite an 'andsome machine,' he said.

'An' I didn't mean what I said about boxin' bein' all brute force,' Eddie told him in the same spirit of generosity. 'I know there's a lot o' skill in it as well.'

Joey clapped Eddie heartily on the shoulder. 'Fancy a pint?' he asked.

'Think they'll serve us?'

'Two future world champions like we are?' said Joey. ' 'Course they'll serve us.'

As Colleen Taylor walked down to the Goldsmiths' Arms, she remembered the first time she had seen Lant Place. How frightened she'd been that day—scared almost half to death of leaving the cosy village where she'd spent her whole life and moving down to the big city. And how strange the cockneys had seemed at first, with their odd accents and their rhyming slang.

'A woman like you, with a good crust on 'er shoulders, should soon be rabbitin' to my old dutch like yer was born under Bow Bells,' Sam Clarke had said to her in the back yard of her new home.

He'd only been taking the mickey out of her, of course—that was how Sam was—but he'd been right when he said that if she was going to live among the natives, she'd better learn to speak their language. And she had: now she could rabbit on with the best of them about how difficult it was to climb up the 'apples' when your 'plates an' pegs' were aching.

Colleen opened the door of the saloon, and walked across to the bar counter, taking note of the customers as she went. Apart from a few regulars like Dick Todd, Fred Simpson and Mary Bates, the pub was virtually empty.

Colleen hated it when trade was like that. She either wanted to be kept busy serving or to chat to one of her chinas on the other side of the bar—and neither of those things looked like a possibility at that moment. It won't last for long, she thought. Give it another half-hour and the place'll be heavin'.

She lifted the flap and stepped behind the bar, to where Mr Wilkins was waiting for her to relieve him.

The landlord looked up at the grandmother clock. 'Right on time, Colleen,' he said approvingly. 'This new nanny of yours is good at her job, is she?'

'George says it's too early to judge,' Colleen replied, 'but then he always was cautious. Me,

I think she's turnin' into a real little treasure.'

Mr Wilkins chuckled. 'A little treasure,' he repeated. 'Yer takin' to bein' an employer like a duck takes to water, ain't you?'

Colleen blushed, but he was right: she wasn't Lizzie's friend or favourite auntie, she was her *employer.*

'Her employer!' she repeated silently to herself, and she had better keep reminding herself of that. George had warned her about getting too attached to whichever girl they took from the workhouse, but Lizzie had only been in the house for a few days, and already Colleen had fallen into the trap.

Mr Wilkins disappeared into the back room. As Colleen started to polish the glasses, she looked across the room at Mary and Fred. Normally, they spent most of their time gazing into each other's eyes like the star-crossed lovers they were, but that night they seemed to be arguing about something.

Fred suddenly stood up. 'Well, I'm fed up with waitin' for yer to get round to it,' he said, loud enough for Colleen to hear. 'Yer'd better tell 'er soon, or we're finished,' and with that, he stormed out of the bar.

Mary pulled her handkerchief out of her bag, and started to dab her eyes.

Colleen lifted up the bar flap and walked across to Mary's table. 'Anythin' I can do for you, love?'

Mary looked up. Her eyes were red and her lower lip was trembling. 'W ... what did yer say?'

'I was just wonderin' if there was anythin' I could do for you,' Colleen repeated.

'No, I ... Why can't I tell 'er, Colleen? I do love 'im, yer know, I really do. An' 'e's dead right when 'e says that I should ...'

'Calm down, Mary,' Colleen said soothingly. 'Calm down an' tell me the whole story. Only this time, it might be better if you started at the beginning.'

Mary stuffed her handkerchief back in her bag. 'There's no point in tellin' *you*,' she said. 'It's not *you* I've got to tell.'

Then she stood up and rushed to the door.

Five minutes after Mary's flight the saloon door swung open and a good-looking woman of around twenty-six, wearing an elaborate, feather-trimmed hat, walked in.

' 'Ello, Maggie,' Colleen said, pleased that someone she could have a natter to had finally entered the bar.

' 'Ello yerself,' Maggie White replied cheerfully, walking up to the counter. 'Give us me drink quick, could yer? I'm fair spitting feathers tonight.' She always said it like that—'Give us me drink'—because Maggie White only ever had the one.

Colleen poured out her usual port and lemon. 'Busy day at the wash house?' she asked.

Maggie took a grateful, almost bird-like, sip from her glass. 'Saturday always is busy. It's when the flower girls usually pay us their weekly visit, yer see.'

'The flower girls?' Colleen repeated.

'Yeah. After spendin' the whole week standin'

out on the street, tryin' to sell their penny bunches, they like to get clean of a Saturday night.'

'I imagine they do.'

'So what they do, yer see, is they each 'ire one of the private rooms an' take off all their clothes 'cept for their skirts and jackets. Then they go into the wash room and give their unmentionables a thorough scrubbing. An' while the unmentionables are dryin', they buy a ticket for the twopenny baths an' give *themselves* a good soak. So by the time they leave us, they're as clean as you please—an' all for threepence 'a'penny.'

Colleen laughed, and then was serious again. 'They must have a hard life, though,' she said.

'Well, I wouldn't like it,' Maggie replied. 'You an' me know we're goin' to get paid every week, but them poor little buggers are livin' from 'and to mouth.' She looked around the bar to see if anyone was listening, then leaned confidentially over towards Colleen. 'I wasn't goin' to tell anybody else this till I'd let me ol' man know about it,' she whispered, 'but I can't keep it in any longer. I've just been to the doctor's, an' ...'

'An' you're expectin'.'

Maggie looked shocked. ' 'Ow did you know that?'

Colleen grinned. 'Well, you wouldn't be so happy if he'd told you you'd got somethin' seriously wrong, now would you?'

'No, I s'ppose not.'

'Well, there you are, then. It could only have

been a baby, couldn't it?'

'Yer right o' course,' Maggie said. 'I'm ever so relieved. Me an' my Sid 'ave been tryin' to 'ave one for ages, an' I'd just about given up on it.'

'I know how you must feel,' Colleen told her. 'Me an' George had the same problem. An' when it did happen, it came as such a surprise that instead of thinkin' I'd finally made it, I thought I must be dyin' of somethin'.'

Maggie's bright, happy face clouded over. 'Don't talk to me about dyin', Colleen,' she said.

'I'm sorry, I didn't want to ...'

'I mean, I've never really worried about it before, but now I'm carryin' a child everyfink's different, ain't it?' Maggie was sounding more panicked with every word she spoke. 'My *baby* could die, couldn't it?' she asked. 'Even before it's born, it could die!'

'Don't talk daft.'

'People do lose their babies, yer know.'

'Yes, some do,' Colleen admitted, 'but you've no reason to think you'll be one of them.'

Now that the idea had occurred to Maggie, there was no shaking it off, though. 'I've never been very strong,' she said. 'I always catch a cold before anybody else does.'

'All you need to do is just take a little extra care, that's all,' Colleen said reassuringly.

'If I lose the baby, I'll die meself,' said Maggie, no longer speaking in whispers but talking so loudly that the whole bar could hear her. 'I'll just die. I know I will.'

'Hush, now. Why don't you have another drink?'

'I only ever 'ave the one.'

'I know you do, but this is a special occasion, and besides, you're a bit upset. Why don't you have another port an' lemon on me?'

'D'you know, I think I will,' Maggie said.

CHAPTER 5

It was Monday morning, and the sky was as grey as only a Monday morning London sky can be. Belinda Benson, as smartly dressed as usual in a knife-pleated skirt, short bolero and blue silk blouse, walked briskly along Moorgate towards London Wall, where the National Telephone Company had its central exchange.

She had been working as a telephone operator for over two years. It was considered by most people to be a very respectable occupation for a young lady. Many of the girls she worked with were the daughters of doctors, barristers and clergymen, and Annie Clarke—Annie *Bates* as she was now— had been the exception which proved the rule.

Belinda missed Annie. All the other operators were so terribly snobbish and boring always talking in an extremely pretentious way about their parents' houses and the balls they were hoping to attend. Yes, Annie had been a breath of fresh air, and somehow the job didn't seem the same without her.

Her thoughts turned to Harry Roberts. She had been his mistress for more than a year now. She grimaced at the word 'mistress'. 'Don't like it,' she told herself. 'Don't like it at all.' So how should she describe their relationship? Say he was her 'master'? That sounded even worse, and certainly didn't sum up how things were between them. Anyway, the *words* were not the point, it was the *situation* she was concerned with. She'd been his lover ...

That was it! Lover. Much nicer than 'mistress'.

... she'd been his 'lover' for quite some time, but now she was starting to feel vaguely dissatisfied with the way things were going. Something was missing. She didn't know what it was, but she definitely knew it wasn't there.

She had reached the door of the telephone exchange. She sighed and turned around to take one last look at the street.

'Another day in the salt mine,' she said to the passing wagons and hansom cabs.

Annie Bates was planning to do a bit of shopping in Lant Street when she ran into Lizzie Hodges, who was just coming out of Mr Southern's shop with a bag of sweets in her hand.

'What have you done with the twins?' she asked chirpily. 'Given them away?'

Lizzie looked horrified. 'Oh no, Mrs Bates,' she said. 'I wouldn't do nuffink like that.'

Annie laughed. 'I was only joking,' she

explained. 'Is it your day off or something?'

'That's right,' Lizzie said.

'What are you going to do with it?'

Lizzie shrugged. 'Well, I've bought me sweets ...'

'Yes?'

'So I'll probably go back to the 'ouse an' eat 'em.'

'Is that it?'

'What else would I do?' Lizzie wondered.

'You're living in London, the capital of the Empire,' Annie told her. 'There are hundreds of things you could do.'

'I can't think of any,' Lizzie admitted.

'We'll go exploring,' Annie said.

'Yer what?'

'We'll go exploring. We'll take the Tube and go and have a look at London.'

'Oh, I couldn't do that!' said Lizzie, with an edge of panic to her words.

'Why not?'

'I just couldn't.'

'Yes, you could,' Annie insisted. 'You're not in the workhouse now, you know. There's nobody to stop you going wherever you want on your day off.'

'I ... I couldn't take up yer valuable time, Mrs Bates,' Lizzie said desperately.

'I wish it was valuable,' Annie said, with just a tinge of regret in her voice. 'Listen, there's no point in us sitting at home moping when we could be out enjoying ourselves.'

'I don't think I know *how* to enjoy meself,' Lizzie confessed.

'Then it's about time you learned,' Annie said, taking her arm and leading her firmly towards the Borough Tube station.

The centre of the London Wall Telephone Exchange was a long room with a pointed roof which had naked steel girders running across it. Switchboards ran all around the walls, but the centre of the room was empty, apart from the large wooden desk belonging to the supervisor, Mrs Barnett, a formidable lady who Belinda Benson had privately christened the Dragon.

The operators were all dressed in over-gowns rather like the ones worn by university students. These were provided free by the telephone company, not in order to save wear and tear on the operators' own clothes, but so that the young ladies should not waste time admiring each other's frocks.

Which is typical of this place, Belinda thought. Just because you happen to be a woman, they automatically assume that you're also a brainless idiot who's only interested in clothes.

As she took her place at her switchboard, she noticed that the girl who usually worked to her left—Emily Hardy—had been replaced by a slightly older woman with a friendly face.

'Are you new?' Belinda asked, speaking out the corner of her mouth so the Dragon wouldn't notice.

'Not exactly,' the other woman replied in the same way. 'I used to work here years ago, but I had to leave.'

'Why?'

'Because I got married, of course.'

Another stupid regulation, Belinda thought. 'So if you're married, what are you doing here now?'

'When the company's short handed, they sometimes call me in,' the woman said.

'I see. So you work whenever it suits *them*, not whenever it suits *you*?'

'I suppose so.'

'Talking is forbidden, Miss Benson, as you well know,' said a stern voice just behind them.

Belinda turned around. Somehow the Dragon had managed to sneak up on her. A tension had been building up inside Belinda for days, and now, suddenly, she felt something snap.

'There were no calls for me to deal with, Miss Barnett,' she said, almost contemptuously.

'I beg your pardon, Miss Benson?' said the supervisor, who never, in her twenty years at her desk, had been addressed in such a manner by one of her operators.

'There were ... no calls ... for me ... to deal with.' Belinda repeated slowly, as though Miss Barnett had missed it the first time around.

'I fail to see what that has to do with anything.'

'I had nothing to do, so rather than sit here like a stuffed dummy, I took the opportunity to have a pleasant conversation with the operator next to me.'

If she had not been conscious of all the other operators watching her, Miss Barnett would have pinched herself, just to make sure she wasn't dreaming.

'But the regulations clearly state that talking at the switchboard is not permitted,' she said, falling back on the Bible which had governed her working life.

'Am I a good operator?' Belinda asked.

'Well, yes,' Miss Barnett admitted. 'I'd go so far as to say that you're an excellent operator.'

'Then as long as I'm doing my job well, why don't you just leave me alone?'

This was outrageous, Miss Barnett thought. It was more than outrageous—it was completely intolerable.

'I shall be talking to the managers later in the day,' she said. 'And when I do, I shall strongly recommend your dismissal.'

Belinda stood up. 'I don't think that will be necessary,' she said, taking off her over-gown and throwing it, with some style, on to the floor.

She turned and looked around the room. All the other operators—even the ones who were dealing with calls—had their eyes glued to her.

'Look, ladies, I'm daring to show my frock in the middle of the exchange,' she said. 'Aren't I wicked? How do you think I'll be punished for doing such a terrible thing? I should imagine I'll burn in hell for all eternity.'

'Miss Benson ...' the Dragon hissed at her through gritted teeth.

Belinda walked over to the door. 'Goodbye, girls,' she said on its threshold. 'I only hope you enjoy your slavery as much as I will enjoy my freedom,' and then she was gone.

None of the other operators dared to cheer her, but they all wanted to.

It was only a short walk from Lant Street to Borough Station, but it was long enough for Lizzie to have three or four panic attacks on the way.

'I don't think this is a good idea, Mrs Bates,' she protested.

'It's an excellent idea,' Annie assured her.

'But I ain't never been underground before.'

'Then you should find it very interesting.'

'An' I ain't got no money.'

'I have.'

Annie half-dragged Lizzie down the steps to the booking office, where she handed over her four pennies and received two tickets in return.

'I don't see no trains,' Lizzie said.

'That's because the tunnel is much further underground,' Annie explained.

'So 'ow are we goin' to get to it?'

'In a lift.'

'I ain't never been in no lift before, either,' Lizzie moaned.

Annie laughed. 'You're going to be doing a lot of things today you've never done before.'

Once on the platform, Lizzie seemed to calm down a little, and take an interest in her surroundings. ' 'Ow far down are we now?' she asked.

'About a hundred feet.'

'An' 'ow did they dig these tunnels, then?'

'How do you think? With picks and shovels.'

'Blimey,' Lizzie said.

The electric train pulled into the station, and when the carriage door slid open, Lizzie and Annie stepped inside.

On the older underground lines—where the trains were pulled by steam engines and the platforms stank of sulphur—there were still three classes of compartments, but on the Twopenny Tube everyone travelled together, and the carriage the two women entered had City gents and office boys sitting side by side.

Lizzie sat down on one of the padded seats. 'Ain't this comfortable?' she said. 'An' ain't it a grand way to travel?'

Annie did her best to hide her smile. 'I thought you'd like it,' she said.

Lizzie gazed up and down Bond Street—at the carriages, then the expensive shop fronts, then back to the carriages.

'Oh Lor',' she said, 'it's 'ard to believe we're still in England, ain't it?'

'Shall we go and have a look round one of the shops?' Annie suggested.

Lizzie's eyes widened even further than they had already. 'Yer mean, go inside?'

'It'll be hard to look around if we stay outside, won't it?'

'But won't they say nuffink? I mean, we're from Southwark.'

'I'm sure there's no law against that,' Annie said, taking Lizzie's arm again and leading her towards the nearest shop.

The stores on Bond Street boasted that they could supply their customers' every need, from stocking their pantries to building their houses—and walking through Woodward's, it was not difficult to believe. There were clothes and carpets, beds and billiard tables, exotic French pastries and tropical plants, but it was the emporium's zoological department which fascinated Lizzie the most.

'Look at them little monkeys,' she said. 'Ain't they luverly? Can yer just buy one if yer want to?'

'If you've got the money—which we haven't!' Annie told her.

Lizzie sighed. 'Maybe one day,' she said wistfully.

Annie noticed one of the assistants heading towards them. He seemed a self-important little man, and had a look on his face which said that he was about to ask them what business they had cluttering up his department.

'I'm going to have some fun,' she whispered to Lizzie. 'Just play along with me.'

The assistant looked Annie up and down. She was wearing her best dress, but it was clear that she didn't pass muster as far as he was concerned.

'Can I help you, *madam?*' he asked.

Annie looked around the room. 'Where do you keep the lions and tigers?' she asked.

'I beg your pardon?'

'The lions and tigers? I don't see them.'

'*You* want to buy a lion?' the assistant asked,

with obvious disbelief.

Annie laughed lightly. 'Of course not,' she said.

'Then I don't see ...'

'But I am acting as the agent of Lord ... well, let's just call him Lord X, and he is very interested in purchasing lions.'

'I see,' the assistant said.

Lizzie chuckled.

'Be quiet, girl!' Annie said harshly.

Lizzie hastily curtsied. 'Yes, milady. Sorry, milady.'

'How many lions is Lord ... Lord X ... interested in acquiring?' the assistant asked.

'Six,' Annie said with conviction. 'But since you do not appear to have any in stock ...'

'We could get them for you, madam ... er ... milady.'

'And how long would it take?'

'That's hard to say. Three months. Perhaps even six.'

Annie tossed back her head haughtily. 'Six months!' she repeated. 'I'm sure that Harrods would never expect me to wait so long. Come, child, let us go to an establishment capable of dealing swiftly and efficiently with our needs.'

With that, she gathered up her skirts and swept regally out of the department, followed by a desperately giggling Lizzie.

The grey skies of the morning had disappeared, and London was bathed in sunshine. It seemed a pity to go straight home, so Annie bought some sandwiches from a confectioner's shop, and suggested that they eat them in Hyde Park.

When they reached the park, they walked down the Ladies' Mile. The unexpectedly warm weather had brought scores of people out. Elderly ladies passed in elegant carriages, which occasionally stopped long enough for a footman to walk one of the ladies' lapdogs. Younger ladies, dressed in full riding habits, cantered past on muscular horses.

'Look at the way they're dressed!' Lizzie said, pointing to two white-robed nurses who were pushing immaculate and obviously expensive prams. 'Maybe I can get Mrs Taylor to buy me one of them uniforms.'

'Somehow, I don't think it would look right in Southwark,' Annie told her.

They walked down to the Serpentine, fed the ducks with the remainders of their sandwiches, and watched the model sailing boats for a while. They strolled to Hyde Park Corner, and joined the crowd of gentry and common folk who had gathered there to wave at Queen Alexandra, as she passed them on her afternoon drive.

And then, finally, it was time to go home.

'I'll never be able to thank yer for what yer've done for me, Mrs Bates,' Lizzie said, as they sat in the Tube travelling back to Southwark.

'Don't be silly,' Annie said, starting to feel embarrassed. 'It was no trouble just to take you into the city, and I enjoyed it as much as you did.'

'Yer've opened up an 'ole new world for me, you 'ave, Mrs Bates,' Lizzie said sincerely.

'That's what yer've done—opened up an 'ole new world.'

Annie had only just arrived home when she heard the knock on the door, and opened it to find her sister-in-law, Mary, standing there, almost in tears.

'I got troubles,' Mary said.

'I can see that,' Annie replied. 'You'd better come in and have a nice cup of rosie.'

They walked down the passageway to the kitchen, and Annie put the kettle on.

'It's Fred,' Mary blurted out as soon as she had sat down at the kitchen table.

'I guessed it would have to be that,' Annie said. 'What's he been doing?'

'It ain't what 'e's been doin', it's what I 'aven't been doin'. 'E wants me to tell me mum about us.'

'And why shouldn't he? He's a grown man, and you're no kid any more. Sneaking around behind your mum's back isn't only wrong—it's ridiculous.'

'Yer don't know me mum,' Mary said. 'She might seem soft an' kind to you, but she's got a will of iron.'

Yes, Annie thought. Anyone who'd brought up four kids single-handed would *have* to have. 'Will of iron or not, you're going to have to learn to stand up to her sooner or later,' she told Mary.

'Maybe if I was a bit older ...'

There was another knock on the front door. 'It never rains but it pours,' Annie said, walking up the passageway and deciding she would tell whoever was calling that she was busy at the moment. Then she saw who the caller was.

'Belinda!' she said. 'What are you doing here on a weekday? Looking for Harry?'

'No, I'm looking for you. We need to have a very long talk, dear girl.'

It never *did* rain without pouring, Annie thought. 'You'd better come inside,' she said.

When they got to the kitchen, Mary stood up. 'Do yer want me to leave?' she asked.

Annie glanced at Belinda.

'No, I don't mind you hearing what I have to say,' Belinda told Mary. Her eyes fixed on the boiling kettle. 'I see you're making a cup of tea, Annie.'

Annie grinned. 'And I suppose you'd like one?'

'Of course I would. In case you've forgotten, you simply can't *get* a decent cup of rosie norf of the river,' Belinda said, in an absolutely awful Cockney accent.

Annie made the tea, and all three of them sat down. 'So what's all this about?' Annie said.

'I had a blazing row with the Dragon,' Belinda said.

Annie frowned. 'Did you, indeed? That wasn't very wise of you, was it?'

'I don't care. I'm sick of all the stupid rules and regulations they impose on us just because we're women.'

'You're going to have to apologise, you know.'

'Never!'

'If you don't, you'll lose your job.'

'No, I won't, because I've already resigned.'

'In writing?'

Belinda grinned. 'Not exactly. I threw my gown on the floor, and marched out.'

Annie did not return her grin. 'Then an apology won't do any good, will it?' she said. 'You really are finished.'

'Exactly, dear girl.'

'So what will you do now?'

'That's the problem. You see, my father provides me with an allowance to live in London ...'

'I thought he must do,' Annie said. 'Nobody earning a telephone operator's salary could ever afford to live in a flat like the one you've got.'

'True,' Belinda agreed. 'Now we come to the ticklish part. You see, he'll keep on paying the allowance as long as I have a *reason* to be in London. Well, I never did care much for being a telephone operator, but at least it gave me an excuse for absenting myself from the ancestral pile.'

'And now that excuse has gone out of the window.'

'Couldn't have put it better myself. So I have to find another job quickly, before dear Pater starts organising the peasantry to welcome the prodigal home.'

'What kind of job?'

'That's just what's been taxing the old brain cells. I don't want to work in a place where I'll be subjected to the same petty regulations I suffered under at the exchange, because I'd be likely to pull another stunt like the one I pulled this morning.'

Now, Annie did grin. 'I expect you would,' she said. 'Once you've got a taste for making the dramatic gesture, it's quite hard to give it up again.'

'So the conclusion I'm forced to reach is that I will simply have to go into business for myself,' Belinda said, ignoring the dig. 'And for that, I shall require a partner. So naturally, I thought of you.'

'Me! But I don't know anything about business. What *kind* of business were you thinking about, anyway?'

'There was a new operator working next to me this morning,' Belinda said. 'It was my talking to her which started the row.'

'So?'

'She was a married woman. The company only called her in because they were short staffed.'

'I still don't get it.'

'I think it was the typewriting machine which changed things,' Belinda said. 'Men love strutting round offices looking important, but when it comes to actually getting down to some good, solid work, they'll leave it to the women every time.'

Annie laughed. 'Are you ever going to get to the point, Belinda?' she asked.

'There are offices all over London which, despite what the men think, are *really* being run by women. And what happens when one of those women goes sick?'

'I don't know, but I'd imagine the other

women share out her work between them.'

'Exactly. But since they're usually overloaded already, that system doesn't really work.'

Annie was beginning to see the way Belinda's mind was working. 'The telephone company has a pool of people it can call on when it needs them ...' she began. 'And if we had a pool of typewriters and women who can file and take shorthand ...'

'Then we could make ourselves a fortune,' Belinda proclaimed triumphantly.

Annie looked dubious. 'I don't know,' she said. 'If it's such a good idea, how is it that nobody's ever tried it before?'

'Because no one else in the whole of London has the famous Benson brainbox?' Belinda suggested hopefully.

'Or because it's a crazy idea which couldn't possibly work,' Annie said.

'But what have we got to lose? My father will advance me the money we need to open a small office, and even if we go broke, he's so rich he'll never notice the difference. And you? You're not making any money at the moment, are you? So you might as well spend your time having fun not making any money with me.'

Belinda was right, Annie decided—it was like betting on a sure thing.

She heard a cough, and realised it came from Mary. With all this talk of setting up businesses, she'd almost forgotten that her sister-in-law was still in the room.

Poor kid! If only she had a bit more self-confidence, she might be able to pluck up the nerve to tackle her mum. But where was that self-confidence to come from? Not from her work. Annie knew from her own experience how small they tried to make you feel at the match factory. If only she could ...

'We'll need a secretary of our own, won't we?' she said to Belinda. 'Somebody to do our typewriting and filing?'

'I expect so,' Belinda agreed.

'What about taking on Mary?'

Mary looked as astonished as Annie had done earlier, when Belinda had first mentioned going into business.

'But I don't know nuffink at all about typewritin' and filin',' she protested.

'You can learn,' Annie said briskly. 'I expect they run all kinds of evening courses down at Borough Polytechnic Institute.'

'I don't think—' Mary began.

'And I'm sure Belinda would pay you a small wage while you were learning,' Annie interrupted her.

'If that means you'll go into business with me, Annie, then of course I will,' Belinda said.

'You were only telling me last week how sick to death you were of the match factory,' Annie said to Mary. 'Well, here's your chance to get out.'

Mary's face was a picture of indecision for about ten seconds, then she squared her shoulders and said, 'I'll ... I'll take the chance an' give it a try.'

'That's the spirit,' Belinda said.

The sound of a key being turned in the front door was followed by footsteps in the passageway.

'Tom's home early,' Annie said.

'If it really is Tom, and not some incredibly noisy burglar,' Belinda said.

It was Tom, and he was looking very pleased with himself. 'I've just 'ad word from 'Arry,' he told them. 'Me application for the Wet Bobs 'as been accepted, an' I'm to go to New Scotland Yard tomorrow for a medical an' some kind of written examination.'

'That's wonderful news,' Annie said enthusiastically. 'You are a clever man.'

'I ain't got in yet,' Tom said cautiously.

'But you will. I know you will,' Annie told him. 'I've got some news for you, too.'

'Oh, yes? An' what's that?'

'Belinda and I are going into business together.'

'Doin' what?'

'Providing temporary replacements for office workers who are off sick.'

'An' I'm goin' to start trainin' to be their secretary,' Mary said proudly.

A look which may have been disappointment or unhappiness—or maybe some emotion even stronger than that—flashed briefly across Tom's face, and then was gone.

'Blimey, this place is gettin' to be just like Clapham Junction today,' he said, forcing himself to smile.

'How do you mean?' Annie asked.

Tom's grin widened. 'All change!' he said.

CHAPTER 6

Tom Bates had never needed an alarm clock to wake him, and at half past six the next morning, just as he'd planned, his eyes were open and he was ready to face the world.

He climbed out of bed slowly and carefully, so as not to wake Annie, and made his way over to the bedroom window. Drawing back the curtain, he looked up at the sky. The last couple of days had started out grey, but that morning the sun shone down on him from out of a cloudless sky.

Maybe that's a sign that there's good luck comin' my way, he thought. He certainly *hoped* it was a sign, because he was going to need all the luck he could get to be accepted by the river police.

He frowned as he remembered what Annie had told him the night before. She was going to set up a business with Belinda—and he wasn't happy about that. Not at all.

He thought back to his own childhood. His mum had always had little jobs to help top up the family budget, but it had been his dad who had been the real breadwinner. The same had been true of Tom and Annie: since they'd got married, he'd had bad weeks and good weeks on the river, but even when they'd had to tighten their belts a little, it was always *his* money which had supported them.

Now it looked as if all that might change. If Annie's business was a success—and he didn't see why it shouldn't be—she could end up earning much more than he did as a waterman. Which was why it was vital that he should be taken on by the Wet Bobs.

He noticed that his heart was beating faster than usual. Its message was clear. 'You need that job,' it said. 'You really need that job.'

He told himself that he was being stupid—that Annie and he loved each other, and it didn't matter which of them was making the most money. Yet he knew deep inside himself that it *did* matter, and that if Annie's income outstripped his, he would find it very difficult to hold his head up high again.

'I'm sorry it's like that, darlin',' he whispered to his sleeping wife, 'but there's nuffink I can do about it. It's just the way I've been brought up.'

Tom walked along the Victoria Embankment, his eyes fixed on the large building with a domed turret on each corner. He'd seen New Scotland Yard hundreds of times, and hardly ever given it a second thought, but he thought about it now.

What would they ask him in there? he wondered. What would he have to do to prove himself worthy to become a river policeman?

He approached the forbidding arched entrance and felt the muscles in his stomach start to knot.

Two policemen stood guard by the door. 'Lost property?' one of them asked Tom.

'What?'

' 'Ave yer come to claim some lost property?'

'No,' Tom said. 'I'm 'ere for a medical and interview. I want to join the Thames River Police.'

The policemen smiled at the mention of their rivals. 'The Thames River Police!' said the one who had spoken before. 'They're not proper bobbies, like we are. All they ever do with their time is mess about in little boats.'

'They seem to put enough criminals away in clink,' Tom said.

'Luck,' the second policeman retorted. 'Pure blind luck. Don't go joinin' the Wet Bobs, son.'

'No, don't,' his partner agreed. 'Try an' find some honest employment instead.'

Tom grinned. 'Me mind's made up.'

The first policeman gave a theatrical sigh. 'All right, then. Yer got yer letter, 'ave yer?'

Tom took out the letter inviting him for an interview, and handed it over.

The second policeman read it, then said, 'That seems to be perfectly in order, but we're still goin' to 'ave to search yer before we let yer go in.'

'Search me?' Tom said, thinking that they were still making fun of him. 'What for?'

'Dynamite.'

Tom grinned again.

'It's no joke,' the second policeman assured him. 'A few years ago, some bloke with dynamite got right inside the buildin'. 'Ad it strapped all over 'im, 'e did.'

The first policeman ran his hands up and down Tom's trunk and legs. 'This young bloke seems clean enough to me, 'Orace,' he told his partner.

'Right,' the second policeman said. 'Yer go through this arch, turn left, and yer'll see the general office. Tell 'em what yer've come for, an' they'll tell yer where to go next.'

'Thanks,' Tom said.

The banter with the two policemen had relaxed him a little, but now, as he walked through the high archway, he felt his nervousness returning.

'Yer sure yer wouldn't rather go an' see the lost property office?' one of the policemen called after him. 'We got all sorts in there. Bicycles, sewin' machines, rabbits—you name it an' somebody's 'anded it in.'

Annie heard the front latch click, and rushed down the passageway to meet her husband. 'So how did it go?' she asked.

Tom shrugged. 'There was this doctor there. 'E gave me a medical examination.'

'And?'

'An' 'e said I was a magnificent physical specimen.'

'So you are,' Annie said impatiently, as she led him back to the kitchen. 'But I didn't need a doctor to tell me that. What else happened?'

'The doctor asked me if I was used to 'eavy outdoor work, an' when I said I was a waterman, 'e said that explained the condition I was in.'

'I could kill you sometimes, Tom Bates,' Annie said. 'I'm not interested in what the doctor said to you or you said to him. I want to know what happened *after* the medical.'

'Well, there was about ten of us, yer see. Or it may 'ave been an even dozen.'

'Tom!' Annie said threateningly.

'Anyway, they took us into this room, an' give us all some tests to do.'

'What kind of tests?'

'Well, yer know.'

'No, I don't know, or I wouldn't be asking you.'

'Readin', writin', 'rithmetic, an' somefink they called an intelligence test.'

'And then?'

'An' then they said that we all 'ad to wait outside while they marked 'em.'

Annie's patience had reached its end. She grabbed her husband by the shoulders, and shook him. 'And what was the result, you lunatic?' she demanded. 'What was the flamin' result?'

'Of the tests, d'yer mean?'

'Of course that's what I mean!'

'Well, it turns out I've got more in me loaf than I ever imagined I 'ad.'

'Are you trying to tell me you passed?'

'With flyin' colours.'

'Told you you would!' Annie said ecstatically. 'Told you you would! Told you you would!'

'I was never in any doubt about it meself—not even for a second,' Tom lied.

'When do you start?'

'Next Monday. I 'ave to report to somefink that they called the Candidates' Section 'Ouse in Kennington Lane. For trainin'. I'll be away for three weeks. D'yer think yer'll be able to manage that long without me?'

'It won't be easy,' Annie admitted. 'I've got used to waking up with you beside me, but yes, I think I'll manage, because I know it'll all be worth it in the end.'

'So what 'ave you been doin' while I've been dazzlin' 'em in New Scotland Yard?' Tom asked.

'Well, Belinda and I went looking for offices.'

'An' ...?'

'We saw quite a number of them.'

'Get to the point.'

Annie smiled wickedly. 'Don't like it when you have your own tricks played back on you, do you?'

Tom grinned. 'All right, it's a fair cop,' he said. 'You tell yer story in yer own way, an' I'll try to contain me impatience better than you managed to contain yours.'

'You're so sharp today you might end up cutting yourself,' Annie said. 'Anyway, to get to the point—like you didn't for ages—we've found an office on Borough High Street that Belinda thinks will do us very nicely.'

'When are yer movin' in?'

'Some time next week. Honestly, Belinda is amazing. She's got so much energy. I wasn't sure of it yesterday, but now I'm certain we can make a real success of the business.'

'An' 'ow much do yer think yer'll be makin' when yer a real success?'

'It's difficult to say, but Belinda told me she wouldn't be the least bit surprised if we ended up earning as much as two pounds ten shillings a week.'

'Twenty-five bob a piece ain't bad goin',' Tom said.

'You've misunderstood me. She didn't mean two pounds ten between us—she meant two pounds ten *each.*'

So even on a Wet Bob's pay, I might end up a kept man, Tom thought gloomily.

The Borough Polytechnic Institute was an imposing Victorian redbrick building with crenellations running around its stern gables. It may or may not have been designed to intimidate, but it was certainly having that effect on Mary Bates, who was standing on the pavement opposite watching all the students and teachers striding confidently in and out.

'Yer don't *'ave* to do this,' Mary told herself, as the butterflies in her stomach did a violent somersault. No, she didn't have to do it. She could simply turn round and go home. Fred wouldn't think any the worse of her for not signing up, and neither would her mum. But she knew that the next morning—when she entered the match factory and saw Miss Hunt glaring at her—*she* would think the worse of *herself.*

'Come on, Mary,' she said aloud. 'It's time yer stopped being so timid. What are yer so worried about, anyway? They're not goin' to bite yer 'ead off in there, are they?'

She forced her legs to move forward, across the street and through the main door.

Just inside the entrance hall, a uniformed porter was sitting behind his desk. He looked, if anything, more imposing than the outside of the building, but Mary had already come too far to turn back now.

'I ... I want to learn to become a typewriter,' she said.

'Do yer now?' the porter said. He smiled, and suddenly looked quite human. 'Go up them stairs an' turn left. It's the third door down. Got a big brass plate on, which says "Commercial Department".'

'Thanks,' Mary said.

The porter smiled again. 'My pleasure,' he told her. 'It's always nice to see a gal 'oo wants to get on.'

Mary sat at one side of the desk in the small office and the woman who was interviewing her—Miss Carpenter—sat at the other.

Miss Carpenter was about forty, and though she was wearing a very severe blouse and skirt, she had a kind smile which almost put Mary at her ease.

'So you've already been offered a position?' she said.

'That's right,' Mary said. 'I'll be working for me sister-in-law an' 'er friend. They're openin' their own business.'

Miss Carpenter raised her eyebrows in surprise. 'Are they, indeed? Well, young women seem to have come a great distance since I was a girl—and good luck to them, I say. As far as you're concerned, though, if you are entering the business world, you'll really need to improve your syntax and pronunciation.'

'Me what?' Mary asked, panicking at the thought that she would have to improve something which she didn't even know she had.

'You must learn to speak more accurate English,' Miss Carpenter explained.

Mary sighed with relief. 'That ain't no problem,' she said. 'If yer've got evening classes in that, I'll go to 'em. I want to go to classes in everyfink I need.'

With a smile on her face, Miss Carpenter filled out the enrolment forms. 'Then we can look forward to seeing you on the first Monday of next month, Miss Bates?' she asked when she had finished.

'I wouldn't miss it for the world.'

Miss Carpenter stood up. 'Well then, Miss Bates ...'

Mary stayed fixed to her seat, her eyes glued to the typewriting machine which sat on Miss Carpenter's desk.

'Miss Bates?'

Mary came out of her trance. 'Can I give it a try?' she asked.

'Give what a try?'

'I know me classes don't start till next month, but could I 'ave a go at typewritin' now—just to see what it feels like?'

'You are keen,' Miss Carpenter said, feeding

a piece of plain paper into the machine. 'All right, Miss Bates. Take my seat and see how you like it.'

Mary made her way around the desk and sat in Miss Carpenter's seat, then she touched the keys on the machine with the tips of her fingers—and something wonderful happened.

An energy, almost like electricity, passed through her fingers and into her hands, until it filled her whole body. She knew then that the typewriting machine had been invented for no other purpose than that she should use it—that she had been born for no other purpose than to put it to use. Though she had not even typed a single letter, she was *sure* that she was going to be a wonderful typewriter, one of the best in London.

She felt like a new woman. No, that wasn't quite true, because up to the moment she had touched the typewriting machine, she had never really felt like a woman at all—just a girl who didn't know what she wanted to do with her life.

That evening May Bates sat in her front parlour-workshop, making paper flowers. It was a fiddly job, and she couldn't say that she was very fond of it, but at least it helped to pay the rent. Now she had lost Tom's wage, she couldn't turn down *any* work, however much she happened to dislike it.

She heard the front door click open. 'Is that you, Mary?' she called out.

'Yes, Mum.'

'Come in 'ere a minute.'

Mary stepped into the parlour. She was wearing her best dress, and her blonde hair—as a result of painstaking hours with curling papers—cascaded in ringlets down to her shoulders. There was something else about her, May thought—a glow which simply hadn't been there before.

'You been out for a walk?' her mother asked.

'No,' Mary replied. 'I've been down to the Borough Polytechnic Institute.'

'The Polytechnic Institute. Whatever for?'

'I've what-d-yer-call-it?—enrolled. I've enrolled for typewritin' classes.'

'Why would you do a thing like that?'

' 'Cos I want to better meself.'

May screwed her eyes up suspiciously. 'These typewritin' classes wouldn't be just an excuse for somefink else, would they, Mary?' she asked.

' 'Ow d'yer mean?'

'They wouldn't be an excuse for gettin' yer out of the 'ouse so yer can see that Fred Simpson?'

'No,' Mary said. 'I really do want to take the typewritin' classes, Mum, but ...'

'But what?'

It would have been so easy to lie, and the old Mary would have done just that, but the new Mary was sick of evasions and deceit. 'I ... I don't think I *need* an excuse to see Fred,' she said.

'Oh, yer don't, don't yer?'

'That's right. If yer must know, I *'ave* been

seein' 'im—ever since our Tom got married.'

An anger which only a few hours ago would have turned Mary to stone flared up in her mother's eyes. 'Seein' 'im?' she said, as if she couldn't believe it. 'Be'ind my back?'

'Yes, but yer mustn't blame Fred for that. 'E wanted everyfink out in the open. It was me that was too scared to face yer.'

'It *is* 'im I blame. 'E's older than you, an' should know better than to go against a mother's wishes.'

'I just don't see why yer've taken so against 'im,' Mary said fiercely. ' 'E's a nice bloke, an' 'e respects me like a man should respect a woman.'

'Yer not a *woman*,' her mother told her, shredding the paper rose she had been so carefully assembling. 'Yer nuffink but a slip of a girl. An' you're not goin' to try an' tell me 'e's never kissed yer, are yer?'

'No. 'E *as* kissed me. Lots o' times. But 'e's never touched me in places where 'e shouldn't 'ave. An' that was 'is choice—'cos I'd 'ave let 'im if 'e wanted to.'

'I can't believe I'm 'earin' this,' May said. 'I just can't bring meself to believe it.'

' 'E wants me to be 'is wife, Mum. 'E wants to marry me as soon as I'm eighteen.'

May flung the shredded rose furiously on to the floor. 'Yer can't get married till yer twenty-one—not without my permission,' she said. 'D'yer think that yer precious Fred'll be prepared to wait that long for yer?'

' 'E won't 'ave to,' Mary screamed back, her

hands clamped defiantly on her hips. ' 'Cos if yer won't let me marry 'im, we'll set up 'ouse together anyway. Then what will yer neighbours say?'

May's mouth opened and closed several times, but no sound came out. She was amazed. More than amazed—she was astounded. Not only was this the first real row she'd ever had with her daughter, but she'd never seen Mary so serious or determined about anything before. If she handled the situation like she'd planned to—the firm, unbending mother—she was going to lose her daughter one way or another. And that would just about kill her, she thought. So what could she say now, to repair all the damage that had already been done?

She searched around for the right words, and finally found them. 'Yer really do love 'im, don't yer?' she said softly.

'I do, Mum,' Mary said, starting to cry. 'I love my Fred with all me 'eart.'

May nodded. 'Then we're goin' to 'ave to come to some kind of agreement,' she said. 'You can keep on seein' 'im ...'

'Thanks, Mum.'

'... but yer've got to make 'im promise not to try an' take advantage of yer.'

'I told yer, 'e wouldn't, Mum. Not even when I gave 'im the chance to.'

'Make 'im promise anyway,' May said firmly. 'D'yer understand what I'm saying to yer?'

Mary sniffed and dabbed her tears with the edge of her sleeve. 'Yes, Mum. I understand. But what about gettin' married?'

'It's still a long way to yer eighteenth birthday ...'

'I know, but—'

'... but if yer still as stuck on each other then as yer obviously are now, I'll give yer me permission to get 'itched.'

Mary hugged her mother. 'Thanks, Mum.'

'Don't thank me yet,' May replied, trying her best to hold back the tears which were forming in her own eyes. 'Yer may live to rue the day I gave in to yer.'

'I won't, Mum. I know I won't. My Fred's so kind an' gentle an' generous ...'

'Well, I s'ppose we'd better 'ave this kind an' gentle an' generous man round for 'is tea on Sunday. If 'e can find the time to come, that is.'

'Oh, 'e'll find the time,' Mary promised. ' 'E'd 'ave been round 'ere long before now, if I 'adn't been so weak an' silly.'

'So 'e's kind an' generous, an' you're weak an' silly. It's a wonder to me that 'e wants to marry yer,' May said smiling. Then her face became serious again. 'What I said about givin' me permission when yer turn eighteen ...'

'Yes, Mum?'

'That's always providin', o' course, that's 'e's still in a position to support yer.'

'Why shouldn't 'e be?' Mary asked. ' 'E's a fireman, an' that ain't goin' to change, is it?'

'Like I said, it's a long way to yer eighteenth birthday,' May said.

CHAPTER 7

It was the kind of August morning that the people of Southwark would look back on with affection from the depths of a cold, snow-bound winter. The sun was warming without being too overbearing, and what few clouds there were in the sky floated lazily along, as if, on a pleasant day like this, they were in no particular hurry to be anywhere else.

Lizzie Hodges was walking along Union Street, pushing the double pram containing Ted and Cathy Taylor. As she crossed Southwark Bridge Road, she looked left to check on the traffic and saw the stark brick walls of St Saviour's Workhouse.

She shuddered. 'Gawd, what an awful place that is,' she said to herself.

There'd been a time when such a thought would never have entered her head. She remembered a talk she'd once had with Ethel Barnes, a washed-out middle-aged pauper who'd only been in the workhouse for three years at that time.

'D'yer know why the Board of Guardians 'ardly ever let us go outside?' Ethel had asked.

'No,' Lizzie had replied.

'It's 'cos they're afraid that if we do, we might start to enjoy ourselves.'

'Why should they be worried about that?'

' 'Cos they think it'll encourage the others.'
'What others?'

'All the people on the outside what are just about gettin' by. See, the board think that if we seem to be 'avin' a good time, folk'll be queuin' at the door to get in. So they do their best to make sure we 'ave a worse life than them as ain't paupers.'

Lizzie had nodded.

'Yer understand what I'm sayin'?' Ethel had asked.

' 'Course I do!' Lizzie had replied, although she hadn't really. The workhouse was all she'd ever known. She was used to living in a long dormitory, going to bed when she was told and getting up when the bell rang. It seemed completely natural to her that she should bathe at the same time every Thursday—in exactly six inches of lukewarm water—and that there should always be a pint and a half of porridge for breakfast.

Who *wanted* to go outside, when the workhouse offered all you could ever possibly need?

Now, she realised what the other woman had been talking about. She *did* understand, and she saw the workhouse for what it really was—as much of a prison as Holloway or Brixton.

Each day away from the confines of St Saviour's was a new adventure, an exciting voyage of discovery. There'd been sausages—not porridge—for breakfast, which she'd loved. And what sights there were to be seen, just walking around the streets—china-menders and chair-repairers going about their business; butchers' vans and doctors' carriages hurrying here and there—and that was just the beginning. Across the river there were amazing shops waiting to be visited, and vast parks which needed exploring.

Yes, it was a wonderful world that the Taylors and Annie Bates had introduced her to, and she would be eternally grateful.

On the corner of Union Street stood an organ-grinder, and on top of his organ he had not a monkey, but a brightly coloured parrot in a cage. 'Tell yer fortune for a penny,' the man called out to Lizzie.

'You don't look like no fortune-teller,' she said, with a boldness which was quite new to her.

The organ-grinder grinned. 'I ain't. It's the bird what does the predictions.'

It seemed worth a penny just to see how the bird did it, but Lizzie was quite happy with life just as it was, and didn't want her fortune told.

She looked down at the babies in the pram. Ted was already starting to develop the solid, dependable look of his father, and when he had a problem—such as an obstacle in his way when he was crawling across the room—he would take his time over thinking how to get round it. Cathy was more like her mum, only without Colleen's big nose. She would be a beauty when she grew up, Lizzie thought, and she was such a sweet-tempered, loving kid already.

'Will the parrot tell one of the baby's fortunes?'

she asked the organ-grinder.

' 'Course it will,' replied the grinder, who wasn't going to let a penny slip through his fingers if he could possibly help it.

'All right, then,' Lizzie agreed, reaching into her bag and taking out a copper. 'Get it to tell the little girl's fortune.'

The grinder picked up a narrow trough full of small slips of paper, and slid it into the cage. The parrot, for his part, strutted self-importantly up and down, then picked up one of the slips in his beak and dropped it through the bars.

'There y'are,' the grinder said, as the piece of paper floated to the ground. 'One fortune, made to order.'

Lizzie bent down and picked it up. 'You will soon be parted from loved ones,' it read.

How awful it would be if that was true, Lizzie thought. But, of course, it was all nonsense. The parrot would have picked the same piece of paper if it had been *her* fortune it was telling, and she didn't have any loved ones to be parted from. Yes, the parrot would definitely have told the same fortune for anyone ... wouldn't it?

Lizzie pushed the pram up to the Union Street stables, where Eddie Clarke had worked before he was taken on as a motor mechanic. The big wooden doors of the stable were open, and through them Lizzie could see the horses in their stalls.

She stopped, and lifted the two babies out of their pram. 'Look at the 'orses, Ted,' she said. 'Ain't they luverly, Cathy?'

One of the grooms saw her standing there.

'Want to bring 'em for a closer look?' he asked.

'That's very kind of yer,' Lizzie said.

She entered the stable. It smelt of polished leather and straw, of horses' sweat and dung. There had been no smells like that in the workhouse.

'Nice 'orses,' she said.

The groom pointed to a huge shire horse. 'See 'im? 'Is name's Samson. 'E pulls one of them brewers' drays yer always seein' around. Very valuable animal, is Samson. 'Ow much would yer say 'e's worth?'

'I've no idea,' Lizzie confessed. 'Five pounds?' she hazarded.

The groom laughed. 'Five pounds!' he repeated. 'Old Samson is worth seventy-five guineas if 'e's worth a penny.'

Lizzie gasped. 'Seventy-five guineas!' She could not imagine anything costing that much.

'Want to stroke 'im?' the groom asked. 'It's all right, 'e won't bite yer.'

'The kids might like to stroke 'im,' Lizzie said, looking first at Cathy and then at Ted, 'but I don't see 'ow I can manage to lift both of 'em up to 'im at once.'

'Give me the little lad,' the groom suggested.

Lizzie handed Ted over, then took Cathy's tiny hand and ran it up and down the horse's head. 'Ain't 'e a nice 'orsey?' she asked, and Cathy gurgled happily.

'They're a luverly pair of kids, ain't they?' the groom said. 'Are they yours?'

'No, they ain't,' Lizzie said, although, in a

way, she felt they were really—especially little Cathy.

It was seven o'clock in the evening when Tom Bates reached his mother's house at the top of Lant Place and knocked lightly on the door of her front parlour-workshop. He was feeling far from light hearted, because his brother, Joey, had entrusted him with a task which he would rather have not been given—but which he knew no one else could perform.

' 'Oo is it?' May Bates called from the other side of the door.

'It's only me, Mum.'

'Well, don't 'ang about in the passage, Tom. Come on in.'

Tom turned the handle and pushed the door open. May was sitting on her usual stool, surrounded by sheets of coloured paper and bits of wire.

'Still on flowers, I see,' Tom said.

'I am.' May looked up and smiled at her son, but her fingers never stopped working on the paper rose she was making.

'Yer shouldn't 'ave to be doin' that kind o'work at your age, old gal.'

May laughed. 'I don't 'ave much choice, now do I? Yer brother an' sisters 'ardly earn enough to pay for their food, never mind anyfink else, an' that miserable old devil of a rent man wants 'is money every Friday whether or not we can afford to give it to 'im.'

It always came down to money, Tom thought. A few bob extra a week could make all the difference to most people, but getting that few bob was always a bloody struggle.

'Maybe I'll be able to 'elp yer out a bit when I've finished me trainin',' he said aloud.

May shook her head. 'I don't want yer money, Tom. Yer'll 'ave little enough for yerself.'

He *wanted* to give her some, though—wanted to relieve his poor old mum of some of the drudgery which had been her life since his dad died. Yet she was right: a Wet Bob's pay was not over-generous, and if he gave some of it to his mum, he'd be even less of the breadwinner in his own home than it already looked like he was going to be.

'When does yer trainin' start?' May asked.

'Next Monday mornin',' Tom said. He hesitated for a few seconds, then decided to plunge straight into his real reason for calling. 'Listen, old gal ...'

'Yes?'

'The ... er ... what's made me come round tonight is that I've been asked to speak to yer on be'half of—'

'If this is about yer sister, that matter's already been settled, thank you,' May told him.

'No, it's not about Mary. It was young Joey 'oo asked me to talk to yer.'

'An' what's so important that 'e 'ad to send 'is big brother in, 'stead of talkin' to me 'imself?'

Tom shifted uncomfortably from one foot to the other. 'Yer know that 'e's been doin' a lot of weight trainin' and sparrin' down at the gym, don't yer?'

'Yes?' May said cautiously.

This was turning out to be just as difficult as Tom had expected it to be. 'Well, yer must 'ave known what it was all leadin' up to, mustn't yer?'

'Leadin' up to? I didn't know it was leadin' up to anyfink. I thought 'e was just buildin' 'imself up a bit.'

Tom had looked straight into the eyes of the policeman who had told him he was to be charged with the murder of Rollo Jenkins. He had not flinched when the magistrate had bound him over, nor when the solicitor had told him he had very little chance of escaping the hangman's rope. So why was he nervous now, facing this grey-haired woman who didn't come up to his shoulder? Because she's me mum, he thought, an' everybody's five years old when they're dealin' with their mum.

'Well, are yer goin' to get it off yer chest or not?' May asked, a little impatiently.

' 'E wants to be a boxer, Mum,' Tom said in a rush.

'But 'e boxes already.'

' 'E wants to do it professionally.'

May's busy fingers stopped working. 'Yer mean, get paid for fightin'?'

'Yes.'

'Well, I'm not 'avin' it.'

'Mum, be reasonable.'

'I'm not 'avin' no child of mine gettin' what few brains 'e 'as beaten out of 'im in a boxin' ring,' May said firmly. 'An' that's me last word on the subject.'

She was reacting just as Tom had expected

her to. He decided to make one last attempt. 'Do yer know them big batteries they 'ave at fairgrounds?' he asked. 'The ones where yer pay an 'a'penny to get an electric shock?'

'I've seen 'em,' May said, as if she sensed her son was leading her into some kind of trap.

'Joey once said it was a funny thing about them batteries. 'E said yer were scared while yer were waitin' for yer go, and it wasn't exactly pleasant while it was 'appenin', but once it was over, yer were glad yer'd done it.'

'That's just kids' talk,' his mother said dismissively. 'It don't mean nuffink.'

'It docs,' Tom disagreed. 'It's about the most grown-up thing 'e's ever said. An' d'yer want to know what else 'e told me?'

'I might as well 'ear it, I s'ppose,' May said, though it was plain from her tone that it wouldn't make any difference one way or the other.

' 'E said that's what 'e wanted 'is life to be like—one electric shock after another.'

'Barmy,' May said.

'That's why 'e joined the Newington 'Ooligans an' got 'imself—an' me—into trouble.'

'An' I 'ope 'e's learned 'is lesson from that.'

'So do I. But don't yer see, if yer won't let 'im box, 'e'll only find some other way to get 'is electric shocks—an' that might be much more dangerous than boxin'.'

'So yer sayin' if I don't let 'im box, 'e might go in for somefink criminal?'

'I don't know if 'e'd ever go that far, old gal,' Tom admitted, 'but it is a possibility.'

May sighed heavily. 'Yer children are a trial to yer, ain't they?' she said. 'A real trial. First there's Mary with that young fireman of 'ers, an' now there's Joey wantin' to get 'imself knocked about. I don't know what to do for the best.' She picked up the paper rose again, and began to put the finishing touches to it.

' 'E's a big bloke, old gal,' Tom said, 'an' even though 'e's a bit on the raw side at the moment, I can see 'e's got the makin's of a good boxer in 'im.'

'All right,' May said. ' 'E can fight.' She lifted her head again and looked into her son's eyes. 'But if anyfink 'appens to 'im, I'm 'oldin' you responsible.'

' 'E'll be fine,' Tom said—and really hoped that he wasn't lying to his old mum.

George Taylor sat at the kitchen table, his evening newspaper spread out before him, feeling perfectly at peace with the world. And why not? After a lean period, trade was picking up again, and business at the wood yard, especially, was doing very well. Then there was his family—he adored his wife, and the kids were a constant joy. He had everything he'd ever wanted out of life.

There was a knock on the front door. 'Don't disturb yerself, sir. I'll get it,' Lizzie called out from the top of the stairs.

Sir! George thought. Nobody called him 'sir'. Even at the wood yard, where a degree of respect was very important if the job was going to get done properly, the men under him only ever called him 'boss' or Mr Taylor.

'But can I train Lizzie to do that?' he asked himself. 'Can I 'eck as like.' Whatever he said, she insisted on 'sir'—even though it made him cringe every time she used the word.

Still, in all other ways she was working out wonderfully. She loved the kids and they loved her, and when she was not looking after them, she was always finding other jobs to do around the house. Yes, George told himself, Colleen had been right about Lizzie—she was turning into a real little treasure.

Lizzie appeared in the doorway. ' 'Scuse me, sir, but there's a bloke outside 'oo says 'e'd like to see yer.'

'Did he give his name?'

'Yes, sir. 'E says 'e's Mr Taylor, like you. Matter o' fact, 'e says 'e's yer brother, though 'e don't look much like you.'

'My brother?' George repeated. It couldn't be Jack, who spent most of his time in Africa, so it could only be Philip.

Philip—who had once sold smutty picture postcards on the promenade at Blackpool, and had ended up serving time in Strangeways Prison for it.

Philip—who had used his brother-in-law Michael's salt blocks as a way of smuggling stolen jewels from Cheshire to London; who had finally started making money with his funny comics, then got bored and jacked it in.

Philip—turning up again like a bad penny.

'Sir?' Lizzie said.

'Yes?' George replied, coming out of his musings.

'What shall I tell 'im, sir?'

'You'd better show him in,' George said heavily.

Philip was wearing a smart double-breasted jacket and trousers with wide turn-ups. In his hand, he carried a bowler hat. He was not alone. The woman who accompanied him wore an extravagant blue dress which seemed all lace and frills, and a hat made up of silk roses.

The two men shook hands, and then Philip said, 'May I have the honour of introducing you to Miss Marie Tomlin, the *chanteuse* and living-pictures star.'

'*Miss* Tomlin?' George said. 'I thought you an' her had got married.'

Philip put his finger playfully to his mouth to indicate that George should say no more. 'We *are* married,' he said in a whisper, though there was no one else in the kitchen to hear, 'but apart from the immediate family, we're keeping the marriage a secret. For professional reasons, you understand.'

'My many admirers would be desolate if they learned I was no longer free,' Miss Tomlin added.

'I see,' George said—though he didn't really. 'Well, I suppose you'd better sit down.'

They sat, though Marie could not do so without a great deal of rustling of silk as she adjusted her skirt.

'Would you like a cup of tea?' George asked.

Philip shook his head. 'No, thank you.'

'We never drink tea,' Marie explained. 'Only coffee passes our lips—and even then, it must be freshly ground coffee made from the finest Colombian beans.'

'A beer, then?' George suggested. 'I think there's a couple of bottles in the cupboard.'

'We're not really thirsty,' Philip interjected hastily, before Marie could make a point of saying that they never drank beer, only champagne.

'Suit yourselves,' said George, who knew his brother far too well to let his guard down yet.

Philip smiled winningly. 'Well, well, well. How long has it been since you and I have seen one another, George? Why, it must be years and years.'

George looked closely at his brother. Philip was not the youngest of the family—Becky was his junior by over a year—but somehow, perhaps because of his slight frame or his irresponsible attitude to life, he had always seemed the baby. Even Becky had felt that—which was why, in the old days, she'd seemed to spend half her time pulling him out of scrapes.

'Yes, years since we've seen each other,' Philip repeated, the winning smile still in place.

'We haven't met since before I got sent out to the Sudan,' George reminded him.

'We really should have written to each other, shouldn't we?' Philip said.

'Maybe we would have done—if you'd bothered to give us your address.'

Philip laughed lightly. 'I always *did* mean to

send it to you, but somehow, what with one thing and another, I never seemed to get around to it.'

George wasn't about to let him off the hook so easily. 'We might even have visited each other,' he said. 'I mean, I assume you don't live too far from here.'

'Oh, good heavens, we live miles away,' Marie said, her tone suggesting horror that George could ever have thought otherwise. 'Well over on the *other side* of the river,' and then she, too, laughed.

She had a voice like a foghorn, George thought. If she really was a star in the living pictures, then it was a damn good job they were silent.

'So what suddenly brings you to see me after all this time?' George asked Philip.

Philip, to give him credit, had the grace to look embarrassed. 'Can't a brother visit a brother for no other reason than that they *are* brothers?'

'Maybe some brothers can, but not you, Philip.'

'I'd like you to do me a favour,' Philip admitted. He held up his forefinger and thumb, only a tenth of an inch apart. 'A very, very small favour.'

'What *kind* of small favour?'

'No doubt you have seen at least some of my masterpieces of living pictures?'

'No, I can't say that I have.'

Philip was astonished. 'But they are shown in music halls all over London.'

'We don't get out to the music hall much. Not with havin' two little kids.'

'Ah yes,' Philip said, as if he had suddenly remembered something. 'When I wrote to Becky for your address, she said you had been graced with children. How are they, by the way?'

'They're very well,' George said drily. 'Thank you for askin'—in the end.'

Philip turned to his wife. 'We should have brought them some presents, my dear.'

'Indeed we should,' Marie agreed, her foghorn voice oozing false sincerity.

'But back to the matter in hand,' Philip said. 'My living pictures—with Marie as the star, of course—have been immensely popular. My *Jewel Thieves* left audiences gasping with fright, while *Tilly's Dilemma*—which is a comedy, you understand—had them positively rolling in the aisles with laughter.'

'How long do these livin' pictures of yours last?' George asked, becoming curious in spite of himself.

Philip looked vaguely uncomfortable again. 'It all depends,' he said. 'The complexity of the plot, the sweep of the subject, the demands of the denouement, all these are factors which must be taken into consideration.'

'But how long would you say that they lasted on average?' George persisted.

'About three minutes,' Philip admitted.

George threw back his head and roared with laughter. 'The complexity of the plot, the sweep of the subject—an' all in three minutes,' he gasped.

'An artist such as myself is capable of great compression,' Philip said haughtily. 'I can contain a whole lifetime in three minutes. Besides, for the moment—but *only* for the moment—it is not technically possible to make them any longer.'

'I'm sorry,' George said, calming down. 'I shouldn't have laughed. Now what was this favour you wanted?'

'I want to make a series of documentary pictures, glorifying British thrift and industry,' Philip said. He spread his hands in an expansive gesture. 'Britain—the centre of the mightiest empire the world has ever known.'

'An' where do I fit into this grand scheme of yours?' George wondered.

'You run a wood yard, don't you?'

'That's right.'

'Well, I'd like to make my first documentary there.'

George's first instinct was to say no—to tell his brother he didn't want him anywhere near the wood yard. Then he had second thoughts. It had been a long time since Philip had been involved in anything crooked. He was older now, a respectable married man—even if his wife did leave something to be desired. There couldn't be any harm in letting him make his living picture in the yard, and anyway, families had a duty to help each other out.

'All right,' he said. 'Give me a time when you'll be comin', an' I'll make all the arrangements.'

'Thank you, George,' Philip said. 'There is

just ... er ... one more thing.'

'An' what might that be?'

'Working on the river as you do, I assume that you have lots of contact with managers of other companies which operate there.'

'Yes, I suppose I do know a few blokes who run other businesses.' George agreed. 'Why are you interested?'

'Because, as I said, I plan to make a *series* of films, and it would make things much easier for me if you would introduce me to some of the people you know. Will you do that?'

'Yes, if you like,' George said, sticking to family loyalty and throwing caution to the wind.

CHAPTER 8

George and Colleen Taylor were having Sunday tea with Sam and Lil Clarke in the Clarkes' front parlour. The parlours in Lant Place were quite large, but thanks to all the furniture Lil insisted on fitting into hers—the three-piece suite in imitation velvet, the walnut veneer sideboard, the circular ebony table, the nest of mahogany coffee tables, the carved display case, the grandfather clock and the cuckoo clock—it was a bit of a squeeze getting people inside as well, even when there were only four of them.

'That tally man must thank 'is lucky stars for the day 'e first met my old dutch,' Sam often said—though never when he was in his wife's hearing. 'Why, 'e must 'ave bought 'imself an ocean-goin' steam yacht out of the money I've given 'im over the years. Probably a big 'ouse in the country as well.'

Though most of the furniture was almost paid for, Sam had no illusions that the tally man would ever stop calling, because long before they were completely out of debt, Lil would decide there was something else—though Gawd alone knew what—she needed to buy for the front parlour.

' 'Ow's young Lizzie turnin' out?' Lil asked Colleen, as she poured her another cup of tea.

'Champion,' Colleen replied. 'Looks after the babies like they were her own.'

'She's always takin' 'em out on little trips, ain't she?' Lil said. 'She 'ad 'em down at the Union Street stables only the other day, yer know.'

A smile came to Colleen's lips. 'Did she tell you that herself?' she asked.

'Well, no, she didn't exactly tell me—not in so many words,' Lil admitted.

Of course she hadn't, but the Sherlock Holmes of Lant Place didn't have to be *told* something to find out about it. As Annie had once said, her mum was always adding two and two, and the remarkable thing was that she often made four.

'So why are you so sure she went to the Union Street stables?' Colleen asked, her smile broadening.

'Well, I just 'appened to run into 'er and the

kiddies in the street,' Lil explained.

'An' you couldn't help noticin' ...'

'An' I couldn't 'elp noticin' that there was a bit of 'orse muck on the tip of Lizzie's boot.'

'There's horse muck all over the streets of Southwark,' George said. 'She could have stepped in it anywhere.'

'True,' Lil said. 'But then, when I was sayin' 'ello to yer little babies, I couldn't 'elp noticin' there was a couple of 'orse hairs inside the pram ...'

'They might have stroked a horse in the street.'

'... an' a bit of straw. So they must 'ave been to a stables, an' the closest one to 'ere is in Union Street.'

Colleen laughed. 'You're right, of course, Lizzie told me she did take them to the stables.'

From the Clarkes' back yard, there came a sudden, loud baa-ing sound.

'It's that goat again!' Lil said in disgust. She turned to her husband. 'I wish you'd never agreed to our Peggy 'avin the smelly thing, Sam.'

Sam grinned. 'Now let me see if I've got this straight. *I* agreed to 'er 'avin' it, did I?'

Lil looked vaguely uncomfortable. 'Well, you are the master of the 'ouse.'

Sam chuckled. 'If I am, it's news to me. But let's think back a bit. It's about two years since Peggy started gettin' on *my* goat about gettin' a goat for *'er*. Ain't that right, Lil?'

'About that,' Lil agreed.

'An' was it me 'oo said she could 'ave one if she bought it 'erself, or got given one for free?'

Lil's discomfort was increasing. 'When I said that, I 'ad no idea Tom would give 'er one as a present,' she said in her own defence. 'She didn't even *know* Tom then.'

'But it was you 'oo made the promise, so 'oo's fault is it that we've been saddled with the goat? Mine or yours?'

'Tom's,' Lil said. 'I don't think I'll ever forgive 'im for buyin' that goat.'

Sam winked broadly at George and Colleen. 'Never forgive 'im?' he repeated. 'She worships that son-in-law of 'ers. Fair thinks the sun shines out of 'is bottom, she does.'

'Sam!' Lil exploded. 'I will not 'ave that kind of language used in me own front room, especially on a Sunday afternoon. It just ain't respectable.'

'Well, yer do, don't yer?' Sam said.

' 'E's a good lad,' Lil cut in, 'an' I'm as pleased as punch 'e's got 'imself a job in the Wet Bobs. You mark my words, 'e won't be a constable for long.'

'Got visions of 'avin' a superintendent in the family?' Sam asked, winking at Colleen and George again.

'Maybe not a superintendent,' Lil admitted. 'Not right away. But I wouldn't be at all surprised if he ain't made up to inspector before long.'

'By Christmas, probably,' Sam muttered.

His wife gave him one of her hard stares to

see if he was taking the mickey out of her. She decided he probably was, and thought it best to change the subject. 'I 'ear that yer brother is goin' down to the wood yard to make one of them livin' pictures that are all the rage now,' she said, turning to George.

'How did you know ...' George began.

'Don't go startin' 'er off on 'er "just 'appened to notice" again,' Sam chuckled.

It was a good point, George thought. Some of Lil's stories could take hours, and even at the end, what made perfect sense to her often left everyone else completely mystified.

'Yes, I did give me brother permission to film at the wood yard,' he said to Lil. 'An' I've arranged for him to take some more livin' pictures at the wool warehouse on Hibernia Wharf an' at the jute factory just up the river.'

'That was kind of yer,' Lil said. 'You're very good to yer brother, George.'

'Perhaps too good,' Colleen said.

It was shortly after twelve-thirty on a cloudy Monday morning. Maggie White had just finished eating her dinner when Clem Davies, the manager of the wash house, brought the tall man in the frock coat into the staff room.

'This gentleman is Mr Harold Bailey, Mrs White,' the manager said to Maggie.

'Pleased to meet yer, sir,' Maggie replied, bobbing down into a half-curtsy.

'A pleasure to meet you, Mrs White,' Bailey replied.

'In case you're wondering what he's doing here, Mr Bailey is a journalist,' the manager explained.

He turned back to the journalist. 'Mrs White is one of the best workers that we have here at the wash house. Isn't that right, Maggie?'

Maggie blushed. 'I ... er ... well, I wouldn't ... If you say so, sir.'

The manager smiled at her discomfort. 'And since Mr Bailey is writing an article on the wash houses of London, it is only proper that he should be shown around ours by one of the best workers, don't you think?'

Maggie's mouth fell open in surprise. 'Me, sir?' she managed to gasp. 'Yer want me to show 'im round? Oh, I couldn't! I wouldn't know what to say.'

The manager's smile broadened. 'I'm sure you'll do fine, Maggie,' he said. 'And now if you'll excuse me, Mr Bailey, I really must get back to my own work.'

Maggie led the journalist into the laundry room. 'It might seem a bit 'ot an' steamy at first, but yer'll find yer soon get used to it,' she said.

Mr Bailey looked up at the ceiling. 'It looks to be well ventilated,' he commented.

'Oh, it is,' Maggie agreed, because he seemed to think this vent-whatever was a good thing, and she wanted him to get a favourable impression of the laundry.

'Shall we go and see the washing troughs first?' the journalist suggested.

The troughs ran the length of the room. Several of them were occupied by women scrubbing hard at their clothes or rubbing them on the washboard. Two or three of the women looked up and smiled.

' 'Lo, Maggie.'

'Keepin' yer busy, are they, Maggie?'

'You seem to be very popular with your customers,' the journalist said as they walked away from the troughs.

Maggie blushed again. 'Well, yer know 'ow it is, don't yer? Washin's 'ard work, even in a modern place like this, and it 'elps if there's a few friendly faces around.'

'How much hot water are they each allowed to use?' the journalist asked.

'As much as they like,' Maggie said proudly. 'We don't put no limit on it.'

She took him to the adjoining room, where there were a number of upright metal cylinders.

'The women bring their baskets of wet clothes in 'ere an' put 'em in one of them wringers,' Maggie explained, pointing at the cylinders.

'Is "wringer" really just another word for mangle?' the journalist asked.

'Good 'eavens, no. They're two entirely different things. Mangles 'ave rollers.'

'So what do these "wringers" do exactly?'

It seemed such a silly question that for a second Maggie was puzzled. Then she burst out laughing. 'Yer've never 'ad to wash anyfink in yer life, 'ave yer?' she asked.

The journalist laughed, too, though his laugh was not quite as comfortable as hers. 'I haven't actually,' he admitted. 'You see, we have servants at home.'

' 'Course yer do, love,' said Maggie, now starting to feel much more relaxed. 'Well, what the wringers do, yer see, is their insides go round an' round, very fast, and nearly all the water that was in the clothes comes out of that tube there.'

'So it's sort of like "spinning" them dry, is it?' the journalist hazarded.

'I suppose yer could call it that,' Maggie agreed. 'Now once the washin's been through the wringer, the customer folds it on one of them tables over there. Or, if they want to iron it first, they can use one of them flat irons that we keep 'eatin' up on the stove.'

'It all seems very convenient,' the journalist said. 'And really very easy.'

Which showed he'd never done any ironing either, Maggie thought. 'But this is the cleverest thing we've got,' she said, taking him over to a cupboard in the wall. 'It's got pipes goin' into it, an' we blow 'ot air through 'em,' Maggie explained.

'Ingenious,' the journalist said. 'And how much do you charge for all these excellent services? I shouldn't imagine it could be any less than sixpence.'

'All it costs is three-'a'pence an hour. Which is not bad considerin' what drudgery washin' used to be for people round 'ere before we opened.'

'Not bad indeed,' the journalist agreed. 'I have found my visit most instructive. It was kind of you to spare the time to show me around, Mrs White.'

'My pleasure,' Maggie said—and was surprised to find that it had been.

It was an hour after the journalist had left that Maggie started to feel the stabbing pain in her stomach—and thought immediately of her baby.

Sid had been over the moon when she told him about it. 'Yer sure?' he'd asked, again and again. 'Yer really are sure that yer expectin' a baby?'

'Yes, I am.'

'Well, ain't this just the most wonderful thing that's ever 'appened to us?'

She'd wanted to say then that she was afraid she might lose the child, but she hadn't had the heart to burst the bubble of Sid's happiness. She still couldn't bring herself to tell him, so she carried the burden of fear alone.

'People do lose their babies, yer know,' she'd told Colleen Taylor in the Goldsmiths' Arms.

'Yes, some do,' Colleen had replied. 'But you've no reason to think you'll be one of them.'

Oh, it was so easy for Colleen to talk—so easy for her to be reassuring. She already had her beautiful twins and all her worries were over.

For one brief second, Maggie hated Colleen Taylor with every ounce of her being. She saw Colleen dead, saw George dead, saw the babies dead, and was glad—because someone who had everything, like Colleen Taylor did, deserved to suffer.

And then the madness passed. 'What's come over yer?' Maggie asked herself. 'Colleen's yer friend an' she's never been nuffink but nice as pie to yer. Yer ought to be ashamed of yerself.'

She felt another stabbing pain, and did her best to believe that it was just a touch of stomach ache.

There were twenty probationary policemen in Tom's group at the Metropolitan Police's Candidates' Section House in Kennington Lane, and it was plain from the start that they were not going to be in for an easy time.

'Good bobbies is few an' far between in this world,' said the sergeant instructor with the massive barrel chest, as he walked up and down the line of new recruits, 'an' lookin' at you lot, I don't see many what's got the makin's of a good one. So what I'm plannin' to do is to make life so difficult for you buggers ...' He had walked past Tom's part of the line, but now he suddenly swung round and pointed his finger squarely at Tom's chest. 'Do yer object to me swearin' at yer, probationer?' he demanded.

Tom squared his shoulders. 'No,' he said.

The instructor walked up to him and put his mouth close to Tom's ear. 'No, *what?*' he bellowed.

'No, *Sergeant!*' Tom said, still looking straight ahead.

'Yer very wise,' the instructor shouted. He walked back down the line again. 'Yer'd all of yer be very wise not to object to *anyfink* I do or say. 'Cos yer know 'oo I am? I'm the bloke 'oo's got yer body and soul for three 'ole weeks.

I'm more important to yer than yer mothers, or yer wives or yer sweet'earts. Now where was I? Can anybody tell me?'

No one was going to fall into that trap, however, and all the recruits kept their eyes on the far wall.

'Oh yes,' the instructor said. 'I'm goin' to make life so difficult for you buggers that by the time I've finished with yer, 'alf of yer won't even *want* to be bobbies any more. An' good riddance to bad rubbish. I'll march yer 'till yer ready to drop, an' then I'll march yer some more. It'll be 'ell on earth—an' if it isn't, then I'm not doin' me job proper.'

Tom thought about his days as a waterman. They were suddenly starting to look like a golden past.

The recruits were given classes in basic criminal law, and had police procedure drilled into them. They were taught how to man an ambulance and assist the Fire Brigade in an emergency. The difference between 'beat' and 'point' duty was explained to them—the former consisting of patrolling a definite round, the latter being to stand in one place for their full tour of duty. They were told that once they were real policemen, they would be given an armlet which they must wear on their left sleeves when on duty. They would also be issued with a whistle and chain, and a stout boxwood truncheon. Handcuffs, they were warned, were only to be carried when they were on their way to arrest someone known to be violent.

There was so much to learn that Tom's

head swam, but the sergeant had been right, and it was the marching—twice a day, in the Wellington Barracks, just up the road from the Section House—which almost finished them all off.

It was during one of the rare and long-awaited rest periods that Tom got talking to another new recruit in the corner of the exercise yard, a black-haired, shifty-eyed man called Reg Wragge. They were squatting on the ground, their backs to the wall, smoking cigarettes.

It was Wragge who spoke first. 'If I'd known it was goin' to be as bad as this, I'd never 'ave joined up in the first place,' he said. 'Still, I s'ppose it'll all be worth it in the end.'

'Yes, the pay's not bad,' Tom agreed, although it flashed through his mind that it was nothing to what Annie could be earning from her business in a few months.

'Yer've got to be bloody jokin', 'aven't yer?' Wragge said. 'Twenty-five shillin's an' sixpence a week to start with, risin' to a maximum of thirty-three an' six! You call that a good wage?'

'It's a lot more than I was makin' as a waterman,' Tom said unenthusiastically.

'It's nuffink compared to what yer can make if yer keep yer eyes and ears open,' Wragge told him.

' 'Ow d'yer mean?'

Wragge looked up and down the yard to see if anyone else was in earshot. Then, satisfied they weren't, he moved closer to Tom. 'Can I trust yer?' he whispered.

'Of course yer can,' Tom told him. 'I've never betrayed a confidence in me life.'

'Well, when yer a bobbie, there's 'undreds of ways yer can find to make money if yer smart,' Wragge said. 'Say yer catch somebody in the act of committin' a crime. Yer've got two choices of 'ow to deal with it, 'aven't yer? You can take 'im down to the station, an' ruin the poor bugger's life. Or yer can make 'im promise never to do it again an' let 'im go.'

'What's that got to do with makin' money?'

Wragge winked. 'Well, 'e'll want to show 'is appreciation of yer kindness, won't 'e? So what 'e's goin' to do?'

'I don't know.'

' 'E's goin' to dig down deep into 'is pocket an' give you whatever money 'e's got on 'im. An' if that's not enough for yer, yer can always go back to 'im at some later date, an' remind 'im of 'ow understandin' you've been.'

Tom shifted slightly and looked down at the brightly glowing end of his cigarette. 'I see,' he said.

'Take another example. There's this honest street trader what wants to operate somewhere where street traders ain't exactly allowed to be. Are yer follerin' me?'

'Yes.'

'Well, yer've got two choices again, ain't yer? Yer can move 'im along right sharpish, but then yer'll be doin' nuffink more than stiflin' the spirit of enterprise what made this country great. Or there's yer second choice: yer can charge 'im a bit of a fee in return for lookin' the other way.'

'D'yer think a lot of bobbies 'ave that attitude to the job?' Tom asked.

Wragge took one last drag of his cigarette, placed it under his heel, and ground it into the concrete. '*Most* of 'em 'ave that attitude. They'd be fools not to, wouldn't they? I tell yer, Tom, there's bobbies all over London livin' in their own 'ouses. Not rented, mind—their own, bought an' paid for. Do you think they've managed that on thirty bob a week?'

'I suppose not.'

'The way I see it, it's doin' a public service. Yer keepin' men out of prison an' their families out of the work'ouse, ain't yer?'

'I suppose so.'

'An' yer makin' a few bob for yerself. So where's the 'arm? Nobody gets 'urt, do they?'

Tom took his cigarettes out of his pocket, and offered one of them to Wragge. 'I'd never thought of it that way before,' he said interestedly.

CHAPTER 9

It was eight o'clock on Saturday evening. The two young men, one tall and broad, the other perhaps a little short for his age, walked purposefully down Southwark Bridge Road.

'Are yer nervous?' Eddie Clarke asked Joey Bates.

'Nervous? Me? O' course not!' Joey replied.

But he was. The time had finally arrived for his first fight, and he was having kittens just thinking about it. He wished that his older brother could be there to cheer him on, but Tom was still in his first week of training and was confined to the Candidates' Section House for the weekend, so Joey was having to make do with a very reluctant Eddie for support.

They crossed Borough Road. A railway engine thundered by on the overhead viaduct, and to Joey its powerful wheels seemed to be screaming a single message: 'Goin' to lose, goin' to lose, goin' to lose ...' over and over again.

'So 'oo's yer opponent goin' to be tonight?' Eddie asked. 'Anybody famous?'

' 'Course it won't be nobody famous, but I won't know 'oo he *actually* is till we get there.'

Eddie sniffed. 'Seems to me it's a funny sort of boxin' match if yer don't even know 'oo yer fightin'.'

'It ain't the National Sportin' Club I'm fightin' in, yer know,' Joey said, with a touch of irritation in his voice. 'Crikey, it ain't even the Whitechapel Wonderland. I'm 'avin' me first fight in a boarded-up railway arch and I'll be expected to take on 'ooever the management tell me to.'

'Talk about startin' right at the bottom of the ladder,' Eddie said dismissively.

'Oh, I'm startin' at the bottom all right, but

I'm 'eadin' for the top,' Joey said with more confidence than he felt.

'Sure yer are,' Eddie replied, and his tone said that *he* didn't believe it either.

They were approaching the arch, inside which, every Saturday night, young hopefuls and old hands battled it out for the benefit of anyone who had a shilling to spend.

Chalkie and Dick, a couple of ex-boxers, were on guard outside, and Joey remembered how they had both made fun of him the first time he'd gone to see a match.

'Been 'ere before, 'ave yer?' Chalkie had asked.

'Lot's o' times,' Joey had replied, unconvincingly.

'Then 'e'll know the drill, won't 'e?' Dick had said, winking at his partner.

Of course, Joey hadn't, and they'd had to show him how to raise his arms while they searched him for weapons. That, at least, was all behind him, thank Gawd! Since that day he'd grown four inches and developed biceps like iron, and the two bouncers always greeted him with some respect.

'Big night tonight, Joey,' Chalkie said.

'Yes, it is,' Joey agreed.

'Nervous, are yer?' Dick asked.

Why does everybody keep askin' me that? Joey wondered. Even if he hadn't been nervous, the constant repetition of the question would have been enough to make his stomach knot.

'I reckon I can take on 'ooever they decide to throw at me,' he said aloud.

Eddie handed over his shilling entrance fee, and Chalkie opened the door for the fighter and his friend to enter.

Eddie had never been to one of these places before, but he looked around with only a little interest. It was like being inside a big brick cave, he decided. There was only one light—a single, furiously burning gas jet in the roof—and it created strange, flickering shadows on the walls. The ring—if you wanted to call it that—was an open square in the centre of the archway, surrounded by tiered, wooden seating.

'You said it wasn't no National Sportin' Club, an' yer wasn't lyin',' Eddie told Joey.

'If it was, it'd cost yer a damn sight more than a bob,' Joey replied, obviously stung. 'Yer'd better go an' get yerself a seat while there's still a few good ones left. If yer really do want to see the fight, that is.'

'Oh, I'll see it,' Eddie said. 'Might as well, now I've come all this way.'

He selected a seat halfway up the tier, while Joey went to the edge of the ring to talk to the other boxers, who were already stripped down to their fighting tights.

Eddie found himself sitting next to a middle-aged man wearing a greasy bowler hat and the look of a bloke who felt at home in this sort of gathering.

'First time yer've been to see a fight, is it, young shaver?' the man asked.

'Yes,' Eddie admitted.

'Yer can always tell,' the man said complacently. He pointed to Joey. 'What d'yer make of that cove down there, the one that's just takin' 'is shirt off?'

Eddie found himself facing mixed emotions. On the one hand, Joey was his friend. On the other, if Joey made a complete hash of his fight, Eddie was not sure he wished to be too closely associated with him.

'Well? Got no opinion on the matter?' the man in the bowler hat asked.

'What do *you* think of 'im?' Eddie asked cautiously.

' 'E'll be murdered.'

Eddie felt an unexpected pang of annoyance. ' 'Ow can yer say that?' he demanded. 'Yer don't know anyfink about 'im. Yer don't even know 'oo it is 'e's fightin' yet.'

'Don't matter 'oo 'e's fightin', 'e'll still be murdered.' The bowler-hatted man shook his head. 'You kids! Yer think the only thing yer need to fight is a bit o' muscle. Well, let me tell you, there's a lot more to it than that. It's experience what counts most of all, an' just lookin' at 'im, I can tell that that young bloke down there ain't got no experience at all.'

A man wearing a flashy check suit stepped into the centre of the ring. 'My lords, ladies an' gentlemen, we are about to start the evenin's entertainment,' he announced.

Eddie looked around at the rest of the spectators. He couldn't see any ladies, and there probably weren't any lords either. In fact, he thought, the master of ceremonies had been pushing it a bit even using the word 'gentlemen.'

'The first fight will be between Sailor Blake and Lightnin' Joey Bates,' the MC continued.

Joey stood up, as did a big square man of about twenty-eight with tattoos of sailing ships and mermaids all over his arms and chest.

'Lightnin' Joey,' scoffed the man in the bowler hat. 'I tell yer, that sailor'll wipe the floor with 'im.'

The bell rang for the start of round one, and both boxers came out of their corners. Joey landed the first punch to the sailor's jaw, and followed through with one to his midriff.

Eddie was experiencing two unexpected emotions. The first was excitement—boxing really could be a thrilling spectacle—and the second, even more unexpected, was pride in his friend.

'Wipe the floor with 'im, will 'e?' Eddie asked the man in the bowler hat gleefully. 'Well, if there's any floor-wipin' bein' done down there, it's my mate that's doin' it.'

'Fight's only just started,' the man replied. 'Yer never said nuffink about 'im bein yer china before.'

'No, I didn't, did I?' Eddie said, and now added shame to his mixed bag of emotions.

'Anyway, keep watchin',' the man in the bowler hat said. 'It's only a matter o' time before yer china comes a cropper.'

Joey was quicker on his feet than the sailor, and by the time they were a minute into the round, Eddie reckoned that his mate had got in about twenty punches to the sailor's six. The only problem was that it didn't really seem to be bothering the sailor at all.

It was two minutes into the round that Joey made his mistake. The sailor lowered his guard, offering Joey an easy target, and instead of asking himself why his opponent had been so generous, Joey fell right into the trap and went on the attack. The sailor side-stepped, so that Joey's blow only caught him lightly on the shoulder, then was back, with both fists working like pistons.

Bam—and Joey's head rocked to one side.

Bam—and a blow to his belly caused him to lean forward.

Bam—and a punch to the nose made his neck snap back again.

The sailor stepped clear, with an amused smile playing on his lips. Joey tottered and did a shaky half-turn.

'Don't go down, Joey,' Eddie found himself praying. 'Whatever yer do, don't go down.'

Joey's legs went first, starting with a buckling of the knees, and then his trunk lurched forward, and he was lying on the ground.

The referee stood over him, one hand raised in the air. 'Er-one,' he counted. 'Er-two ... er-three ... er-four ...'

By now, most of the audience was joining in. 'Er-five, er-six, er-seven.'

'Get up, Joey,' Eddie pleaded silently. 'Get up an' show 'em what yer can really do.'

'... er-eight, er-nine ...'

Joey raised himself weakly on one elbow.

'... er-ten. Out!'

The crowd were whistling and stamping their feet.

'Call yerself a fighter?' someone shouted at Joey, who was now climbing groggily to his feet.

'Couldn't punch yer way out of a wet paper bag!'

'Told yer that was 'ow it would end up,' the man in the bowler hat said to Eddie.

The MC lifted the victorious sailor's arm in the air, and the spectators cheered. Joey slunk back to the bench, and sat down. Eddie, still sitting in the middle of the baying mob, felt almost as miserable as his defeated friend looked.

The nearest pub to the archway was called the Green Man, and that was where Eddie took his battered friend.

The landlord looked at Joey's face suspiciously. 'We don't want no trouble in 'ere,' he said.

' 'E ain't been fightin',' Eddie said. 'Leastways, not on the street. E's a boxer.'

'Is that right, son?' the landlord asked.

'Well, I thought I was until about 'alf an hour ago,' Joey said miserably.

They took their pints over to a corner table. ' 'Ow are yer feelin' now?' Eddie asked.

'I've never been so 'umiliated in me life.'

'It was only yer first match.'

'Yes, an' I think it'll be me last one. Gawd alone knows what me mum's goin' to say when she sees me boat race. I look a real proper mess, don't I?'

Eddie examined his friend. Joey's left eye was puffed up, his nose was swollen and there was a nasty-looking cut on his lip. 'Yer do look a *bit* of a mess,' Eddie admitted, 'but that ain't no reason for givin' it up.'

'That's plenty o' reason.'

'That sailor must 'ave 'ad dozens o' fights in 'is time—maybe even 'undreds.'

'That don't alter the fact that 'e beat me.'

'Yer was a lot quicker than 'e was. 'E just knew more tricks, that's all.'

'Yer suddenly seem very keen to 'ave me go back in the ring,' Joey said.

'I am.'

'Why? So I can 'ave me boat race rearranged again?'

'No, it ain't that.' Eddie hesitated for a second. 'We're chinas, ain't we?'

'Well, o' course we are.'

'*That's* why I want yer to keep fightin'.'

'Yer not makin' much sense to me,' Joey said. 'Am I still punch-drunk or somefink?'

'No, yer not. Listen, if I 'ave a crash when I'm tryin' to break the speed record, I'll want yer to encourage me to start again.'

'Why?'

' 'Cos racin's what I've got me 'eart set on, an' I think it's the same with you as far as boxin' goes. What yer want most in the world is to be a good boxer.'

Joey grinned, then winced as the movement stung his lip. 'Yer right. An' yer a bloody good mate into the bargain.'

Eddie looked embarrassed. 'Get on with yer,'

he said. 'Yer want another pint?'

'What, an' 'ave to face me mum when I've 'ad a skinful?' Joey asked. 'Don't yer think I'm goin to 'ave enough trouble with 'er as it is?'

Working in the wash house six days a week didn't leave Maggie White much time for doing her own household chores, and it was generally while her Sid was sleeping off the effect of his Sunday dinner—which was always meat and three veg—that she managed to catch up on herself.

On the Sunday afternoon after Joey Bates' disastrous fight in the archway, she decided that rather than risk disturbing Sid, she would start her cleaning upstairs. Windows first, she thought, because it was two or three weeks since she'd last done them, and they were definitely starting to look a little grimy.

She climbed the steep, narrow stairs carefully, because she didn't want to slip and damage the baby.

'A couple more months an' you'll 'ave to take over this job from me, Sid,' she said to her husband, whose loud snores followed her up the stairs. She'd try to spare him from the housework as long as possible, because it was hard graft down at the docks and he put in even longer hours at work than she did.

She washed the inside of the bedroom window first, then raised the sash and sat carefully on the sill, so that when she pulled the sash down on her legs, the rest of her was on the outside, overhanging the street.

'Luverly day, ain't it, Mrs White?' somebody called from down below her.

Maggie turned her head and saw that the speaker was the local chimney sweep, looking quite different now he had scrubbed away his weekday sooty covering.

'It *is* a luverly day,' she agreed. 'I think I might even go for a little walk later.'

The sun reflected on the glass as she polished it. She *would* go for a walk, she decided. It would do her good. 'And what's good for you is good for your baby,' the doctor had told her.

Good for *her* baby. She still felt a tingle every time she heard those words. It would be a beautiful baby, she was sure of that. And she was equally certain that it would be a little girl.

She pictured Sid, holding the infant in his arms, his face flushed with pride. She had an image of the christening, with little Ellen—which was what she was going to call the baby—screaming furiously when the vicar splashed the water on her head.

Her thoughts rushed ahead to even later in her as yet unborn child's life: Ellen's first day at Lant Street Board School; her daughter bringing her first, nervous young man home for tea; the wedding, which they would start saving for now, so that it would be the biggest Suffolk Street had ever seen. Yes, it was all going to turn out wonderfully.

The window gleamed in the sunlight. Maggie lifted the sash again and stepped back into the bedroom. She'd do the dusting next, she thought, but first, she'd nip down to the kitchen and make herself a cup of rosie, because all that rubbing had made her feel a little light-headed.

She was at the top of the stairs when her vision started to blur. She groped for the banister rail, but though she knew exactly where it was, she couldn't seem to find it.

'Don't move!' she told herself. 'Whatever yer do, Maggie White, don't move,' but her body refused to obey her, and was swaying towards the edge of the step.

'Sid!' she screamed to her still-snoring husband. 'Sid, wake up! Yer 'ave to come an' 'elp me!'

Then her legs gave way beneath her, and she was tumbling down the stairs.

At first, everything was just a blur, then Maggie's eyes began to focus on the plaster mouldings on the ceiling. But there weren't any plaster mouldings on the ceiling—not in the little house she shared with her Sid. The bed felt wrong as well. It was far too narrow for both her and her husband to fit into comfortably.

She turned her head to one side. The effort hurt her quite a lot, but it did allow her to see that she was lying in a long, thin room filled with beds. 'Ospital! she thought, with rising panic. They've brought me to 'ospital.

There was a woman standing at her bedside, wearing a long white apron and a high white cap. 'How are you feeling, Mrs White?' she asked.

'Sid!' Maggie croaked. 'Where's my Sid? I

want to see my Sid right now.'

The nurse smiled sympathetically. 'And so you shall, Mrs White. Just as soon as you've had a word with the doctor.'

As if he had been waiting to hear his cue, a young man in a white coat appeared from out of nowhere. 'How long has she been conscious?' he asked the nurse.

'Only a couple of minutes, Dr Robinson.'

The doctor bent over slightly, so that Maggie could see and hear him more easily. 'You had a very bad fall, Mrs White,' he said in a soothing voice.

'Stairs,' Maggie mumbled. 'Standin' at the top of the stairs. Feelin' dizzy.'

'That's right,' the doctor agreed. 'And then you lost your balance and fell all the way to the bottom. There were some internal injuries and we had to operate on you immediately. You're very lucky to be alive, you know.'

'Is the baby all right?' Maggie asked desperately.

The doctor shook his head slowly and regretfully. 'No, I'm afraid I have to tell you that you lost it.'

'What was it?'

'Mrs White ...'

'What was it *goin'* to be?'

'At times like this, it's usually better not to ask questions about what might have—'

'I want to know what it was goin' to be,' Maggie insisted in a voice which would have been a scream if she'd been feeling strong enough.

'It was a girl,' the doctor told her reluctantly.

'I knew it,' Maggie said. 'I could *feel* it was a little girl that was growin' inside of me.'

'I'll leave you now,' the doctor said. 'Your husband will be with you in a few minutes.'

'What can I tell 'im?' Maggie asked. 'Can I say we'll 'ave other babies?'

A look of hesitancy crossed the doctor's face. 'It's always difficult to say with absolute certainty in these cases ...'

'But *you* don't think I can, do yer?'

'Given the nature of your injuries and the operation we were forced to perform, I would think it highly unlikely.'

She couldn't have babies, and without them, life was not worth living. Maggie buried her face in the pillow, and sobbed with what little strength she had left.

CHAPTER 10

Annie was clearing away the dinner plates when Belinda arrived at the door, excitedly waving the first edition of the evening paper in her hand.

'What's all this about?' Annie asked as they walked down the passageway towards the kitchen.

'Our advertisements,' Belinda told her.

Annie stopped dead in her tracks. 'Our advertisements?' she repeated. 'And what advertisements are they?'

'For the company, dear girl. I wrote some out and sent them off to the paper. D'you want to see them?'

There'd been a part of her, Annie realised, which had never really quite accepted that anything would come of her friend's scheme, and now here was Belinda, steaming ahead like an express train, with advertisements in the papers.

'Well, *do* you want to see them?' Belinda asked impatiently.

'I suppose I'd better,' Annie replied.

'Then don't stand in the passage like a zombie. Let's go into the kitchen.'

With a feeling which could not quite be described as one of impending doom, Annie covered the rest of the distance to the kitchen.

Once they were inside, Belinda spread the newspaper out on the table. The advertisement really did look quite impressive:

YOUNG LADIES WANTED

A newly established company is looking for young ladies with all types of office skills. We guarantee that we will double your present income.

Apply in writing to Benson, Bates and Co. Ltd, 75 Borough High Street.

'Good, isn't it?' Belinda said.

'Yes, I suppose so,' Annie said doubtfully.

Belinda frowned. 'What's the matter?' she asked. 'Did I miss something out?'

'Well, not exactly, but you do sort of give the

impression that they'll be working for us.'

'They will, won't they?'

'In a way, but from the advertisement, it looks like they'll be working in our office in Borough High Street.'

'Doesn't say that anywhere,' Belinda said, scanning the advertisement herself.

'No, but it suggests it. And was it wise to promise to double their present income?'

'Wise!' Belinda repeated. 'My dear girl, no one ever got anywhere by being wise. Have a look at the other one.'

The second advertisement was even bigger than the first.

TO ALL BUSINESSMEN

As an old-established company, experienced in the field of bankruptcy receivership ...

Annie read. She looked up at Belinda. 'An old-established company?'

'Certainly. We were established last week, although, strictly speaking, we're not legally a company.'

'Experienced in the field of bankruptcy receivership?'

'Read on, dear girl,' Belinda urged. 'Read on.'

... we understand your problems. Our extensive research in the field has shown that most enterprises fail due to a lack of qualified office staff. Our surveys have indicated that even the short sick leave of a filing clerk can result in lost orders which will plunge an enterprise into penury. To prevent such tragedies, we have established an exciting new company which will provide temporary clerical help for any organisation which requires it. Our staff are of the highest calibre, and our charges are more than reasonable. Contact Benson, Bates and Co. Ltd, 75 Borough High Street.

Annie put down the paper. 'It's all lies,' she said.

'Not lies at all,' Belinda said airily. 'Nothing more than a case of exaggeration.'

'Do you think we can get away with it?'

'I have no idea, but I think it should be tremendous fun finding out.'

Annie shook her head. 'You're incorrigible, Belinda.'

'I think I shall take that as a compliment.'

Annie reached for her jacket, which was hanging from a hook on the kitchen door.

'Are we going out?' Belinda asked.

'We certainly are,' Annie said. 'After reading about all the experience we've had and the surveys that we've carried out, this half of Benson, Bates and Co Ltd, could do with a stiff drink down at the Goldsmiths' Arms.'

The Hibernia Wharf, where George Taylor managed his wood yard, ran from London Bridge to the dock at the end of Church Street. From the wood yard itself, there were magnificent views of some of the most important edifices in London: Billingsgate Market and the Tower to the right, St Paul's to the left. An' if you ever get tired of lookin' at the buildin's, there's always the Thames to keep you amused, George thought fondly, shifting his gaze from the opposite bank on to the water.

The river was busy that day, as it had been most days in the previous few weeks. Ships steamed past on their way to the East India Docks. Watermen plied their trade in their small skiffs. A convoy of heavily laden lighters slid slowly upstream, all pulled by one plucky little tug.

George wondered how many people's livelihoods depended on the river. A hundred thousand? Maybe more. Without the mighty Thames running through its centre, London would still be nothing but a quiet little village.

He took his silver watch out of his waistcoat pocket, and checked the time. It was a quarter to two. He had told his brother that if he wanted to shoot his living pictures, he should make sure that he arrived by one. He was not surprised that Philip was late—reliability was not one of his strong points.

George turned around and surveyed the wood yard. It was rectangular in shape and had a high fence running around its perimeter. Most of it was open to the sky, but around two sides of the fence ran a lean-to with a sloping tin roof, where some of the more valuable timbers were stored. The only other building in the yard was the office, a square brick structure tucked neatly away in one corner.

George thought about the first time Colleen had seen the office, and grinned at the memory.

'But it's awful!' she'd said. 'It's all so ... so bare an' cold an' uninvitin'.'

'It's a wood yard office, not somebody's front parlour,' George had told her.

Colleen was having none of that. 'A nice pair of curtains would help. I'm sure I've got some material in my trunk that would do you a treat. An' carpet—'

'Carpet!'

'I've seen some off-cuts down at the market which would go champion with the blue wallpaper.'

'But there isn't any blue wallpaper,' George had said, looking at the bare brickwork. 'There isn't any wallpaper at all.'

'There will be—as soon as the plaster's dried.'

George had laughed. 'You never used to be like this. It's livin' next door to Lil Clarke that's changed you.'

'It is not,' Colleen had said crossly, as she turned away to hide her blushes. 'It's just that I think you should have a nice place to work, that's all.'

Now that his wife's transformation of the office was completed, George had to admit that it *was* pleasant to get away from the starkness of the yard once in a while, and grab a few minutes' relaxation behind his floral curtains.

The door which led on to the road swung open, and Philip stepped into the yard, carrying his camera over his shoulder. He had not come alone. With him, he had brought his wife, and five slim young men.

'Who the hell are them fellers?' George asked, when his brother had joined him by the loading bay.

'They're my actors.'

George shook his head in amazement. 'Why did you have to go to all the expense of hirin' yourself actors? You could've taken your livin' pictures of my men for free.'

Philip laughed. It was a light, frivolous laugh, which he seemed to have been deliberately cultivating. 'Your men?' he said, then glanced around the yard until his eyes settled on a large Irishman who was stacking a consignment of Baltic pine. 'Him, for example?' he asked.

'Why not? He's a good worker, an' he's fairly typical of the people I've got workin' for me.'

'Just *look* at him,' Philip said.

'What's wrong with him?'

'He's so ugly.'

George sighed. 'I employ me men for their strength, not their looks,' he said. George surveyed the actors, who were standing in a tight circle and giggling. 'Your fellers look like they couldn't chop sticks, let alone heft great pieces of timber around.'

'That may be the case, but even so ...'

'You'd still rather use your lot.'

'Exactly. Living pictures create a magic world, a world of beauty and elegance, a world of—'

'Is your missis goin' to be in the picture as well?' George asked jokingly.

'Of course she is,' Philip said, as if it

was inconceivable that his brother could have thought otherwise. 'Marie appears in all my living pictures. She has become my trademark.'

'An' how do you think you're goin' to be able to explain away a woman dressed up in all her finery, standin' in the middle of a workin' wood yard?'

Philip smiled. 'I've already thought of that,' he said smugly. 'We will have a caption to explain that she's come to buy a consignment of timber.'

George shook his head. 'It doesn't work like that,' he said. 'You see, most of our buyers never actually—'

'It doesn't matter whether it really works like that or not,' Philip said, a trifle impatiently. 'My only concern is to make sure I entertain my public.'

'Oh, right,' George said. 'Well, you'd better get on with it, hadn't you?'

The living picture might only end up as three minutes long, but Philip took hours to shoot it. George looked on, bemused, while the slim actors his brother had brought with him minced across the yard, carrying one plank between two of them, and then stacking it delicately on a pile in the corner.

If we really ran this yard like that, George thought, we'd be bankrupt within the week.

Watching Marie act was even worse than watching the others. She'd chosen to wear an off-the-shoulder silk dress with a pearl brocade, and when she played the part of the customer ordering wood, she did it so melodramatically that she might have been reporting the death of a loved one.

'You should have seen her in *Alice the Orphan,*' Philip confided to his brother. 'There was one magnificent scene where she wanders through the snow, and then, seeing there is no hope left in this cruel, cruel world, she simply lies down and dies. I tell you, George, she was breathtaking.'

'She's takin' my breath away right now,' George said. And she was—but only because he was trying so hard not to laugh out loud.

Finally the filming was over.

'I need somewhere to process it,' Philip said. He pointed across to the office. 'Can I use that?'

'How long will it take?' George asked.

Philip shrugged. 'I couldn't say for sure. Sometimes it can take hours.'

'Well, in that case, I'll have to say no, because I've got work to do, and bein' kept out of the office for anythin' longer than half an hour just isn't—'

Philip looked alarmed. 'Half an hour would do me perfectly,' he said hastily. 'I was forgetting we were using the special film today. One that develops much quicker than the stuff which we normally use. So can I use your office?'

'Well ...' George said dubiously.

'Please! Otherwise the film might be ruined. I promise I won't be longer than thirty minutes.'

'Oh, all right. Go on, then.'

Philip let out a soft sigh of relief. 'I'll need to

draw the curtains,' he said, 'and it's imperative that no one—not even you—comes in while I'm working. Even a single shaft of light could destroy the whole process.'

'I'll keep my men away,' George promised.

Philip carried his heavy camera over to the office, closed the door behind him and drew the curtains.

George looked around the yard. The slim young actors had left, but Marie was still standing there, though *posing* there might have been a better way to describe it.

She saw him watching her, and strolled over to join him. 'Did you not think that I was wonderful?' she asked in that foghorn voice of hers.

'Yes,' George agreed. 'I have to admit, it was a real education watching you.'

'I *was* that customer,' Marie told him. 'I could feel her take me over completely—the urge to buy the wood, the desperate need to own the Baltic pile ...'

'Baltic pine,' George corrected her.

'Whatever,' Marie said airily. 'I had to have it, you see. My life would simply not have been complete without it.'

Philip placed the camera in the corner of George's office, then tightly closed the floral curtains which Colleen had lovingly hung over the windows. Satisfied that no one could now see him, he took a box of matches out of his waistcoat pocket and struck one. In its flickering fight, he saw that the gas mantle was situated, very conveniently, right over George's desk.

'Excellent!' he said to himself, as he lit the mantle and turned it up to full.

Since George had only given him half an hour, speed was of the essence. He sat down in the chair and grasped the handle of the top drawer, praying that it was not locked.

The drawer slid open, and at the very top of it was a stack of papers clipped together. Philip placed them on the desk. 'Hibernia Wharf Timber Company,' he read. 'Trade Invoice.' That was a stroke of luck, he thought, coming across them straight away like that.

From his jacket pocket, he extracted a notebook and pencil, and jotted down all the details of the top invoice. One down, and—by the thickness of the bundle he was holding—a dozen or more still to go. He carefully detached the top invoice, laid it flat on the desk, and began to copy the information from the second one.

He hadn't exactly been lying to his brother when he'd said he wanted to make one of his living pictures in the wood yard. There had been film in the camera, and what he'd shot that day would eventually end up being shown in the Lambeth Hippodrome and the Mile End Paragon, but the filming had been nothing more than a pretext for the visit. Getting into the office—that was what he'd been aiming at all along.

'You've come up with some good dodges in your time, Philip,' he told himself, 'but there is absolutely no doubt that this is the best one of the lot.'

Marie was still strutting around the yard, her hat cocked jauntily and her parasol resting lightly on her shoulder.

George wished she would stop distracting the men: the labourers' eyes followed her every move, and she was loving it. In a way, George didn't really blame his workers. He couldn't honestly say that he liked Marie as a person, and her voice grated more every time they met, but there was no arguing about it, she was a stunning-looking woman.

George checked his watch. Philip had already been over three quarters of an hour. He decided to give him five more minutes, then knock on the office door and tell him that ready or not, he was going to have to come out.

Suddenly the floral curtains were drawn back, then the office door opened and Philip emerged, carrying the heavy camera on his shoulder.

'You took your time,' George said, a little gruffly. 'What have you been doing in there? Readin' through my private business papers or somethin'?'

Philip looked alarmed again. 'No, of course not, George, I wouldn't. Nothing could induce me—'

'Take it easy,' George said. 'I was only makin' a joke. What interest would a livin'-pictures "artist" like you have in dusty old business statements?'

Philip smiled gratefully. 'Of course,' he said.

'What interest could I possibly have in them?'

'So have you finished processin' the film, or whatever it was you were doin'?'

'Indeed I have, and when it is shown at one of the more select music halls in the area, I will make sure that you and your lady wife receive complimentary tickets.'

'I'm lookin' forward to it,' George said, though he was just being polite.

Philip bit his lower lip, as if he were unsure of his next move. 'About the other matter,' he said finally.

'What other matter?'

'Don't you remember? You promised that you would give me introductions to some of the managers of the other businesses along the water.'

'Oh aye, so I did. You want to make your livin' pictures of them an' all, don't you?'

'That's right,' Philip agreed. 'When you talk to them, be sure to tell them how little disruption I cause, and how wonderful it is to watch the filming.'

'I'll do that,' George said, forcing himself to hide his laughter again.

'And don't forget to tell them that immediately the filming is over, I shall require the use of their offices for half an hour, just as I did with yours.'

'I won't forget.'

Philip held his hand out to his brother. 'It's been lovely to see you again after all this time,' he said. 'You really must come up west and dine with me some time.'

CHAPTER 11

Napoleon, Peggy Clarke's goat, stood in the back yard, munching away at some grass cuttings which Peggy had collected for him from the posh garden in the middle of Nelson Square.

He looked up for a second, and saw that, because of the warm weather, Lil Clarke had left the back door open when she'd gone out shopping. He returned to the grass feeling vaguely dissatisfied. Grass was all right as far as it went, but the open door offered far richer pickings.

The goat turned his attention to the back wall, where the other end of the chain which was attached to his collar was anchored to the brickwork. If he was free of that chain, he thought, he could go wherever he pleased.

He tried a tentative tug. The chain held firm, but it seemed to him that it was a little closer to giving way than it had been the last time he tested it. He gave another tug. The chain held. He backed right up to the wall, took a deep breath and made a dash towards the kitchen door.

When he reached the point at which the chain was stretched to its maximum, he half-expected to be jerked violently backwards, as had happened on so many occasions before—but this time there was a sound of crumbling brickwork, and then the chain clanked along the ground.

He was free at last! He stepped through the back door and into the kitchen.

As Lil Clarke walked along Lant Place, her shopping basket full of groceries from Mr Southern's shop, she could not help reflecting on how well things seemed to be going with the family.

Traffic was brisk at St Katherine's Dock again, so for the moment Sam had plenty of work. Annie's Tom had a good, steady job with the Wet Bobs now, so it shouldn't be long before they were thinking of starting a family. Eddie was settling in to his work at the garage, which might be dirty, but at least was safe—and very possibly respectable. Even Peggy seemed to be losing some of her vagueness and had started taking her school work seriously at long last. And finally, after all her years of striving, she had the house just how she wanted it—a real home.

Yes, Lil thought, life really was pretty good, whichever way you looked at it.

She heard the tearing noise in the parlour as she was putting her key in the front door. 'Burglars!' she said aloud.

For a second, she considered calling for help, but *only* for a second. If anyone had dared to violate her precious home, they would have her to answer to, and no one else!

She flung the front door open and stepped into the hallway. The tearing sound was louder.

If the burglars had heard her enter, they were obviously not worried, and neither was she! It was anger, not fear, which was driving her.

She opened the parlour door. The goat, who had happily been ripping his way into the mock-velvet sofa, looked up and realised that he was in trouble.

Napoleon once more chained in the yard, Sam, Lil and Peggy stood in the front parlour amidst the wreckage of what had once been Lil's pride and joy.

'Napoleon didn't mean no 'arm to yer furniture, Mum,' Peggy said plaintively.

'No 'arm!' Lil repeated, picking up a large handful of horsehair stuffing and waving it in front of her younger daughter's eyes. 'No 'arm, yer say. 'E's only gone an' ruined me sofa, an' one of the easy chairs.'

' 'E'll not do it again. Honest 'e won't,' Peggy promised. 'Cross me 'eart an' 'ope to die.'

'I know 'e won't do it again,' Lil told her, 'because 'e won't be given the chance to. I want that 'orrible smelly creature out of this 'ouse. Right now!'

'Where can 'e go?' Peggy wailed. She had started to cry, an act which was normally guaranteed to soften her mother's heart, but which appeared to be having absolutely no effect on Lil Clarke this time.

'I don't know where 'e can go, an' I don't care,' Lil said, standing firm.

'We can't just put 'im out on the street,' Sam said, as reasonable as always.

'Why not?' Lil demanded.

' 'Cos if we did, we'd be 'avin' the bobbies round summonsin' us for causin' a public nuisance. An' that ain't very respectable, now is it, Lil?'

Lil nodded her head to acknowledge that it wasn't. 'Take 'im up to Battersea Dogs' 'Ome, then,' she said. 'Tell 'em what 'e's done to my 'ouse, an' see if they'll put 'im to sleep in that machine they've got there.'

There was a part of Sam which found all this comical—as he found most things in life comical—but he knew how important it was to his wife, so instead of making a joke of it, he just said, 'I don't think they 'andle goats.'

'Then take 'im to Battersea Goats' 'Ome.' Lil said, now crying almost as hard as her daughter was. She took a despairing look around the parlour. 'Can't yer see the terrible thing what 'e's done to me beautiful 'ome?'

'It's nuffink that can't be repaired,' Sam said. 'That sofa was gettin' past it anyway, an' I expect the tally man'll be delighted to find yer a luverly one to replace it.'

'Maybe 'e will,' Lil sniffed, then, when she saw that her daughter was looking up at her hopefully, she added, 'but I'm not givin' that 'orrible goat a second chance to destroy me 'ome. So yer can give 'im away, or yer can drop 'im off Southwark Bridge in an old sack. I don't care what yer do with 'im, Peggy, but 'e's not goin' to stay 'ere.'

Peggy looked up at her father, her eyes begging him to intervene on her behalf. 'You like Napoleon, don't yer, Dad?' she said. 'You wouldn't see 'im thrown out on the street.'

Sam squatted down so his eyes were at the same level as his daughter's. 'This is yer mum's 'ouse,' he told her gently.

'I know Dad, but ...'

'An' if she says Napoleon 'as to go, 'e 'as to go.' Then, just as Peggy was about to give up all hope, he looked across at his wife and said, 'But yer 'ave to give 'er a bit of time to find a new 'ome for it, Lil. That's only fair.'

'What good would givin' 'er time do?' Lil wanted to know. ' 'Oo in their right mind would ever agree to take in that smelly, 'ome-destroyin' creature?'

'It beats me,' Sam admitted, 'but at least give our Peggy a chance to find somewhere.'

Peggy held her breath while her mother weighed the matter up in her mind.

'All right,' Lil said finally. 'Peggy's got three days to find it another 'ome.'

'Only three days? That ain't no time at all, Mum!' Peggy protested.

'It's more than 'e deserves.'

'I tell yer what,' Sam said. 'Give 'er a week, an' I'll make sure the chain is really secure this time.'

Lil folded her arms across her chest. 'A week,' she said, 'but not a day more. An' if she 'asn't come up with somefink by then, I'll take it down to the slaughter'ouse meself.'

The offices of the old-established firm of Benson, Bates and Co. Ltd, consisted of two rooms.

The larger one had a view over Borough High Street, and had been christened by Belinda 'the directors' room'. The smaller one, with a view over the back yard, was to serve as Mary's office and general waiting room.

With a recklessness which was absolutely typical of her, Belinda had spent the last of the money her father had advanced her on expensively furnishing the place.

'Got to create the right impression straight away, dear girl,' she told Annie.

The directors' room was furnished with a polished walnut double desk, a sofa, two easy chairs and a coffee table. Mary's office had a more functional metal desk, eight straight-backed chairs and a row of impressive-looking filing cabinets which—for the moment at least—were almost completely empty.

Annie and Belinda sat behind the double desk in their new office. Another chair had been set up in front of it for interviewing the typewriters and secretaries who had answered their advertisements in the evening papers.

'I'm ever so nervous,' Annie confessed.

'No need to be,' Belinda told her. 'Just watch what I do, and you'll soon get the hang of it.'

'But you're not used to doing this kind of thing yourself,' Annie pointed out. 'How will *you* know what to say?'

Belinda laughed. 'A Benson has never been lost for words yet,' she said.

'But if you do it wrong? Make a mistake?'

'We're not afraid of making mistakes either,

because even if we commit the most crashing great blunder, we'll never admit it—not even to ourselves.'

Mary opened the door from the outer office. She looked very smart and efficient in the new tailored suit Belinda had bought her.

'It's only just turned 'alf past ten an' there's six young ladies outside already,' she whispered.

'Excellent,' Belinda said crisply. 'Then you'd better show the first one in, hadn't you? And Mary ...?'

'Yes, Belinda? I mean, yes, Miss Benson?'

'Don't get so flustered that you forget to announce her properly, will you?'

' 'Course not,' Mary said, unconvincingly.

She retreated into the back office, quickly reappeared, said, 'Miss Harding,' and stepped to one side so that the interviewee could enter the room.

Miss Harding was around twenty-four or twenty-five. Her blonde hair was tied back in a tight bun, but Annie guessed that once it was released, it would flow down well below her shoulders. She was wearing a check business suit which effectively disguised what was probably a very good figure, and had a pair of plain, studious spectacles perched on her nose.

'Take a seat, Miss Harding,' Belinda said, pointing to the chair in front of the desk.

Miss Harding didn't sit down, however. Instead, she looked around the room as if she were expecting to find someone lurking in one of the corners.

'Is there a problem?' Belinda asked.

Miss Harding looked understandably confused. 'I was ... er ... well, I was rather expecting to talk to either Mr Benson or Mr Bates,' she confessed.

'My father is *Lord* Benson,' Belinda told her, 'and as for Mrs Bates, her father's name is Taylor.'

Miss Harding appeared to be shocked. 'Do you mean to say that you're ...?'

'Yes, we are the people you've come to see,' Belinda said. 'Won't you take a seat, Miss Harding? Just seeing you standing there is making me feel tired.'

With some show of reluctance, Miss Harding walked over to the chair and sat down.

'It is normal on occasions such as this for the people behind the desk to interview the person in front of it,' Belinda told her. 'However, from the expression on your face, I suspect that this time it might be the other way round.'

'Yes,' Miss Harding admitted. 'I rather think it might be.'

'Very well,' Belinda said. 'Perhaps first I might clear up a minor misunderstanding.'

'What kind of misunderstanding, exactly?' Miss Harding asked suspiciously.

'My partner, Mrs Bates, has pointed out to me that our advertisement in the newspaper could have led you to believe that you would be working for us.'

'Yes, it did.'

'That is not quite the case. We intend to provide temporary replacements for office workers who are sick or on holiday. We would charge you a small fee for these services, but you would keep most of the pay you received.'

'But nobody in London—nobody anywhere, as far as I know—does things that way!' Miss Harding said.

'Exactly,' Belinda agreed. 'Nobody else does it. That is why the business is simply bound to be such a huge success.'

'Are you sure about that?'

'Of course. Our filing cabinets are already crammed with requests for temporary help,' Belinda lied.

It was only shock that was keeping Miss Harding in her chair, Annie thought, and any minute she would recover, stand up and walk out. Women just didn't work for women, not in the business world. It really was the craziest of crazy schemes that Belinda had talked them both into.

'Consider the advantages, Miss Harding,' Belinda pressed on. 'We cannot guarantee you will work every day, but when you *do* work, your daily rate will be much higher than it is now, and I would be very surprised if, in addition to extra leisure time, you did not find yourself considerably better off.'

'But as you said, you can't guarantee that—'

'And we will free you from the tyranny of man,' Belinda said, as if she were playing her trump card.

'I beg your pardon?'

Belinda smiled. 'I think you can take your spectacles off now, Miss Harding.'

'I can?'

'Of course. They are only plain glass, aren't they?'

Miss Harding gasped. 'How did you know?'

'You let your hair down at the weekend, don't you?' Belinda said, answering Miss Harding's question with one of her own.

'Well, yes, I do.'

'Any woman who cares as much about her appearance as you do, Miss Harding, would not have bought such ugly spectacles if she really needed them. They are there for effect, aren't they?'

'Employers expect—' Miss Harding began.

'Employers—*male* employers—not only expect you to do your work perfectly—which is all they legitimately have a right to demand—but are not happy unless you look exactly as *they* think you should look,' Belinda interrupted. 'They not only want slaves, they also want worshippers.'

'I never thought of it like that,' Miss Harding said, as if all this were coming as a revelation.

'Have you ever been the victim of un-gentlemanly advances from men whom you work with?' Belinda asked.

Miss Harding blushed.

'I see that you have,' Belinda said.

'Well, yes, it has happened to me once or twice,' Miss Harding told her.

'And have you reported it to your employer?'

Miss Harding looked down at the floor. 'No, I haven't.'

'Why ever not?'

'Because ... well, you know.'

'Because men always stick together?'

'I suppose so.'

'Yes, they can be such swine, can't they?' Belinda said sympathetically. 'If you worked for us, Miss Harding, such things would not be allowed to happen. If you were treated improperly, the employers would have *me* to deal with, and if the guilty party was not punished, we would withdraw our services.'

'Really?'

'Really,' Belinda confirmed. 'You would also have more freedom over your choice of clothing. There would be no need to disguise yourself as a frump. You could wear exactly what you wished to, and if the employers did not like it, they could go elsewhere—except that there is nowhere else to go.'

Miss Harding could manage nothing more than a gasp of astonishment this time.

'They will need us more than we need them,' Belinda told her, 'and when have we women ever been able to say that before?'

Miss Harding raised her head again. The expression on her face seemed to say that she thought she was in the presence of a madwoman, but she was not quite sure. Then she removed her spectacles and smiled.

'When can I start?' she asked.

By the middle of the afternoon, Belinda and Annie had found eleven young ladies who were prepared to start working for the firm of Benson Bates, once they had served out their notice with their current employers.

'So that's one side of the operation successfully

completed,' Belinda said, and picked up the telephone.

'Can I help you?' asked the operator, after a few seconds had passed.

Belinda thought she recognised the voice from her old days at the exchange. 'Is that you, Sarah?' she asked.

'Yes,' the operator replied, surprised.

'Belinda Benson here. I want to place calls to the warehouses on Tooley Street.'

'I'm sorry, I don't think I quite understand. Which warehouse in particular do you wish to contact?'

'All of them.'

'All of them?' the astonished operator repeated.

'Yes. And after we've worked our way through them, we'll start on the City offices.'

Joshua Spiggot was a bulky man, with a red face which was only partly the result of his great liking for single-malt whiskies. He had been a customer of the Hibernia Wharf Timber Company since long before George Taylor had taken over as manager, and had always expressed his complete satisfaction over the way the company had dealt with him. Now, however, as he sat in the wood yard's brick office, his hands clenched tightly on his lap, it was plain that he had something unpleasant on his mind.

'So what can I do for you, Mr Spiggot?' George asked, with more heartiness than he was really feeling.

Spiggot fixed his eyes on a spot on the wall, a couple of feet above George's head. 'I've ... er ... come to tell yer that I'm afraid I shall be takin' me business elsewhere in the future, Mr Taylor,' he said awkwardly.

George frowned, although he'd been half-expecting this. 'Have we done something wrong, Mr Spiggot? Because if we have, you've only to tell us, and we'll soon put it right.'

'No, o' course you ain't done anyfink wrong,' Spiggot said, still gazing at the wall.

'If one of our consignments has fallen below the usual standard in any way ...'

'The quality from this yard's excellent, Mr Taylor. It always 'as been.'

'Then why ...?'

Spiggot finally forced himself to look at George. 'I like dealin' with you, Mr Taylor. Yer a very efficient bloke. Honest, an' all, an' that's rarer than yer might think on the river.'

'Thank you,' George said. 'So what's the problem?'

'Like I've said before, yer've been always more than fair with me, but yer 'ave to see it from my point of view, don't yer? Business is business, when all's said and done.'

'I'm not sure I'm followin' you,' George told him. 'You've just given me several good reasons why you should stay with us, and now you're sayin' you're goin' to take your custom elsewhere. It doesn't make sense.'

Spiggot sighed. 'It's the price, yer see, Mr Taylor.'

'But we're very competitive.'

'Not any more, yer not. There's one company —an' don't ask me to name 'em, 'cos I won't—which is undercuttin' yer by ten per cent. In fact, that's just what they said as soon as they come to see me. Their very first words: "We'll undercut what yer've been payin' the 'Ibernia Wharf by ten per cent." '

'Wait a minute,' George said, realising that he was on to something. 'Am I right about this? You didn't go to them for a quote—it was them who came to you?'

'That's correct.'

'An' without even knowin' what you were payin' us, they offered to undercut us.'

Spiggot was looking very uncomfortable. 'It wasn't quite like that,' he said.

'Then how was it?'

'Well, they quoted me a price.'

'You're losin' me again.'

'They quoted me a price that was exactly ten per cent less than what you were chargin'. Yer see what I'm gettin' at?'

George did. 'To do that, they must have already known all about our business dealings.'

'Exactly.'

'Perhaps somebody from your company has been tellin' them how much—'

'I 'andle all the accounts personally, Mr Taylor,' Spiggot said. 'Nobody else sees any of 'em, so if anybody's been blabbin' about yer prices, it's come from your end.'

'You won't change your mind about changing suppliers?' George asked, without much hope.

Spiggot shook his head. 'Ten per cent off the

raw materials can make a lot of difference in a business like mine.'

George levered himself up. 'In that case, there's nothing more to be said.' He held out his right hand. 'It was a pleasure to do business with you, Mr Spiggot.'

'Likewise, I'm sure,' Spiggot said, quickly shaking hands and then beating a hasty retreat.

George stood at the door of his office, and though his eyes watched Spiggot leaving the yard, his mind was elsewhere.

Losing one customer was not a disaster, but Spiggot was the third who'd left him within a couple of days. Wood yard managers who kept losing customers at that rate very soon found themselves out of a job.

He remembered coming home from the Sudan, his new wooden leg still chafing him, and seeing other limbless ex-servicemen selling matches on the London railway stations. It had seemed that that bleak but almost inevitable prospect was all he, too, had to look forward to. Then, because he'd been a sergeant and knew how to handle men, he'd landed the job of a manager at a wood yard in Northwich, and from there to London.

But what next? If he lost this job—if he was dismissed with poor references—what could he do? He had a wife and children to support now.

At least Spiggot had had the decency to come to the wood yard himself, instead of just sending a curt cancellation like the others had done, George thought, and because of that, he now knew *why* he was losing customers.

He glanced around the yard. A new consignment of teak had arrived from Africa that very afternoon, and several of his workmen—most of them personally trained by him—were stacking it with a speed and efficiency which would have pleased even the most demanding manager.

Which of them was betraying him? he wondered. Which of these fellers, whom he'd trusted and would have done anything for, was selling his trade secrets to the competition and would probably end up costing him his job? With his training, it should have been obvious to him, but it wasn't.

He shook his head despondently. 'An' to think, you always prided yourself on bein' a good judge of men,' he said aloud. 'Well, George, you must be losin' your touch.'

That didn't mean he was going to give up, though—he was too much of a fighter for that. He would study all his men carefully, searching for any signs of disloyalty, and eventually he would discover the Judas who had sold him out.

An' when I do find you, God help you, George thought. Whoever you are.

CHAPTER 12

The police rowing boat glided smoothly under Tower Bridge with two men at the oars. One of them was Sergeant Harry Roberts, whose experience made him almost a veteran. The other was a raw recruit called Tom Bates.

Just ahead of them, at Fresh Wharf two large boats with brightly painted funnels were building up a head of steam.

'A few minutes, and they'll be off,' Harry said knowledgeably.

'Where are they goin'?' Tom asked.

'Just down the river. Takin' day-trippers as far as Ramsgate an' Walton-on-the-Naze.'

The passengers were already starting to embark. They were mostly young couples. The men wore flannel trousers and nautical peaked caps, while most of the women wore white dresses, with shoes and stockings to match. As they ambled lazily up the gangplank, they were greeted with popular tunes from the small orchestra which had been hired to entertain them.

The music drifted across the water to the police boat. 'It's all right for some, ain't it?' Tom said grumpily.

' 'Oo'd want the life of the idle rich?' Harry asked, and when Tom didn't reply, he continued, 'Well, not me, for a start.'

They rowed towards the centre of the river. A dozen or so steamers with foreign names were anchored there, and scores of lighters were taking on their cargoes and ferrying them to the wharves on Tooley Street.

'I like to see people bein' kept busy,' Harry said. 'Good honest work. Yer can't beat it.'

The rowing boat drew level with a floating firefighting tender. At that moment, it was moored close to Pickle Herring Stairs, but should a fire break out further up the river, the powerful tug anchored next to it could have the tender on the move in under a minute. A couple of firemen were standing on the deck of the tender. They waved cheerfully to Harry, and he waved back.

'Mickey Dodd an' Jack Cartwright,' Harry informed his new partner. 'Good blokes. Two of the best.'

'Hmm,' Tom replied, And it was plain that his mind was somewhere else entirely.

Ever since the police rowing boat had passed under Tower Bridge, Tom had been back on familiar territory. He had worked this stretch of water for years—ferrying impatient wharfingers out so they could inspect newly arrived cargoes; taking sailors whose shore leave had expired back to their ships.

All them years, takin' me boat out in every kind of weather, an' what 'ave I got to show for it? he thought. *I* can't put on flannel trousers an' take the day off to go to Ramsgate. All I've got is a roof over me 'ead—which I could lose if I fall be'ind with the rent—an' a few sticks of furniture. Nuffink really!

'Yer went to see the Super this mornin', didn't yer?' Harry Roberts asked. 'What did 'e want to talk to yer about?'

Tom shrugged. 'Nuffink really. Said 'e just wanted to 'ave a little chat since it was me first day.'

'An' what was this chat about?'

'The usual stuff. 'E told me yer'd taken a big chance when yer recommended me, an' 'e pointed out that the Wet Bobs was a good career if yer kept yer nose clean an' got on with the job.'

'He's right, there,' Harry agreed.

' 'Course, things are a lot easier for you than they are for me, ain't they, 'Arry?'

' 'Ow d'yer figure that out?'

'Well, I mean, you're a sergeant, an' I'm only a constable. Come the end of the week, you must be takin' 'ome eight or nine bob more than I am.'

'Yes, I am,' Harry said, 'but I've earned that extra bit of cash in me pocket. Seven year's solid service. That's what I've put into the Thames River Police.'

'Does that mean I'll 'ave to wait that long before I get promoted?' Tom asked.

'Yer might 'ave to wait even longer.'

'Longer!' Tom repeated, as if the thought didn't please him one little bit.

'Yer might *never* get promoted,' Harry pointed out. 'There's an awful lot of blokes that stay constables right up until the day they retire.'

'I suppose yer right,' Tom said. 'So they're not earnin' much more when they leave the Force than they were when they first joined up, are they?'

Harry gave him a penetrating glance. 'No.'

They were almost level with Battle Bridge Steps, where Tom had worked from when he was a waterman. Several of his old mates were lounging on the steps, waiting hopefully for customers.

'D'yer mind if we pull over?' Tom asked. 'I'd

like a word with the lads.'

Harry's slightly worried expression disappeared, and he grinned. 'What are yer goin' to do?' he asked. 'Show off yer new uniform to them?'

'Somefink like that.'

Harry consulted his watch. 'We're not makin' bad time today, so I suppose I could give yer ten minutes to catch up with their news,' he said.

Tom stepped out of the boat, and the watermen of Battle Bridge Steps crowded around, as proud of him as if he were one of their own family.

'Don't you cut a dashin' figure with yer broad trousers an' yer cap with a brass anchor?' Dick Sharp said.

'Yes, ain't 'e just the one?' Bill Rose agreed.

' 'Oo'd 'ave ever thought, when you was arrested for that murder, that instead of endin' up at the end of a rope, yer'd be joinin' the Wet Bobs?' Bandy Chambers chipped in.

Tom smiled, accepting all their praise and congratulations with due modesty, but there was a faraway look in his eyes which suggested that renewing old friendships was not the real reason for his visit to Battle Bridge Steps. Finally, after two or three minutes of being told what a fine bloke he was, he said, 'I much appreciate all yer good wishes. I really do. Now if yer don't mind, I'd like to 'ave a few quiet words with Dick 'ere before I go back on patrol.'

'Anyfink for the Law,' Dick Sharp said, and all the other watermen laughed.

'Let's go for a bit of a walk along the wharf,

shall we, Dick?' Tom suggested.

'Certainly, Officer,' Dick replied, and got another giggle from his mates.

They walked towards Pickle Herring Steps. A consignment of tea was being unloaded at the first warehouse they passed, but the wharf in front of the second one was deserted.

'This is far enough,' Tom said.

Dick Sharp grinned. 'So what's all the mystery about, Tom?' he asked.

Tom's face turned to stone. 'So what's all the mystery about, *Constable Bates,* is what yer mean, ain't it, Dick?' he said.

Dick Sharp's mouth dropped open in astonishment. 'Yer what?' he asked.

'Say it, Sharp!' Tom told him. 'I want to hear yer call me "Constable Bates".'

'Oh, for Gawd's sake, Tom, you an' me 'ave known each other for years.'

'Say it,' Tom insisted.

'Constable Bates,' Dick muttered reluctantly.

'That's better,' Tom said. 'Still do a bit of smugglin' on the side, do yer?'

'Pardon?'

'You 'eard.'

'I 'eard, but I didn't believe it.'

'I'll tell yer 'ow this little racket of yours works, shall I?' Tom said. 'A ship comes in from America with bales of tobaccer, yer see. Now all the way across the Atlantic, the crew 'ave been shavin' them bales. Not much, not so it'd be noticed on any one bale, but by the time they anchor in London, they've got a fair weight set aside.'

'Tom ... Constable Bates ... I—' Dick Sharp interrupted.

'Shut up an' listen. Now the only problem these bent sailors 'ave is gettin' the tobaccer ashore. That's where you come in. Yer take yer lights off yer boat, an' some time in the middle of the night yer row across an' pick it up. Then yer sell it off, an' split the money with the crew.'

Dick had gone very pale indeed. 'I swear that I've never—' he began.

'If me memory serves me well, the two ships yer used to deal with most often were the *Pride o' Richmond* an' the *Baltimore Castle,*' Tom said. 'There ain't many secrets on the river. Watermen tell each other things, an' I used to be a waterman meself. But now that's all be'ind me.'

'Are yer goin' to run me in?' Dick asked fearfully.

For the first time, Tom smiled. 'Run yer in? An old china like you, Dick? 'Course I ain't.' The smile vanished as quickly as it had appeared. 'But I shall be wantin' yer to show yer appreciation of me generosity,' he continued in a much harsher tone.

'Yer want payin' off!' Dick gasped. 'You, of all people. Well, I'd never 'ave thought it of you.'

'You 'ave to plan for the future,' Tom told him. 'Wet Bobs don't earn enough for trips to Ramsgate.'

'Trips to Ramsgate? I'm not followin' yer.'

'Yer don't 'ave to follow me. All yer 'ave to

do is come up with the money.'

'But I'm already payin' off one of your blokes as it is,' Dick Sharp protested.

' 'Oo might 'e be?'

'Constable Downes. I give 'im five bob a week to keep me out of bother like this.'

Tom laughed. 'Well, it don't look like it was money very well spent, does it? An' now yer goin' to 'ave to come up with *ten* bob a week, ain't yer?'

' 'Ow can I pay yer both?' Dick whined.

'Yer'll just 'ave to work 'arder, won't yer? There's plenty o' work for a good smuggler on this river.' Tom put his hand on Dick's shoulder. 'I tell yer what, I won't start collectin' till next week. That should give yer time to get organised, shouldn't it?'

'Maybe,' Dick mumbled.

'An' if you mention our little arrangement to Constable Downer—' Tom tightened his grip on Dick's shoulder—'yer'll wish I *'ad* arrested yer, 'cos what yer'll be gettin' is somefink much worse.'

'I won't. I swear on me mother's grave, I won't.'

Tom walked down the steps and climbed back into the police duty boat.

'What was goin' on there?' Harry asked, pulling on his oar.

'Goin' on where?'

'You know what I mean. What was it yer were talkin' to Dick Sharp about?'

'Oh that,' Tom said easily. 'We was just 'avin'

a rabbit about old times.'

Harry looked far from convinced. 'Then why did yer 'ave to do it away from all yer other chinas?' he asked. 'It looked to me like yer was arguin'.'

Tom grinned. 'Yer've got a sharp eye, you 'ave, 'Arry. Yes, we were arguin' all right. See, what 'appened was, a few months back I lent Dick Sharp a few bob to tide him over. Well, now I need tidin' over meself, an' the tight bugger 'ad the nerve to tell me he couldn't pay me back yet.'

'I see,' Harry said. 'Look, if yer want me to, I'll sub yer until payday ...'

'No, yer've done enough for me already,' Tom replied. 'I'll manage some'ow.'

The gymnasium was located just off the New Cut. From outside, it could have been anything from a warehouse to a small factory, but once inside there was no questioning its purpose.

It was a great barn of a place, with two rings at one end of it and various pieces of training equipment at the other. It smelt of sweat and Sloane's Liniment, and was filled with the sounds of grunting boxers and of leather gloves thudding against sand-filled punch bags.

Joey Bates and Eddie Clarke stood in the doorway. 'That's the bloke I'm goin' to be takin' on,' Joey said, and pointed to a large man with a broken nose who was lifting what seemed to Eddie to be impossibly heavy weights.

'What's 'is name?' Eddie asked.

'Dave Donning.'

'Never 'eard of 'im.'

'A few years ago, 'e used to be one of the best fighters in the 'ole of London.'

'Might 'ave been good once, but now 'e looks past it,' Eddie said, as Donning added yet another weight to each end of his barbell and picked the whole thing up with ease.

A middle-aged man in shirtsleeves walked over to where they were standing. 'Oo's yer mate?' he asked Joey.

'This is Eddie,' Joey said. 'Eddie, I'd like yer to meet Mr Fuller, 'oo runs the gym.'

'I also do a bit of refereein' when me legs is up to it,' Fuller said. 'Pleased to meet yer, Eddie. Are yer about ready, Joey?'

'Just about.'

Fuller looked across at Donning, who was still hefting weights. ' 'Ow about you, Dave?' he shouted. 'You ready?'

'Any time,' Donning called back, lowering the barbell and reaching for his gloves.

Fuller climbed up into the ring. Joey waited until the referee had moved across to the far corner, then turned to Eddie. 'I'm nervous,' he said.

'Yer shouldn't be. There's nuffink to be nervous about,' Eddie assured him.

'But I ain't 'ad a fight since that sailor flattened me under the archway.'

'Yer ain't 'aving a *real* fight now. This is only sparrin'. It's like when I take the motorcar out into the countryside, just to open out its engine a bit. It's practice, not the real thing.'

'I suppose yer right,' Joey agreed.

Donning was already in the ring. When Joey reached for the ropes to pull himself in, the other fighter smiled sarcastically and held out a hand for Joey to grab on to.

'I don't need that,' Joey told him, pulling on the ropes and climbing into the ring unaided.

Donning grinned. 'Sorry. It's just that I 'eard yer needed 'elpin' *out* of the ring the other night, so I thought yer just might need 'elpin' *in*, as well.'

Joey felt what little confidence he had left start to ebb away. 'It wasn't as bad as that,' he said defensively.

'Yer lasted a minute an' an 'alf, from what I was told. Was that the best yer could do?'

' 'E caught me off me guard,' Joey said weakly.

'I'll catch yer off yer guard! Yer make me sick, you young boxers,' Donning said bitterly. 'Yer all think yer can be as good as I was when I was in me prime. Well, let me tell yer, yer never will be.'

Mr Fuller walked over to them. 'Let's keep it friendly, shall we?' he said.

'Oh, it'll be friendly enough,' Donning replied, through clenched teeth. 'I'm just about to teach this lad 'ere a *friendly* lesson about real boxin'.'

Donning went on to the attack immediately. He was slower than he'd once been, but he still knew exactly where to hit to cause the maximum harm. This wasn't sparring to Dave, Joey realised. This was as important a contest to him as any he'd ever fought.

'I forget 'ow long yer lasted with that sailor,' Donning said, as he delivered a blow to the side of Joey's head. 'A minute an' an 'alf, was it? Well, yer shouldn't even last that long against a proper boxer like me.'

Though he didn't want to, Joey suddenly found himself seeing red. Donning was out to humiliate him. Well, he'd just have to show his opponent what a strong young fighter could do against an ageing, over-the-hill one.

Joey went in with both fists flying, an angry human windmill—and before he knew what was happening, he was lying on the floor.

It was the fight in the archway all over again.

Donning had not mauled Joey as much as the sailor had done, but the landlord of the pub near the gym raised the same quizzical eyebrow as the one in the boozer near the archway had, and once again Eddie was forced to explain that his friend was not a hooligan, but a boxer.

'Well, that's it,' Joey said, when they were sitting down with their pints in front of them.

' 'Ow d'yer mean, that's it?'

'I'm not prepared to spend the rest of me life polishin' floorboards with me nose.'

'If yer give up now, yer'll live to regret it,' Eddie said. 'Yer'll always be wonderin' what yer could 'ave done if yer'd decided to stick at it.'

'I already know what I could 'ave done. I could 'ave done nuffink, 'cos I'm no bloody good.'

'Yer know what I think? I think yer 'andlin'

it wrong,' Eddie said tentatively.

Joey shot his friend a hard look. 'A couple o' weeks ago yer'd never even been to a boxin' match, but now yer an expert on it, are yer?' he demanded.

'No,' Eddie admitted. 'I'm not an expert on boxin', but I'm an expert at drivin'.'

'That's nuffink like the same thing.'

'I think it is. See, the aim of racin' motorcars is to go as fast as yer can, but yer can't go at yer fastest speed all the time, because there's bends in most roads, an' if yer don't slow down, yer'll never get round 'em.'

'Is there some kind o' message in that for me?' Joey asked aggressively.

'Yes,' Eddie said. 'Both times I've seen yer fight, yer was in far too much of an 'urry to get it over with. So instead of 'oldin' back a little, yer went in there at top speed, an' as a result, yer crashed before yer'd really shown 'em what yer could do.'

For perhaps a minute, Joey was thoughtfully silent. Then he said, 'Maybe yer right.'

' 'Course I am.'

Joey nodded his head slowly. 'I'll tell yer what I'll do. I'll give it one more chance down at the archway. I'll 'old back a bit, like you say I should, an' if I still end up bein' counted out, I'll give the 'ole thing up as a bad job.'

'But if yer win ...?'

Joey grinned for the first time since they had entered the pub. 'If I win, then there's still a chance yer'll be able to brag about 'avin' a world champion boxer as yer best friend.'

Eddie clapped his hand on Joey's shoulder. 'That's the spirit,' he said.

It was a fair distance from Wapping Police Station to Lant Place, but after six hours sitting in a rowing boat, Tom Bates thought his legs could do with a good stretch, and decided to walk it rather than take a tram.

By the time he had reached the hop warehouses and asbestos works near the top of Southwark Bridge Road, the board schools had finished for the day, and the kids were out on the streets. Tom stopped for a minute and watched them running off the energy they'd been forced to suppress while they were in their classrooms.

A few boys were playing cricket with an old piece of timber and a rag ball, while a group of girls skipped furiously over a rope which was tied at one end around a gas mantle. One little lad on his own was running a few yards, bending down to draw an arrow on the pavement, then running on again.

'Are you the 'are?' Tom called after him.

'I am, mister,' the boy replied, looking back.

'Then yer better get a move on, 'adn't yer? The 'ounds'll be after yer soon.'

The boy grinned. 'They'll never catch me, mister. I'm too fast for 'em.'

He had only just finished his boast when a small pack of boys suddenly appeared from around the corner, yelping at the top of their voices.

'Told yer,' Tom said, as the boy began to

run as if his life depended on it.

Tom waited until both the hare and hounds had disappeared down Townshend's Yard, then set off towards home again.

Kids! he thought. They were so innocent, but then they could afford to be, because unlike grown-ups, they weren't always having to face the harsh realities of life.

He was just level with the workhouse when he noticed a bloke who looked familiar hanging about outside the pub on the corner of White Cross Street.

'Wally Cooper!' Tom said to himself, and strolled across the road towards him.

Wally saw him coming and smiled. 'Well, blow me down if it ain't Tom Bates,' he said. 'I 'aven't seen yer for ages. 'Ow yer doin', young Tom?'

'Fair to middlin',' Tom replied.

'Are yer still workin' as a waterman down at Battle Bridge Steps?'

'That's right,' Tom said. He looked up and down the street, then moved closer to Wally. When he spoke again it was in a whisper. 'An' are you still a bookie's runner?'

'Now why d'yer want to know about that?' Wally Cooper asked suspiciously.

Tom smiled. 'Why d'yer think I want to know?' he said. ' 'Cos I've just got meself an 'ot tip from one of me chinas, an' I want to place a bet on it.'

Wally checked the street, just as Tom had done. 'What's the 'orse, an' 'ow much do yer want to put on it?'

Tom smiled again, but this time there was no humour behind it. 'Yer know I told yer a couple of minutes ago that I was still workin' as a waterman?'

'Yes?'

'Well, I was lyin'. I jacked that in nearly a month ago. An' d'yer know what I am now?'

'I 'aven't a clue.'

'I'm a Wet Bob,' Tom told him.

Cooper's jaw dropped. 'Yer never are!'

'If yer need convincin', I can always show yer me warrant card,' Tom said.

'Oh, bloody 'ell,' Wally groaned.

'I could run yer in, yer know ...'

'Tom, be reasonable!'

'... but I won't if yer make it worth me while not to.'

'But I'm already payin'—'

'Somebody else for protection? An' 'oo might that be?'

'Constable Battersby.'

Tom shook his head. 'Well, I might 'ave a word with Constable Battersby,' he said, 'an' then again, I might not. But either way, you'll say nuffink about it to 'im, and from now on, yer'll be payin' five bob a week to me as well.'

Tom thought back to the conversation he'd had with Reg Wragge in the Kennington Lane Candidates' Section House. Wragge had been right about the extent of corruption among the bobbies. Tom had only approached two villains so far, and both of them had admitted to paying off the police—so either Tom had been very lucky or there was a lot of it about. That was hardly surprising, Tom decided, because it was an awfully easy way to make money. Here he was, just starting out, and he had already increased his wage by ten bob a week.

When Tom finally reached home, he was greeted by the delicious smell of steak and kidney pie wafting up the passageway from the kitchen.

'What's the special occasion?' he asked when he'd sat down and his wife had brought it to the table.

'What do you think the special occasion is?' Annie replied. 'It's a reward for my hero, coming home after his first day at work.'

'I don't s'pose I can expect this treatment every day, can I?' Tom asked.

Annie laughed. 'You most certainly cannot,' she said, leaning over and pecking him on the cheek. 'So if I was you, I'd take advantage of it while it's there.'

'I'll do that,' Tom said. He saw there was only one plate. 'Ain't yer 'avin' any of it yerself?'

'No, I've already eaten,' Annie said. It was a lie, but best steak was very expensive, and she could always grab a bit of bread and cheese later.

'Well, I really am bein' spoiled, ain't I?' Tom said, tucking into the pie with relish.

Annie sat down opposite him. 'So are you going to tell me how your day went, then?'

Tom finished chewing a piece of tender steak. 'There's nuffink much to tell,' he said. 'Me an' my sergeant—that's Sergeant 'Arry Roberts, yer know?'

'Of course I know it's Harry.'

'We rowed our way down the river for a bit, an' then ...' He paused for dramatic effect.

'And then?'

Tom grinned. 'An' then we turned around an' rowed back.'

A twinkle came to Annie's eye. 'So you didn't catch any dangerous criminals? Not even one?'

Tom shook his head. 'Maybe tomorrow. An' 'ow's *your* business with Belinda goin'?'

'Very well!' Annie said enthusiastically. 'When we'd paid off all our expenses last week, we had thirty-five shillings left over. That's seventeen and sixpence each. Belinda said that's only a start. By the end of the year, we should be earning more than—'

'More than a Wet Bob?' Tom asked.

Annie frowned. 'Well, perhaps,' she said. 'That won't bother you, will it?'

'No, of course not,' Tom lied.

Annie's frown became even more serious. 'You know, when I first started going out with you, my mum was dead against it.'

Tom speared a juicy kidney with his fork. 'I know. I'm not likely to forget it, am I?'

'She said once a hooligan, always a hooligan, but you told me you'd given all that up, and I believed you.'

'An' yer were quite right, too.'

'Then you were arrested for Rollo Jenkins' murder, and everybody else seemed to think that you'd done it, but I still kept my faith in you.'

'Is all this rakin' over 'istory leadin' us anywhere?' Tom asked, popping a piece of crisp pastry into his mouth.

'We've shown them, haven't we? We've shown them all what you can do when you put your mind to it.'

'You reckon?'

'Of course we have. You need to be a special kind of bloke before they accept you in the police force. Intelligent, brave and—above all—honest.' Tears started to pour from her eyes.

Tom put down his fork and took his wife's hand in his. 'Whatever's the matter now?' he asked.

'It's just that I'm so proud of you,' Annie sobbed. 'So very, very proud.'

CHAPTER 13

It was Thursday, six days since Peggy Clarke's goat had disgraced himself, and only one day before Lil Clarke would carry out her threat and take Napoleon down to the abattoir. The sky overhead was as grey as Peggy's mood as she walked up to the house at the end of Sturge Street and knocked tiredly on the front door.

The woman who answered her knock wore a flowery apron and had a turban on her head. She was holding a feather duster in her hand, and looked as if she wasn't very pleased at being called away from her work.

'Yes?' she said brusquely. 'What d'yer want?'

'I was wonderin' if yer might be in the market for a goat,' Peggy said.

'A goat?' the woman repeated. 'Why in 'eaven's name should I want to buy a goat?'

'Oh, I'm not sellin' 'im,' Peggy said hurriedly. 'If I can find 'im a nice 'ome, I'll give 'im away.'

The woman's eyes narrowed. 'Give 'im away?' she said suspiciously. 'What's the catch?'

'There ain't no catch.'

'If yer don't want any money, there must be somefink wrong with 'im.'

'There ain't nuffink wrong with 'im. Honest!' Peggy protested. ' 'E's a very good goat, my Napoleon, 'ealthy an' even tempered. 'E'll play with yer kids—'

'They've all grown up.'

'An' if yer got 'im a little cart, yer could make a fortune usin' 'im for runnin' errands.'

'So why ain't you makin' a fortune yerself, 'stead of tryin' to give 'im away?'

Peggy looked down at the doorstep. 'Yer've made a luverly job of donkey-stonin' this,' she said. 'I bet it's the cleanest doorstep in the street.'

The woman was not to be sidetracked. 'I said, why ain't yer making a fortune yerself?' she repeated.

'Me mum don't like goats.'

'Why not?'

'She's taken what yer might call an unnatural dislike to 'em. But as me dad said to 'er, the sofa an' chair were just about due for replacin', anyway.'

'What are yer telling me?' the woman demanded. 'That the goat ate yer sofa?'

' 'Course not,' Peggy replied. ' 'Ow could a little goat like 'im eat an 'ole sofa?'

'So what did 'e do?'

'Well, 'e did tear it a bit,' Peggy admitted, 'but that was an accident. Yer might easily 'ave done the same thing yerself. I've given 'im a stiff talkin' to, an' told 'im never to do it again. So won't yer take 'im, missis? Yer won't regret it. If yer don't, me mum's goin' to take 'im down to the slaughter'ouse.'

'From what yer've just told me, that sounds like the best place for 'im,' the woman said. 'An' now, if yer'll excuse me, I do 'ave me 'ousework to do.'

'Please!' Peggy said, but the woman was already retreating into her front passage.

'Yer won't regret it,' Peggy told the closing door.

A tear trickled down her cheek. She had been to every house in Struge Street, and every one in Queen's Court, Little Suffolk Street, William Street and Toulmin Street. Nobody in the whole of Southwark seemed to have any interest in keeping a goat.

The Mariner's Arms was sandwiched between two gloomy warehouses, and had a sign hanging over its door showing a jolly Jack Tar, a clay pipe in his mouth, coiling a rope. It was not a boozer which George Taylor patronised very often, but it was the closest one to the wood yard, and at that moment George felt like he really needed a drink.

'Pint, Mr Taylor?' the barman asked.

'Yes,' George said. 'An' yer better give me a whisky chaser to go with it.'

He leaned against the bar, and when the whisky arrived he knocked back half of it immediately. He was in big trouble, and he knew it. He'd lost another customer that morning—making it four in a week—and though no one from the company had said anything yet, he was sure that his job was hanging in the balance. 'But who the hell's behind it?' he asked himself for the hundredth time.

He thought back to his days in Burma. Funds had gone missing from the officers' mess, and because he'd already had a reputation for getting to the bottom of things, he'd been asked to investigate it. Two days, it had taken him to come up with the guilty party—a corporal who'd been fiddling the books. Just two days!

Then there'd been the bloke in Moore's wood yard in Northwich. He'd been selling off some of the yard's stock for years, right under Mr Moore's nose, but George had been on to him from the day he started the job as manager.

So why was he having no success this time? Why, in spite of watching his men like a hawk, did he still have no idea who the guilty party was?

'Think it through logically,' he ordered himself, 'just like you used to do when you were plannin' a patrol.'

To get the information, the traitor would have needed access to the files in the office, but the men were not allowed in there unless George was present. If any of them had tried to sneak in while he was in the yard, he was bound to have noticed, and when he *wasn't* in the yard, the office was always locked.

'I'll 'ave the same as Mr Taylor's 'avin',' a voice said behind him, and turning round, George saw Albert Howard, a grey-haired, thin-faced man who managed the wool warehouse at the other end of Hibernia Wharf. Howard did not look well. His eyes were bloodshot, and he seemed to have developed a nervous tic in the left side of his mouth.

'Had a rough day, Albert?' George asked.

Howard nodded. 'Though it'd be more accurate to say I've 'ad a bloody rough week,' he told George. 'Do yer know, I've lost three customers. Three! I've never known anything like it. Even when times were bad, I've never 'ad—'

'Do you know *why* you lost them?'

'Yes, I bloody well do know. It's because some bugger is undercuttin' me.'

'An' this bugger who's undercutting you—does he seem to know what prices you normally charge?'

'Accordin' to one of me customers—one of me *ex*-customers, I should say—'e does. An' 'e 'asn't just got a rough idea, neither. 'E knows down to the last penny.'

If the same thing was happening to the wool warehouse as was happening to the wood yard, then maybe one of his men wasn't to blame after all, George thought. So where did that leave him? Maybe there was a gang operating along the wharfs—a gang which used a very good locksmith, and broke into offices at night.

'Enough of this gloom an' doom,' Howard said, cutting into George's thought process. 'Let's talk about somefink pleasanter. 'Ave yer got them complimentary tickets to go an' see yer brother's livin' pictures yet?'

'No, I haven't,' George admitted. 'I'm expectin' to receive 'em any day now.'

'Marvellous what they can do with science these days, ain't it?' Howard said. 'I'm lookin' forward to seein' them meself, but I must confess it'll feel strange to see the old wool ware'ouse up there on a screen.'

'What?' George said, puzzled. And then he realised what Howard was talking about 'Oh, of course, he had his camera round at your place an' all, didn't he?'

'He did. An' he brought a bunch of pansy actors round with 'im as well.'

George laughed. 'An' I suppose he also took that ridiculous wife of his?'

Howard joined in the laughter. 'Oh yes, she was there. I wasn't goin' to say anyfink about 'er—not with 'er bein' yer sister-in-law an' everyfink—but now yer've brought the subject up, I 'ave to say it was 'ard for me to keep me giggles down.'

'Was she playin' a customer, like she was at the wood yard?' George asked.

'No. She was supposed to be me secretary. Yer

should 'ave seen 'er, sittin' over the typewritin' machine. She 'ad no idea what to do, which is just as well—'cos if she'd tried typewritin', I swear she'd 'ave got them long nails of 'ers caught between the keys.'

'Do you want another drink?' asked George, who was starting to feel better.

'Might as well,' Howard replied. 'Think I'll do without the whisky this time, though.'

'I think we could probably both do without the whisky this time,' George said.

'One thing I didn't understand about the way yer brother works,' Howard said as they attacked their second drinks. 'He didn't seem to have no chemicals with 'im.'

'Chemicals? Why would he want chemicals?'

'Well, 'e asked if 'e could borrow me office so 'e could process 'is film.'

'So what? He did the same at the wood yard.'

'Well, I don't know much about photography, but I do know about wool an' fabrics, an' when we go about "processin" somefink, we always 'ave to use chemicals.'

'I see what you mean. Maybe the chemicals were already in the camera.'

'Maybe,' Howard said dubiously.

And then it hit George like a thunderbolt. 'Or maybe him wantin' to go inside our offices had nothin' to do with livin' pictures at all!' he said.

Peggy was at her wits' end. She seemed to have knocked on every door in Southwark, and nobody would take Napoleon off her hands. What was more, when she'd asked her mother for more time to find Napoleon a home, Lil had stuck to her guns and said that she would tolerate the smelly, ' 'ome-destroyin' creature' for one more day, and after that he definitely had to go.

'So what am I goin' to do?' Peggy asked herself mournfully as she walked, head bowed, up Lant Place. 'I can't let me goat down. I can't just stand by an' watch my Napoleon end up as somebody's Sunday dinner.'

'When a young gal starts talking to 'erself like that, yer can bet it's not long before other people start talkin' *about* 'er!' said a friendly voice.

Peggy looked up and saw Fred Simpson walking towards her, with Mary Bates on his arm.

'Oh 'ello, Mr Simpson, 'ello Mary,' she said miserably.

Fred Simpson pulled a face. 'Now what's the matter with you?' he asked. 'Yer look so sad anybody 'ud fink the sky was about to fall in on yer.'

'It is,' Peggy said. 'I've only got one more day left to find an 'ome for me goat, Napoleon, an' if I can't, me mum's goin' to 'ave him butchered.'

Fred squatted down on the pavement in front of her. 'I think yer'd better tell me all about it,' he said.

So Peggy did—from the moment when she had first seen Pedro the Gypsy's goat on Highgate Heath that August Bank Holiday, right up until the second she had begun to tell Fred the story.

'I think I remember this goat of yours now,' Fred said. 'Wasn't 'e the one that was tied up to a lamppost outside the Goldsmiths' Arms durin' Tom's weddin'?'

'That's right. Tom gave 'im to me as a present for bein' a bridesmaid.'

But Fred was no longer listening to her. Instead, he was staring into Mary's eyes. 'That was the first time we ever danced together, wasn't it?' he said.

Mary smiled back. 'Yes it was. An' I was so frightened about askin' yer, that I 'ad to pretend me mum 'ad made me come an' invite yer to dance.'

'An' I was so stupid that I didn't realise what was goin' on, an' told yer you were under no obligation.'

Peggy coughed. Loudly. 'Me goat,' she reminded them. ' 'Ave yer got any ideas about what I can do with me goat?'

Warm memories faded away, and both Fred and Mary started to look properly concerned.

'Isn't there anyfink you can do about findin' an 'ome for it, Fred?' Mary asked.

'Me?' Fred replied. 'I'm in a worse position to 'elp her than most people. I live in a dormitory, don't forget. 'Ow d'yer think the other firemen would feel if I suddenly walked in with a goat an' tied it to the foot of me bed?'

'They might get quite fond of my Napoleon in time,' Peggy said hopefully. 'I mean, 'e don't smell or nuffink. Well, not too much, anyway.'

'An' I'm sure they'd be over the moon when your Napoleon ate their boots,' Fred said.

' 'E's not really very partial to firemen's boots,' Peggy said unconvincingly.

' 'E's probably never 'ad the chance to become partial to 'em,' Fred said, 'an' I'm sure that I'm not goin' to be the one to give 'im the opportunity.'

'So it's 'opeless,' Peggy said, tears beginning to form in the corners of her eyes.

'Oh, never say die,' Fred told her. 'There must be somebody 'oo can find a use for a go—' He stopped, suddenly, and a smile came to his face.

' 'Ave you thought of somebody?' Peggy asked.

'I might 'ave,' Fred said cautiously, 'but I don't want to go raisin' yer 'opes too 'igh, 'cos it might not come to nuffink.'

Peggy looked at Fred adoringly. 'Yer know what you are? Yer my 'ero,' she told him.

'Mine as well,' Mary said.

It was a cool early evening when Harry Roberts walked down Battle Bridge Lane in the direction of the steps. He was out of uniform, but he was not off duty, because as long as there was even one unsolved crime anywhere along the river, he never considered himself to be off duty.

'An' if my suspicions are correct, a crime 'as been committed,' he said to himself. 'Right before me eyes.'

When he reached the steps, he found the

usual collection of watermen around, waiting hopefully for work. They had a hard life, but for all that, most of them stayed honest, which was why it angered Harry so much to think that someone who had been offered a better living should take advantage of it to line his own pocket.

The watermen saw him approaching. 'It's Constable ... I mean *Sergeant* Roberts,' Bandy Chambers called out. ' 'Ow yer doin', Mr Roberts?'

'Can't complain, Bandy,' Harry said, then he turned around to look at Dick Sharp. 'I'd like a word in private with yer, if yer don't mind, Dick.'

If Harry had needed anything to confirm his suspicions, then the shifty look which suddenly appeared in Dick Sharp's eyes was more than enough.

'Me, Mr Roberts?' Sharp asked. 'Yer want a private word with me?'

'Yes, you,' Harry said.

They walked along the wharf. It was a quiet time, and there was no one to hear their conversation, but Harry did not stop until he had reached the spot where he had seen Sharp arguing with Tom Bates.

'So what can I do for yer, Mr Roberts?' Sharp asked, with a slight tremble in his voice.

'I'm on to yer,' Harry told him.

'Yer what?'

'Yer could go inside for what yer've been doin', yer know,' Harry bluffed. 'Couple o'years. Maybe more. It all depends on what mood the judge is in that mornin'. Do yer know what it's like inside, Dick?'

'No, I ...'

' 'Course yer don't. 'Ow could yer? Well, I'll tell yer—it's bloody awful. Yer've got no mates, 'cos the authorities never let yer talk to anybody except the prison officers an' the chaplain. An' they use the birch in there. Ever been birched, Dick?'

'Mr Roberts, please ...'

'Neither 'ave I,' Harry said, 'but I've seen blokes 'oo 'ave been. Big strong blokes, most of 'em were—blokes yer'd think could stand anyfink—but when they come away from the birchin', they was cryin' like babies.'

Dick Sharp had turned very pale, and his hands were beginning to tremble. 'Be reasonable, Mr Roberts,' he pleaded.

' 'Ow d'yer mean, reasonable?'

'I just can't come up with no more money in pay-offs, 'owever 'ard I try.'

So he *had* been right, Harry thought. Tom complaining about a constable's pay, the way he had seemed to be arguing with Dick Sharp—yes, it all added up to a sickening conclusion.

' 'Ow much are you payin' Constable Bates for lookin' the other way?' Harry demanded.

'Five bob a week. Only 'e ain't been round for 'is first payment yet.'

'An' are any of the other watermen payin' 'im anyfink?'

Dick Sharp shook his head. 'I don't think so.'

'Right,' Harry said. 'Now listen carefully. I

don't want yer money, an' I'm not after seein' you banged up. It's Constable Tom Bates that I want to nail.'

Dick Sharp took a greasy handkerchief out of his pocket, and wiped his brow. 'Thank 'eavens for that.'

'Yes, I want to nail that bugger, and you're goin' to 'elp me, Dick.'

The panic was back in Sharp's eyes. 'What do yer want me to do?' he asked.

'It's not so much what I want yer to do, as what I *don't* want yer to do,' Harry said. 'I don't want yer to refuse to pay 'im 'is money just 'cos yer know I'm after 'im. An' I don't want yer to tell 'im yer've even been talkin' to me. Do yer think yer've got that, Dick?'

Dick Sharp bowed his head. 'Yes, Mr Roberts, I think I've got it,' he said.

Belinda Benson was lying in her bed. She was totally naked, and she was feeling very dissatisfied. She rolled over, pulled a cigarette from the packet on her night table, and lit it. She inhaled deeply, letting the smoke caress her lungs, then twisted round to face her visitor.

Harry Roberts, also naked, was on his back, and was gazing at the ceiling as if there were magic words written on it that only he could see.

'Are you going off me, Harry Roberts?' Belinda asked. 'Because if you are, you only have to say so, you know. I mean, I would really hate to have you think that you had to go to bed with me out of any mistaken notion of charity.'

Harry continued his silent contemplation of the ceiling as if he hadn't heard her.

'Oh, for God's sake, pay attention, Harry!' Belinda exploded. 'This is serious.'

Her words seemed to break whatever spell he was under, and Harry rolled over on to his side. 'Did yer say somefink?' he asked.

'Indeed I did. I wanted to know whether you were getting fed up with me.'

'Well, of course I ain't,' Harry said. 'Why should yer ever think that?'

'Because, my dear man, I must have let you have your wicked way with me at least two hundred times in the last year, and never, in all that time, have I known you put on such a lacklustre performance as you did tonight.'

Harry frowned. 'Are yer tryin' to tell me that I wasn't very good?' he asked.

'Not very good? That would be an understatement. You were positively awful.'

Harry looked shamefaced. 'Sorry.'

'And if your falling so far below your usual standards isn't because you no longer find me attractive, then I would very much like to know what the reason *is*.'

Harry moved closer to Belinda and put his arms around her. 'We could always try again,' he suggested. 'Maybe I'll do a bit better next time.'

Belinda pushed him away. 'Perhaps later we could try again, but first of all, you're going to tell Aunt Belinda exactly what's on that mind of yours.'

'It's nuffink. Just a problem to do with me

work,' Harry said evasively.

'It must be a very big problem to put you off your stroke like this, and I rather think I'd like to know about it.'

'I don't want to burden yer.'

'A problem shared is a problem halved, or so they say,' Belinda told him.

Harry looked up at the ceiling again. 'All right,' he said, 'maybe it might do me some good to talk about it to yer. The problem is Tom Bates.'

'Tom? Isn't he shaping up as a Wet Bob? I should have thought that a bright young man like him—'

'It's a lot more serious than that,' Harry interrupted. 'I've found out 'e's been black-mailin' one of the watermen on Battle Bridge Steps, an' 'e may 'ave 'is finger in a lot of other pies as well. I just don't know yet.'

'But that's awful!' Belinda exclaimed. 'Are you absolutely sure that he's guilty?'

'I'm sure.'

Belinda nodded. 'Yes, knowing you and the way you work, you probably are.' She took another deep drag of her cigarette. 'So what are you going to do about it?'

'First of all, I'm goin' lookin' for more evidence.'

'But why, if you're so certain?'

'Because if there's only one charge, Tom Bates just might be able to wriggle 'is way out of it. When I give me report to the Super, I want to 'ave a rock-solid case against 'im.'

'Oh my God, I've just thought of something,' Belinda said.

'What?'

'You staked your reputation on Tom working out right. If he goes down, you go down with him. You'll lose your job, Harry, as sure as night follows day.'

'Yes, there is a chance of that,' Harry admitted.

'There's more than a chance. You know that as well as I do. You positively adore being a Wet Bob.'

'Ain't that the truth.'

'What will happen to Tom once you've handed in the report to your boss?'

' 'E'll be arrested an' tried.'

'And then?'

' 'E'll be found guilty, an' e'll go to prison.'

'Have you thought about what it will do to Annie—to all the Clarkes?'

'Of course I've thought about it. I've not thought about nuffink else all day. But 'e 'asn't left me with no choice.'

'Couldn't you just tell him that you're on to him and he'd better stop this blackmailing game immediately?'

'I could,' Harry admitted, 'but 'ow do I know that 'e really would? An' if I find a reason to let one criminal off, 'ow long is it goin' to be before I find a reason to let another off, an' then another? I can't live that way, darlin'.'

'No,' Belinda said sadly. 'I know you can't. Surely there must be some way we can ...'

'I've looked at it from all the angles, an'

there's only one thing I can do.'

Belinda lit a second cigarette from the stub of her first. 'Poor Annie,' she said. 'What a bloody, bloody mess.'

CHAPTER 14

Peggy lay awake for most of Thursday night, praying that the light which marked the start of Napoleon's last day in Lant Place would never come. Some time before dawn, she heard the sound of the local milk cart, clattering down the street on its way to meet the milk train at Paddington Station.

'Get on, yer idle bleeder,' Dick Todd, the milkman, called to his horse. 'Yer goin' to make me late again.'

'If yer don't like yer horse, why don't yer 'ave Napoleon instead, Mr Todd?' Peggy said softly into her pillow, but she knew that her little goat could never manage to pull such a big cart.

She heard her mother get up and go downstairs, then her father's footsteps as he followed her fifteen minutes later. By now the sun had started to rise, casting a crimson glow over Southwark—casting its light on the hopelessness of Napoleon's cause.

Eddie's door opened, and mumbling something about 'infernal combustion engines' to himself, he made his way downstairs. Peggy hugged her pillow tightly to her, and asked

God for a miracle, but if he answered, she didn't hear him.

Finally, at just after eight o'clock, Lil Clarke walked to the foot of the stairs and called up, 'It's time you were down 'ere, 'avin' yer breakfast, gal.'

With a very heavy heart, Peggy climbed out of her bed.

Lil was in the kitchen, cooking up something in her big, cast-iron frying pan.

'Hmm, that smells wonderful,' Peggy said ingratiatingly. 'What is it, Mum?'

'Fried bread, a bit o' sausagemeat, an' tomaters,' Lil replied, without looking up.

'Delicious,' Peggy said, sitting down at the table. 'Yer are a kind mum, ain't yer, Mum?'

'Nice to be appreciated for a change,' Lil said, transferring the fry-up from the pan to a plate. She walked across to the table and laid the plate in front of Peggy. 'There yer are. Tuck in.'

Peggy picked up her knife and fork, but did not touch her food. 'Mum?' she said.

'Yes, what is it now?'

'Yer 'aven't changed yer mind, 'ave yer?'

'About what?'

'About lettin' Napoleon stay.'

Lil folded her arms across her chest. 'No, I 'ave not changed me mind,' she said firmly.

'But Mum ...'

'I was very attached to the sofa that smelly creature of yours went an' destroyed.'

'Dad said it was past its best.'

'It might 'ave been, but you wouldn't 'ave been born if it 'adn't been for that sofa.'

' 'Ow do yer mean?'

Lil looked suddenly embarrassed. 'Well, that was where me an' yer father ... I mean we ... oh, stop asking so many questions. The fact of the matter is, that goat is goin' to 'ave to go. Now eat up yer breakfast an' get off to school.'

'I'm not 'ungry,' Peggy said, pushing her untouched plate to one side.

'There's many a starvin' mite would think 'e was in 'eaven if 'e was given a breakfast like that,' Lil said, 'so I'm not goin' to 'ave you wastin' it. Now, eat!'

'I can't, Mum,' Peggy said. 'I'd be sick if I did. Me belly's all knotted up.'

A look of deep sympathy flashed across Lil's face. 'Well, yer are puttin' on a bit of weight,' she lied, 'so maybe it won't do yer any 'arm to miss yer breakfast for once.'

Peggy sensed the weakening. 'Can I miss school as well?' she asked. 'It'd give me more time to find a new 'ome for Napoleon, yer see.'

'You certainly cannot play truant because of that goat!' her mother said. 'The very idea. I'd be summonsed before the school board if I let yer stay away without a good reason.'

'They'd never find out,' Peggy said.

'There's attendance officers roamin' the streets every day, just lookin' for kids 'oo should be in school. If yer get caught, it's a twenty-shillin' fine, yer know. 'Ave you got the odd twenty shillin's to spare?'

'No, Mum. I did 'ave once, but yer made me give it away to the Battersea Dogs' 'Ome.'

'Yes, an' we all know 'ow yer got that money, don't we?' Lil said. 'Beggin' and trickin' people so you'd 'ave enough to buy a goat. Yer see what I mean about them animals? They're trouble even before yer get 'em.'

'It wasn't Napoleon's fault I was playin' the broken-milk-jug dodge,' Peggy protested. ' 'E wasn't even born then.'

'I'm not goin' to argue no more,' Lil said. 'You're goin' to school, an' that's final. Do you understand?'

'Yes, Mum,' Peggy said miserably.

'An' make sure yer don't get lost on the way, 'cos I'll be down there at playtime to make sure yer in school.'

'I'll be there,' Peggy promised, seeing one of her last ounces of hope flying out through the window.

It was two o'clock in the afternoon. Peggy sat at her desk, itching to be free, yet knowing there were still hours to go before the final bell rang.

All around her, her classmates—the other fifty-eight girls who made up Miss Crosby's class at Lant Street Board School—were probably feeling the same way she was. None of them dared show it, because Miss Crosby had eyes in the back of her head and a tongue sharp enough to cut through a brick.

What am I goin' to do? Peggy thought. 'Ow can I save me poor little Napoleon?

Fred Simpson had said that he'd try to do something, and that had sounded promising the day before, but now Peggy was not certain he *could* do anything, what with him being a fireman and living in a dormitory.

'Well, Clarke?' said Miss Crosby's sharp voice. 'Are you going to make us wait all day for your answer?'

Peggy looked up at the blackboard and saw a sum written on it in white chalk. 'Is the answer seven an' an 'alf, Miss Crosby?' she hazarded.

The other girls all tittered, but only for the second it took their fearsome teacher's eyes to sweep once around the room.

'The answer might have been seven and a half, Clarke—if we'd still been doing arithmetic,' Miss Crosby said witheringly. 'But since, for the last ten minutes, we have been practising our spelling, I hardly think that seven and a half *can* be right. Do you?'

'No, Miss Crosby,' Peggy said. 'Sorry, Miss Crosby, but yer don't want a goat, do yer?'

There was more laughter.

'A goat!' the teacher exploded. 'Are you trying to be impertinent, girl?'

'No, miss. But me mum said that me goat—'

'You have wasted the class's time, and so I will waste yours,' Miss Crosby told her. 'You will stay behind after school. Do you understand, Clarke?'

'Yes, miss,' Peggy mumbled. Which meant she had even less time left to find a new home for Napoleon.

It was ten to five before Miss Crosby finally decided that Peggy had been punished enough, and five o'clock by the time that the girl got home.

Lil was in the kitchen, her arms white up to the elbows from the pastry she had been making. 'Yer very late today,' she said. 'What's the reason?'

'I was kept in,' Peggy admitted.

'Kept in! Yer've never been misbe'avin', 'ave yer? Kids from respectable 'omes don't misbe'ave in school.'

'I wasn't misbe'avin' really. I just asked Miss Crosby if she wanted Napoleon.'

'Did yer tell her that 'e was your goat?'

'Yes. I said that 'e'd been livin' in our back yard, but that you'd said ...' Peggy dried up, because it was plain from the look on her mother's face that Lil thought it was the worst possible thing she could have told her teacher about the Clarke family.

'The shame of it!' Lil said. 'Even now that we're on the point of gettin' rid of 'im, that goat of yours is still causin' us nuffink but trouble.'

'When's ... when's it goin' to 'appen, Mum?' Peggy said, almost in tears.

'As soon as I've finished me bakin', I'll take 'im ... take 'im for a walk,' Lil said.

'Just give me one more day to find 'im a new 'ome, Mum,' Peggy pleaded.

'It wouldn't do any good,' Lil said, touched by her daughter's distress and hoping she wouldn't start crying, too. 'You've 'arassed everybody yer know—an' a lot of people yer don't—an' it's got yer nowhere. One more day ain't goin' to make no difference.'

The slightly dingy street was just to the south of Hampstead Heath, and George was surprised when the hansom cab pulled up at a house roughly in the middle of it.

He turned round to look at the cabman, who was sitting on the high seat behind him. 'Are you certain that this is the right place, driver?' he asked.

'It's the address what you give me, all right, guv,' the cabby replied.

George paid off the cabby and examined the house. He supposed it was in *quite* a respectable area, and it was—as Philip's wife, Marie, had pointed out—some way north of the river. But it was part of a terrace, just like his own little home in Lant Place, and somehow, after hearing Philip talk about it, he'd been expecting to find something much grander.

'You should have known better,' he told himself. Should have known better than to believe anything his brother said to him. Should certainly have known better than to let Philip anywhere near the wood yard—or any of the other businesses which operated on or around Hibernia Wharf.

He lifted his big fist and knocked heavily on the front door. There was a sound of shuffling feet in the corridor, then the door opened and Philip was standing there.

'George!' he said. 'What are you doing here? Shouldn't you be at work?'

All the speeches that George had prepared previously went completely out of his mind at the sight of his brother. 'You look bloody awful,' he said.

And Philip did. He hadn't shaved for days, and had probably not had a proper wash, either. His hair was a tangled mess. His eyes were bloodshot and he wasn't even wearing a collar.

'I ... uh ... haven't been sleeping too well,' Philip said. 'You still haven't said what you're doing here.'

'We need to talk.'

'Then you'd better come inside.'

George followed him down the corridor to the kitchen. *At least he hasn't quite forgotten where he's come from,* George thought, *because when there was serious talking to be done back home, it had always been in the kitchen.*

Philip offered George a chair, then picked up a bottle of whisky which was standing on the Welsh dresser and held it up to the light. There was only about an inch of liquid left.

'Only bought it this morning,' Philip mumbled. 'Still, there's enough left for one shot each.'

'I don't want a drink, an' I don't think you should have one,' George said.

'Maybe you're right,' Philip agreed, flopping down in the chair opposite his brother.

'When you were in my office, supposedly developin' your film, you looked through confidential files, and then you sold the information to me competitors,' George said accusingly. 'An' you did the same in Albert Howard's wool warehouse.'

Philip nodded tiredly. 'You're quite right, of

course,' he said. 'I pulled the same trick at the jute warehouse and the asbestos manufactory.'

'It's got to stop.'

'Yes, I know.'

'More than got to stop. You're goin' to have to go to the people you sold the figures to, an' tell 'em that if we don't get all our customers back, we're takin' the whole matter to the police. If we do that, I think you're goin' to find that you an' your mates'll be in very hot water.'

'I'll tell them,' Philip said, 'and you'll get your customers back. The people I deal with don't want trouble with the bobbies any more than I do.'

'What made you sink so low as to betray your own brother?' George asked.

Philip shrugged. 'What do you think? I desperately needed the money.'

'Mam an' Dad were down on their uppers now an' again, and there've been occasions when me an' Colleen have been a bit pushed to make ends meet,' George said. 'In fact, I don't think there's ever been a time when our family *couldn't* have used a bit of extra money—but you're the only one of us who's ever stolen to get it.'

'It was different this time,' Philip said weakly. 'I didn't do it for myself.'

'Then who *did* you do it for?'

'For Marie, of course.' Philip spread his hands out in a gesture of desperation. 'You've no idea what working in the living-pictures business is like, George. Film is very expensive to buy, but do the owners of any of the music halls ever take that into account? No, they don't!'

'Are you sayin' you don't earn much?'

'They pay me such a pittance for showing my pictures that sometimes I actually lose money on them.'

'If that's the case, you should start lookin' for some other line of work.'

'I can't ... or anyway, I *couldn't*. You see, before Marie would agree to marry me, I had to promise her I'd make her a big star.' Philip laughed bitterly. 'I sometimes wonder if that's the only reason she agreed to be my wife.'

'Well, I should *stop* wonderin' if I was you, because it's fairly obvious to me,' George said mercilessly. 'Where is she, anyway?'

'Gone.' Philip laughed again. It was a hollow, broken sound. 'You think it was bad enough I sold your competitors some of your secrets?' he asked. 'Imagine how you'd feel if your wife had run off with one of your competitors.'

'She's done that, has she?'

'Oh, I can see *why* she's done it. Charlie Tooke has got pots of money. In his last living picture, he used a hundred actors in one scene alone. If only I'd had Charlie Tooke's money, then I could have staged bigger productions ...'

'You're not really sorry about stabbin' your own brother in the back, are you?'

'If there'd been some other way to raise the cash in a hurry ...' Philip said.

'When I came here tonight, I was goin' to give you a damn good thrashin'.'

Philip looked down at the kitchen table. 'I probably deserve it,' he admitted.

'You *do* deserve it,' George told him. 'But I can't hit a man when he's down.'

'If I can just have one really big success, she'll come back to me,' Philip said. 'I know she will.'

'You're a bloody fool, Philip,' George told his brother sadly.

Philip lifted his head and stared straight into George's eyes. 'Don't you think I know that?' he asked.

Lil Clarke placed the cake she'd been making in the oven, took off her apron and washed the flour off her arms. She looked around to see if there was anything else she could do to put off the dreadful moment, but the kitchen was spick and span.

She sighed. 'Well, I s'ppose I'd better get it over with.' She looked up at the ceiling, knowing that above it Peggy was lying on her bed and sobbing her heart out. 'I'm sorry, love,' she whispered, 'but you know there really ain't no other way.'

Lil was on the point of going to collect the goat from the back yard when she heard a knocking on the front door.

'Now I wonder 'oo that can be?' she said to herself as she walked down the passageway.

She opened the front door to find a grinning Fred Simpson standing there.

'Can I 'elp yer, Mr Simpson?' she asked.

'Well, not really,' Fred replied. 'It's your Peggy that I've come to see.'

'Is it about the goat?'

'Yes, as a matter o' fact, it is.'

There was the sound of feet pounding down the staircase, and then Peggy, panting from her dash and with excitement, was standing next to her mother.

'Yer've found an 'ome for my Napoleon, 'aven't yer?' she said, in between gasps. ' *'Aven't yer?'*

Fred's grin spread even wider. 'Would yer mind if I borrowed yer daughter an' 'er goat Napoleon for 'alf an hour or so, Mrs Clarke?' he asked.

Lil smiled with relief. 'As long as the only one yer return to me is our Peggy,' she said.

'I think I can guarantee that,' Fred told her. 'Come on, Peggy, we're goin' to take yer goat for a little walk.'

It was only a short journey, just down Lant Place, past the Goldsmiths' Arms and round the corner to the Fire Brigade headquarters.

'Yer are goin' to let me goat live in yer dormitory, after all,' Peggy said.

Fred laughed. 'There's no chance of that. The other blokes would be up in arms.'

'Then if 'e can't sleep in yer dormitory, where the bloomin' 'eck is 'e goin' to sleep?'

'Just be patient for just a few more minutes an' yer'll see,' Fred teased.

He led Peggy through the archway into the yard where the firemen did most of their training. Some of them were there at that moment, running up and down ladders and squirting jets of water at an imaginary fire.

Watching them was a very important-looking fireman with white hair.

'That's the commander,' Fred said. They walked up to him, then stopped.

Fred saluted. 'This is Peggy, sir,' he said.

'How do you do, young lady?' the commander said.

'Pleased to meet yer, sir,' Peggy replied.

The commander looked down at Napoleon. 'So this is the goat, is it? I think he'll do very nicely.'

'Do very nicely for what?' Peggy asked, alarmed. 'Yer don't want to take him out to fires with yer, do yer? Napoleon's not very good at fightin' fires.'

The commander laughed. 'No, we don't want to take him out to fires with us, but we would like to use him as our mascot.'

'Mass-what?'

'Mascot. A sort of good luck charm.'

'Would 'e 'ave to do anything to earn 'is keep?' Peggy asked, still suspicious.

'Not much. Sometimes we have parades, and he'd take part in them.'

' 'Ow d'yer mean?'

'We'd dress him up in a coat of gold cloth, and he'd walk in front of the Fire Brigade band.'

Peggy sighed. 'Think of that. My Napoleon in a big parade. I'd be ever so proud of 'im.'

'Does that mean we can have the goat, Miss Clarke?' the commander asked.

'Would I be able to come an' visit 'im sometimes?' Peggy asked.

'Of course you would. Any time you wanted to.'

Peggy looked down at the goat, then back at the commander. 'Then yer can 'ave 'im,' she said.

'Splendid. I'm sure you won't regret it.'

Peggy bit her lip, trying hard not to cry. 'D'yer mind if I 'ave a couple of minutes just to say goodbye to 'im?' she asked.

'Of course not.'

The commander and Fred stepped back a few paces to give Peggy and Napoleon a little privacy. The girl knelt down and put her arms around the goat.

'Now you be good,' she whispered into the goat's ear. 'No eating fire 'oses or any of them ropes, 'cos the firemen need 'em to do their job. An' when yer on parade, I want yer to 'old yer 'ead up an' look straight in front of yer.'

Fred watched the whole scene with a smile on his face. Despite a few tears, Peggy was happy—and that made him happy, too. He had no way of knowing then that it would be a long time before he would experience even a snatch of happiness again.

Maggie White poked her key at the front door, trying to fit it in the lock, but the lock wouldn't stay still—would insist on moving first to the left and then to the right.

Maybe the best thing to do is to take it by surprise, she thought, pretend to go away and then twirl round suddenly an' catch it off its guard. She giggled at the idea.

'Shh!' she told herself. Best not to give anything away, because the lock was listening and would know she was planning a trick.

She turned away, then spun round, but somehow things had gone wrong. The door was open now. She could see the gas mantle in the passageway and a blurred figure standing under it.

'Is that you, Sid?' she slurred. 'Sid, me beloved 'usband? For richer or poorer, for better or worse, eh, Sid? Well, we've certainly got landed with worse, ain't we?'

'Yer should come inside before the neighbours complain,' her husband told her.

'Don' wan' come inside,' Maggie said. 'Wan' to dance in the street. Dance with me, Sid.'

She waltzed around, like she used to in the dance halls before they were married, but all that spinning was not good for someone who had drunk as much gin as she had. She swayed from one side to the other, then her legs gave way from underneath her, and she fell into her husband's arms.

Maggie sat in the kitchen, drinking hot, sweet tea. She was not exactly sober yet, but she was better than she had been half an hour earlier. Better—but also worse. Now she was no longer so drunk, she was remembering why she'd started hitting the gin in the first place.

'I've tried to be reasonable,' Sid said to her. 'Ain't that true, Maggie?'

'I lost my baby! I lost me little Ellen,' Maggie said, tears starting to trickle down her cheeks.

'I know yer lost yer baby. It was my baby as well. But life 'as to go on.'

'I can't 'ave more.'

'The doctor says yer *probably* can't 'ave any more. That's not the same thing at all.'

'It is to me,' Maggie sobbed. 'I'm a woman, an' I know what's possible an' what ain't.'

'Yer don't know nuffink,' Sid told her. 'An' even if yer *can't* 'ave no more kids, all this drinkin' yer doin' ain't the answer to any of yer problems.'

'If yer felt like me—' Maggie began.

'I talked to Mr Davies today.'

Maggie looked at him blankly. 'Mr Davies?'

'Yer boss. Yer remember that, at least, don't yer? Mr Davies. The manager of the wash'ouse.'

'Oh, 'im.'

'Yes, 'im. 'E told me that yer used to be one of the best workers 'e 'ad. But now, 'e says, yer a liability. Them's 'is very words. A liability. 'E says if yer don't buck up soon, 'e's goin' to 'ave to give yer the sack.'

Maggie shrugged apathetically. 'It don't matter if 'e does sack me,' she said. 'Nothing matters to me now I 'aven't got no family to look forward to.'

Sid's face flooded with sadness. 'Do yer still love me, Maggie?' he asked.

His wife tried to focus on him, and faded. 'Well, of course I still love yer.'

'Then you'll give up all this drinkin',' Sid told her, ' 'cos things can't go on like this—you comin' 'ome pissed every night.'

'What are yer sayin'?' Maggie demanded.

'I'm sayin' that if yer can't get a grip on yerself, I'll 'ave to leave yer.'

Maggie wiped her tears away with the sleeve of her dress. 'I'll try,' she promised. 'I'll really try.'

But neither of them really believed she could do it.

CHAPTER 15

Saturday night had come round again—the night when the women of Southwark visited the New Cut market to do last-minute shopping for the Sunday dinner, and the men either strolled down to the boozer or went off in search of some other form of entertainment.

The usual crowd was gathered in the boarded-in archway to watch the young hopefuls and seasoned pros battling it out. Eddie Bates climbed up to the third row of tiered seats and sat down next to the man with the greasy bowler hat.

'So you're 'ere again, are yer?' the man asked.

'That's right.'

'An' is yer china fightin' tonight?'

' 'E is.'

The man shook his head in wonder, and his bowler hat wobbled. 'Some people never learn, do they?' he asked.

'Joey'll do better this time,' Eddie told him,

without any real conviction in his voice.

'Well, 'e couldn't do much worse, now could 'e? If 'e gets the floor wiped with 'im one more time, 'e might as well apply for a job as a mop.' The man laughed, and dug Eddie in the ribs. 'Did yer 'ear that? I just made a joke.'

'I 'eard it. 'Ilarious,' Eddie said grimly. 'Side-splittin'. Yer ought to be on the stage.'

Was I right to encourage Joey to try again? Eddie wondered. Say 'e gets beat this time. 'E's goin' to feel worse than 'e ever 'as in 'is 'ole life, an' 'oo's 'e goin' to blame? Me—because I talked 'im into it.

The Master of Ceremonies, wearing a different, but equally loud check suit, stood up and welcomed all the lords, ladies and gentlemen to the evening's entertainment.

'The first fight of the evenin' is between Lightnin' Joey Bates ...' he announced.

'Lightnin' Joey?' somebody in the crowd called out. 'Faintin' Joey'd be a better name for 'im.'

'Yeah, 'e's rubbish! Send 'im 'ome to 'is mum, and let's see a decent fight,' a second man shouted.

'Give the kid a chance!' a third man said. He paused, for dramatic effect. 'After all, it ain't as if 'e'll be 'oldin' up the evenin's entertainment for long!' The crowd roared with laughter at this last piece of wit.

Eddie looked down at Joey. He was standing at the edge of the ring, patting his gloved knuckles together, looking halfway between worried and miserable. I've just gone an' lost me best friend, that's what I've done, Eddie thought.

The MC waited until the noise had died down a little, then said, 'An' facin' 'im, in a grudge return match, will yer give a big 'and for Sailor Blake!'

Eddie's heart sank as he saw the cocky, tattooed sailor strut across the ring to the cheers of the spectators. Of all the opponents that Joey could have drawn, the man who had humiliated him and almost destroyed his confidence the last time he'd fought was easily the worst possible choice.

The man with the bowler hat dug Eddie in the ribs again. 'Now we'll 'ave some fun,' he said.

The bell rang, and the two fighters stepped into the centre of the ring. The sailor had a smile on his face which said this was going to be easy work, hardly worth turning up for. Joey's face was pale and strained, and even from where he was sitting, Eddie could see that the young fighter was biting his lower lip.

Joey launched out with his left fist and then his right, catching the sailor two mostly deflected blows, one on the chin and the other on the shoulder.

'Yer goin' too fast,' Eddie muttered, trying desperately to transmit his message to Joey. 'Keep on at that speed, an' yer'll be off the road at the first bend.'

But the message was not getting through. Joey was dancing around and landing weak punches by the half dozen.

' 'Ow long d'yer think 'e'll last this time?' the man with the bowler hat asked Eddie.

' 'E's goin' to win,' Eddie said, though it was obvious to him that Joey wasn't.

The man chuckled. 'Win, yer say? Do yer want to put a small bet on that?'

'Yes,' Eddie said. It would be just like throwing money down the drain, he thought, but he didn't see that he had any choice but to be loyal to his best friend.

' 'Ow much shall we bet?' the man with the bowler hat asked Eddie, as Sailor Blake delivered what was obviously a punishing blow to Joey's left eye.

'A bob?' Eddie suggested.

'A bob!' the man scoffed. 'A bob ain't a proper bet. If yer really serious, yer'll put at least a quid on yer china winnin'.'

A pound! Eddie did actually have a pound to his name—one pound one and sixpence to be more exact. He kept it in a tin box in his bedroom, and on a wage of five shillings a week, it had taken him nearly a year to save it up.

'Well?' the man next to him said. 'What about it? Are yer goin' to put yer money where yer mouth is?'

Eddie looked down at the ring. The state of the fight had not changed at all. Joey was still landing three times as many punches as Sailor Blake—with about half as much effect.

'A pound it is,' Eddie said.

The man with the bowler hat chuckled again. 'Money for jam,' he said.

The sailor deliberately dropped his guard, as he had done just before the sudden end of his last fight with Joey and it took all of Eddie's self-control not to shut his eyes. Any second now, he thought, Joey would go into the attack full throttle, and then it would all be over.

But Joey didn't. Instead, he stepped back slightly. The sailor looked surprised that things had not gone the way he'd planned, and Joey—putting all his strength behind the blow—caught him with a left hook to the jaw.

The sailor tottered for a second, the surprised look still on his face, then dropped to the floor.

The referee, with his arm raised in the air, stepped over the fallen boxer. 'Er-one ...' he counted, '... er-two ...'

Now Eddie did close his eyes, terrified that the sailor was only temporarily dazed, and would be back on his feet within a second or two.

'... er-three ... er-four ... er-five ...'

'Stay down,' Eddie pleaded silently. 'Just stay down for another five seconds.'

'... er-six ... er-seven ... er-eight ...'

Just two more seconds to go, and still Eddie could not bear to look into the ring.

'... er-nine ... er-ten.'

'Out!' the crowd screamed.

Eddie opened his eyes. The sailor was climbing groggily to his feet—but it was too late!

And Joey? Joey stood there, as proud as Punch, while the referee lifted his arm high in the air and announced to the audience that he was the winner. The crowd had laughed at him earlier, but now they cheered him as if he'd always been the local favourite.

Eddie turned to the man with a bowler hat. 'What did yer think?' he asked.

'Not bad.'

'Not bad?' Eddie repeated.

'All right, it was very impressive,' the man said grudgingly.

'Yes, it was, wasn't it?' Eddie agreed. 'An' now I believe yer owe me a quid.'

The following Monday afternoon had been a glorious day for rowing up the river, but Harry Roberts had not got any of his customary pleasure out of it. Now the shift was over, Tom Bates had gone home, and Harry sat in the duty room at Wapping Police Station.

He looked up at the frowning portraits of long-dead superintendents. Hard, unyielding men, most of them—but in *their* job, they'd had to be. He shifted his gaze down to the cardboard folder in his hands, the folder which, in a few minutes' time, he intended to present to the current superintendent.

Conducting his investigation into Tom Bates' corruption, and coming up with four rock-solid examples of it, hadn't been the hard part, he decided. The hard part had been working with Tom, day after day. It had put a real strain on Harry to pretend that they were still friends and everything was normal, when all the time he'd been uncovering new dirt and despising Tom more and more.

Yer could 'ave 'ad a real career in the Bobs, Tom, Harry thought. Yer could 'ave brought up a nice little family in security. Yer could 'ave made Annie really 'appy. But there was no chance of that now.

Harry wondered if Annie would ever forgive him for sending Tom to gaol. It didn't seem likely. He sighed. Over the last year or so, the Clarkes and the Bates had become like family to him, but that was all over now.

Harry checked his watch. Two more minutes and he would be in the super's office, spilling the beans that would lose him both his friends and his job. It was still not too late to change his mind—but he knew that he wouldn't.

It was exactly five o'clock when Harry knocked on the door of Superintendent Drummond's office.

'Come in,' the superintendent said.

Harry turned the handle and stepped into the office, glad that the chance for a moment of weakness was finally over.

Drummond was sitting at his desk, his pipe in his mouth and clouds of blue-grey smoke swirling around his head. 'Punctual as usual, Sergeant Roberts,' he said, 'and from the look on your face, I'd guess you have something very grim to report.'

'I 'ave, sir,' Harry confirmed. 'I've been collectin' evidence of corruption on the part of one of me fellow officers.'

Drummond raised his bushy eyebrows. 'Have you, indeed?' he said. 'I think that you'd better sit down and tell me about it.'

It took a lot to fluster Harry, but being asked to sit down in his boss's presence threw him into a minor tiswas. 'I couldn't do that, sir,' he said. 'It wouldn't be right.'

'I'm the man who decides what's right and wrong in this office,' the superintendent said firmly. 'And since this talk of ours is likely to be quite a long one, *I'd* be more comfortable if I wasn't looking up at you all the time. So sit yourself down, Sergeant Roberts, and *that's* an order.'

'That's very kind of yer, sir,' Harry mumbled as he did as he was ordered.

Superintendent Drummond took his pipe out of his mouth and poked around in the bowl with a long thin spike he kept on his desk, then he returned the pipe to his mouth, and sucked. Satisfied he had cleared whatever blockage there'd been, he packed the pipe with naval shag, and lit it again.

'Now tell me about this corrupt officer,' he said. 'Let's start with his name, shall we?'

'I'm sorry to inform yer that the man in question is Constable Tom Bates, sir.'

The superintendent's eyebrows rose again. 'Ah, Constable Bates,' he said. 'The man who, if my memory serves me well, you personally recommended.'

'Yes,' Harry agreed. 'The man I recommended.'

'And what exactly has he been up to?'

Though Harry knew the details off by heart, he was a careful man and consulted his notes before speaking.

'I don't know whether I've managed to uncover all 'is nasty little rackets, sir, but I do know that I've got enough to 'ave 'im sent inside for a very long time. Number one: 'e's started takin' bribes from one of the watermen 'oo works from Battle Bridge Steps, a bloke by the name of—'

'Dick Sharp,' the superintendent said.

'That's right, sir,' Harry said, surprised.

'Go on.'

'Number two: 'e's takin' money off a very dodgy wharfinger on Tooley Street—'

'Thadeus Lloyd?'

'Yes, sir.'

'Anything else?'

'There's this bookie's runner in Southwark ...'

'Wally Cooper?'

'He's the bloke.'

'Is there more?'

'Yes, sir. Just one. A shippin' clerk 'oo works down at St Katherine's Dock ...'

'Yes, that would be Obediah Babcock.' Drummond smiled. 'Congratulations, Sergeant Roberts. You missed three or four others, but then you didn't have the resources at your disposal which I have at mine. So, on the whole, I would say that you have once more conducted the kind of thorough police investigation that I've come to expect from you.'

Harry was still finding it hard to believe the way the interview was going. 'If yer don't mind me askin' yer, sir,' he said, ' 'ow is it yer already know everyfink I came to tell yer? 'Ave yer been on to Tom Bates all along?'

'As I told you earlier, you're a very good policeman,' the superintendent said, with a hint of mild rebuke in his voice, 'but you shouldn't go beyond that and start believing you're the *only* good policeman we have working in this station.'

'No, sir. I'm sorry, sir,' Harry said, accepting the criticism as justified.

'Do you remember when you asked me to recommend Bates for training?' Drummond asked. 'You said something then about setting a thief to catch a thief.'

'I think that was *you*, sir,' Harry corrected him. 'What I said was that 'avin' once been a minor villain 'imself, 'e knew somefink about the criminal element. But what I never thought was that 'e might use 'is knowledge to—'

'Whichever of us said it, it got me thinking,' the superintendent interrupted. 'I always suspected we had some corrupt policemen working here—there's corruption in every line of business —but up until that point, I'd no idea how to root them out. With Tom Bates on the Force, though ...'

'I don't think I'm followin' yer, sir,' Harry said. 'Maybe I missed somefink.'

'From his old days as a waterman, Constable Bates already knew that Dick Sharp did a bit of tobacco smuggling on the side, but when he put the pressure on Sharp, it wasn't to get him to pay up five shillings a week.'

This was getting crazier and crazier with every minute, Harry thought. 'So if 'e didn't do it for the money, then why the devil *did* 'e do it, sir?' he asked.

'To find out if Sharp was paying off any other

policemen—which, indeed, he was.'

Harry suddenly saw the astonishing truth. 'Yer mean 'e was workin' for you, sir?'

'Right from the start. And thanks to the work he's done, there are three policemen in this division and two in the Met who will shortly be having their collars felt.'

'Well, bugger me sideways!' Harry blurted out, before he could stop himself.

The superintendent smiled again. 'No, thank you, Sergeant,' he said. 'In case you've forgotten, *that* is a criminal offence.'

Harry pushed open the doors of the Goldsmiths' Arms and entered the saloon. Colleen Taylor, who was standing behind the bar, saw him and gave him a friendly wave. Harry waved back, then looked around him.

Fred Simpson and Mary Bates were sitting in one corner, holding hands and looking into each other's eyes.

Nice to see young love, Harry thought. I 'ope things work out for 'em.

His gaze moved across to the other side of the room. Maggie White was leaning with both elbows on the table, as if without the support, she would fall over. Her hat was askew and there was an empty gin glass in front of her. It crossed Harry's mind that it would be an act of kindness to go across and talk to her, but he quickly rejected the idea because he didn't know her very well, and didn't feel he had the right to go intruding on her private grief.

There were other people in the saloon

he knew: Dick Todd, Southwark's champion grumbler; George Taylor, who was listening to one of Sam Clarke's stories with obvious amusement; Mrs Gort, the local midwife ... Lots of people he was well acquainted with, but not the one he needed to talk to. He walked up to the bar and ordered himself a pint of best ale.

It was ten minutes before Tom Bates entered the bar and made straight for his partner.

'Didn't expect to see you 'ere,' Tom said cheerily. 'I'd 'ave thought that by now yer'd be on the other side of the river with that lady friend of yours.'

'I should 'ave been,' Harry replied, 'an' maybe I will go an' see Belinda later. But first I think that I owe yer a drink an' an apology.'

'An apology?' Tom said.

'I've been to see the Super this afternoon ...'

'Oh, yes?'

'... an' 'e told me all about the special job yer've been doin' for 'im.'

Tom grinned. 'I see.'

'Yer don't get the point. Do yer know *why* I went to see the Super?'

'Oh, I think so,' Tom replied. 'The job I've been doin' is top secret, so if 'e told yer about it, it must 'ave been because 'e felt 'e 'ad no choice. Which can only mean that the reason yer went to 'im was to report me.'

'That's right,' Harry agreed. 'I really thought yer was takin' bribes all along the river, an' even though you're me china—an' Annie's 'usband—I was goin' to shop yer.'

Tom slapped Harry on the shoulder. 'Well, of course yer were,' he said. 'When yer become a policeman, yer swear to up'old the law, so that's just what yer 'ave to do. In your place, I wouldn't 'ave acted no different.'

'Thing was, with you always moanin' about 'ow poor the pay was in the Wet Bobs, I thought yer'd decided to do somefink about makin' more money.'

'I 'ave,' Tom said. 'I want promotion, an' I want it fast. I know this thing I worked out with Superintendent Drummond won't get me me sergeant's stripes right away, but it'll go somewhere towards it, won't it?'

'Yes,' Harry agreed. 'Catchin' five rotten apples in a couple o' weeks is bound to 'elp yer.'

'An' after sergeant, there's inspector,' Tom said. 'That's where me evenin' classes come in.'

'What evenin' classes?'

'I got the idea from me sister, Mary. I said to meself, if she can go down to the Borough Polytechnical Institute at night, what's to stop me doin' the same thing? So when we're not on night shift, I go down there to catch up on me learnin'.'

'Yer never mentioned that before.'

Tom shrugged. 'I s'ppose I kept quiet about it 'cos I was embarrassed.'

'Embarrassed? Why?'

'I wasn't sure that I could 'andle it. I never was much of a scholar at the board school—couldn't see the point of all that learnin'—but I reckon I might give it another try, 'cos now I know just where I'm 'eadin'.'

'Bloody 'ell, you really are serious about gettin' on, ain't yer?' Harry said.

'Never been more so.'

Harry signalled to Colleen. 'I'd better buy yer that drink, then,' he told Tom.

'There's no need,' Tom replied. 'Yer did right by goin' to the Super. You don't owe me nuffink.'

Harry grinned. 'That's not why I'm buyin' it for yer,' he said. 'I've got an even better reason for payin' for yer ale now than I 'ad when I walked through the door.'

'An' what's that?'

' 'Cos I don't think it's ever too early to start butterin' up yer future boss.'

PART TWO

The Worst Few Days of Their Lives

CHAPTER 16

It was the morning of the last Friday in August. Only two more days, people told themselves, as they toiled away in the stables, factories and warehouses of Southwark, and it would be the Sabbath the one time in the week when they could lie in bed, mend the rabbit hutches in their back yards, or do whatever else took their fancy. Thank Gawd for Sunday.

The weather was mixed that day. The sun shone early in the morning, was eclipsed by clouds at ten, and by eleven had fought its way out of the grey mass again. A breeze blew in from the river, carrying with it toffee wrappers, bits of fly posters, and other assorted rubbish.

On Southwark Bridge Road, the orderly boy was at work as usual, dashing between the wagons and hansom cabs and buses, his scoop at the ready to clear up all the dung he could before reaching the safety of the other side of the street. On the corner of Marshalsea Road, a rat charmer, with his pet rodents already clambering over his shoulders and arms, waited to charm a few coppers out of the workmen going for a dinnertime drink.

The walking sick entered or left the Evelina Hospital, a few pious souls made their way up Pepper Street to All Hallows' Church, and in Fire Brigade headquarters, near the corner of

Lant Place, all was quiet—for the moment.

The alarm bell rang loudly through the length and breadth of the fire station, spreading pandemonium everywhere.

In the recreation room, games of draughts and billiard matches were immediately abandoned, cups of tea were left half-drunk, and newspapers —normally carefully folded out of consideration for future readers—were carelessly flung to one side.

In the gymnasium, dumbbells were already being lowered on to their stands and skipping ropes dropped, and one fireman, who had been somersaulting over the horse when the bell went off, hit the ground running.

Men converged on the tackle room from every corner of the station. The duty firemen reached for helmets, pulled on their boots and tucked their axes into their belts.

Speed was all-important and concentration was total. No one asked where they were going, or what kind of fire it was—they would find that out soon enough.

Down in the stables, a groom touched the spring which in three easy movements would release the cords which secured the horses to their stalls, drop collars over their heads, and pull the rugs from their backs.

'Come on, me beauties,' he cooed as he led them rapidly away from their stalls. 'Yer needed again.'

The engineer was already in the garage, checking that the steam boiler on the fire engine was burning fiercely enough to generate the pressure they would need to pump water.

'Just about right,' he said, examining the gauge.

The groom arrived with the horses, which were quickly strapped between the shafts of the fire engine. The duty firemen had by now assembled, and were taking their previously assigned places behind the driver.

A little over three minutes had elapsed since the alarm had gone off. The bell had indeed spread pandemonium, but it was *organised* pandemonium!

The double gates of the fire station swung open, and the engine, pulled by the two powerful white horses, was off up Southwark Bridge Road, heading for the blaze which had been reported in nearby Keppel Street.

People ahead had heard the furiously ringing fire bell, and stood by the side of the road to wave and cheer the firemen on. None of the crew waved back. There would be time for friendly gestures later—now there was just a job to do.

Sitting close to the boiler, Fred Simpson felt as he always did on such occasions: excited, tense and just a little afraid, although the fear would go away once he was in action—it had never failed to yet.

They rushed past the end of Marshalsea Road, where the rat charmer now stood alone, as those he had been entertaining turned to watch a much more exciting spectacle.

Fred could see the smoke, rising in a long

black column above the railway arches. The fire must be somewhere near the hop warehouses, he guessed, and it looked like it was a big one.

The fire engine passed under the railway arches, crossed the top of America Street and then turned left. All the houses along Keppel Street were three storeys high, and many of them would have at least six families living in them—none of which made the firemen's task any easier.

The fire was at number twenty-six. It looked as if it had started on the first floor, but it was already spreading to the other two. A small crowd had gathered outside, and two local policemen were doing their best to hold it back.

The driver reined in the horses, and the firemen quickly climbed down.

'Usual men on the hoses!' Leading Fireman Harris bellowed. 'You, Simpson, go an' check the bottom floor to see if there's anybody still in there.'

'Sir!' Fred shouted, to show that he had heard.

He rushed to the front door. It was wide open, and through the gap he could see that the fire was burning strongly near the top of the stairs.

If anybody's trapped up there, they'll 'ave to use ladders to get 'em out, he thought. That was not his concern, though, so he wiped it from his mind. Checking downstairs was the task he had been entrusted with, and the sooner he got on with it, the better.

The air was smoky but much more bearable than it would be on the second floor. The heat was tolerable, too. Fred had been on worse jobs than this—much, much worse.

He tried the first door leading off the passageway. It was locked. He pulled his axe from his belt, and struck the door just at the level of the lock. The wood splintered. He hit it again, and felt his axe connect with the metal bolt. One more blow and the lock was ruptured. Fred pushed the door open and stepped inside.

An oven and washing copper were the first things he saw, and after that a door in the far wall, which was closed.

He wiped his hand across his brow. It was hotter in this kitchen than it had been out in the corridor, which probably meant that the fire was burning at its fiercest immediately overhead.

'Is there anybody still in here?' he shouted out at the top of his voice.

Only silence greeted him. Everybody in the flat was probably long gone, but he knew that he would have to check all the other rooms anyway. He made his way across the kitchen towards the door which led to the rest of the flat.

The ceiling gave way with no warning. One second the bulge in it was so slight that it could hardly be noticed, the next, plaster and lathes were falling like a summer rainstorm. Fred had just a moment to look up in horror before the large wooden beam caught him a glancing blow on the side of his head—then everything went black.

Standing on the pavement, Leading Fireman Harris looked up at the blazing first floor. Three hoses were trained on it, and were pumping gallons of water into it every second.

Any poor bugger trapped in there is already dead, Harris thought. Or as good as, anyway. There was still hope for anyone left alive on the second floor however, which was why he had already sent a two-man team up their ladders to check it out.

His men were in place and knew what they were doing, and Harris was at last free to devote himself to another task. He turned his attention to a middle-aged woman in an old grey shawl, who said she was one of the tenants.

'Is everybody out?' he asked.

' 'Ow should I know?' the woman asked.

Harris sighed. It was often like this—people were so shocked by being burned out of their homes that they just couldn't bring themselves to think clearly.

'You know 'oo's usually at work at this hour an' 'oo's usually at 'ome, don't yer?' he said.

'Yes,' the woman agreed, though it was obvious that she still couldn't see what he was getting at.

'An' the people that was inside ain't goin' to walk away, are they? Not with their 'omes burnin' down?'

'I s'ppose not.'

'So just 'ave a butcher's at the crowd an' see if there's any faces missin'.'

The woman looked around. 'Well, let me

think,' she said. 'I don't see Mr Makepeace—'e works shifts, so 'e's normally sleepin' at this time of day. Oh no, look, it's all right. There 'e is, standin' over there by that bobbie.'

'Anybody else?' Harris asked. 'Think 'ard, missis. It could be important.'

The woman pursed her brow. 'I can't see Mrs Ryder,' she said, 'but I know she's out, 'cos I was talkin' to 'er a couple o' minutes ago. An' there's Mrs Owen, so she's all right. I think that's just about everybody 'oo should have been—' She stopped suddenly and a look of horror came to her face.

'What's the matter?' Harris asked.

'Oh my Gawd—Mrs Burr!'

'What about 'er?'

'She's an old woman—bedridden—an' 'er daughter Queenie's out at work.'

'What flat is she in, woman?' Harris demanded. 'Quickly! I need to know now!'

'Ground floor. At the back.'

The leading fireman relaxed. He'd sent Fred Simpson in to check the ground floor, and as young as he was, Fred knew the job better than most. Yes, you could always rely on Simpson. He would definitely have reached the back flat by now, and would already be bringing the old lady out.

When Fred came to, he was lying on an unfamiliar floor, covered in plaster and wooden lathes. His head was throbbing, and he wasn't at all sure where he was or what he was doing there.

He pulled himself painfully to his feet. It was very hot in the room, and when he looked up, he could see the reason why. There was a hole in the ceiling and beyond it was a blazing fire.

'Bloody 'ell! I'd better get out of 'ere as quick as I can,' he told himself.

He walked groggily down the passageway, and out into the road. A crowd had gathered on the opposite pavement to watch the fire, and it seemed to him that it would be a good idea to join it. Brushing the plaster dust off his clothes, he crossed the street.

He'd been standing with the other gawpers for perhaps a minute or two—and really enjoying the spectacle—when one of the firemen who were fighting the blaze came up to him. The man looked vaguely familiar, though Fred couldn't actually recall where he'd seen his face before.

'What are you standing around here for, Simpson?' Leading Fireman Harris demanded angrily. 'When you've finished one job, yer report to me an' I give yer another. An' just what have you done with the old woman you brought out?'

'What old woman?' Fred asked, bemusedly.

'The old woman in the back flat. You did check the back flat, didn't yer?'

'I don't remember,' Fred confessed.

'Bleedin' Norah!' Harris said, then he turned and ran towards the front door of the burning building.

The fire had advanced nearly to the bottom of the stairs and the corridor was thick with choking black smoke.

This was going to be a lot harder than it would have been a few minutes earlier, Harris thought, and keeping his head down, he advanced along the passage to the back flat. He tried the handle. The door wasn't locked, which was one mercy at any rate.

He pushed the door open, and found himself in a kitchen. He crossed it quickly, and opened the door in the far wall. The room that lay beyond it might once have been somebody's front parlour, but now it contained a large, cast-iron bed, in which lay a white-haired old woman.

'Are yer all right, missis?' Harris asked.

The old woman opened her mouth, but she was so terrified that no words came out.

'Don't worry about a thing, we'll soon 'ave yer out of 'ere,' Harris said.

He quickly stripped off the bedclothes, then wrapped the old woman in a blanket. There was an enamel water jug standing on the bedside table, and Harris picked it up and poured the water all over the blanket.

The old woman found her voice at last. 'What 'ave yer gone an' done that for?' she moaned.

'Bein' damp'll protect yer when we're goin' out of 'ere,' Harris explained. If they *were* goin' out! he thought. If it wasn't already too late for them to make an escape.

He slung the old woman over his shoulder and carried her into the corridor. The smoke was thicker than ever, and the heat was now so intense that he knew that neither he, nor the woman he was trying to save, could survive it for long. He began to advance towards the front door in long strides.

He stopped to assess the situation just before he reached the staircase. The fire had reached the bottom of the stairs, but it had still left him a clear passage. Harris shifted the old woman slightly so that she would be as far away from the blaze as possible, fixed his eyes on the open front door, and started moving again.

He felt the familiar prickle as flames began to scorch his skin. He heard the crash as the weakened staircase finally gave way, but by then he was out in the open, gulping in fresh air and listening to the applause of the crowd.

Two of his men appeared. 'Anyfink we can do, Mr 'Arris?' one of them asked.

'Yes, yer can look after this old lady for me,' Harris said, passing Mrs Burr into the man's arms.

'Right, sir.'

'An' *you* can get me some of that green ointment before this bleedin' stingin' drives me completely out of me bonce,' Harris told the second fireman.

'Got it 'ere, Mr 'Arris,' the fireman said, holding out a tin of the stuff.

The leading fireman rubbed the ointment over his face and hands. It started to alleviate the pain immediately, but there was something else which was still stinging him—something which no medicine could relieve.

'Get me Simpson,' he said. 'I think I'd like to 'ave a few words with the yeller bastard.'

Fred stood in the 'at ease' position—legs spread, hands linked behind his back. He was facing a large oak desk, behind which sat Commander Wells, whose every word was like the voice of God to the men who served under him.

'I would like you to tell me exactly what happened to you during that fire in Keppel Street, Fireman Simpson,' the commander said in a tone which by no means could have been described as friendly.

'I wish I *could* tell yer, sir,' Fred said, 'but I can't. All I know is that one second I was inside the buildin', and the next I was out on the street, watchin' the fire.'

'In other words, you're saying that you disobeyed the orders of Leading Fireman Harris, and left the building before you had checked all the rooms?'

'It does look that way, sir,' Fred admitted. 'Otherwise I'd 'ave found the old woman meself, wouldn't I? But like I said, I really can't remember.'

'Leading Fireman Harris had to do your job for you, and because by then the fire had had time to spread, it was a much more difficult job to do.'

'I realise that, sir.'

'Do you also realise, therefore, that you must take the responsibility for putting Harris's life needlessly at risk?'

'I ... I don't think I would 'ave done that on purpose, sir,' Fred said helplessly.

The commander made a note on the pad of paper which lay in front of him. 'Have you ever lost your nerve on a job before, Fireman Simpson?' he asked.

'I don't know for sure that I lost it *this* time, sir,' Fred pointed out to his chief.

'Just answer the question, if you don't mind,' the commander said coldly.

'No, sir, I 'aven't.'

The commander wrote something else down. 'There will have to be an investigation,' he said, 'and following that, a Board of Inquiry to rule on this case. Do you understand what that means?'

'I'm not sure that I do exactly, sir. Would yer mind explainin' it to me?'

'Very well. A senior officer will be appointed to collect evidence from both your comrades and any civilian witnesses to the fire. When he has completed his task, a board—headed by myself—will decide whether or not you were derelict in your duty.'

'I see.'

The commander consulted his calendar. 'The board will meet a week on Monday. Is that clear?'

'Yes, sir.'

'In the meantime, whilst you may continue to live in the dormitory, you are suspended from duty.' A look which might almost have been compassion flickered across the commander's face. 'It doesn't look good, Simpson.'

'I know it don't,' Fred said.

It was half past seven in the evening, and the Goldsmiths' Arms was just starting to get busy.

Colleen Taylor pulled a pint of bitter for a Billingsgate Market porter who lived on Little Suffolk Street, then surveyed the rest of the customers in the saloon bar.

Maggie White was there, hitting the gin again. A rumour was going round the district that her husband, Sid, had kicked her out of their house. Well, if that was true it was very sad, but really, after the way she'd been behaving since she lost her baby, Colleen could not help but feel sympathy for Sid.

'If Maggie comes up here an' asks me for another gin, I'm goin' to refuse to serve her,' Colleen told Mr Wilkins.

The landlord shrugged. 'You do what yer want,' he said. 'If she can't get served 'ere, she'll only go somewhere else, though.'

'Maybe she will,' Colleen agreed. 'But if she does, least it won't be me that's helpin' her to drink herself to death.'

Mr Wilkins went to the other end of the bar, and Colleen turned her attention to Fred Simpson and Mary Bates. They were sitting in their usual corner—but that was the only thing that was usual about them. Instead of holding hands and gazing into each other's eyes, as they normally did, it looked like they were having a very earnest discussion. Maybe it had something to do with Fred's work, Colleen thought. The Lant Place grapevine had hinted that something had gone terribly wrong at the fire station that day. No details had emerged yet—but they would. They always did.

Mary Bates looked just about as worried as anybody could. 'I still don't understand,' she said. 'What will 'appen if this board of whatever-yer-call-it ...'

'Board of Inquiry,' Fred said.

'What will 'appen if this Board of Inquiry finds against yer? Could yer go to prison?'

Fred shook his head. 'It's cowardice, not crime, that I'm bein' accused of.'

'Then what will they ...?'

'I'll be dismissed without references, which is even worse than goin to prison.'

' 'Ow can yer say that, Fred? 'Ow can yer even think it?' Mary asked.

'It's true,' Fred told her. 'If I went to prison, then when I came out again I could at least say that I'd served me time an' paid me debt to society. But this way, I never can. I'll be branded as a coward for as long as I live.'

Mary sighed heavily. 'I'm sure this Board of yours will decide yer did the right thing,' she assured him. 'But say they don't? It ain't the end of the world, is it?'

'Ain't it?'

'O'course it ain't. Yer a big, strong bloke with a good loaf on yer shoulders. Yer'll soon get yerself another job.'

'Yer've got to be jokin', Mary!' Fred said bitterly. ' 'Oo in 'is right mind would give a job to a coward? I know I wouldn't, if I was an employer meself.'

'We could move away to somewhere nobody knows us,' Mary said desperately. 'Southend or Brighton. Somewhere nice, by the sea. We could get married right away, an' you could—'

'If I lose me job, we won't be gettin' married at all,' Fred interrupted.

'Won't be gettin' married?' Mary repeated, fighting back her tears. 'Why not?'

'Because that was the deal yer made with yer mother. Remember? If I still 'ad good prospects, she'd give yer permission to marry me when yer turned eighteen.' He hesitated and looked down into his beer glass, as if he could see a hidden message in it. 'Besides ...'

'Besides what?'

'Mr 'Arris and the commander are both experienced firemen—a lot more experienced than what I am—an' they seem to think that I'm as guilty as sin.'

'That don't mean that yer are, though, does it?'

'If I could remember, it might be different. But like I told yer, from the time I went into that kitchen until the moment that I 'eard Mr 'Arris say I'd got a yeller streak so wide 'e could drive a fire engine down it, me mind's a complete blank.'

'What exactly are yer sayin', Fred?' Mary asked with a tremble in her voice.

'I'm sayin' that maybe they're right. Maybe I did see all them flames and lose me bottle. I wouldn't be the first bloke 'oo's ever done that, yer know.'

'I'm sure it didn't 'appen that way,' Mary said.

' 'Ow can yer be, when I'm not even sure of

it meself?' Fred asked. 'If it turns out I really was a coward ...'

'Yes?'

'... then I can't ask you to marry me, because I'll not be worth anything—not to you an' not to anybody else, either. Not even to meself.'

CHAPTER 17

If it had been raining on the Monday morning after Fred Simpson was suspended from duty, things might have turned out differently. Instead of rain, though, there was an almost cloudless sky—just the right sort of weather for Lizzie Hodges to take the Taylor twins for a really long walk.

It was while Lizzie was manoeuvring the pram down the narrow passageway that she noticed there was a long, diagonal scratch along its front.

'I didn't do that, Mrs Taylor,' she said in a panic, pointing it out to Colleen. 'Honest, I didn't.'

Colleen laughed. 'Don't worry, Lizzie. I know you're not responsible for it. It was me own clumsiness gettin' the pram out yesterday that caused that.'

'Thank 'eavens!' Lizzie said with relief.

'I'm glad you told me, though,' Colleen said. 'You should always tell me if you break or lose anythin'. I promise you, I won't be cross.'

'It's luverly workin' for you, Mrs Taylor,' Lizzie said. 'Yer must be the kindest boss in the 'ole world.'

'Get on with you,' Colleen said, embarrassed.

'I don't know 'ow I'll ever be able to repay yer for what yer've done,' Lizzie pressed on.

'Well, you can start by takin' the twins for such a long walk that they're too tired to cause any trouble this afternoon.'

Lizzie grinned. 'I'll do that, Mrs Taylor,' she promised.

Lizzie pushed the double pram down Lant Place, towards Southwark Bridge Road. 'So where shall we go today, babies?' she asked the twins. 'Up towards yer dad's wood yard? Or down towards the Tower, where the king used to 'ave people's 'eads cut off.'

Ted frowned, as if he were really giving the matter his serious consideration, and Cathy gurgled as if either of the two plans was perfectly all right with her.

'I think we'll go to the Tower,' Lizzie decided. 'Then I can learn yer a bit of 'istory.'

She pushed the pram up Borough High Street towards London Bridge Station. 'When yer a bit older, maybe I'll take yer on a train,' she told the babies. 'I wouldn't mind doin' that meself. Mrs Bates took me on the Underground, yer know—we went up west—but I've never been on a real train.

'Look at 'im,' Lizzie said, seeing a sandwich man up ahead of them. 'Reason 'e wears them boards on 'is chest is 'cos they're advertisements,' she explained to the children. 'That's why they call 'em sandwich men, yer see. 'Cos they're sandwiched between the boards.'

The board on the sandwich man's chest said, 'Kent's Pet Emporium, for the finest animals in London,' and he had a little black and white dog by his side as a walking advertisement.

Lizzie did not normally talk to people in the street, but because of the dog, and because the sandwich man seemed to have a kind face, she decided that she would now. She brought the pram to a halt next to him.

'Would yer mind if I showed yer little puppy to the babies?' she asked.

The sandwich man smiled. ' 'Course yer can show 'em the pooch, gal,' he replied. 'Only, yer'll 'ave to pick 'im up yerself, 'cos I can't reach the ground with these boards on me.'

Lizzie bent down. 'Don't be frightened of me, little puppy,' she said softly, but far from being frightened, the dog wagged its tail furiously and licked her hand.

Lizzie picked up the puppy and held it over the pram for the twins to see. 'Ain't he luverly?' she asked Ted and Cathy. 'Ain't *everyfink* luverly?'

She put the puppy down on the pavement again. It looked up at her, hopeful of more caresses, then got bored with waiting and turned its attention to what was going on further up the street.

'Yer've got a nice job, ain't yer, mister?' Lizzie said to the sandwich man. 'Walkin' around the streets of London all the time. That must be really interestin'.'

'Oh, it ain't bad, apart from the pay,' the sandwich man said. 'Except for days when it's windy, o' course. I really 'ate it when it's like that.'

'Why? I like a nice bit o' wind meself. It blows away some o' the smoke.'

The sandwich man laughed. 'Yer can tell you've never worn boards,' he said. 'Get a bit o' wind under 'em, an' as sure as twelve pence makes a shillin', it'll knock yer over.'

'So what do yer do when it's windy?'

' 'Old on to a lamp-post an' 'ope for the best.'

The thought of the sandwich man gripping tight to a lamp-post made Lizzie giggle, and Cathy joined in, as if she thought it was very funny, too.

'Are they your kids?' the sandwich man said.

People were always asking her that, and on other occasions she'd told the truth, but now, for some reason she did not fully understand herself, she found herself tempted into a lie.

'I'm just lookin' after Ted, the little boy,' she said, 'but Cathy, the little girl, is mine.'

It gave her such a wonderful warm feeling to say those words that she kept repeating them in her head. *Cathy's* mine. Cathy's *mine. Cathy's mine.*

'Funny that, I could 'ave sworn they was twins,' he said.

They'd told her in the workhouse that one lie always led to another, Lizzie thought, and how right they'd been. ' 'E's me sister's son,' she said. ' 'E was born at nearly the same time as my Cathy.' There it was again! My Cathy! And the feeling of warmth was stronger than ever.

'Yeah, well, if the two of 'em are cousins, that'd explain it,' the sandwich man said.

It was time to move on before she was forced into any more lies, Lizzie decided. She smiled at the sandwich man. 'It's been nice talkin' to yer, mister.'

'It's been nice talkin' to *you* as well,' he replied. 'It's always a pleasure to spend a bit o' time with a pretty gal like you.'

Lizzie felt herself turning red. Nobody had ever told her she was pretty before. She pushed the pram hurriedly on, before the sandwich man could see her blushing.

She listened to the rubber wheels of the pram, swishing along the pavement. 'Cathy's mine,' they seemed to be saying. 'Cathy's mine ... Cathy's mine ...'

Colleen Taylor was not due at the Goldsmiths' Arms until four o'clock, and with the twins out of the way for a while, she decided it was a good time to get on with some of the household tasks she'd been neglecting recently. The grate could do with blackleading, for a start, and it was ages since she had dusted under the beds.

She started with the kitchen, and then worked her way upstairs. She was on her knees, cleaning under the bed—and discovering her suspicions had been correct and it really *was* dusty—when she heard the squeak of a pram coming along Lant Place.

Prams were funny things, she thought. They nearly always squeaked, however much they cost, but no two squeaked in exactly the same way, so she could say with absolute certainty that the one she could hear now contained the twins.

Yet there was something different about the squeak from the pram that day. It seemed much noisier than it normally was. No, not noisier, she corrected herself. Quicker! Lizzie must be moving at a hell of a rate.

Colleen checked the wall clock. Lizzie had had the kids out for over three hours, and now it was nearly dinnertime. That would explain her hurry. Still, you had to admire the energy of the girl—practically running at the end of such a long expedition.

Colleen heard the key being turned in the lock, followed by the noise of the pram being pushed into the passageway.

'Did you an' the babies have a good long walk, Lizzie?' Colleen called.

There was no answer.

'I said, did you have a good long walk this mornin', Lizzie?' Colleen repeated.

The front door clicked closed, and Colleen heard someone running in the street below.

'Lizzie?' she said for a third time. 'Is there somethin' the matter, Lizzie?'

She was starting to get worried. She stood up and walked to the top of the stairs. She could see the pram's handle.

'Are you there, Lizzie?' she asked. Worry was rapidly developing into fear. She took the narrow steps two at a time.

It was a wide pram, and it almost blocked the passageway. Ted was lying sound asleep, a serious expression on his face, but where Cathy should have been, there was only a pencilled note in Lizzie's semi-educated scrawl.

'I'm sorry,' it said.

Colleen squeezed frantically past the pram and flung the front door open. It was so close to dinnertime by then that there was hardly anyone on the street—and there was definitely no sign of either Lizzie or Cathy.

Colleen put her elbows on the kitchen table and rested her head in her hands.

'I can still hardly believe it of her,' she moaned. 'I can still hardly believe that Lizzie Hodges would have done anythin' as terrible as this to us.'

'Yer don't know these work'ouse girls like I do,' said Detective Inspector Walton, a stocky man with piggy eyes and a wide, humourless mouth. 'If yer did, yer'd soon start believin' that they're capable of anyfink.'

'The point is, what are you doin' to get our daughter back?' George said, doing his best to sound calm and collected.

'All officers on patrol 'ave been issued with a description of this Lizzie 'Odges,' the inspector said. A new thought suddenly came into his head. ' 'Ave yer noticed any money gone missin?'

'She's not a thief,' George said.

'Yer didn't think she was a baby snatcher until an hour ago,' Walton reminded him.

The policeman was right, George thought. He reached behind him, opened the drawer in the Welsh dresser, and took out the cash box. 'How much should be in this?' he asked his wife.

Colleen shrugged. 'I'm not sure exactly. About eleven and sixpence, I think.'

Even though his hands were trembling, George forced himself to count the coins carefully. 'Eleven and fourpence 'alfpenny,' he said finally. 'Lizzie wouldn't have stolen three 'a'pence an' left the rest, would she?'

'No, that don't seem likely,' the inspector admitted. 'Does this 'Odges girl 'ave any money of her own?'

'I don't pay 'er much,' Colleen said, 'but I suppose she might 'ave saved up a few bob.'

Walton nodded. 'She'll not get far on a few shillin's, but I'll ask the railway police to look out for 'er, anyway. An' I'll give 'er description to all the work'ouses an' doss 'ouses, in case she tries to bed down for the night in one of 'em.'

'When will we get our baby daughter back?' Colleen asked desperately.

The inspector scratched his nose. 'That's difficult to say for sure, madam.'

'But we *will* get her back, won't we?'

Walton put on what he considered his sympathetic expression, and only succeeded in looking shifty. 'We 'ave a very 'igh success rate with this kind o' crime,' he said, 'especially when the criminal is an uneducated little toe-rag like this Lizzie 'Odges.'

'You haven't answered my wife's question,' George said, gripping Colleen's hand tightly.

'Yer've a very good chance yer'll get 'er back,' the inspector said, 'an' we're doin' all we can to make sure that yer do.'

'It's all my fault,' Colleen said, when the detective inspector had finally left.

'You mustn't blame yourself,' George told her.

'If I hadn't insisted that we should get a girl from St Saviour's Workhouse ...'

'Hush, Colleen.'

'If I hadn't insisted we should get a girl from the workhouse, none of this would have happened,' Colleen persisted.

'It was my decision to engage her,' George said. 'So if anybody's to blame, it's me. But passin' the blame around isn't goin' to get us anywhere.'

A flash of hope came to Colleen's eyes. 'You don't think all this is just some kind of terrible mistake, do you?' she asked. 'You don't think that Lizzie's goin' to come walkin' in in a few minutes, with Cathy in her arms?'

George shook his head. 'No, I don't.'

'But it's possible,' Colleen said wildly. 'She could have decided that Ted was tired, but Cathy could do with a bit more fresh air. Couldn't she?'

'It's nearly four hours since she brought Ted back. Anyway, there was the note—she said she was sorry for takin' Cathy.'

'Nettie Walnut!' Colleen said.

'What are you talkin' about?'

'When Nettie Walnut was here in the spring, she read Ted's future in his hand, but she wouldn't read Cathy's! I should have known then. I should have taken better care of her.'

'You couldn't know ...'

Colleen grabbed George's hand so tightly that her nails dug into his flesh. 'Do you think she's dead?' she sobbed. 'Is that it? Do you think she's already dead?'

'Of course she isn't,' George assured his wife. 'Lizzie may have done a very wicked thing, but she only did it because she loves Cathy so much. She'll be with her now, lookin' after her like she's always done. I promise you she will.'

Lizzie Hodges pushed open the door of the saloon bar of the Mariner's Arms, and stepped inside. It was the first time that she had ever been into a pub, but people always said that in times of crisis, a drink helped. An' right now, I need all the 'elp I can get, she thought, as she made her way up to the bar.

The barmaid, an oldish woman with her iron-grey hair pulled into a tight bun, looked suspiciously at the young girl standing uncertainly in front of her. 'An' just what can I do for you, gal?' she asked.

'I'd like a drink, please,' Lizzie said.

'A drink of what?'

What *did* people drink? Lizzie wondered. 'Port,' she said. 'I'd like a glass of yer best port.'

'D'yer want lemon in it?'

'No, just port. Right up to the top.'

The barmaid's suspicions deepened. 'Are yer sure yer old enough to be in 'ere?'

Old enough? Lizzie was so weary she felt like she was a hundred and one. ' 'Course I'm old enough,' she said. 'Look, if yer'd rather I took me custom elsewhere ...'

The barmaid hesitated. Trade had been slack that week, and since the police had paid a visit to the pub only the day before, they were unlikely to be putting in an appearance that night. She reached for the bottle. ' 'Ere yer are,' she said. 'One glass of port filled right up to the top.'

Lizzie took the glass over to the table. She sat down, and sipped at the deep red liquid. It tasted very sweet to her, but it was not unpleasant.

What am I goin' to do? she wondered. She could get away from London, but where would she go? She hardly even knew what life was like on the other side of the river, so any other town would be almost a foreign country.

Maybe she could move just a mile or two along the Thames, change her name and start a new life. But what kind of life? She wasn't trained for anything, and she knew that it was difficult for girls with little education to earn money—unless it was their bodies they were willing to sell.

She looked down at her glass, and was surprised to see that it was empty. She would have another glass of port, she thought. That would help her to see things more clearly.

'I 'ates night duty,' Constable Baxter complained to his partner, Constable Cox, as they made their way up Marshalsea Lane. 'I 'ates it with a passion.'

'An' you 'ates mornin' duty an' afternoon duty, Len,' Cox replied good naturedly. 'Not to mention point duty an' traffic duty. Let's be honest, you just 'ates duty.'

'Yer could be right there, Arfur,' Baxter agreed.

They had reached the corner of Southwark Bridge Road. In front of them loomed the grim shape of St Saviour's Workhouse. It was not late, but there were few lights burning in the workhouse—paupers did not merit wasting the gas.

'We could 'ave our tea now,' Cox suggested.

'There's a good thought,' Baxter agreed.

The two men took their flasks out of their pockets. Cox struck a match and lit first the small spirit stove built into the underside of his flask, and then the one in his partner's.

'I do like a smoke with me cup o' rosie,' Baxter said. 'Think we could risk it for once?'

Cox shook his head. 'Yer never know when the sergeant's comin' round to check on us,' he said, 'an' I don't want no black mark against me name.'

'I s'ppose yer right,' Baxter said gloomily.

It did not take the spirit stoves long to do their work on the cold tea, and soon the world was looking a better place, even to Baxter. It was just as they were putting their flasks away that they saw the young woman staggering up Peter Street towards them.

'Looks to me like the first drunk an' disorderly of the night,' Cox said.

'An' probably it'll be one of many,' Baxter said. 'I 'ates drunk and disorderlies.'

The young woman had stopped walking and was fumbling with her bag when the two policemen approached her.

' 'Ave you been drinkin', miss?' Cox asked.

'I've 'ad ... I've 'ad four ports, filled right up to the top,' the young woman slurred.

'What's yer name, gal?' Baxter asked.

'Me name's Lizz— Annie Bates, an' I've 'ad four ports, filled right up to the top.'

'Yer weren't goin' to say Annie Bates just then,' Cox said. 'Yer were about to tell us yer name was Lizzie somefink.'

Lizzie stuck out her chin, defiantly. 'No I wasn't,' she said, and then she giggled.

Cox held up his lantern, so it was shining into her face. 'We've been asked to look out for a girl called Lizzie 'Odges,' he said. 'You're not 'er by any chance, are yer?'

The grin disappeared from Lizzie's face, and she began to cry. 'Yes, that's me,' she admitted. 'I'm the one yer lookin' for. I'm the guilty one.'

CHAPTER 18

Just going through the process of getting arrested had been enough to help sober up Lizzie, and the two cups of hot strong tea followed by a cold wash had completed the process. Now she sat at a table in the police station interview room.

It was a bare, soulless room. The walls were painted a dark brown, and the single window looked out over a stark courtyard. The only furniture, apart from the table, was two straight-back chairs, and the whole place smelt of disinfectant and desperation.

Lizzie looked up at Detective Inspector Walton, who towered over her like an angry god.

'Let's start at the beginnin' again,' Walton said.

'B ... but I've already told yer everfink three times,' Lizzie stammered.

'Then this'll be the fourth, won't it? From the beginnin', yer little work'ouse toe-rag.'

'It ... it was a nice day, so I decided to take Ted an' Cathy for a walk ...'

'Normally do that, do yer? Take 'em out for a walk if it's a nice day?'

'Yes, they like bein' in the fresh air, an' I ... I like to show 'em things as we're goin' along.'

' 'Ow far did yer go on this walk of yours?'

'As far as Lime'ouse Reach.'

Walton's eyes narrowed with suspicion, as they had done each and every time she had described her walk to him. 'Lime'ouse Reach? That's a long way to go.'

'Like I said, it was a nice day, an' ... an' bein' able to go where I want is so new to me that—'

' 'Ow many people did you talk to while you were out walkin' all the way to Lime'ouse?'

'Just one.'

'An 'e was ...?'

'A sandwich man on Southwark Bridge Road.'

'What was 'is name?'

'I don't know. I didn't think to ask.'

' 'Ow very convenient,' Walton sneered. 'Do yer make a point of talking to men yer don't know?'

'No, but 'e 'ad a kind face ...'

'A kind face!'

'... an' 'e 'ad this little black an' white dog with 'im, yer see, an' I wanted to show it to the babies.'

Walton shook his head as if to suggest she should be able to come up with a better story than that.

'So when yer reached Lime'ouse what did yer do?' he asked.

'Turned round and came back.'

'An' yer didn't stop at all?'

'No. At least, not until I got to Mr Southern's shop, which is on Lant Street.'

'Oh yes, Mr Southern's shop. Yer reached the shop, an' yer decided to go inside. Is that what yer tellin' me?'

'Yes. I fancied some sweets. We never 'ad sweets in the work'ouse, yer see, but now I've got a bit of money of me own, an' I like the odd sweet.'

'So yer parked the pram outside?'

'That's right.'

' 'Ow long were yer inside the shop?'

'A couple o' minutes. There were two other customers before me—a little lad 'oo wanted a twist of tea, an' a lady in a bonnet 'oo wanted 'alf a pound of bacon.'

'Got a good memory when yer want to 'ave one, ain't yer?' Walton said menacingly.

'It's the truth.'

'O' course it is, an' I believe every single word of it. What 'appened next?'

'When the old lady in the bonnet 'ad paid for 'er bacon, I bought me sweets.'

'So yer were lyin' earlier, were yer?'

'No, I ...'

'Then explain this. You said you only talked to this one man—the sandwich man in Southwark Bridge Road—so 'ow did you buy your sweets? With mime?'

'Oh, I forgot about Mr Southern!' Lizzie said.

'Yes, an' I'm willin' to wager there are a few other things yer've conveniently forgotten as well. But we might as well 'ear the rest of it. What did yer do after yer'd bought the sweets?'

'Went back to the pram, o' course.'

'An, ...?'

'An' ... an' Cathy wasn't there any more. I

267

looked up an' down the street, but there was no sigh of 'er.'

'So yer took the other kid—the one yer 'adn't managed to lose—back to 'is mum.'

'Yes. I pushed the pram into the passageway, an' left Mrs Taylor a note to say I was sorry.'

'Why did yer run away?'

'Because I was scared.'

'You 'adn't done anyfink wrong, 'ad yer?'

For a moment, surprise overcame Lizzie's fear. 'Of course I 'ad,' she said. 'I was s'pposed to be lookin' after Cathy, an' I let somebody take 'er.'

Walton put his two big fists on the table. 'I'm gettin' tired of all these stories o' yours,' he said. 'I know what really 'appened, an' you know that I know. Yer either wanted the baby for yerself, or—what's more likely—yer sold it to somebody else 'oo wanted a baby. In either case, yer know where she is now, so why don't yer come clean an' tell me?'

Lizzie felt tears forming in her eyes. 'I don't know where she is. Why won't yer believe me?'

Walton turned to the constable who was standing near the door. 'Take 'er away,' he said. 'A few hours down in the cells with the rats should loosen 'er tongue.'

It was well after midnight, but the gas lights still burned in the Taylor's kitchen.

George and Colleen were not alone: they had been joined by Sam and Lil Clarke, and by Annie and Tom Bates. Though it was late, and though one of the company occasionally stifled a yawn, no one said they were tired and no one suggested going home. They were neighbours, and they would sit out the ordeal together.

'It's been over twelve hours now since she went missin',' Colleen said.

'I'm sure the bobbies are doin' all they can, gal,' Sam Clarke said. 'The London police are the finest in the world. They'll find 'er, you can be certain of that.'

'But why is it takin' so long?'

'London's a big city.'

'We should never have left Marston,' Colleen said, looking reproachfully at George, then she saw the hurt in his eyes, and was ashamed. 'It was my decision as much as yours, luv,' she told him. 'An' like you said, it doesn't do any good to start handin' out the blame.'

The loud knocking on the front door startled them all. Colleen was about to jump to her feet, but Tom beat her to it and put a restraining hand on her shoulder.

'I'll get it,' he said, because while the knock was bound to bring some sort of news, there was no telling whether it would be good news or not.

Tom walked quickly down the passageway and opened the door to find himself facing an old enemy.

'What are you doin' 'ere, Bates?' Detective Inspector Walton demanded.

'I'm a friend of the family,' Tom said.

'Is that right? A friend of the family, eh?'

' 'Ave yer found little Cathy?'

'What I 'ave to say is for the ears of Mr an' Mrs Taylor,' Walton told him. 'Not for the likes of some ex-gaolbird—even if 'e 'as managed to wangle 'is way into the police. So if yer wouldn't mind steppin' to one side an' lettin' me in ...'

Tom turned and walked back towards the kitchen. Walton followed him.

'Have you ...?' Colleen said, when she saw it was the inspector. 'Is my ... is my baby all right?'

'We 'ave no reason to believe that any 'arm 'as come to her,' Walton said, 'an' we 'ave arrested Lizzie 'Odges.'

'Then you *must* have Cathy.'

'Unfortunately not, madam. 'Odges managed to 'ide your baby before we arrested 'er.'

'Won't she tell you where Cathy is?' Tom asked.

Walton gave him a look of pure loathing. 'As I told yer earlier, Bates, I'm addressin' me remarks to the parents of the missin' child and not to some—'

'I'd like to hear an answer to Tom's question, if you don't mind,' George said.

'She *claims* that she didn't 'ave nuffink to do with stealin' the baby. Says it was taken out of the pram while she was in Southern's shop on Lant Street.'

'Then why didn't she come straight home an' let my wife know what had happened?'

Walton sneered. 'Exactly, sir. What she says, o' course, is that she was too frightened to do that.'

'Maybe she's tellin' the truth,' Tom said.

'The truth!' Walton echoed. 'A little gutter-snipe like 'er wouldn't know the truth if she fell over it.'

'I'm her friend,' Annie said. 'If she really does know where Cathy is, she'll tell me.'

'Then yer'd better talk to 'er,' Walton said.

Annie stood up. 'Where is she? At the local police station?'

'I was goin' to keep 'er at the police station, an' then I 'ad a better idea,' Walton said, with a self-satisfied look on his face. 'I decided to 'ave 'er transferred to 'Olloway Prison as a way of impressin' upon 'er the seriousness of 'er predicament.'

'Then I must go to Holloway immediately.'

'I'm afraid that won't be possible at this time o' night, madam,' Walton said, 'but I'm sure I can arrange for yer to see 'er first thing in the mornin'.'

Colleen slammed her hand down hard on the table. 'For God's sake, my baby's missing!' she screamed. 'An' I want her back as soon as possible. If Annie thinks Lizzie will tell her where Cathy is, why won't you let her see the girl now?'

'It is not up to me, madam,' Walton told her. 'Prisons 'ave their regulations like everywhere else, an' I can assure you that they do not include allowin' night-time visits.'

Colleen cradled her head in her hands and started to sob. Lil Clarke bent over her and stroked her hair.

'Don't upset yerself,' Lil crooned. 'Lizzie wouldn't 'ave left yer baby anywhere she might come to 'arm, an' in a few hours yer'll 'ave 'er back with yer as if nuffink 'ad ever 'appened.'

'George said Lizzie would never leave Cathy at all,' Colleen sobbed, 'but she did. She must have done, or I'd have me baby back with me right now.'

Inspector Walton coughed loudly. 'If 'Odges does tell yer anyfink, madam,' he said to Annie, 'I will expect yer to communicate it to my officers immediately.'

'I will,' Annie replied, with an edge to her voice which suggested that he had insulted her for even thinking he had to tell her that. 'Finding Cathy is all any of us want, and we'll do anything we can to see that happens.'

'Quite,' Walton said drily. He turned to George. 'Well, if yer'll excuse me, sir, I 'ave to be about important police business.'

'Of course,' George said abstractedly, his eyes still fixed on his weeping wife.

Tom started to stand up, but Walton raised an imperious hand to stop him. 'I'd rather see meself out than be shown to the door by you,' the inspector said.

Tom waited until the sound of the inspector's heavy boots had receded down the passageway, then, after making sure that Colleen's head was still cradled in her arms, he caught George's attention.

'The man's a fool,' he mouthed silently.

George nodded, sadly.

The warehouse was located just off Morgan's Lane. Until a few weeks earlier, it had been used for storing tea, but then the company which had rented it had gone into liquidation. The stock had been sold to pay off the debts, and now the place stood boarded up, waiting for new tenants.

If there had been a nightwatchman on duty, he might have noticed that some of the boards on one of the side windows had had their nails pulled out, and were now merely resting on the windowsill, but there was no nightwatchman. Why shell out extra wages when there was no need for it?, the owners of the warehouse had argued. Apart from a few dozen broken tea chests, there was nothing to steal in the empty building.

The building wasn't *quite* empty, however. On the first floor, in a corner on the river side of the structure, a sad, demented woman had set up her home.

She had everything she needed for her comfort: bedding, crockery, a spirit stove to cook with, and an oil lamp for lighting. She even had running water, since the owners had decided it wouldn't be worth their while cutting it off. Yes, she had everything she needed there—including the baby.

She looked at the child, sleeping somewhat fitfully inside an old orange crate.

'Yer'll settle down,' she crooned softly. 'By this time next week, yer'll 'ave forgotten all about yer real mother, an' it'll only be me that yer love.'

The woman lit the spirit stove and boiled up some water for tea. In the daytime, it was noisy outside, what with all the tugs on the river and the clip-clopping of horses' hooves up and down the street. But at night it was more peaceful, with only the occasional hoot of a steamer or the footsteps of late-night drinkers to break through the silence.

She liked the warehouse. She knew that she and the baby could not live there for ever, that eventually a new business would take it over and they would have to move on, but for the moment she was quite content.

The kettle came to the boil, and she filled her tin mug with the steaming water.

'There's nuffink like a good cup of rosie for steadyin' the nerves,' she told herself.

She leaned over the orange-box again. The infant seemed to have quietened down a little.

'Yer my baby now, Ellen,' the woman whispered. 'Yer my baby, an' I'll never give yer back. Yer do believe that, don't yer? 'Cos it's true. I'd kill the both of us before I'd let them take yer away from me.'

CHAPTER 19

Annie Bates looked out of the window of the tram at the unfamiliar scenery which was rattling past her. The last time she'd been so far north of the river had been over two years earlier, when—as Annie Clarke—she had gone to the August Bank Holiday celebrations on

Hampstead Heath with Harry Roberts. Then, as now, it had been a complicated journey, involving several changes of trams. Unlike her previous excursion, however, this one promised no entertainment of any kind at the end of it. Instead of searching for pleasure, she was doing all she could to try and rescue Colleen Taylor's baby.

The final tram dropped her at the top end of Camden Road, directly in front of a formidable row of tall iron railings. Annie walked across the road and gazed through the railings at the large brick building which lay beyond. She examined the arched wooden doors—big enough to drive even the largest wagon through—and the crenellated towers on each side of them, which seemed to be frowning down disapprovingly at her.

It looked to her just like a castle where the wicked king in a story book might live. It wasn't a castle, though, it was Holloway Prison, the place where Detective Inspector Walton had sent Lizzie Hodges in the hope that it would make her come to her senses and tell him what he wanted to know.

The room Annie sat in had a flagstone floor and contained only a table and two chairs. There was a window set high in the wall, and though it did not look large enough for even a child to squeeze through, there were bars on it.

The door of the room creaked open, and two people walked in. The first was Lizzie Hodges. She was wearing the clothes she'd been arrested in, but somehow she seemed to have shrunk, so that now they hung loosely on her. Behind Lizzie came the wardress, wearing a long severely cut black dress, with a thick leather belt around her waist, from which hung a dozen or so intimidating large keys.

'Sit down, Prisoner Eight-Eight-Seven,' said the wardress in a voice as chillingly cold as the Arctic winds which sometimes blew through Southwark.

Lizzie, keeping her eyes firmly on the floor, shuffled over to the free chair and sat down. The wardress stepped back and took up a position by the door.

'Do you think you could possibly leave us alone for a few minutes?' Annie asked her.

The wardress shook her head. 'Can't do that, madam. It's against the prison regulations. But yer can speak freely. I won't be listenin' to yer.'

Lizzie was looking at the table now, as if on its bare surface there was the most intricate and fascinating pattern that she had ever seen in her life.

Annie leaned forward. 'Why did you do it, Lizzie?' she asked. 'How could you ever think you could get away with it? Don't you realise what suffering you're causing to poor Colleen Taylor? George Taylor, too, for that matter?'

Lizzie lifted her head. Her eyes were very red indeed, and Annie guessed she had been crying all night.

'It *is* my fault, ain't it?' she said. 'I told that sandwich man that Cathy was mine, an' now

God's punishin' me for it. 'E's punishin' us all for it.'

'You shouldn't have taken the baby,' Annie said gently. 'You know that, don't you? But you can make partial amends by telling us where she is now.'

'I don't know where she is, Mrs Bates,' Lizzie said. 'I told that 'orrible policeman again and again that she was taken from outside Mr Southern's shop while I was buyin' sweets, an' that's the honest truth. You 'ave to believe me.'

She sounded sincere, Annie thought. Was this wide-eyed, simple kid who she'd got to know on their trip up west capable of lying so convincingly? Annie leaned even further forward.

'No touchin' the prisoner, madam,' the wardress warned her.

'Sorry,' Annie said. She turned her attention back to Lizzie Hodges. 'Look at me, Lizzie,' she coaxed. 'Lift your head up, and look me straight in the eyes.'

'I'm not sure I can,' Lizzie mumbled. 'I feel so guilty about everyfink that I can't ...'

'Try!'

Slowly and reluctantly, Lizzie raised her head until her eyes met Annie's.

'Now tell me one more time that you didn't have anything to do with Colleen's baby going missing,' Annie demanded.

'I didn't,' Lizzie said. Her voice was shaky, but her eyes never wavered. 'I swear on me mum's grave I didn't. Do yer believe me, Mrs Bates?'

'Yes,' Annie said, slowly and thoughtfully. 'Yes, I rather think that I do.'

A brave, grateful smile came to Lizzie's lips, lingered there for a second, and then was gone again. 'But it won't do me no good that you believe me, will it?' she said. ' 'Cos that 'orrid bobbie ain't ever goin' to believe I didn't do it.'

'Don't give up hope like that, Lizzie,' Annie said. 'My husband Tom's already out looking for Cathy, and when we find her, then whoever took her will be able to tell the police you had nothing to do with it.'

'Time's up, madam,' the wardress said.

'Couldn't we 'ave just a few more—' Lizzie began.

'Silence, Prisoner Eight-Eight-Seven,' the wardress barked.

Annie stood up. 'I'll come and see you again,' she said.

'Don't tell anybody about the sandwich man, will yer, Mrs Bates?' Lizzie begged. 'I'm so ashamed of what I said to 'im. Please don't tell anybody, will yer?'

'No,' Annie promised. 'I won't tell anybody.'

While Mr Southern handled the morning rush, Tom Bates looked idly around the shop. It was only a small place, but like many of the other stores around Lant Street, it sold almost everything you could want—from butter in churns and tins of baked beans to zinc buckets and mousetraps.

Mr Southern dealt with his last customer, then turned to Tom with a broad smile on his face.

'An' 'oo are you 'ere as today?' he asked. 'Tom Bates, 'oo used to try an' cadge gobstoppers off of me when 'e was nuffink but a nipper, or Constable Bates, out on official police business?'

'A bit o' both,' Tom admitted. 'I am on police business, but it ain't exactly official—if yer know what I mean.'

Mr Southern's face clouded over. 'It's about that little kiddie that went missin', ain't it?' he said.

'That's right,' Tom agreed. 'The Taylor family are neighbours of mine.'

'Is it true that Lizzie 'Odges was the one what did it? Why, she was in 'ere only yesterday ...'

'That's what I come about,' Tom said. 'So she *was* 'ere, like she claimed to be?'

'Just before dinnertime. I remember it quite distinct, because I could smell me missis's cookin' comin' from the back room. Toad in the 'ole, it was.'

'An' yer sure this was yesterday?'

'Certain. There was some ragamuffin in at the same time, buyin' a twist of tea an' sugar. An' Mrs Butler—'er that always wants 'er bacon sliced so thin I nearly cut me finger off every time I serve 'er—she was in, too.'

'It could 'ave been the day before,' Tom persisted.

Mr Southern shook his head. 'No, it couldn't,

'cos when I 'eard the news—at about five o'clock, I believe it was—I remember thinkin' to meself, it's only a few hours since them babies was parked outside me shop.'

Tom nodded, satisfied. 'Do you remember what she bought, by any chance?'

'I always remember what me customers buy from me,' Mr Southern said with pride. 'She 'ad a quarter of mixed sweets, like she always does.'

'So it wasn't the first time she'd bought sweets?'

'That's what I'm tellin' yer. She was in two or three times a week. Couldn't get enough of 'er sweets.'

'Did she seem nervous?'

'No, I wouldn't say so. She seemed pretty much 'er normal self to me.'

'I see,' Tom said thoughtfully.

'Is there anything else I can do for yer?'

'Yes,' Tom said. 'This Mrs Butler 'oo was in the shop at the same time as Lizzie was—yer wouldn't 'appen to know where she lives, would yer?'

'I don't know 'er exact 'ouse number, if that's what yer mean, Tom, but I *do* know that she lives somewhere near the top end of Rodney Street.'

When Tom knocked at number fifty-nine Rodney Street, the door was opened by a little old woman in a bonnet which had gone out of fashion at least twenty years earlier.

'I ain't done nuffink wrong,' she said, looking

at Tom's police uniform.

'Are you Mrs Butler?'

'Yes, that's 'oo I am, all right—but I still ain't done nuffink to bring the bobbies round.'

Tom smiled his most winning smile. 'I'm sure yer 'aven't, Mrs Butler, but if yer don't mind givin' me a few minutes of yer time, I'd like to ask yer a few questions.'

The old woman looked rapidly up and down the street, to see if any of her neighbours were watching. 'Questions?' she repeated. 'What kind o' questions?'

'You were in Mr Southern's shop on Lant Street yesterday mornin', weren't yer?'

'Yes,' the old woman said cautiously.

'Do yer, by any chance, remember seein' a young girl in there at the same time?'

'I do, an' a scruffy little urchin buyin' a twist of tea, as well. Didn't 'e pong? I know soap's expensive, but there's no excuse for not 'avin' a wash at least once a week.'

'It's the girl I'm concerned with,' Tom said. 'Did she seem nervous to you?'

'Not particularly.'

'You left the shop before 'er, didn't yer?'

'Yes, I did.'

'An' did yer 'appen to notice a pram?'

'Nearly fell over it. People should've more consideration, if yer ask me.'

'Was there anyfink unusual about the pram?'

'Depends exac'ly what yer mean by unusual,' the old woman said cunningly.

'What would *you* mean?' Tom asked.

'Well, it was one o' them double prams,' Mrs

Butler admitted, 'but there was only one baby in it.'

'You're sure of that?'

'I may be gettin' on a bit, but me eyesight's nearly as sharp as it ever was. If I saw one baby in that pram, then that's 'ow many there were.'

'Did you see anybody else in the street?'

'A few people,' the old woman said, back on her guard again.

'Did you see anybody carryin' a baby?'

'No, I didn't,' Mrs Butler said. 'No, 'ang about a minute. There was a woman walkin' towards Southwark Bridge Road. She 'ad a bundle in 'er arms, an' I thought at the time it was 'er washin'. But I s'ppose that *could* 'ave been a baby.'

'Did you recognise this woman?' Tom asked, feeling the hairs on the back of his neck start to bristle.

Mrs Butler shook her head. 'Too far away to get a proper look at 'er,' she said. 'Although I 'ave to admit, there was *somefink* familiar about the way she walked. Maybe I've seen 'er once or twice on the trams or in the wash'ouse.'

Tom did his best to contain his disappointment. After all, he told himself, even if Mrs Butler couldn't identify the woman with the bundle, he'd still got a lot further with his morning's work that he'd ever dared to hope.

'Thanks for yer 'elp, Mrs Butler,' he said. 'If yer remember anyfink else, yer will tell the policeman on the beat all about it, won't yer, now?'

The old woman smiled. She had very few teeth left, and most of the ones she did have were rotten. 'I don't normally talk to bobbies,' she said, 'but an 'andsome young bloke like you can come round 'ere any time.'

For most of London south of the river, Tuesday was very much a normal day. At the docks and on the wharves, ships from the four corners of the globe were being unloaded. In the workhouses, the paupers picked oakum, paused for a lunch of bread and cheese, and then picked oakum again. Street cleaners cleaned streets, clog dancers danced in their clogs for the entertainment of passers-by. Everything was as it had always been, and, so many people imagined, as it always would be.

Only around Southwark was the normal pattern of life disrupted. Uniformed policemen, working overtime shifts, searched the cheap boarding houses and derelict buildings for any woman who had recently appeared with a young female child in her arms. Men from the detective branch checked the scores of modest hotels for the same thing. Everyone was touched by the disappearance of a baby. Everyone wanted the little girl returned to the safety of her mother's arms. However, as the day waned and the hint of a moon appeared in the sky, the investigation was no closer to finding Cathy than it had been early that morning.

There were eight of them around the table in the Taylors' kitchen. George and Colleen sat at one end of it, holding hands. Next to them were Sam and Lil Clarke. Beyond Lil sat Annie, and facing George and Colleen was Tom. On the other side of the table sat Harry Roberts and Fred Simpson, who—despite his personal misery—had offered to do what he could to help find Cathy.

'Accordin' to this Mrs Butler,' Tom said, 'Cathy was already missin' when Lizzie was buyin' the sweets from Mr Southern.'

'What's yer point?' Harry asked.

'Me point is that it simply don't add up. Say it was really Lizzie what stole Cathy. 'Ow would she do it?'

'You tell us 'ow *you* think she'd do it,' Harry said.

'She'd bring both kids back 'ere, an' then snatch the little girl. What she *wouldn't* do is leave Cathy somewhere else, an' then bring Ted back 'ome.'

'Why not?' George asked.

'Because that's too risky. Say she was walkin' along Lant Street with only Ted in the pram, an' she met somebody she knew. They'd be bound to ask where Cathy was. Say she even met *Colleen*—then the fat would really 'ave been in the fire.'

'True,' Harry agreed.

'Stoppin' to buy sweets is just plain mad, because leavin' the pram outside for anybody to see just doubles the risk. Besides, people 'oo are kidnappin' babies 'ave a lot more important things on their minds than toffees.'

'So yer sayin' she's innocent?' Harry said.

'That's exactly what I'm sayin'.'

'After seeing her for myself, I don't believe that she could have done it,' Annie added.

'You'll have to let the police know what you've found out,' George said.

'I've already seen Detective Inspector Walton,' Tom told him. ' 'E ain't interested.'

'Not interested!' Colleen gasped. 'How can he not be interested? That's—'

'Just typical of the bloke,' Tom interrupted. ' 'E's got it into that thick 'ead of 'is that Lizzie 'Odges is the one an' only key to findin' Cathy, an' 'e don't want no inconvenient new theories gettin' in the way of that.'

'So we're on our own,' George said. 'Just like we were when Tom was in prison.'

'It ain't quite the same, 'cos even if Walton's investigation's goin' in the wrong direction, the uniformed branch are still out lookin' for Cathy,' Harry said.

'But without them knowin' who snatched her, what chance do you think they've got of findin' her in a city the size of London?' George asked gloomily.

Harry shrugged. 'Not much,' he admitted, 'but yer never know, they might get lucky.'

'We're not just going to sit on our backsides and hope for a lucky break, are we?' Annie said.

'No, we ain't,' Tom agreed. ' 'Arry an' me will be carryin' out our own investigation, 'cos that's what we've been trained to do.' He turned to Lil. 'It'll be your job to 'elp out George an' Colleen any way that yer can ...'

'You mean it'll be her job to see that I keep

off the bottle,' Colleen said.

Tom looked embarrassed. 'Well, if I remember rightly, there was a time ...'

'I know there was, but that's long past. Still, we are goin' through a very bad time,' Colleen said, 'an' it'd be nice to know that Lil was there as a shoulder to cry on.'

'Well, o' course I'll be there, gal.'

'Is there anyfink the rest of us can do?' Fred asked.

'Yes,' Tom said. 'You can keep yer eyes an' ears open for anyfink that might give us a lead. An' every time yer talk to anybody, remind 'em that little Cathy's still missin'.'

'That don't seem very useful.'

'Oh, but it is,' Tom said emphatically. 'Look, yer know 'ow these things go. For the first couple o' days, everybody's keen as mustard an' on the lookout for anyfink suspicious. Then it starts bein' old news, and, 'uman nature bein' what it is, people get sloppy. So somefink that they might 'ave noticed early on slips right past 'em after a week or two.'

'A week or two?' Colleen said dully. 'Do you think it will take as long as that?'

'No,' Tom said hastily, 'but we 'ave to be prepared to cover all possibilities.'

Colleen turned her gaze on to Harry. 'You've been a policeman for a long time,' she said. 'You must surely have handled cases like this one before?'

'Not really. Little babies don't usually go missin' on the river, yer see.'

'But you do *know* about other cases?'

'Well, yes.'

'So, as the closest thing we've got to an expert, how long do *you* think it will take to get Cathy back?'

Harry considered fobbing her off with a bland, reassuring answer, but the steely look in Colleen's eyes told him that would not be a good idea. 'I'll be honest with yer,' he said. 'Sometimes they're back within hours—well, that 'asn't 'appened. In other cases, it's a couple o' days, but sometimes it takes a week, or even a month.'

'An' sometimes the parents don't ever get their babies back, do they?'

'That only 'appens in rare cases.'

'But it *does* happen.'

'Yes, it does.'

A brooding silence descended over the table, and it was something of a relief to all of them when there was a loud knocking on the front door.

'I'll get it,' Annie said.

She walked up the passageway, half-expecting it to be Detective Inspector Walton, but when she returned half a minute later, it was George's brother, Philip, she had with her.

'What are you doin' here at a time like this, Philip?' George demanded roughly. 'Thought up another good way to steal some money from me, have you?'

Philip looked down at his hands. 'I ... I read about your daughter in the evening paper,' he stuttered. 'I want you to know how very sorry I am.'

'Aye, well, that's very kind of you,' George said unrelentingly. 'Thanks for comin', and now you've said your piece, you can go away again.'

Philip was still examining his slim fingers. 'I didn't just come to give you my sympathy, George. I ... I want to help.'

'Oh aye? And what use do you think *you'd* be? Is police work yet another job you've tried your hand at?'

'Don't, George,' Colleen said softly.

'Well, he makes me sick,' George told her. 'He lives just across the river, but he's never once been to see our Cathy. And now she's gone missin', he comes crawlin' round here givin' us his sympathy an' offerin' to help.'

'Do you care so little about your daughter that you can afford to be too angry—or too proud—to hear what he has to say?' Colleen asked.

George bowed his head for a second. 'You're right,' he admitted, and looked up at Philip. 'You'd better tell me how you think you can help us,' he said.

'Do you happen to have a recent photograph of your Cathy?' Philip asked.

'We had one taken only last week. Why?'

'I still have some contacts in the printing world from the days when I ran my comic. If you can give me the photograph, I can get posters printed up of it with some sort of heading like, "Have you seen this baby?" and have them plastered over the whole of London.'

George looked questioningly at Harry. 'What do you think of that,' he asked.

'That's not a bad idea, George,' the Wet Bob said. 'In fact, it's a bloody *good* idea.'

'Could you go and get the photograph, Colleen?' George asked his wife.

'Right away,' Colleen said. She stood up, and as she walked past her brother-in-law, who was still standing awkwardly near the door, she said, 'Thank you, Philip.'

The hard expression which had been on George's face since his younger brother had entered the room, softened a little. 'Yes. Thanks, Philip.'

Philip shrugged uncomfortably. 'After the way I've treated you in the past, it was the least I could do,' he said.

Philip Taylor and Fred Simpson sat in the saloon bar of the Goldsmiths' Arms, moodily sipping at their pints. All around them, other customers were doing exactly the same thing. There was no joy in the whole pub that night. Everybody had heard about what had happened to the baby, and the Taylors' loss was Lant Place's loss.

'Don't worry about what George said to yer,' Fred told Philip. ' 'E didn't mean 'alf of it, but when yer upset like 'e is, it's only natural that yer—'

'He was right,' Philip said.

'Yer what?'

'When he said I'd shown no concern over Cathy before, he was quite right. I could have walked from where I live in a little over an hour, yet until I wanted something from George, I never did. And even when I was in his house, I didn't even bother to ask if I could go upstairs and take a look at the children. I've never seen my niece, Fred, my own flesh and blood, and now maybe I never will. I feel so incredibly guilty.'

'It don't do no good to think about things like that,' Fred said. 'What's the point in blamin' yerself for being thoughtless now? It wouldn't 'ave changed anyfink. Even if yer'd been the kindest uncle in the world, it wouldn't 'ave stopped little Cathy from bein' snatched from her pram.'

'I know all that,' Philip said, 'but you have to understand that I've never really felt guilty about anything before, and I'm not sure I know how to deal with it.'

'If yer ask me, the best way's to 'ave another pint of ale,' Fred told him.

'You're probably right,' Philip agreed, signalling across to the barman that they were ready for fresh drinks.

The pints were pulled, and when Philip opened his wallet to pay, he noticed the two tickets. 'Would you have any use for these?' he asked Fred.

'What are they?'

'Tickets for Thursday night's performance at the Lambeth Hippodrome.'

'Money's a bit tight at the moment,' Fred said. 'I might not even 'ave a job by next Monday afternoon.'

'Oh, I don't want paying for them. They're complimentaries. The Hippodrome's showing the living pictures which I took in George's wood yard as part of the evening's entertainment. I got them for him, but I don't suppose he'll be interested in going now. So if you feel like whiling away a couple of hours ...'

Fred shrugged, then held out his hand. 'Thanks, Philip,' he said. 'I think I probably will use 'em. I could do with a bit of cheerin' up at the moment.'

'Couldn't we all?' Philip said, handing over the tickets.

The fire station—with its shift system—was never really quiet. At any time of the day or night, there would be men in the recreation room waiting to go on duty, or feeling the need to relax once they had come off it, and when Fred Simpson entered it on his return from the Goldsmiths' Arms, there were half a dozen of his comrades playing billiards or just lounging around.

Fred's arrival was like an icy wind suddenly blowing through the room. Conversations stopped abruptly, ivory billiard balls ceased to clack.

Fred thought of turning round and walking out, but his pride would not let him, so instead he said, 'Evenin', lads.'

Three or four of the other firemen grunted a reply, but none of them looked at him. Fred went over to one of the easy chairs and picked up a newspaper. Only when he had been pretending to read it for a couple of minutes did the recreation room return to normal.

The billiard game finished, and one of the players said, 'Right, that's it. I'm turnin' in for the night.'

Fred put his paper down and walked over to the table. 'I'll give yer a game, Alf,' he said to the remaining player.

'No, er, thanks,' Alf said, looking away. 'I think I've 'ad enough meself.'

Fred turned to face the remaining four firemen. 'Does anybody else fancy a game?' he asked, and when his only answer was silence, he added, 'All right, then, I'll play by meself. I could use the practice, anyway.'

He was just bending over the table to take his first shot when a voice behind him, which Fred recognised as belonging to a fireman called Wilf Eccles, said, 'Can you smell somefink funny in 'ere all of a sudden, Ozzie?'

'I'm not sure,' Ozzie replied. 'What kind of smell is it yer've got in mind, Wilf?'

'It's 'ard to say, exac'ly. Bad eggs? It could be that.'

Fred struck the cue ball, but he had misjudged the shot, and after it hit the spot, it was deflected across the table and rolled into one of the pockets.

'No, I know what it is!' Ozzie said loudly. 'It's the smell yer get when somebody shits 'imself. 'Course, the bloke I'm thinkin' of didn't shit 'imself today. If my memory serves me well, it was last Friday 'e did it. But some'ow, 'owever

much he washes 'imself, he can't get rid of the pong.'

Fred put down the cue and turned round. 'If yer've got anyfink to say, say it to me direct, Wilf,' he said.

'All right, I will,' Wilf replied. 'Yer yeller streak nearly cost us 'Arris, 'oo's ten times the man that you are.'

Fred felt his hands bunching up into fists. 'Yer want to finish this argument outside?' he asked.

Eccles laughed. 'So it's a fight yer want, is it? O' course it is, 'cos yer know yer could beat me any day of the week! It's easy to be brave when yer sure that yer goin' to win. But bein' brave when yer know yer just might get burned to death, well, that's a different matter, ain't it?'

'I'll tell yer what—I'll fight yer with one 'and tied be'ind me back,' Fred said.

'Yer talkin' like a loony. With that kind of advantage on me side, I'll murder yer.'

'I'll do it anyway.'

Eccles shook his head. 'No, I won't fight yer, Simpson,' he said, 'but I'll tell yer what I will do. I'll apologise to yer for what I've just said—straight after yer've told me, 'and on 'eart, that yer didn't lose yer bottle last Friday.'

Fred tried to force the words out, but they just wouldn't come. 'I'm goin' to bed,' he said.

'I thought that'd be yer answer,' Eccles told him.

CHAPTER 20

George Taylor tossed and turned fitfully in his bed. He did not know what time it was, only that it was still very black outside. The ceiling glowed a faint white in the light of the gas lamp outside the window, and from the distant river he heard the faint sound of a steamer's warning horn.

He closed his eyes. He knew he would not sleep, but somehow total darkness made his load a little easier to bear.

George heard a rustling sound in the corner of the room. He opened his eyes again, and saw a woman standing there, surrounded by a strange eerie light. He did not know who she was, only that there was a mad expression on her face. She was holding a bundle in her arms, and he thought that it was her washing at first. Then the bundle began to struggle and cry, and he realised it was not washing at all, but his little Cathy. He wanted to get up and help, but—though he could feel no ropes—he appeared to be tied to the bed.

The bundle had stopped struggling and began to grow, until it was so big that the madwoman had to put it on the floor. Still it continued growing, until it had stopped being a child, and was already the young woman that Cathy might one day become.

George wanted to call to her, but his tongue, like the rest of his body, refused to move. Still, she seemed to sense his wish, because she left the corner and walked over to the bed. He tried to speak again, but it was no good, and he could only lie there while his own daughter gazed down at him with calm, unrecognising eyes.

Bored by this helpless stranger, Cathy turned and walked back to the corner. The madwoman held out her arms to her and the two of them joyfully embraced.

"This shouldn't be happening!" George's fevered brain shrieked. 'She isn't your baby—she's ours!'

Cathy began to shrink again. Now she was only twelve, now seven, now two. And she was once more just a bundle.

The madwoman picked the bundle up, but it didn't struggle this time. She tickled it under the chin, and there was no reaction. She opened her mouth, and let out a single, silent scream, then dropped the lifeless baby to the floor, as if it were of no more use than a worn-out rag doll.

And George, watching it all with horror, could do nothing.

He woke up with a start, his heart pounding furiously, his body drenched with sweat. It was light outside now, and he could hear the clip-clopping of cart horses in the street below. Colleen's side of the bed was empty.

George lay perfectly still for a minute or two—until his heart had slowed down, and the nightmare vision had faded a little—then got up, washed, and dressed. As he made his way downstairs, the smell of cooking wafted up towards him.

Colleen was standing by the stove, basting some eggs in her frying pan.

For some reason, George discovered a sudden rage building up inside him. 'I hope you're not cookin' any of that for me,' he said.

Colleen looked up from her work. The expression on her face was as neutral and unrevealing as a blank piece of paper. 'Two of the eggs are for you,' Colleen told him. 'The other two are for me.'

'How can you think of eatin' anythin' at a time like this?' George demanded.

'Our bodies need food, George. Even if we don't feel like it, we've got to eat to keep our strength up.'

George sat down heavily at the table. 'All I want is a cup of tea,' he said.

Colleen slid the eggs on to two plates, put one of the plates in front of George, then sat down opposite him. 'You've always been the practical one,' she said.

'An' just what's that supposed to mean?'

'It means what it says. Whenever we've had a crisis before, you've always kept your head, because you knew that was the best way to get through it.'

'This is different.'

Colleen sliced off a piece of egg, speared it with her fork, and put it into her mouth. She didn't look as if she was enjoying the experience, but she swallowed it anyway. 'Try an' eat a bit yourself, George,' she said.

'It *is* different,' George said, though she had not contradicted him out loud. 'It's me daughter that's gone missin'.'

'She's my daughter, too, George,' Colleen reminded him. 'But do you really think it's goin' to do our Cathy any good to have us both losin' our heads?'

'God, but you're a hard woman!' George said.

For a second Colleen looked deeply wounded, and then her face returned to the blank expression it had been wearing since George entered the room.

'I'm bein' sensible, not hard,' she said. 'Our lives can't just stop until we get our Cathy back, because we ... we have to face the fact that we might never get her back.'

George slammed his big fist down on the table, rattling the crockery. 'Don't say that!' he shouted.

'We have to consider the possibility, George,' Colleen said firmly. 'If that's what *does* happen—if we don't get her back—we'll just have to learn to tell ourselves that whoever took Cathy loves her, and is makin' her very happy. An' we'll have to force ourselves to be happy *for* her, as well.'

'But anybody could have taken her,' George said. 'A match girl without two ha'ppenies to rub together. Or a tramp even—an alcoholic bloody tramp! Have you thought of that?'

A slight flush rose to Colleen's cheeks. 'I'm

Cathy's mother,' she said. 'Of course I've thought of it! But don't you see, what we have to make ourselves believe is that it isn't like that at all.'

'You're mad!'

'I'm not mad, love. Thinkin' like that's the only way that we'll get by.'

'I'm not sure that I want to get by, if that's how I'm goin' to have to do it.'

'You don't have any choice in the matter. You've got responsibilities to little Ted, an' any other babies we might have. They've got a right to expect a happy life—an' we can't give 'em one as long as we're mournin' for Cathy.'

George stood up, his face white with fury. 'If we don't get our Cathy back, I don't *want* any more kids,' he said, and stormed out of the room.

Colleen sat perfectly still until she heard the front door slam behind her husband. Then she buried her head in her arms and sobbed until she had run dry of tears.

It was eleven o'clock in the morning. Philip had had the posters of little Cathy printed with remarkable speed, and they were going up all over Southwark. Tom Bates and Harry Roberts, for their part, had positioned themselves on the pavement in Lant Street, close to Mr Southern's shop.

'The way I figure it,' Tom had explained earlier, 'is that anybody 'oo's around 'ere at this time o' day on Wednesday might also 'ave been around at the same time o' day on *Monday*.'

'That's possible,' Harry had admitted.

'An' if they *were* around, then they might 'ave got a better look at this bundle—which could 'ave been the Taylor's baby—than old Mrs Butler did. If they saw the bundle, then they must 'ave seen the woman 'oo was carryin' it as well.'

'There's no arguin' with that.'

The theory was solid enough, but the practice was simply not working out. It wasn't that people minded being stopped and interrogated—they had all heard what had happened, and were eager to help—the problem was that there was very little they *could* do to help.

'I was over in Lambeff on Monday,' one man they stopped said to them. 'Never came nowhere near Lant Street.'

'I went to Southern's shop meself,' a young woman told them, 'but that was hours before the baby went missin'.'

'If I 'adn't stopped for a drink in the Goldsmiths', I'd 'ave been walkin' right past when it happened,' the Billingsgate Market porter who lived up Suffolk Street volunteered.

At twelve o'clock Mr Southern closed down his shop for his dinner hour, and both horse and foot traffic on Lant Street all but disappeared.

'Might as well go an' 'ave a bite to eat ourselves, 'adn't we?' Harry suggested.

'In a minute. I think I'll just 'ave a word with this bloke first,' Tom said, pointing to a sandwich man who was walking down the street towards them. The man was leading a small black and white dog, and on his boards were written the words: 'Kent's Pet Emporium, for the finest animals in London.'

Tom stepped forward to block his path. 'Would yer mind answerin' a few simple questions which might be of 'elp to us in our inquiries?' he asked.

The sandwich man grinned good naturedly. 'Always willin' to do anyfink that will 'elp the Law,' he said. 'Ask away.'

'Do yer always come down Lant Street at this time o' day?' Tom asked.

'No. Sometimes I don't come down it all. I like to vary me route, yer see.'

' 'Ow about Monday? Were yer 'ere then?'

The sandwich man frowned with concentration. 'Monday? Let me see. No, Monday I was up an' down Southwark Bridge Road in the mornin', an' then in the afternoon, I was on Tooley Street. What's this about, anyway?'

'Don't yer know?' Tom asked. ' 'Aven't yer seen all the posters that are goin' up? 'Aven't yer been readin' the papers?'

'Can't read. I did go to school for a couple o' years, but I could never seem to get the 'ang of readin', some'ow.'

'Well, what 'appened was that on Monday somebody stole a little baby from right near 'ere.'

The sandwich man shook his head. 'A bad business, that kind of thing,' he said. 'I like kids meself. I saw two little babies on Monday, luverly little things they was an—'

'Wait a minute!' Tom said. 'When yer said yer saw two babies, do yer mean two babies together—in one pram?'

'That's right. A boy an' girl.'

Tom and Harry exchanged glances.

'I asked if they was twins,' the sandwich man continued, oblivious to the exchange. 'The girl pushin' said they wasn't, but I could tell they was. Still, I didn't let on that I knew she was fibbin'. She wasn't much more than a kid 'erself, an' there was no real 'arm in it, now was there?'

'This girl. Was she about so 'igh,' Tom said, raising his hand to chest height, 'with light brown 'air an' a slightly pointed face?'

'That sounds like 'er. Wait a minute. Are you sayin' it's one o' them two babies that was stolen?'

'Yes. The little girl.'

The sandwich man shook his head again. 'Terrible thing to 'appen,' he said. 'It makes it worse, some'ow, now that yer've told me that in a manner o' speakin' I knew the little mite.'

'Was the pram she was pushin' a blue one?' Tom asked, just to make certain they *were* talking about the same babies.

'It was, now I come to think of it,' the sandwich man said. 'It was in luverly condition, but 'ad a big scratch down the front. I was goin' to mention it to the gal, then we got talkin' about somefink else, an' it must 'ave slipped me mind.'

Harry looked questioningly at Tom.

'The Taylors' pram has a scratch like that,' Tom said. 'Colleen did it herself, on Sunday.

She told me about it when we was both round at me mum-in-law's for tea.'

'Where exactly did yer see this girl with the twins?' Harry asked the sandwich man.

'Top end o' Southwark Bridge Road.'

'An' what time was that?'

'Let me see now. It must 'ave been around 'arf nine or a quarter to ten.'

It was disappointing news for the two policemen. If the sandwich man had seen her on her way *back* from the walk, then he might have had something interesting to tell them. However, Lizzie had talked to him at the start of the walk, and that was no good at all.

'Well, thanks for yer time,' Tom said resignedly.

'Wait a minute,' the sandwich man said. 'I've just remembered somefink.'

'What?'

'Well, this girl says she got to go, an' says it's been nice talkin' to me. I tell 'er it's mutual, 'cos it's always nice to talk to a pretty little thing like 'er. Anyway, I don't think she's used to bein' given compliments, because she got all flustered like an' left me in a real 'urry.'

'I don't see 'ow that's goin' to 'elp us,' Tom said.

' 'Ang on a minute, I'm gettin' to that part,' the sandwich man said. 'She'd only just gone when another woman came rushin' right past me. Me first thought was that she must be followin' the girl with the pram. Then I told meself I must be goin' soft in the 'ead. I mean, why *should* she 'ave been followin' the girl? But now, after what yer've just told me ...'

'This other woman,' Tom said excitedly. 'Did yer get a good look at 'er?'

'Yes, I did.'

'An' could you describe 'er to us?'

' 'Course I could. Easiest thing in the world. I've got a good memory for faces. Sort of made it me 'obby to study 'em, yer see, what with spending so much time on the street an' all. She 'ad dark 'air an' a thin face, around twenty-six or twenty-seven. She was wearing a feather 'at, an' was swayin' a bit, like she'd been drinkin'.'

'An' yer sure she was followin' the girl with the pram?' Tom asked.

'Can't be sure of *anyfink*,' the sandwich man told him. 'But like I said, me first thought when I saw she was in such a 'urry, was that was what she 'ad to be doin'.'

'Yer goin' to 'ave to take the rest of the day off work, me old china,' Harry said.

'I can't go doin' that,' the sandwich man protested. 'I'd lose me job for sure.'

'We'll square it with yer gov'nor,' Harry promised, 'but we really need yer to come with us right now.'

'Go where with yer?'

'To see the police artist.'

A few rays of sunlight filtered through the small, barred window high in the wall, but they did little to relieve the gloom of the visitors' room of Holloway Women's Prison.

Annie looked across the rough wooden table at Lizzie Hodges. The poor girl had been in this awful place for less than two days, and she was already as pale as if she hadn't seen the sun for years.

' 'Ow is everybody back in Lant Place?' Lizzie asked. Then she laughed bitterly and added, 'That's a stupid question for me to ask, ain't it? Poor Mrs Taylor must be out of 'er mind with worry, an' it's all my fault.'

'It isn't your fault, and you mustn't blame yourself,' Annie said fiercely.

'If I 'adn't left the kids outside Mr Southern's shop while I went in for some sweets ...'

'Everybody leaves their kids alone sometimes. And no matter how careful you are, if someone really wants to steal your baby, they'll find their chance.'

'I s'ppose yer right, Mrs Bates, but I still can't stop meself from feelin' guilty.'

Annie glanced up at the grim-faced wardress, who was standing by the door and making a great show of ignoring their conversation, then turned back to Lizzie. 'How are they treating you in here?' she asked, almost in a whisper.

Lizzie shrugged. 'Oh, I can't complain. In some ways, it ain't even as bad as the work'ouse. But the difference is, yer see, that when I was in the work'ouse, I didn't know no better. Now I've 'ad me chance to see what life's like on the outside, an' that makes this place terrible 'ard to bear.'

'We'll get you out soon,' Annie protested.

' 'Ow can yer? That Inspector Walton is

convinced that I 'elped 'ooever took the baby.'

'It's like I told you the last time I came. Tom and Harry are out looking for the kidnapper right now, and when they find her—Harry's almost certain it's a woman who's taken Cathy—she'll be able to tell the police that you had nothing at all to do with it.'

'An' what if they *don't* find 'er?' Lizzie asked.

'They will.'

' 'Cos Inspector Walton told me that kidnappin's a very serious offence. Almost as bad as murder. 'E said I could get twenty years for it.'

Even though she didn't know whether George would be coming home or not, Colleen went through all the motions of preparing her husband's supper.

'Stick to the routine,' she ordered herself. 'Carry on as if everythin' was normal.' Now she no longer had her husband's support, she knew that without that routine, that normality, she was in danger of coming apart at the seams.

It was just after half past six when she heard the front door open, and the clump, clump, clump of George's wooden leg as he walked down the corridor. Then the kitchen door opened, and he was standing there.

'I've made your supper,' she said flatly, bracing herself, even as she spoke, for some new verbal attack from him. 'You don't have to eat it if you don't want to, but I've made it anyway.'

'I've been thinkin',' George said, speaking in that slow, careful way of his.

'Oh yes? What about?'

'About what you said this mornin', an' about what I said. I called you a hard woman.'

Colleen felt tears forming in her eyes, but she wouldn't cry! She wouldn't! 'I don't need remindin' of what you called me, thank you very much,' she said.

George leaned heavily on the table, as if standing were a harder effort than usual—as if even talking were hard. '*It* was wrong an' *I* was wrong,' he told her. 'I was confusin' hard with strong. You're a strong woman, Colleen. Maybe the strongest I've ever met, an' I realise now that if we're ever to come through this terrible mess, we'll have to come through it together, like we've always done.'

It was a long speech by George's standards, and for a moment Colleen just stood there by the stove, taking it all in. Then she rushed across the kitchen, flung her arms around her husband and buried her head deep in his massive chest. 'I do so love you, George,' she said.

'An' I love you. I don't think I've ever loved you more than I do right now.'

There was a knock on the front door, and they both froze, imagining the worst.

'Say somethin', George,' Colleen pleaded.

'It's not locked,' George called down the passageway, at the same time as he gently lifted his wife's arms from his shoulders.

There was the sound of two sets of footsteps and a voice which called out, 'It's us. Tom an' 'Arry.'

'Have they found her?' Colleen gasped, the moment the two policemen entered the room.

Tom shook his head sadly. 'But we really are gettin' somewhere,' he said. 'We found a bloke 'oo we think might 'ave seen the woman 'oo took Cathy,' Tom explained. ' 'E's just been down to the station with us, an' described 'er for the police artist.'

Harry reached into his pocket, pulled out a piece of drawing paper and handed it over to Colleen. 'We think this is the woman we're lookin' for.'

Colleen examined the pencil sketch of the woman in the feathered hat, and as she looked, an expression somewhere between shock and revelation came to her face.

'Oh my God!' she gasped.

'Do yer recognise 'er?'

'How could I have been so stupid?' Colleen asked, hitting her forehead hard with her left fist. 'After the way I've seen her goin' downhill with me own eyes, how could I not have thought of her before?'

'D'yer know 'er name?' Harry asked.

'Of course I do.'

'Then 'oo is she?'

'You must have seen her yourself hundreds of times in the Goldsmiths' Arms,' Colleen told him.

'Maggie White!' Harry exclaimed.

'That's right,' Colleen agreed. 'Maggie White!'

CHAPTER 21

It was Thursday morning, nearly three full days after Cathy Taylor had been kidnapped. Tom Bates and Harry Roberts stood outside Detective Inspector Walton's office, waiting for the Great Man to find time to see them.

'Which of us do you think should do the talkin' when we get in there?' Harry asked.

'It 'ad better be you,' Tom replied. ' 'E 'ates me for gettin' off that murder charge.'

Despite the tense situation, Harry grinned. 'An' 'e 'ates *me* for gettin' yer off.'

Tom grinned back. 'Maybe we'd better just play it by ear,' he said. 'You start the talkin', an' I'll join in if I think it seems like a good idea.'

The door swung open, and a harassed-looking uniformed sergeant emerged. 'The inspector says he'll see yer now,' he told the two waiting men.

Tom and Harry marched smartly through the door and stood to attention in front of a desk which was piled high with a confusion of documents, many of them faded and dog-eared. The inspector himself was sitting behind the desk, his chair tipped back so far that it touched the wall.

'Well, well, well, if it isn't Sergeant Roberts an' Constable Bates,' he said, sounding surprised though he knew full well that they'd been outside for over an hour. 'To what do I owe this unexpected honour, Officers?'

Harry cleared his throat. 'We think we may 'ave information relatin' to the missin' Taylor baby, sir.'

Walton smiled the sort of smile which terrifies small children. 'Do yer now?' he said. 'Do yer indeed? Then I think yer'd better tell me all about it.'

Harry told him about Mrs Butler from Rodney Street, sketched out Tom's theory that if Lizzie was going to steal the baby she would have done it after she'd taken Cathy home, and finally talked about their conversation with the sandwich man.

'We got the police artist to make a sketch from his description, sir,' he said, 'an' several people 'ave recognised the picture as bein' of a Mrs Margaret White.'

'All this seems extremely fanciful to me,' Inspector Walton said dismissively.

'We know for a fact that Mrs White lost 'er own baby a few weeks back ...'

'Lots of people lose their babies. It doesn't make 'em into kidnappers.'

'... an' that she took it very badly.'

Walton sighed theatrically. 'I suppose I could bring 'er in for questionin',' he said. 'When I get round to it.'

'I'm afraid that probably won't be possible, sir.'

Walton scowled. 'An' what, exactly, do yer mean by that?' he demanded.

'She lost 'er job at the wash 'ouse some time ago, due to 'er 'eavy drinkin', an' 'er 'usband, Sid, 'as finally thrown 'er out—for the same reason. She's been seen now an' again in the neighbour'ood around Lant Street, but nobody that we talked to seems to 'ave any idea where she's livin'.'

'I see,' Walton said. 'So what yer've brought me, in fact, is a dubious suspect—at best—'oo yer can't even lay yer 'ands on.' He waved his hand dismissively towards the door. 'Thanks for comin' in, Sergeant. Yer've been a great 'elp, an' if there was more bobbies like you, there'd be no crime left in London.'

Harry held his ground. 'We still 'ave the picture the police artist did of 'er, sir. What do yer want us to do with that?'

'Well, I suppose yer could always frame it an' 'ang it on yer wall, couldn't yer?'

'We thought it might be more useful to 'ave it printed up as a poster an' plastered all over the area, sir,' Harry said, his face completely deadpan.

'Oh, yer did, did yer?'

'Yes, sir.'

'Takes time to get posters printed, but I expect that bein' only a sergeant, yer wouldn't know about that.'

'Mr Taylor's brother could 'ave 'em done in a couple of hours, sir. All we want from you is permission to stick 'em up.'

Walton frowned, as if he hadn't liked being contradicted over how long it would take to print the posters, then said, 'Based on the flimsy evidence yer've given me, I don't think there's any grounds for puttin' up posters.'

'I always felt bad about the Rollo Jenkins case, sir,' Harry said, apparently changing the subject.

'Yer what?'

'Well, I made a mess of collectin' the evidence in the first place, which led you to arrestin' young Tom 'ere.'

'Oh, it did,' Walton agreed. 'I remember it well.'

'Then, before yer 'ad time to see what rubbish me evidence was, I got lucky and came up with the real killers, which I'm sure you'd 'ave done through *proper* police work—no luck at all—if yer'd 'ad a couple more days.'

'You're right, there,' Walton agreed, but he sounded neither convinced nor convincing.

'So what 'appened?' Harry continued. 'I got all the glory out of it, an' you came away with egg on yer chin. Now that wasn't fair, was it, sir?'

'No,' Walton growled. 'It wasn't.'

'Which is why this missin' baby case is worryin' me, sir,' Harry explained. 'Yer see, say I got lucky again? Say it really is Maggie White 'oo took the baby, an' I find 'er? Me! On me own!'

'What are yer sayin'?'

'Well, it's goin' to make you—with all the men yer've got at yer disposal—look stupid again, ain't it, sir? An' I would 'ate for that to 'appen.'

Walton ran his index finger up and down

his nose several times. 'It couldn't do any real 'arm to put a few posters up, could it?' he said finally.

'No 'arm at all,' Harry agreed.

'All right, we'll do it,' Walton said decisively. 'It might even turn out to be the best idea I've 'ad all week.' He waved his hand again. 'Yer can go now.'

'There is one other thing, sir,' Harry said.

'Yes?'

'Lizzie 'Odges.'

'What about 'er?'

'Now we've got a stronger suspect than 'er, couldn't yer let the poor gal out of the clink?'

'Certainly not!'

'But sir—'

'Even if it turns out that this Maggie White woman did take the baby, I am still convinced that Lizzie 'Odges 'ad *somefink* to do with it,' Walton said. 'An' I shall make it my business to see she's punished with the full rigour of the law.'

Maggie White looked down at the orange box in which little Cathy was sleeping.

'I've got to go out to do a bit of shoppin', darlin',' she said softly. 'Now if I'm not back when yer wake up, yer mustn't worry that I've left yer, 'cos I'd never do that. I love yer, Ellen. I love yer with all me 'eart.'

It was half past one when she climbed into the alley and made her way towards Tooley Street. When she reached Morgan's Lane, she saw a policeman standing on point duty, and for a second, she almost turned back. Then she told herself she was only being stupid.

' 'E ain't goin' to bother you, gal,' she said aloud. After all, why should he? It was true that there were posters with the baby's photograph on them all over the district, but nobody knew who had taken her, and unless someone saw them together, there was nothing to connect her with the kidnapping. She walked past the policeman with the calm and innocence of any ordinary citizen. He didn't even give her a second glance.

Tooley Street was its usual busy self. Trams crammed with penny passengers, wagons loaded with tea chests, and brewers' drays weighed down with oak casks, rumbled endlessly up and down. Wharfingers in frock coats scurried along the pavements with wads of shipping manifests tucked under their arms, and the bill stickers were out in force, as they were most afternoons.

A new poster was going up. From a distance, Maggie could see that it looked like it had a pencil sketch of a face on it. Well, it couldn't have anything to do with her baby, could it, because they'd used a photograph on her poster? Still, there was no harm in checking.

As she got closer, she could see the writing above the sketch. 'HAVE YOU SEEN THIS WOMAN?' she read. When she was near enough to see the sketch clearly, she realised, with horror, that they were on to her. Though the words were swimming before her eyes, she forced herself to read the rest:

> The Metropolitan Police wish to interview Margaret White, 27, in connection with the abduction of a small child from Lant Street last Monday. Anyone with information as to the whereabouts of this woman should contact their local police section house immediately.

Maggie's mind was racing. The posters were only just going up, but soon they would be all over the area, and she would be a marked woman. If she acted quickly, though, she might be able to escape before the trap finally closed.

She realised that she was standing right next to the poster, as if inviting any passer-by to make the comparison, and moved quickly away. Before she did anything else, she needed to disguise herself, but she had no idea how to go about it.

'Get rid of yer 'at!' a voice screamed loudly in her head. 'Get rid of yer hat an' yer'll already 'ave gone 'alfway to changing yer appearance.' However, a woman without a hat would stick out like a sore thumb. Suddenly Maggie remembered a second-hand clothes store just next to the butcher's. She could get herself a new hat there.

It was possible that the people in the store had already seen the posters, and she had to force herself to walk through the door, but instead of pointing an accusing finger at her, the young woman standing behind the counter merely smiled and said, 'What can I do for yer, gal?'

Maggie made herself smile back, though it took a huge effort. 'I'd like a new 'at,' she said, taking off the one she was wearing before the assistant could get a really good look at it.

'I don't blame yer,' the assistant said. 'I don't think there's nuffink like a change of 'ats for makin' yer feel like a new woman.' She pointed to a pile of hats in the corner. 'There yer are. See if yer can find one o' them that takes yer fancy.'

Maggie felt the urge to pick up the nearest one, but she knew that would look suspicious, so instead she made a show of examining several hats, before finally selecting one with a wide brim and a trim of artificial flowers.

'Looks luverly on yer,' the assistant said, as she counted out the money Maggie had given her.

'Thanks,' Maggie replied. 'An' yer were right. I *do* feel like a new woman.'

She stepped out on the pavement, a little more confident now she was wearing her new disguise.

What next? she wondered. Food! That was what she'd come out for in the first place, before the sight of the poster had knocked her off balance. She still had some of her savings left. She should buy enough food so that she didn't have to leave the warehouse again until all the fuss about the kidnapping had died down a bit.

At the provision store a few doors up from where she'd got the hat, she bought corned beef, biscuits, tinned peaches, and milk for the baby. Then, though she'd not touched a drop of alcohol since she'd found the baby, she went into the jug and bottle department of the nearest pub and bought two bottles of gin.

'We should both be safe enough if we just stay in hidin',' she told herself, although she knew that she had to face the possibility that the bobbies might come across her hiding place.

She'd promised the baby that they'd never be separated, and it was a promise she intended to keep. She went into an ironmonger's shop and purchased the biggest carving knife he had on sale.

Thursday afternoon drifted slowly into early evening. The posters with Maggie White's picture on them had gone up several hours earlier, but when Tom Bates went to visit the Taylors it was with the heavy news that their baby had still not been found.

'I was so sure that the posters would help,' Colleen said despondently, after Tom had sat down at the kitchen table, opposite her and George.

'They 'ave 'elped,' Tom said. 'I've just been down to the section 'ouse, and the sergeant there told me that they've been contacted by a couple o' people 'oo think they may 'ave spotted Maggie White just before the posters went up.'

'Spotted her?' Colleen gasped. 'Did she have my little Cathy with her?'

Tom shook his head. 'No, she didn't, but then that's 'ardly surprisin,' is it? After the pictures of

Cathy went up, she'd 'ave to be a fool to risk bein' seen on the street with the baby. She'll 'ave left Cathy somewhere safe while she went out on 'er own.'

'When and where was she spotted?' asked George, speaking crisply and clearly, because he always fell back on his precise military training in times of trouble.

'She was seen on Tooley Street,' Tom told him. 'Early this afternoon, it was.'

'What was she doin' there? Just walkin' around without any purpose?'

Tom shook his head. 'No, far from it. She 'ad a very definite purpose.'

'Which was?'

'To buy food. She went to a provision store on the corner of Stoney Lane an' bought 'alf the shop up.'

'She's goin' to ground,' said ex-Sergeant George Taylor. 'That's just what I'd do if I was in her position.'

'You said a couple of people spotted her,' Colleen said. 'The man in the provision store must have been one. Who was the other?'

Tom looked distinctly ill at ease. 'Just another shopkeeper,' he said evasively.

Colleen was not going to be fobbed off with that. Knowing Maggie as she did, she already had her own suspicions about what else the woman might have bought. 'What sort of shopkeeper was this second one, exactly?' she demanded.

Tom sighed. 'If yer must know, it wasn't, strictly speakin', a shopkeeper at all.'

'I think that you'd better tell us the worst, Tom,' George said gravely.

'It was the barmaid at the Red Lion on Vine Street 'oo saw 'er,' Tom admitted.

'What was she doin' goin' into the Red Lion?' Colleen asked.

'She went there to buy somefink from the Lion's jug an' bottle department.'

'What?' Colleen said, determined to drag the full story out of the young policeman.

'A couple o' bottles o' cheap gin.'

Colleen gripped her husband's hand as tightly as she could.

'Yer shouldn't worry,' Tom told her. 'Like George said a few minutes ago, she's gone to ground. She bought enough food to last her for a long time, and that's probably why she bought two bottles o' gin as well. If she only 'as the occasional drink, Cathy won't come to no 'arm.'

'So the woman who stole my baby has got enough booze to drink herself unconscious—maybe even kill herself?' Colleen said, and there was an edge to her voice which said she expected the truth.

'Yes,' Tom admitted. 'Yes, she 'as.'

As evening approached, the sky had begun to cloud over, and the wind—blowing in from the river, and funnelled along the alleyways which led from the wharves—had a biting edge to it.

The two policemen who had been assigned the job of checking the area around Morgan's Lane for the missing baby, made their way towards the tea warehouse.

'I 'ate these extra duties,' Constable Len Baxter complained. 'The way I see it, we've already done our bit on this case.'

' 'Ow do yer work that out?' his partner, Arthur Cox, asked.

'Well, it was us what caught that Lizzie 'Odges, wasn't it?' Baxter asked.

Cox laughed. 'We didn't so much catch 'er as 'ave 'er fall into our arms,' he said. His face grew more serious and concerned. 'Anyway, the *real* job ain't arrestin' anybody, is it? It's gettin' that little baby back to 'er mum.'

'Maybe it is,' Baxter admitted, 'but if yer ask me, we're never goin' to do it by lookin' round 'ere.'

'What makes yer say that?'

'Well, I'll tell yer what I think, Arfur. This Maggie White woman must be pretty smart, or we would 'ave caught 'er long before now. An' if she *is* smart, then she'll know that if she stays 'ere, we're bound to find 'er sooner or later, so she'll 'ave 'ightailed it out of the area. It's other places, like Stepney an' Poplar, that we should be searchin', not right 'ere in 'er own backyard.'

Cox shook his head dubiously. 'I don't know about that, Len. There was all that food she bought—'

'If it really was 'er,' Baxter interrupted, 'an' I'm far from convinced that it was.'

'If it *was* 'er,' Cox conceded, 'then that would suggest that she's found 'erself a really good 'iding place where she thinks we'll never look.'

They had reached the empty tea warehouse. A sign on the big double doors said, 'THIS PROPERTY TO LET.' A thick iron bar ran the length of each door, and the doors were joined in the middle by a hasp, to which was fastened a huge padlock.

'Somewhere like this ware'ouse would be a good place to 'ide out,' Cox said.

'Do you think so?' Baxter asked, taking the padlock in his hand and feeling its weight. 'Well, as far as I can see, there's no evidence of forcible entry 'ere.'

'I think I'll just nip down the alley an' see if everyfink looks all right there,' Cox said.

Baxter frowned. 'All right, if yer feel yer must. But try an' be sharp about it, will yer? After all this searchin', I could really murder a cup of rosie.'

Cox disappeared down the alley, and Baxter fiddled with his whistle, wishing, for the hundredth time, that his partner wasn't quite so enthusiastic.

Cox was away for a little over two minutes, and when he returned there was a slightly disappointed look on his face.

'Well, did yer find anyfink?' Baxter asked, though it was obvious that his partner hadn't.

'There's a couple o' windows round the side,' Cox said, 'but they're both boarded up.'

'It's like I said: she'll be long gone,' Baxter told him. 'Can we 'ave that tea now?'

'I suppose so,' Arthur Cox said.

From a small window on the first floor of the tea warehouse, Maggie White watched as the two policemen walked slowly back up Morgan's Lane.

'That was a close one, wasn't it just, Ellen?' she said over her shoulder.

The baby made no response. Sometimes she cried, and sometimes she was quiet, but since the moment she'd been snatched from her pram there had been no signs of the joyousness which she'd so often shown in the past.

Maggie walked over to the box. 'Yes, it was close.' She looked down at the large carving knife in her hand. 'Still, they've gone away now, so I won't be needin' to use this, will I?'

She placed the knife on the floor, and reached for the gin bottle. It was half-empty, which surprised her because she didn't think she'd drunk that much. 'You ain't been drinkin' it, 'ave yer, Ellen?' she asked. 'So it must 'ave been me.'

She'd better slow down, she told herself. Just one nip a day, that was the ticket.

Still, those policemen had put the wind up her, and she really needed something to calm her down. 'An' what 'arm can another small one do, Ellen?' she asked the baby. 'Can't do no 'arm at all, can it?'

With a shaky hand, she lifted the bottle to her mouth and took a generous swallow.

CHAPTER 22

Each time the door swung open, the customers in the saloon bar of the Goldsmiths' Arms would look up hopefully. Then, realising that the person entering was not bringing news of little Cathy Taylor, but just—like they themselves—searching for consolation in a drink, they would return moodily to their pints.

The posters of Maggie White had raised hopes in Lant Place, but those hopes had not been fulfilled. If the Taylors did not get their baby back, then life in the Place would eventually have to return to normal, but for the moment Cathy's disappearance was casting a cloud of despondency over the whole neighbourhood.

Fred Simpson and Mary Bates sat at their usual corner table, sharing in the general gloom of the saloon bar, and adding to it a little of their own.

'I come up before the Board of Inquiry on Monday mornin',' Fred said gloomily, 'so it's only another four days before we're told the worst.'

Mary tried to force an optimistic smile to her lips. 'Or the best,' she pointed out. 'It could always be the best.'

Fred shook his head. 'I don't think so.'

'But yer can't be sure till after the inquiry.'

'They've got a way of sensin' 'ow these things

will go down at the station,' Fred said. 'They can almost smell it out. Most of the men are already treatin' me like I've got some kind of disease that's catchin', so it's the 'igh-jump for me, there's no doubt about that.'

Mary bit her lower lip quite hard. 'An' yer still 'aven't changed yer mind about ...?'

'About not marryin' yer if I'm discharged?'

'Yes.'

'I couldn't marry yer, Mary. If the board decides I've dishonoured me uniform, it'll be like I don't know meself any more.' He waved his hands helplessly, as if he knew what he wanted to say, but couldn't find the right words. 'It'll be like all these years I've gone around thinkin' I was one kind of person, an' now it turns out that I've really been another.'

'Yer'll still be my Fred,' Mary said, reaching across and stroking his hand.

'No, I won't be,' Fred said, pulling his hand away. 'That's the trouble.'

They sat in silence for a few more minutes, then Fred said, 'D'yer fancy goin' to the music 'all tonight? When I was in 'ere with George's brother Philip the other night, 'e gave me tickets for the Lambeff 'Ippodrome. Yer want to go?'

'I don't know,' Mary confessed. 'It don't seem right, some'ow, us goin' off to an entertainment. Not with Mrs Taylor's baby still bein' missin'.'

'An' yer think that if we stay 'ere, it'll 'elp the police to find little Cathy any quicker?'

'I s'ppose not,' Mary said. 'All right. If it'll make yer feel any better, we'll go to the music 'all.'

'Well, the way things are, it certainly couldn't make me feel any worse,' Fred said.

A long and varied queue lined up outside the Lambeth Hippodrome that night. There were groups of young men, out on the town, who laughed at old jokes and punched each other in the ribs. There were families, with mothers who fussed over their sons' collars and straightened their caps, and courting couples like Fred and Mary—though most of them were in much better spirits than the young fireman and his girlfriend.

For anyone looking down from the windows above the queue, it must have been like watching a sea of hats—women's hats with silk roses and feather trim; men's top hats and bowlers; children's caps and sailor hats—all slowly rolling forward towards the entrance.

'I've never been to the music 'all before. What are we goin' to be watchin'?' Mary said.

'It's all on there,' Fred said, pointing to a poster which had been pasted on to the wall.

LAMBETH HIPPODROME
Proudly Presents an All-star Cast
to Rival Any Show in the West End

★ ★ ★ ★

MR CHAS GILLIORD
in a special twenty-minute version of *Hamlet*

Miss TILLY HARVEY
Chanteuse

TAFFY JONES
the Cardiff Comedian

MR JOCK MCVIE
Comic Cyclist

MR PETER SMITH
and His Performing Dogs

MR MICHAEL MILLS
Hypnotist

'I don't see no mention of Mr Taylor's brother, Philip, on that notice,' Mary said.

'There it is,' Fred told her, pointing his finger downwards. 'Right at the bottom: "Mr Philip Taylor's Living Pictures: A Day at the Wood Yard." '

'It's written in much smaller letters than all the other acts are,' Mary said.

'Well, it's bound to be, ain't it? Them livin' pictures'll never catch on.'

They were finally through the door and in the music hall. Seats in the gallery cost threepence, but the complimentary tickets Philip had given Fred were one and sixpenny ones, and their seats were near the stage.

Mary looked around her at all the fine dresses and silk hats. 'I feel ever so awkward, sittin' 'ere among all these posh people,' she whispered into Fred's ear. 'They're all wearin' such nice clothes.'

'That's 'cos they've got more bees an' 'oney than we 'ave. But yer shouldn't measure things by money, Mary. Yer may not 'ave much in the Post Office, but yer the finest lady 'ere.'

Mary put her hand on his arm, and nuzzled her face up against his shoulder. 'I love yer,' she said.

'An' I love you.'

Which made it all the more tragic that on Monday morning they would almost certainly lose their only chance of happiness, Mary thought, as she felt her eyes sting with the tears she was trying to fight back.

The show began, and, for the moment at least, Mary forgot about her troubles. She laughed at the comedian until it hurt, giggled at the amusing antics of the troupe of performing dogs, and gasped every time the trick cyclist seemed about to lose control and hurtle off the stage into the audience.

'You seem to be enjoyin' yerself,' Fred said to her, when the cyclist had finally made his wobbly-skilful way off the stage.

'Oh I am,' Mary admitted. 'This was such a good idea of yours. An' 'ow about you? Are *you* enjoyin' yerself?'

'Yes, I am,' Fred said. In fact, there were whole minutes at a time when he was so caught up in the performance that he almost forgot about the ignominy which awaited him at the Board of Inquiry.

A new 'artiste' walked confidently on to the

stage. The tall, thin man in evening dress was billed as Mr Michael Mills the hypnotist.

'Ladies and gentlemen, for my performance tonight, I shall require a volunteer from among the audience,' he said. 'Do I have such a volunteer?'

'I'll do it!' shouted a man from the middle of Fred and Mary's row of seats.

'Excellent,' the hypnotist said. 'A true sporting gentleman. Would you care to come up on to the stage, sir?'

The volunteer made his way to the end of the row. He was a cocky young man of around twenty-five, wearing flashy trousers with turn-ups, a coat but no waistcoat, and a straw boater with a bow on it. He mounted the steps with a swagger, and when he reached the top he turned around and grinned at the audience. 'Load o' rubbish, this, ain't it?' he said.

The hypnotist frowned. 'Do I take it that you do not believe in the power of hypnosis?' he asked.

The volunteer's grin widened, until it looked like it would split his face in two. ' 'Course I don't believe in hypno ... hypno ... whatever yer call it. 'S'all a trick.'

'Is it indeed?' the hypnotist asked. 'We shall see.' He pulled a watch out of his pocket. 'Would you mind keeping your eyes firmly fixed on this, sir?'

'Anyfink to oblige,' the young man said.

The hypnotist swung his watch slowly from side to side, and his volunteer followed it with his eyes.

'You are feeling very sleepy,' the hypnotist said, as the young man's head began to slump forward. 'I am now going to count slowly to five. When I reach the number five, you will wake up, but you will be in a trance and will do whatever I tell you to do. One ... two ... three ... four ... five.'

The volunteer opened his eyes.

'You are walking by the Thames,' the hypnotist said. 'Can you see the river?'

The volunteer nodded.

'You want to cross the river. There aren't any bridges, but that doesn't matter because as long as you do it on tiptoe, you can walk across water.'

While the audience howled with laughter, the young man tiptoed across the stage.

'Oh dear!' the hypnotist said. 'You're right in the middle of the river now, and unfortunately you suddenly seem to have forgotten *how* to walk on water.'

The young man collapsed immediately, and then began thrashing his arms and legs around.

'That's it,' the hypnotist encouraged. 'Not far to the bank now. There, you've made it. Pull yourself ashore.'

The volunteer got on to his hands and knees, and crawled along for a few feet.

'You're wet, aren't you?' the hypnotist said.

'Absolutely blinkin' soppin',' the volunteer agreed.

'I think you'd better take your jacket off, then. Don't you?'

'Take me jacket off, that's the ticket,' the

young man said, and removed it immediately.
'It might also be a good idea to get out of
those wet shoes and socks.'

These were discarded, too, and the young
man was just beginning to unfasten the belt on
his flashy trousers when the hypnotist said, 'No,
that's quite enough, thank you. Would you like
to come and stand next to me?'

The volunteer obeyed.

'I will count up to five again, and when I
reach the number five, you will come out of
your trance and remember absolutely nothing
of what has happened in the last few minutes.
One ... two ... three ... four ... five.'

The young man blinked, and then grinned at
the audience. 'See, I told yer it was all a fake,'
he said.

'A fake is it?' the hypnotist asked. 'Then
would you mind explaining to the ladies and
gentlemen how you came to take off your socks,
shoes and jacket?'

The volunteer glanced down at his feet, and
a look of horror came to his face.

'They're over there,' the hypnotist said,
pointing helpfully to the part of the stage
which, a few moments earlier, his volunteer
had imagined was a river bank.

Blushing furiously, the young man picked
up his clothes, and, without bothering to put
them on, rushed down the steps towards the
anonymity of the darkness beyond the footlights.

'Hypnotism can do many wonderful things,'
the hypnotist told his audience, 'but perhaps the
most wonderful of all is that it can take you right

back to a time you had forgotten, and let you see things as clearly as if they were happening now. For my next demonstration, I shall ask for a volunteer who is willing to be taken back to his earliest childhood.'

After what they'd seen happen to the cocky young man, however, none of the audience seemed very eager to step forward and be made complete fools of.

'Come on, ladies and gentlemen,' the hypnotist urged. 'What you've observed so far was only my bit of fun. I promise you, this will be a serious scientific demonstration.'

Still, no one raised a hand.

'Fred, you should go up!' Mary said, with a sudden excitement in her voice.

'Me go up? Why should I? I don't 'ave no wish to go back to me child'ood.'

'Maybe not, but there *is* somefink yer've forgotten that yer really want to know, ain't there?'

'I don't understand yer.'

'*Fink about it,*' Mary urged.

And then Fred saw what she was getting at. 'Yer a genius,' he said, kissing her quickly on the lips.

'Isn't there anyone brave enough to face their own past?' the hypnotist asked plaintively.

Fred stood up. 'I'll do it,' he said.

'Good for you!' the hypnotist replied. 'Give him a big hand, ladies and gentlemen.'

With the sound of applause ringing in his ears, Fred made his way down the row and up the steps to the stage.

'I am going to take you back to the time when you were two years old,' the hypnotist told him.

'I don't want to go back to when I was two,' Fred said. 'Only to last Friday afternoon.'

The hypnotist looked annoyed. 'I don't really see the point in taking you back a mere week, young man,' he began. 'Now if you would consent to let me return you to your second birthday—'

'Last Friday afternoon,' Fred said firmly.

'What's so special about that day?'

'There's somefink very important that I need to remember—an' I can't, 'owever 'ard I try.'

The hypnotist turned to the audience. 'Is there no one else prepared to journey back into their childhood?' he asked, and when it was plain that there wasn't, he sighed and said, 'Very well. Last Friday afternoon. Any particular time?'

'About one o'clock.'

The hypnotist sighed again. 'One o'clock it shall be.' He pulled out his watch again, and dangled it in front of the young fireman. Fred quickly slipped into a trance. 'What is the day and date?' the hypnotist asked.

'Thursday, the third of September, 1903.'

'We're going to travel back in time. It is no longer Thursday, but Wednesday ... Tuesday ... Monday ... Sunday ... Saturday ... Friday ... Do you understand?'

'Yes.'

'What is the day and date?'

'Friday, the twenty-eighth of August, 1903.'

'Good. It is one o'clock in the afternoon. Tell me exactly what you can see.'

A three-storey house—part of a row. Bright orange flames pouring out of the first-floor windows. A crowd already gathered in the street, with two policemen trying their best to hold them back.

Fred could hear the loud ringing of the fire bell in his ear, could feel the vibrations of the truck and could smell the smoke from the boiler.

'We're outside this burnin' 'ouse on Keppel Street,' he said, 'an' Leadin' Fireman 'Arris tells me to go an' see if there's anybody left inside.'

'So you're a fireman?'

'Yes.'

'Go on.'

The heat in the passageway, the crackling of the fire at the top of the stairs.

'I check the first room—the kitchen—an' I'm just about to cheek the second when ... when ...'

'When what?'

A sudden crashing sound, a hailstorm of crumbly plaster, a heavy old beam smoked black by years of open fires.

'... when the ceilin' collapses an' I get 'it on the 'ead by this beam. It ... it knocks me out cold ...'

'Please continue.'

'... an' when I come round again, I don't know 'oo I am or what I'm supposed to be doin' there.'

'Obviously concussion,' the hypnotist told the

audience. 'A classic case.'

'So I go outside, an' join the crowd that's watchin' the fire. Then the leadin' fireman comes up an' shouts at me, an' that's when I start rememberin' things again.'

The hypnotist turned to the audience. 'You have just witnessed the true power of hypnotism, my friends,' he said, and bowed to thunderous applause. 'I will now count to five, and when I reach five you will come out of your trance,' he said to Fred. 'But you will not forget what you have just told me. Rather, it will be as vivid to you then as it is now. One ... two ... three ... four ... five.'

Just like the young man before him, Fred blinked once, then turned to where Mary was sitting.

'I ain't a coward,' he shouted joyfully to his sobbing girlfriend. 'I ain't a coward after all.'

CHAPTER 23

Maggie White opened her eyes, looked all around her, then quickly closed them again.

Where the 'ell am I? she wondered. What had happened to all the bedroom furniture that she and her Sid had spent so much time choosing from out of the tallyman's catalogue? And how long had they been able to see Old Father Thames through their window? Come to that, she thought, since when had there been the space in their tiny bedroom for such a vast window as this one? It wasn't easy to work things out properly when your head was pounding like it was being hit with a dozen hammers all at once, but Maggie did her best.

Slowly, memories started to seep back. Sid's proud smile when she told him she was expecting ... losing her baby after that terrible fall down the stairs ... having the odd drink because that helped to ease the pain ... finding that just *one* drink didn't do the job any more ... taking the new baby from out of her pram in front of Mr Southern's shop ...

'I'm in a ware'ouse,' she said aloud. 'I'm in a ware'ouse at the end of Morgan's Lane.'

She opened her eyes again. The light seemed far too bright at first—almost blinding—then slowly she got used to it. She climbed shakily to her feet and walked across to the box where the baby was still sleeping.

'They're lookin' for us, Ellen,' she said softly. 'They want to take yer away from me. They don't know that we'd both rather die than be parted.'

It was time for a little sip of gin—just enough to get her going again. She reached for the bottle, and saw that it was empty. Good thing she'd bought another one. She picked up the second bottle, and saw that it was empty, too—no wonder she had a headache.

She rubbed the second bottle between her hands, as if she were one of the metal wringers in the wash house, trying to squeeze the last few drops of moisture out of newly washed clothes.

A wasted effort. She remembered she'd done exactly the same thing with the bottle the night before, so it wasn't surprising that it had no effect now.

She didn't want to, but she started to cry. 'There ain't none of the gin left, Ellen,' she told the baby. 'What am I goin' to do without me gin?'

She would have to buy some more. She knew it was madness to go out on to the street, where a picture of her was pasted to the wall every few yards, yet without the gin to help her along she didn't know how she was going to cope.

'Don't you worry yer little self, Ellen, I'll be careful,' she promised the baby. 'An' I'll be back 'ere with yer before yer even know I've gone.'

When Constables Arthur Cox and Len Baxter had worked the midnight shift, as they had the previous evening, it had become a firm habit of theirs to call in for a pint—just the one—at the Crown and Anchor. Which was why Baxter was surprised when Cox announced that on that particular Friday morning, he was going to go straight home.

'What's the matter, Arfur?' Baxter asked. ' 'As yer old dutch been 'en-peckin' yer or somefink?'

'No, she 'asn't,' Cox said defensively. 'I just don't feel like a pint, that's all.'

'So what yer sayin' is, I'll 'ave to go an' 'ave a drink all by meself, will I?'

'Not all by yerself. There's usually a few other bobbies in the Crown.'

'There might be other bobbies, but that ain't like drinkin' with yer partner, is it?'

Cox considered telling Baxter the truth—which was that whatever his partner believed about the missing woman and baby already being miles away, he himself was convinced that they were still somewhere in the Tooley Street area, and he wanted to give Morgan's Lane one more going over.

'Well, are we goin' up to the Crown for that pint or not?' Baxter asked.

'I really don't fancy it,' Cox replied, having decided that he'd rather risk his partner's temporary irritation than go through weeks of ribbing for having wasted his time on a futile search.

'Please yerself, then,' said Baxter, suitably irked.

Maggie waited until there was silence in the alley outside, then cautiously removed one of the boards from the window and peered out. There was traffic moving along Morgan's Lane, but who would think to look down the alley to see if anyone was climbing out of the warehouse window?

'It's safe enough,' she said. She was lying to herself—and she knew it—but the thought of spending a whole, long day without a single drink was intolerable to her.

She removed the rest of the boards, hitched up her skirt, and slipped through the window.

She checked around the alley.

'Still safe,' she whispered.

She leaned through the window and replaced the boards. Then she stepped back and examined her work. Perfect. Nobody would ever guess that there was a way into the warehouse through there.

As she walked up the alley, she began to feel better. Her headache was going away, and very soon she would have bought what she needed.

'I'll get three bottles this time,' she decided. Or maybe four bottles—just to make certain that she didn't run out again.

It was as she turned on to Morgan's Lane that she saw the policeman coming towards her.

Arthur Cox was still some distance from the empty tea warehouse when he saw the woman emerge from the alley.

She was the same height as the suspect, and the right age and build, as well. Still, there were hundreds of women in the area who would have fitted the same description. But then he asked himself what she was doing coming out of the alley next to the warehouse? Where had she been? And where was she going?

When he saw her turn and run, he knew for certain that she was the one everybody was looking for.

Maggie dashed back down the alley, pulled away the boards and climbed through the window. She knew she should have replaced the boards, but there was no time, because the bobbie was not far behind, and she couldn't let him stop her from getting back to her baby.

Already gasping for breath, she dashed across the room towards the stairs to the first floor.

The boards lay haphazardly in the alley, and the open window was there for all to see.

'I should 'ave noticed it when I was 'ere yesterday,' Constable Cox told himself, but if he'd missed it then, at least he had noticed it *now*—and that was the main thing.

He climbed through the window with more ease than Maggie had, and found himself in a big, square room which still contained a few dozen empty tea chests. 'Fire 'azard,' he said to himself automatically. 'Should never 'ave been allowed.'

He wondered whether he'd made a mistake—whether the open window really had anything to do with the woman he'd chased down the alley—but that would have been far too much of a coincidence.

'I know that yer must be in 'ere somewhere, missis,' he shouted out, and his words echoed back at him: '... 'ere somewhere ... 'ere somewhere ...'

He saw the flight of iron stairs at the other end of the room. That had to be where she'd gone—upstairs. He walked over to them and started to climb.

They taught new officers caution in the Force, and when Cox reached the trapdoor at the top of the stairs, it was with caution that he opened it. The two flaps of the trapdoor crashed heavily onto the floor above. For a full ten seconds, Cox did nothing, then he slowly climbed a little higher so that just his head appeared through the gap.

The first floor looked similar to the one below it, but where the ground floor had been free of any human inhabitants, this one wasn't. In the very corner of the room, next to the window which overlooked the Thames, was a woman leaning over a box.

Cox began to climb again—very slowly and smoothly, so as not to frighten her.

'Don't you come any closer to us than you are now!' the woman screamed.

'Mrs ...' Cox began. He had forgotten the woman's bloody name, he realised. What the devil was it? Winters? Wilson? White! That was it. Maggie White.

'Mrs White, don't yer think it's time yer started actin' sensibly?' he asked. All the time he was talking, he was moving further up the iron stairs.

'I'm warnin' yer ...' Maggie White said.

'We've found yer now. It's all over.'

Another two steps, so that now all of him above the knee was visible on the first floor.

'Why don't yer leave us alone?' Maggie asked. 'My baby an' me just want to be left alone.'

Cox stepped clear of the trapdoor. 'She ain't your baby, Mrs White. She's Mrs Taylor's baby.'

'She *is* my baby,' Maggie protested. 'My little Ellen. She belongs to me, an' I belong to 'er.'

Cox moved a little closer. 'I know 'ow yer

must feel about 'er, Mrs White, but yer 'ave to give the baby back to 'er rightful mother sooner or later.'

Suddenly a wicked-looking knife appeared in Maggie White's hand—pointed at the baby's tiny body.

'If yer love 'er ...' Cox said, coming to a halt.

'Of course I love 'er!' Maggie said. 'An' she loves me. Don't yer see, that's why I can never give 'er up? We'd both rather die than be separated.'

'She's only a baby, Mrs White,' Cox said gently. 'How can yer know that she feels the same as you do?'

'A mother always knows,' Maggie White said, moving the knife closer to the baby's chest.

Cox gauged the distance between him and Maggie White. They were about thirty feet apart, he estimated. Even if he ran like the wind, she would easily be able to plunge the knife into the baby long before he had reached her.

He was out of his depth, he realised. This situation was well beyond the competence of a simple constable—nothing they had taught him in Kennington Lane had prepared him for it.

'If I do somefink for you, will you do somefink for me, Mrs White?' he asked.

'What?'

'If I promise to go away, will yer promise that as your part of the deal yer'll take the knife away from the baby's head?'

Maggie thought about it. 'All right,' she agreed finally. 'But if anybody else comes ...'

'Let's worry about that when it 'appens, shall we?' Cox said. 'What I'm goin' to do, Mrs White, is I'm goin' back towards the trapdoor. Then I'm goin' down the stairs. Yer can wait till yer can only see me 'ead in the gap, but before I finally leave, I want to see yer put that knife down. Is that fair?'

'I s'ppose so.'

Cox backed slowly. He felt the heel of his boot bang against the trapdoor and began to descend. 'I'm almost gone, Mrs White,' he said. 'Will yer put the knife down now, please?'

But Maggie didn't. Instead, she clutched the handle as firmly as ever.

A couple more steps and Cox knew that she could only see his head. 'Come on, Mrs White, play fair,' he implored her. 'We 'ad a deal, you and me, didn't we?'

Maggie White stared intently at the knife as if she was considering using it then and there. Then, after a second's hesitation, she placed it on the floor.

'Now I want yer to stay calm, Mrs White,' Cox said. 'I'm goin'—like I promised—but I expect that later there'll be somebody else 'ere to talk to yer ...'

'I don't want to talk to nobody.'

'Don't say that, Mrs. White. Maybe yer vicar or yer husband could convince yer ...'

'I don't want to see no vicar, an' me 'usband doesn't love me no more.'

' 'Ooever it is 'oo comes to see yer, Mrs White, I don't want yer pickin' up that knife again the moment yer 'ear 'im comin' up the stairs.'

'Leave us alone!' Maggie White screamed. 'Leave us alone, or I'll kill 'er right now!'

Cox sighed. 'All right, Mrs White,' he said. 'Just keep calm. I'm goin'.'

He took the steps very slowly, so as not to scare the madwoman. It wasn't particularly warm inside the warehouse, but when he finally reached the ground floor he realised that he was bathed from head to foot in sweat.

Maggie listened carefully to the policeman's gradually retreating footsteps.

She needed a plan, she realised. Leaving the warehouse was going to be impossible, because even if the bobbie went away, he was almost certain to leave someone else on watch. What could she and her baby do? She wished that there was just a little bit of gin left—but there wasn't.

'A cup o' rosie,' she told herself. 'A cup o' rosie is always good for calmin' down yer nerves.' She struck a match, lit the spirit stove and put the kettle on top of it.

'They've beat us, Ellen,' she told the baby in the box. 'They've beat us good and proper, but it don't matter, do it? We don't mind dyin' if we 'ave to, 'cos we know that we'll be together in 'eaven.'

She'd bought plenty of food, but hadn't eaten any of it—hadn't eaten anything at all for over two days—and now she was starting to feel giddy, just as she had that day when she'd fallen down the stairs.

'I mustn't let meself faint,' she said, as she tried her best to focus her eyes on the swirling floor. 'Whatever else 'appens to me, Ellen, I mustn't let meself faint.'

And then she fell, sprawling across the floor and knocking the blazing spirit stove into her bedding.

CHAPTER 24

As Philip Taylor set up his camera on the corner of Battle Bridge Lane and Tooley Street, he had only half his mind on his immediate task. The other half was thinking about the little niece he hadn't seen while he'd had the chance—and of the living picture which he was going to dedicate to her. There'd be nothing clever in the title of this one. It would simply be called *Kidnapped—Cathy's Story*.

He had the picture all planned out in his head. It would start with the abduction of the baby from outside Mr Southern's shop, then would show Mrs White walking down Tooley Street to buy her gin and provisions. And it would end—he prayed to God that it would end—with the police finding Cathy and returning her safely to her loving mother and father.

He looked through the camera at the actress in the broad feathered hat who was standing in front of him. She's no Marie, this one, he thought. With Ellie Dawes, there wasn't any of the fuss that he'd had to put up with when he'd worked with his wife. Ellie didn't spend hours getting into the role, and hours after the filming telling him that she felt ... she really felt ... that she *was* that kidnapper. You told Ellie what it was you wanted her to do, and she just went right ahead and did it.

Philip decided on his camera angle and shifted his unwieldy apparatus slightly to the left. Though he had not yet shot a foot of film, he knew that this was going to be the most powerful living picture he had ever made. His only reservation was that Ellie—with her black hair which hung down in ringlets, her deep brown eyes and her wide, amused mouth—was perhaps a little too pretty to be the villain of the piece.

Everything was finally ready. 'Right,' Philip said. 'I want you to walk up the street, Ellie, and when you get to the pub, I want you to stop. Hesitate for a few seconds, like you're wondering what to do, then suddenly, as if you've finally made your decision, go into the jug and bottle department. Have you got that?'

'Yes, Mr Taylor.'

Mr Taylor! In some ways, he liked her calling him that, and yet in other ways he didn't. He wondered what she'd say if he invited her out to dinner one night.

Quite a crowd had gathered to watch the filming. Up until that point, the spectators had been quiet—almost reverential—but now an excited buzz ran through them.

Most of what was being said was lost to Philip in the general hum, but he did manage to pick up enough to give him some idea of what was going on.

'Big fire!'

'Fire?'

'Where?'

'Ware'ouse on Morgan's Lane.'

Instantly, Philip's fickle spectators deserted him. However, there would have been nothing for them to see if they'd stayed, because Philip was already packing up his camera and wondering which was the quickest way to get to Morgan's Lane.

The alarm rang in the fire station and there was the usual flurry of activity. Fred Simpson stood close to the engine—though not too close to be in the way—watching the other firemen getting ready, and wishing he could go with them. But that wasn't allowed—not when you were under suspension while an inquiry into your conduct was taking place.

He was more sure than ever of what the result of that inquiry would be. He knew now that he'd acted bravely at the fire in Keppel Street, but he did not see how he would ever be able to convince the grey-haired men who would be judging him. He imagined himself telling the board that a hypnotist had taken his mind back to the fire and shown him the truth. They'd laugh at him first, and then despise him for not taking his punishment like a man. No, he would not put himself through that final humiliation. So it was suspension until the hearing on Monday, and then a dishonourable discharge from the brigade.

'Accordin' to some information we've just received from the bobbies, there's a woman an' a baby trapped in that ware'ouse on Morgan's Lane!' Leading Fireman Harris shouted over the hubbub. 'So move yerselves.'

Fred felt the hairs on the back of his neck prickle. 'It's the missin' baby,' he told Harris.

'Don't know anyfink about that.'

'It 'as to be,' Fred said. 'It just 'as to be. Let me go with yer, Mr 'Arris,' he pleaded.

'In case yer've forgotten, yer under suspension, Simpson,' Harris said.

'But I just *'ave* to go with yer. That little baby is me niece,' Fred lied.

'All the more reason for yer to want to leave 'er rescue in the 'ands of real professionals 'oo ain't goin' to bottle out at the last minute,' Harris said harshly.

The horses were already between the shafts, and the men were on the engine. The big double doors swung open and, bell ringing furiously, the fire engine left the station.

Fred waited until it had turned on to Southwark Bridge Road, then turned himself, and went straight up to the tackle room to get his helmet.

The floating fire station had many advantages over the conventional fire engine, Leading Fireman Bains thought.

For openers, since many of London's biggest fires broke out in the warehouses around the wharves and docks, the floating station was very often near at hand. Even if it wasn't, the streets were usually so full of traffic that the floating station, pulled by its powerful tug, regularly arrived at the scene first. Then there was the fact that before the ordinary fire engine could go into action, the firemen manning it had to find some source of water, whereas the floating station was already connected to an almost infinite water supply—the mighty River Thames.

However, there was one big drawback to the floating station, inasmuch as it was always at the mercy of the tides. Sometimes, with a low tide, the floating station simply couldn't get close enough to the bank to do much good, and the firemen on it would be forced to sit in the middle of the river and look on, frustrated, as their comrades did all the work.

At least it was a fairly high tide that day—thank Gawd—Bains thought, as the tug towed the floating station closer and closer to the burning warehouse on Morgan's Lane.

'Looks like a pretty bad one,' one of his crew said, gazing up at the burning building.

It looked like a *very* bad one. The fire was at its worst on the first floor, but was starting to take a hold over the floors above and below it. As was always the case, the big danger was it would spread even further.

Bains examined the buildings on either side of the burning warehouse. Employees were gathered at all the windows and loading bays. If the fire *did* start to spread, these people would soon be dumping tea, sugar, wool, or whatever else they were storing, straight into the river, in the hope that by sacrificing the stock, they could at least save the building.

The floating station was level with the warehouse now, and Bains' crew had already taken up their positions. It only remained to issue the order.

'Give it all yer've got, lads!' Bains bellowed.

Three hoses simultaneously shot jets of water at the crimson flames belching forth from the warehouse. Behind him, Bains could hear the boiler bubbling furiously and the pump spluttering as it forced the Thames water through it. They were giving this fire their maximum effort—but from the way the flames were still spreading, it did not look as if that would be enough. We're goin' to lose this one, whatever we bloody do, Bains thought gloomily.

Every second the fire gained more ground. Flames licked at the roof now and even through all the smoke and the furious jets of water, Bains could see that a section of the wall of the first floor was starting to buckle.

Suddenly the wall buckled no more, but broke away from the building and plunged down towards the floating fire station.

Bains looked up at the fiery brickwork cascading towards him. 'Bloody hell! Jump for it, lads!' he screamed.

He need never have delivered his order. The rest of his crew were already in the water.

Looking up at it from Morgan's Lane, the warehouse seemed, to Leading Fireman Harris, to lurch to one side.

'One of the supportin' walls must 'ave just given way,' said Fireman Wilf Eccles, confirming his boss's suspicions. ' 'Oo will yer be sendin' in, Mr 'Arris?'

'I'm not sendin' *anybody* in,' Harris told him. He pointed to the right side of the building. 'Look, there's just one corner that's not burnin' like merry 'ell. That'll catch soon, then 'ooever's up there will be trapped.'

'I thought yer said that there was a woman an' a little baby in there.'

'That's right, Eccles. But if they're on the first floor, they'll be dead by now.'

'An' if they're on the second?'

'Then it's only a matter of time.'

'I'm still willin' to 'ave a go at tryin' to get 'em out,' Wilf Eccles said.

'I know yer willin', Wilf,' Harris said, 'but I'm not goin' to let yer do it.'

'But Mr 'Arris—'

'Listen, I expect the men under me to take risks—that's all part of the job—but I ain't goin' to be responsible for sendin' nobody out on a suicide mission.'

A street urchin rushed up and tugged urgently at the hem of Harris's jacket. 'You the guv'nor 'ere?' he asked.

'What's it to do with you?'

'Only if yer are, I thought yer might like to know that that floatin' fire station of yours is blazin' away like billy-oh, an' all the men what was on it are bobbin' up an' down in the ol' river as if they was corks.'

'Bleedin' 'ell!' Harris said. He looked up the building, then back at Eccles. 'Can you manage things 'ere?' he asked.

'I should think so,' Eccles replied.

'Right,' Harris said. 'You take charge, an' I'll go an' see what I can do about them poor buggers from the floating station.'

The crowd was swelling by the minute, but Fred was in his full uniform, and it was not too difficult for him to push his way to the front.

'What are you doin' 'ere, Simpson?' Wilf Eccles demanded. 'Yer on suspension.'

'*Was* on suspension,' Fred replied, looking round to see if there was any sign of Leading Fireman Harris. 'The commander said that on a big fire like this, we needed every man we've got.'

'That's true enough,' Eccles agreed. 'Right, Simpson. What I want yer to do is—'

'I've already got me orders,' Fred lied. 'From Leadin' Fireman 'Arris 'imself. 'E said I was to go in.'

'But not five minutes ago, 'e told me that it would be suicide to send anybody in.'

Fred shrugged. 'Then somefink must 'ave 'appened to make 'im change 'is mind, mustn't it?'

Eccles looked at Fred suspiciously. 'I'm not sure that I believe yer,' he said.

'So what are yer goin' to do?' Fred asked.

'Wait till Mr 'Arris comes back an' wants to know why nuffink's been done? 'Cos if yer do that, it *will* be too late to do anyfink.'

Eccles hesitated for a second, then said, 'You two men! Get a ladder up to that second-floor window.'

The firemen put the ladder in place with a speed which was almost unbelievable to the onlookers.

'Right, off yer go,' Eccles said gruffly.

Fred strode over to the ladder, his eyes on the fire which was greedily swallowing up the building he was about to enter. He had his foot on the first rung when he felt a hand on his shoulder.

He turned, and saw Wilf Eccles had followed him. 'Good luck, me old china,' Eccles said.

Fred smiled, 'Thanks, Wilf,' he said, and began to climb.

The initial part of the climb—past the ground floor—was easy, because, at that level, the fire was mostly restricted to the other side of the building, but by the time Fred had reached the first floor, the flames were so close that they almost touched the ladder.

He pressed on, trying to ignore the prickling of his skin. In his mind's eye, he could almost see his helmet in the station's museum, next to those of other firemen who had died on duty.

The names of the dead men flashed through his head now: Barratt, who had fallen into a lake of boiling oil; Jacobs, who had succeeded in pushing his comrade through a small window, but had been too large to go through it himself; Ford, who had dragged six people from an inferno before finally being trapped himself. Somehow it didn't seem right that his own helmet should be displayed with theirs—he didn't feel worthy enough.

He had reached the second floor. He tried to open the window and discovered that it was securely bolted from the inside. It was almost like Maggie White didn't really want to be rescued.

He pulled his axe from his belt, turned his head away, and swung the hatchet at the window. He heard the sound of breaking glass, and felt a sting as a small piece embedded itself in his cheek.

Fred turned back to the window. Most of the glass was gone, but the wooden frame was still holding firm. He began to hack away at crosspieces. It was all taking too long, he thought—far, far too long.

The last crosspiece fell away. Fred slipped his axe back into his belt, gripped the wall firmly with both hands, and pulled himself through the window into the room.

Leading Fireman Harris had satisfied himself that the crew of the floating fire station were all safe and well, and now made his way back to his own team on Morgan's Lane.

He noticed the ladder up to the second-storey window the moment he was clear of the crowd. 'What the bleedin' 'ell's that doin' there?' he demanded angrily.

'I thought that was yer orders, Mr 'Arris,' Wilf Eccles said.

'My orders! Why, in Gawd's name, would I want yer to put a ladder up against the buildin' when I've no intention of sendin' anybody in there?'

'But ... but somebody *is* in there.'

'Yer what?'

'Fred Simpson said yer'd told 'im to go in. I didn't believe 'im at first, but 'e seemed so sure of 'imself ...'

'Let me get this straight,' Harris said. 'You *allowed* Fred Simpson to enter that buildin', even though yer could see for yerself the state it was in?'

'I ... I thought that I was only doin' what yer wanted me to, Mr 'Arris.'

Harris looked up at the blazing warehouse, at the flames which were getting ever closer to the ladder. 'You bloody fool, Simpson!' he said. 'You bloody 'eroic fool!'

The second floor was thick with grey smoke, threaded with the golden sunlight which shone in through the gap where the wall had collapsed. It took Fred Simpson's eyes a couple of seconds to adjust to the gloom, but when they had, he could just make out the vague shape standing in the corner. And then he heard a baby crying.

Keeping low to avoid most of the smoke, Fred made his way across the room. He could see the woman now and recognised her from the saloon bar of the Goldsmiths' Arms. She was holding

Cathy in one hand and a large carving knife in the other.

'We tried to get downstairs, but the fire 'ad cut us off,' Maggie told him. 'So we came up 'ere instead.'

Fred took another step forward.

'Don't come no closer,' Maggie croaked.

Fred stopped in his tracks. 'But I'll *'ave* to come closer if I'm goin' to rescue yer,' he said.

'My baby an' me don't want no rescuin',' Maggie told him. 'My baby an' me want to die together.' All the time, she was watching him with her mad eyes—waiting for him to try some trick which would force her to use the knife.

He needed time to deal with this situation, and time was just what he didn't have, because even without looking round he could tell that the fire was getting closer.

'Listen, Mrs White ...'

'She wasn't my baby till I took 'er out of 'er pram, while that girl was busy in the shop. But she is now. They don't believe it—none of 'em believe it—but she is.'

What could he tell her? Fred wondered. What could he say to make her hand over Cathy?

The wood yard cart could get no further than the edge of the crowd, but Tom and Harry were waiting there to escort George and Colleen to the very front of the mêlée.

'Oh my God!' Colleen said, looking in horror

at the warehouse. 'Are you sure they're in there?'

'They were there before the fire started,' Tom said gently, 'an' the guard the bobbie posted said nobody came out, so they must still be in there.'

Colleen started to cry. 'I wish they'd got away,' she sobbed. 'I'd rather my little Cathy had been brought up by a drunken washerwoman than that she end up like this.'

'There's 'ope yet,' Harry said. 'Fred Simpson's gone in after 'em, and whatever they're sayin' about 'im down at the station, Fred knows what 'e's doin'.'

'I know you're only tryin' to help, Harry,' George said grimly, 'but I wish you wouldn't. False hope isn't goin' to do us any good. We have to prepare ourselves for the worst.'

The smoke was getting even thicker, the air even hotter, but Maggie White had not moved an inch, and her knife still hovered over little Cathy's head.

'Yer know what yer said about the baby bein' yours?' Fred asked desperately.

'She *is* mine.'

'I know she is. I didn't believe yer when yer first told me, but now I do.'

Maggie White's mad eyes flashed with rage. 'Liar!' she screamed. 'Bloody liar!' She moved the knife closer to the baby's head. 'Me an' my Ellen just want it over with. That's all we want.'

'An' d'yer know *why* I believe yer?' Fred

asked shakily. 'I believe yer, 'cos I know yer love 'er enough to 'and 'er over to me, so I can save 'er.'

'I told yer, she don't want savin'.'

'Just look at 'er, Maggie,' Fred said. 'Look at 'er luverly little nose an' 'er perfect little eyes, an' then tell me she don't 'ave a right to live.'

'She don't want to live. She wants to go to 'eaven with me,' Maggie said stubbornly.

'You won't be goin' to 'eaven,' Fred told her.

Uncertainty crept into Maggie's expression. 'Not go to 'eaven?' she repeated.

'Yer know what it says in the Bible, don't "Thou shalt not kill." Well, if yer don't give Cathy to me now, that's what yer'll be doin'— killin' 'er.'

Fear had replaced the madness in Maggie's eyes. 'Not go to 'eaven?' she said for a second time. 'But me other baby's waitin' for me in 'eaven.'

'It's still not too late for yer,' Fred said softly. 'Give me Cathy now, an' I'm sure God will forgive yer.'

Maggie took a halting step forward, then another.

'That's it,' Fred coaxed. 'Yer doin' fine. Now why don't yer drop the knife?'

Maggie opened her right hand, and the carving knife clattered to the floor.

'Now give me the baby. Come on, Maggie. Yer know it's the right thing to do.'

Maggie held out the baby with both hands.

Moving very slowly, so as not to frighten the madwoman, Fred reached out and took Cathy from her.

The moment he had Cathy in his arms, he headed for the window, and it was not until he was nearly there that he realised Maggie wasn't with him. He spun round and saw that she was standing at the far side of the room next to the gap in the wall.

'Yer'd better get goin',' Maggie said.

'We'd all better be goin'.'

Maggie shook her head. 'I'll not be comin' with yer.'

'I can manage the both of yer.'

'I said, I'm not comin'.'

'I can't leave yer 'ere.'

'Yer can if I'm dead,' Maggie said.

'Let me 'elp yer, Maggie,' Fred begged. 'Please, for everybody's sake, let me 'elp yer.'

'You just look after the baby,' Maggie told him. 'That's yer main job now.'

She turned, and Fred realised that she was about to jump. He rushed towards her, but by the time he reached the jagged edge of the building, she was already gone.

He looked down into the river. He could see the circles in the water where she had landed, with a few bubbles rising from the centre, but Maggie did not come up again.

He thought of jumping himself, but there were no boats close enough to rescue him—and he had never learned how to swim.

The ladder to the second floor had gone long

ago, burned away by the fire on the first floor. Now, the crowd looked on in horror as the flames reached the right-hand end of the building, and licked their way greedily around the window through which Fred had entered.

'Well, that's 'im gone, poor devil,' said one man.

'Right enough,' another agreed.

The people with most to lose from the fire stood in a tight group at the front of the crowd. Colleen Taylor was softly sobbing into her husband's powerful shoulder, and George, his own face a mask of pain, was doing his best to find comforting words for his wife.

'Cathy won't have suffered,' he said. 'The fumes will have got to her before the fire did, an' it'll have been just like fallin' asleep an' never waking up again.'

Next to the Taylors, Tom Bates was talking to his sister, Mary, who had just arrived. 'It was Fred's choice,' he was saying. ' 'E knew the risks, but it was what 'e wanted to do. Yer should be very proud of 'im.'

The last member of the group, Harry Roberts, had no one to talk to, and so he stood alone, wishing that Belinda was there to take away some of the pain that he was feeling for his friends.

Another minute passed. Harry tapped George on the shoulder. 'I think it's time we got the women away from here.'

Colleen looked up. 'I don't want to go,' she said. 'I can't desert my baby now.'

'Yer not doin' yerself any good by stayin'

'ere,' Harry told her. 'I really think it's for the best that we all leave.'

'He's right,' George said. 'There's no point in torturin' ourselves any longer.'

He guided his wife through the crowd. Tom, half-carrying Mary, followed, and Harry brought up the rear.

Once they were clear of the spectators, Harry turned around and took one last look at the burning warehouse. The frame around the window on the second floor glowed a bright crimson red, and then, suddenly something was coming through it—a man.

The crowd saw the feet first, then the trunk and finally the head. For a split second, the body hung crazily in mid-air, parallel to the ground. Then it was falling, and as it fell, it twisted round, so that now the booted feet were pointed at the street.

The people below held their breath as the man plummeted towards the ground at a terrifying speed. Down and down he went, first just reaching the top of the first floor, then the ground floor, and then he was landing—to the relieved cheers of the crowd—right in the middle of the jumping sheet.

Leading Fireman Harris was at the other end of the building when Fred Simpson jumped, so by the time he reached the sheet Fred was already out of it and leaning against the fire engine with his arms crossed over his chest.

'Are yer all right, Simpson?' Harris asked.

'I got a few superficial burns an' a couple

of cuts from the glass, but I think I should survive.'

'Yer were takin' a chance, weren't yer?' Harris said. 'Yer couldn't 'ave known for sure that we 'ad the jumpin' sheet in place when yer dived out of that window.'

'I didn't 'ave much choice. Either that worked, or nuffink did. Anyway, yer've got to 'ave confidence in yer comrades, 'aven't yer?'

'Yes,' Harris said thoughtfully. 'Yes, I suppose yer 'ave. I'm sorry yer didn't succeed in what yer were tryin' to do.'

' 'Oo says I didn't succeed?' Fred asked. He uncrossed one arm, so that Harris could see nestling inside his thick fireman's jacket the tiny head of a baby. 'This is Cathy. Say 'ello to Leadin' Fireman 'Arris, Cathy.'

'Blimey!' Harris said.

'An' 'ere's somebody else 'oo'll probably be wantin' to have a word with 'er,' Fred said, seeing Colleen push her way through the crowd.

CHAPTER 25

It was the Monday morning after the fire at the warehouse, and Harry Roberts found himself standing in front of Detective Inspector Walton's desk once again.

'So what's it about this time, Roberts?' the inspector asked impatiently. 'Is it really so important that yer 'ad to go botherin' me so early in the day?'

'I've been tryin' to get in touch with yer all weekend, sir,' Harry said.

'Yes, well, I've been away, ain't I? Thought I deserved a little 'oliday after solvin' me latest case.'

'Yer latest case?'

'The little baby that went missin' from Lant Street. I found 'er, didn't I?'

Harry had to fight back the urge to smile. 'So yer did, sir,' he said. 'I was forgettin'.'

'That's why I'm an inspector and you're still a sergeant,' Walton told him. 'I never forget anyfink. An' yer still 'aven't told me what yer've come to see me about.'

'It's connected with the Taylor case, sir. Lizzie 'Odges is still in gaol.'

'An' why shouldn't she be? I've told yer before that I'm convinced she was part of the kidnappin'.'

Harry reached into his uniform pocket, produced a piece of paper, and laid it on the desk in front of Walton.

'What's this?' the inspector asked, as if he couldn't be bothered to read it himself.

'It's a sworn statement from Fireman Frederick Simpson, sir.'

'An' 'oo's 'e when 'e's at 'ome?'

' 'E's the fireman 'oo saved little Cathy Taylor from the burnin' ware'ouse.'

'Very commendable, I'm sure,' Walton said, 'but what's all this got to do with me?'

'Which means that 'e was also the last person

to see Maggie White alive.'

'So?'

'She said to 'im, an' I quote, "She wasn't my baby till I took 'er out of 'er pram, while that girl was busy in the shop." '

'What's yer point?'

'Ain't it obvious, sir?'

'If it was, I wouldn't be askin' the question, would I?'

Harry sighed. 'If Lizzie 'ad 'ave been involved in the kidnappin', Maggie White would 'ave used 'er name, instead of just callin' 'er "that girl", wouldn't she?'

'It's possible,' Walton admitted.

'An' she wouldn't 'ave said, "While she was busy in the shop", 'cos that would suggest that Lizzie knew nuffink about what was goin' to 'appen.'

'So what do you think she would 'ave said?' Walton asked aggressively.

'Somefink like, "While Liz was in the shop, like we'd agreed she'd be", or, "After Lizzie 'ad gone into the shop, like I'd told 'er to". That would make more sense if Lizzie really 'ad been involved, don't yer think?'

Walton picked up a pencil from his desk, and ran his fingers up and down it. 'Maybe yer right,' he said cautiously, 'but 'ave yer considered the other possibility?'

'An' what's that, sir?'

'That Maggie White could 'ave been lyin' to cover up for her associate.'

Harry sighed again. 'She was in a burnin' buildin' which was on the point of collapse. Is it likely that coverin' up for 'er associate was the most important thing on 'er mind?'

'No, it's not likely,' Walton conceded, 'but like I said, it is a possibility.'

'Maggie White killed 'erself shortly after she told Fred that,' Harry pointed out.

'I know that.'

'Which makes it 'er dyin' declaration, an' the law takes dyin' declarations very seriously.'

Walton frowned. 'I don't like lettin' people go once I've arrested 'em,' he said. 'It makes me look bad.'

'Yer'll look even worse if it comes to court an' Lizzie's found not guilty.'

'Per'aps yer right,' Walton said. 'I'll see to it that she's released tomorrow.'

'There's a lot of bad feelin' about Lizzie's arrest down Lant Place way. There's even talk about raisin' a fightin' fund so they can 'ire a really sharp shyster to get 'er off.'

The pencil in Walton's hands snapped in two. 'I'll see to it that she's released today,' he said.

Harry smiled. 'Yes, I think that'd be yer best course of action. Can I go now, sir?'

'Yes, yer can go,' Walton growled, but when Harry was nearly at the door, he said, 'There is one more thing.'

'Yes, sir?'

'If yer were so keen on gettin' Lizzie 'Odges released from 'Olloway, why didn't yer bring this fireman of yours down 'ere with yer as a witness?'

The triumphant smile instantly disappeared

from Harry's face. 'Fred's a bit busy today,' he said. 'Got a few troubles of 'is own, the poor lad 'as.'

Fred Simpson, accompanied by the solicitor who the Firemen's Association had appointed to argue his case before the Board of Inquiry, walked across the fire station quadrangle towards the commander's office.

'Good luck, Fred!' Wilf Eccles called to him from across the yard.

'Yes, good luck!' echoed Leading Fireman Harris, who was standing next to him.

Fred and the solicitor entered the building and came to a halt in front of a door with a large brass plate on it which read: 'Commander Wells'.

Fred coughed nervously.

'I told you not to worry,' said the solicitor.

'With respect, Mr Keatin', sir, it's all very well for you to say that, but you're not the one 'oo's in great danger of losin' 'is job,' Fred replied.

Now that he knew he was not a coward, he no longer had any qualms about marrying Mary. However, if he lost his position—if he was so destitute that he was forced to take a job as a casual labourer at the docks—he did not see how Mary's mother would ever give her consent to the union. And who could blame her?

The door was opened by one of the commander's two deputies. 'Fireman Simpson?' he asked formally, though he saw Fred nearly every day, and knew exactly who he was.

'Yes, sir.'

'You and your legal representative may now come inside.'

The commander and his other deputy were sitting behind the commander's oak desk, in front of which had been placed two chairs. 'Please be seated,' Wells said.

Fred and the solicitor sat down. The young fireman looked across the desk at the three men who held his future in their hands, and his heart sunk as he saw the grim expression each of them had on his face.

'I will outline certain facts about this case, and you will say whether or not they are true,' the commander told Fred. 'Do you understand, Fireman Simpson?'

'Yes, sir.'

'On the twenty-eighth of August, you were part of the team led by Leading Fireman Harris which was called to a fire in twenty-six Keppel Street. Is that correct?'

'Yes, sir.'

'Leading Fireman Harris assigned you the task of entering the building to see whether or not it had been fully evacuated. Also correct?'

'Yes, sir.'

'The next time that Leading Fireman Harris saw you, you were standing in the crowd, watching the fire. You had not checked the whole building, as is evidenced by the fact that there was still an old lady at the back of the house—an old lady who Leading Fireman Harris then rescued. Correct?'

'Yes, sir.'

'And are you aware of the fact that, due

to the delay, Leading Fireman Harris's rescue operation was considerably riskier than any rescue operation carried out by you would have been? In other words, that your failure to carry out your duty endangered one of your comrades?'

'Yes, sir, I am aware of that.'

'What is your explanation for your conduct?'

'I believe I was sufferin' from concussion, sir. I think that when the ceilin' collapsed, I got 'it on the 'ead.'

The commander looked questioningly at his two deputies, and then returned his gaze to Fred. 'I see. Can you prove that assertion?' he asked.

Fred thought back to the hypnotist. 'No, sir,' he admitted, 'but I really believe that's what 'appened.'

The commander and his deputies put their heads together and started whispering.

They don't believe me, Fred thought. Yer can tell just by lookin' at 'em that they don't believe me.

The whispering had stopped and the commander was looking at him again. 'In the fire service, our most valuable piece of equipment is not an axe or a ladder,' Wells said. 'It is the trust we have in our comrades, and the trust they have in us. We must know that we can rely on them. We cannot operate in any other way, given the dangerous circumstances under which we work.'

'I know that, sir.'

'Leading Fireman Harris trusted you when

he sent you into the building—and, on the evidence, you would seem to have betrayed that trust.'

'Officer Simpson did behave with considerable courage at a fire in a warehouse on Morgan's Lane, just last Friday,' Fred's solicitor pointed out.

Commander Wells frowned. 'While he was under suspension,' he said. 'That is another disciplinary matter which we must deal with, *if* Officer Simpson can satisfactorily answer the present charge.' He turned back to Fred. 'The question we on the Board must ask ourselves is, "Did you, in fact, suffer from a failure of nerve at the fire on Keppel Street?" We will listen to what you and your attorney have to say, but I must tell you that based on the evidence, it is very likely that our verdict will be that you did. Do you understand that?'

Fred looked straight into his commander's eyes. 'Yes, sir. I do understand it.'

'Very well,' the commander said. He turned to the solicitor. 'You may begin your plea, Mr Keating.'

Lizzie Hodges stepped through the front gate of Holloway Women's Prison, and gulped in the first lungful of free air she'd tasted for a week.

'I never thought they'd let me out!' she shouted at the traffic passing by on the Camden Road. 'I thought they was goin' to keep me in there for ever.'

She'd had good reason for such thoughts.

Inspector Walton had made it quite plain that he was convinced she was guilty, and so would the jury be when she came to trial. Even without Walton's chilling words, why should she ever have assumed that things would go her way? She'd had bad luck all her life. The only good thing that had ever happened to her was when George and Colleen Taylor ...

She frowned. She was going to have to see Mr and Mrs Taylor, to apologise for the way she had behaved. It would be a hard thing—mumbling her words under their reproachful gaze—but it was still something she wanted, and needed, to do.

And after she had had her say, and they'd shown her to the door? A shiver ran through Lizzie.

'I ain't *really* escaped prison at all,' she told herself, because once she had left the Taylors' home, she would have no choice but to go straight from Lant Place to St Saviour's Workhouse.

She walked on, head down, her whole body racked with the worst kind of misery.

'Lizzie,' said a voice to her left.

She looked up and saw Colleen standing there. 'Oh, Mrs Taylor!' she said.

'My husband would have been here as well,' Colleen told her, 'but work down at the wood yard has been rather neglected over the past week, you know, an' he decided he'd better go in an' do some catchin' up.'

Lizzie took Colleen's right hand in both of

hers. 'Can yer ever forgive me, Mrs Taylor?' she asked.

'I hated you at first because I thought that you'd stolen my little baby ...'

'Oh, I never would 'ave, Mrs Taylor. I'd never 'ave done anyfink to 'urt you.'

'Then I hated you because you'd run away without tellin' me what had happened ...'

'I couldn't face yer. I felt so guilty about not takin' better care of 'er.'

'An' then, yesterday, I realised that even if you had come and told me, it probably wouldn't have made any difference, because whatever had happened, Harry and Tom would have conducted their investigation in the same way.'

'It was still wrong of me,' Lizzie said.

'Yes, it was,' Colleen agreed. 'But I put myself in your shoes for a minute, an' I can't say for certain that I'd have acted in any other way.'

'So yer've forgiven me?' Lizzie asked hopefully.

'Yes, I've forgiven you, Lizzie,' Colleen said, 'an' so has my husband.'

Tears came to Lizzie's eyes. 'Yer both too good, Mrs Taylor,' she sobbed. 'Far too good. I don't know 'ow I'll ever be able to thank yer for yer kindness.' She reluctantly let go of Colleen's hand, and turned to walk down Camden Road.

'And just where do you think you're goin', young woman?' Colleen asked.

Lizzie shrugged. 'I don't know. Maybe I'll try one of the other work'ouses, 'stead of goin' back to St Saviour's. At least it'll be a change.'

Colleen put her hands on her hips. 'I never thought you could be so selfish.'

'Selfish?'

'Yes, selfish. So selfish that you'd leave me to handle the twins on my own.'

Lizzie's eyes widened with astonishment. 'Does that ... does that mean yer'll 'ave me back?' she gasped.

'Not just *have* you back,' Colleen said. '*Want* you back.'

Lizzie threw her arms around Colleen. 'Yer more than just good,' she said. 'Yer a bloomin' saint, that's what you are.'

Colleen smiled. 'St Colleen,' she said. 'I don't think there's been one of them before.'

This is it, Fred thought, as his solicitor, Mr Keating, stood up to present his defence before the Board of Inquiry. The moment he'd been dreading for over a week had finally arrived, and—as the commander had pointed out—the odds were heavily stacked against him.

'I would like to request that the Board adjourn for a few minutes and reconvene in the fire officers' recreation room,' Mr Keating told the three men on the other side of the desk.

The commander frowned. 'Reconvene in the recreation room? That would be a highly irregular procedure, Mr Keating. What purpose would it serve?'

'The recreation room is the place where we have set up the equipment necessary for us to carry out our demonstration,' the solicitor told him.

'What demonstration?'

'It is a little difficult to explain to non-specialists such as yourselves,' Keating said, with what sounded like genuine regret in his voice, 'but if you will just bear with us for a few minutes, all will become clear.'

The commander looked at his two deputies, who both nodded their agreement. 'We will do as you ask,' the commander said, 'but I warn you that if this turns out to be nothing more than a waste of time, it will damage your client's case even further.'

'I promise you that this will definitely not be a waste of time,' Keating said.

Fred, rising from his chair, wished that he could feel half as confident as his attorney sounded.

The recreation room had been transformed. The billiard table, normally the centre of the firemen's interest, was covered over with planks, and on the planks stood a large metal box with two arms projecting from it.

'What is that?' the commander asked.

'I don't know the technical term,' the solicitor admitted, 'but it's used to show living pictures.'

'And are living pictures to play a part in your so-called demonstration?'

'Indeed, they are central to it.'

A slim blond man, who had been carefully fixing reels to the machine's metal arms, now came over to join them. 'This gentlemen is Mr Philip Taylor,' Keating said. 'It is his living pictures we will shortly be watching.'

Philip smiled and pointed to rows of chairs which faced a white sheet pinned to the wall. 'If you would care to take your seats, gentlemen,' he said.

The puzzled Board sat down, and Philip turned to his other piece of equipment—a gramophone—and slid a record into place.

'What is going on here?' the commander demanded, seeing what Philip was doing. 'We're here to conduct a serious Board of Inquiry, not listen to music.'

'The sound of the projector is sometimes rather distracting if you're not used to it ...'

'The projector? Is that the box you use to show your living pictures with?'

'Exactly. As I said, it can be distracting. Music tends to deaden the noise, and so enables you to concentrate more on what you're actually seeing.'

What he'd said was true, in a way, but that was not the main reason that Philip had decided to use the gramophone as part of his strategy. He'd had a lot of experience of putting on shows, and he knew that however dramatic the pictures were to begin with, music always made them seem even more intense.

'Very well, we will have the music,' the commander said reluctantly, 'but I warn you again, Mr Keating ...'

'I'm sure you'll find it a very satisfactory demonstration, Commander,' the solicitor said.

An' if he don't, I'm out on me 'ear, Fred thought, taking up a position behind the commander's chair.

Philip closed the heavy curtains and, apart from the single light on the projector, the room was plunged into darkness.

'Would you mind starting the music now, Mr Keating?' Philip asked the solicitor.

Keating placed the needle on the record. A hiss was followed by the opening strains of the William Tell Overture. Philip, for his part, switched on the projector.

At first, there was just a flickering white light on the sheet, and then the image of the empty warehouse in Morgan's Lane appeared, with a large crowd gathered outside it and a team of firemen attempting to put out the blaze.

'Remarkable!' said Commander Wells, who had never seen living pictures before.

A ladder was quickly positioned against the wall, and Fred started climbing. On the screen, the flames looked even closer to the ladder than they had been in real life, and Commander Wells whistled softly to himself.

As the music sped up, Fred disappeared through the second-floor window. The camera moved around, showing anxious faces in the crowd, and then returned to the window.

Philip, standing next to the projector, grinned. He always knew when he had his audience gripped, and this one was actually holding its breath.

The window frame caught fire, burning—on the screen—as brightly as the midday sun, and then, through the inferno which surrounded the window, came a pair of legs. The camera followed Fred's fall from the window to the moment he hit the landing sheet.

The scene changed again, and the camera was closer to Fred, filming both him and the little child he held protectively inside his coat.

The screen went blank, and the members of the Board of Inquiry realised that they were applauding furiously.

Philip opened the curtains again, and Mr Keating walked around the chairs so that he was standing in front of the board.

'Gentlemen, having seen those living pictures, how can you doubt my client's courage?' he asked. 'Would a man who went up the ladder under those conditions have been afraid to enter the ground floor of a building which was scarcely burning at all? Would a man who jumped from a second-floor window—not even knowing if the landing sheet was in place underneath—have had any hesitation about carrying an old lady from a room at the same level as the street? Of course not. You must either decide to believe my client, gentlemen, or you must dispute what you have just seen with your own eyes. I can think of no third alternative.'

'And neither can I,' Commander Wells said with considered gravity. 'Fireman Simpson?'

'Sir?'

'Would you please come here and face the Board.'

Fred walked around the chairs and took up a position next to Mr Keating.

'It is the decision of this Board that you were guilty of no misconduct at the Keppel Street fire,' Commander Wells said, 'and you will be reinstated immediately.'

'Thank you, sir.'

'With regard to the other matter—the Morgan's Lane fire,' the commander continued, 'you were under suspension at the time, and clearly had no business going up the ladder at all. Such breaches of discipline cannot be ignored and you will have to be punished. Do you understand that?'

'Yes, sir.'

The commander's face broke into a broad grin. 'I'm sure a small fine would prove an adequate penalty,' he said.

It was one o'clock in the afternoon, and Fred Simpson was standing at the counter of the saloon bar in the Goldsmiths' Arms, arguing with Mr Wilkins, the landlord.

'An' I'm tellin' you that you can't buy any drinks 'ere, Fred, an' that's final,' the landlord said firmly.

'I just want to buy one for 'im,' said Fred, pointing to Philip, who was sitting at one of the tables in the corner.

' 'E came in 'ere with *you*, so the answer's no.'

' 'E's just been an' saved me bacon. Won't yer let me at least pay for 'is beer?'

The landlord looked across at Philip, and then back at Fred. 'Yer can buy one for 'im,' he said reluctantly, 'but yer not buyin' one for yerself.'

'But Mr Wilkins ...'

'Yer've got a week's free beer in this place,

whether yer like it or not. An' if that doesn't suit yer, yer can take yer custom elsewhere. Fair enough?'

Fred grinned. 'Fair enough,' he agreed.

Fred took the drinks over to the table. ' 'Ere yer are,' he said, sliding Philip's pint across to him. 'Yer did a brilliant job for me with that Board of Inquiry.'

'Yes, it wasn't bad, was it?' Philip said modestly. 'I was working on it all weekend.'

'Not bad?' Fred repeated. 'When I saw meself jumping out of that window, even *I* was worried about me. 'Owever did yer manage to make it look so frightenin'?'

'Easy,' Philip said. 'It *was* frightening. Oh, I admit I did cut it around a little to increase the tension, but mainly what you saw was what you did.'

Fred took a sip of his drink. He'd not really enjoyed his beer since he'd been put on suspension, but this—the first pint after his exoneration—tasted marvellous.

'I'll never be able to pay yer back for what yer've done for me,' he told Philip.

Philip smiled. 'Don't worry about it.'

'I like to pay me debts.'

Philip's smile broadened. 'You already have. You just don't know about it yet.'

' 'Ow d'yer mean?'

'Think about it,' Philip told him.

'I 'aven't got a clue what yer talkin' about, Philip. Honestly, I 'aven't.'

'Your Board of Inquiry was thrilled by my living pictures, weren't they?'

'Well, of course they were. That's why they let me off.'

'They're experienced firemen, who've seen a lot in their time with the Brigade, so if *they* were thrilled, just think how the general public's going to feel.'

'Yer mean ...?'

'I mean that what you've given me, Fred, is the living picture that's going to make my name.'

CHAPTER 26

George Taylor and Fred Simpson looked around the upstairs room of the Goldsmiths' Arms. Three tables had been set out in a horseshoe shape, and each of them was positively weighed down with vast quantities of food.

George ran his eyes over the eels, oysters, slices of chicken and best ham, pies and pastries. 'He always does a good job, does Ollie Wilkins,' he said with satisfaction.

'He does,' Fred agreed. 'I remember Tom an' Annie's weddin'. That was the first time I danced with Mary.'

'You mean it was the first time she danced with you?' George said. 'If I'm rememberin' things right, it was her what did the askin'.'

Fred had changed a great deal since that day. The baby-faced features which had been his curse had melted away to reveal a strong jaw and handsome nose, but he had never quite got out of the habit of blushing, and he blushed now.

'Well, maybe she did do the askin',' he admitted, 'but I'd 'ave got round to it.'

'Maybe you would—eventually,' George said drily. 'Do you know what Sam Clarke told me—in this very pub—the day that me an' Colleen moved into Lant Place?'

'No. What?'

'He said that when it comes to bein' crafty about gettin' their own way, women are halfway round the track before we've come out of the startin' gate.'

Fred grinned. 'Sam's probably right, but I'm still glad I'm marryin' my Mary next year.'

'So you should be. She's a lovely lass. An' thank heavens women *are* crafty, because if they always left things up to us, we'd be in a real mess.'

'Now yer *definitely* right there,' Fred agreed. He hesitated. 'George, about payin' for all this lot ...'

'That's already taken care of.'

'I've got some savin's.'

'I'm sure you have, a careful lad like you, but you'll need all of 'em—an' more—when it comes to settin' up home.'

'It is my engagement party,' Fred protested.

'An' it's *my* way of sayin' how grateful me an' Colleen are to you for rescuin' our Cathy.'

Fred shrugged awkwardly. 'That was nuffink. All part of a day's work.'

'So you're always jumpin' out of blazin'

second-floor windows, carryin' babies are you?'

'Well, maybe not *every* day,' Fred admitted.

'You're a real hero, Fred, an' don't try to argue about it. I may have just missed the jump, but I've seen our Philip's living pictures of it half a dozen times.'

'It was the way 'e put it together that made it look so excitin',' Fred said. 'Anyway, I didn't do nuffink any other fireman wouldn't 'ave done in my place.'

George nodded his head, as if he agreed, then said, 'So why are they givin' you a medal for it?'

Fred looked suddenly very sheepish. 'Well, yer know 'ow it is with medals.'

'Yes,' replied George, who had a few of his own. 'I believe I do.'

The guests started to arrive at around half past four, and by five o'clock the big room was packed and buzzing with conversation. May Bates and her family—as was only right—sat at the top table with Fred Simpson, but apart from that, there was no formal seating plan, and the people of Lant Place changed their seats almost as quickly as they swapped gossip.

The party was already a success, George Taylor decided, and when the band arrived, it would be even better. He found himself remembering other parties he had attended. The one that Colleen's parents, Paddy and Cathy O'Leary, had held to celebrate their twenty-fifth wedding anniversary, after which Philip had run away to work with the magic lantern man. The big one his brother-in-law, Michael, had thrown to welcome the arrival of the new century, when, in the glow of a dying bonfire, George had first kissed Colleen and told her that he'd loved her for years. Tom and Annie's wedding party, held in this very room ...

They all seemed like yesterday, but some of them were already long in the past.

The kids are only babies now, but I'll be a grandfather before I know it, he thought—and was surprised to discover that he found the prospect rather pleasing.

Despite Lil Clarke's firmly held belief that families should stick together on occasions like this—because, after all, that was the only respectable thing to do—Eddie Clarke had finally managed to detach himself from his parents and was sitting next to his best mate, Joey Bates.

'Do yer know yet when yer next fight is goin' to be?' Eddie asked Joey.

'Week on Saturday. An' guess what? I'm toppin' the bill. I mean, it's nuffink to get excited about. I know it's only a boarded-up archway I'll be fightin' in—'

'There's nuffink wrong with the archway,' Eddie interrupted. 'Yer get good experience in the archway. Imagine it—only a few weeks ago, yer were the warm-up fight, an' now 'ere yer are, at the top of the bill.'

'Yes,' Joey said. 'Worryin', ain't it?'

'Why is it worryin'?'

' 'Cos if I'm top of the bill, it stands to reason

I'll be comin' up against the best fighter in the 'ouse.'

'No, it don't,' Eddie said. 'It means yer'll be comin' up against the *second* best fighter in the 'ouse.'

A puzzled expression came to Joey's face. 'An' just 'ow do yer work that out?' he asked.

Eddie grinned. ' 'Cos you're the best, ain't yer?'

Joey smiled back gratefully. 'Thanks, Eddie. I think yer the best pal a bloke ever 'ad,' he said.

'The feelin's mutual,' Eddie said awkwardly.

There were a few seconds of uncomfortable, embarrassed silence, then Joey said, ' 'Ow's things at the garage?'

'Fine,' Eddie replied. 'We've nearly finished the modifications on the Renault Sixteen.'

'So when will yer be racin' 'er?'

Eddie looked up the table to make sure his mother was fully occupied. 'Unless the weather turns bad, it should be in the next few weeks,' he whispered.

'I can see the newspaper 'eadlines now,' Joey said. ' "Eddie Clarke—the new world champion. Southwark boy's amazing drive smashes all records." '

'I wish it was as easy as yer makin' it sound,' Eddie said, 'but there's goin' to be a lot of competition. I've 'eard about this bloke in France 'oo's—' He stopped suddenly, and gazed, wide eyed, across the room.

'What yer lookin' at?' Joey asked.

'That,' Eddie said, pointing to the space

between the tables, where the Taylor twins were crawling around on the floor under the supervision of Lizzie Hodges.

'What exactly is it I'm supposed to be watchin'?' Joey said. 'Ted an' Cathy?'

Eddie snorted. 'No, not the kids!'

'Then what?'

' 'Er! Lizzie!'

Joey cocked his head to one side. Lizzie was wearing a new blue dress with white lace cuffs and collar. Her brown hair seemed less mousy than it used to, and shone in the sunshine which filtered in through the window, and her face had lost its pinched look now she was off workhouse food and getting her daily ration of Colleen Taylor's cooking.

'Oh, I see what yer mean now,' Joey said. 'She's turnin' into a bit of a cracker, ain't she? Yer know, I really wouldn't mind chancin' me arm with 'er.'

Eddie gave his friend a hard look. 'That's just what I was thinkin' about meself,' he said.

Peggy Clarke was sitting in between her parents, where—Lil said—she couldn't get into trouble.

'Did I tell yer that I went to see me goat today?' she asked her parents.

'That's not news,' her mother said disdainfully. 'Yer go to see yer goat nearly *every* day. I can't understand what yer see in 'em, meself. Nasty, smelly creatures, goats are. It don't make no sense to 'ave anyfink to do with goats—not when yer've been brought up so respectable.'

' 'Ow is old Napoleon?' Sam asked.

'Luverly,' Peggy replied. ' 'E's as proud as punch of 'is golden coat. He likes it at the fire station, 'cos sometimes they give 'im old fire 'oses to eat 'is way through.'

'With chips?' Sam asked.

Peggy shook her head. ' 'E don't like chips. They're too greasy for 'im—give 'im a bad stomach.'

'I know 'ow 'e must feel,' Sam told her. 'I've often felt meself, when I was munchin' me way through a bag of chips, that an old fire 'ose might make a nice change.'

' 'Ave ycr, dad?' Peggy asked.

'Of course 'e 'asn't,' Lil said. ' 'E's just tryin' to be funny again. I don't know where 'e gets that sense of 'umour of 'is from. 'Is mum an' dad were such nice, quiet people.'

'Anyway, I'm glad now that Napoleon's livin' at the fire station,' Peggy said, ' 'cos—'

'If ycr ask me, there'll soon be another romance bloomin' in Lant Place,' Lil interrupted.

'Now what makes yer say a thing like that, me old dutch?' Sam asked.

'Well, I was just lookin' across at our Eddie—'oo, by the way, should be with 'is family instead of consortin' with a street fighter—when I couldn't help noticin' ...'

Whatever Lil couldn't help noticing, Peggy would never find out, though, because she had drifted off into her dream world. 'Yes, I'm glad Napoleon's gone,' she said quietly to herself, ' 'cos 'e'd never 'ave got on with the performin' seal I want to talk me mum into lettin' me buy.'

At the top table, George and Colleen Taylor were talking about Maggie White.

'You know, there's times I can't help feelin' sorry for her,' Colleen said.

'Sorry for her!' George repeated. 'In case you've forgotten, the woman kidnapped your baby, put you through days of anguish, an' in the end would have let our Cathy die in a blazin' buildin' if Fred hadn't stepped in to prevent it. An' you can still say that you feel sorry for her?'

'She wasn't bein' herself,' Colleen said. 'Not actin' like the woman that I used to know at all. Who's to say what any of us would do if we'd been through what she had?'

'You'd never have stolen another woman's baby, I do know that.'

Colleen smiled. 'Just like a man.'

'What do you mean?'

'Men are always such experts on everythin' under the sun, aren't they? They *know* how it must feel to carry a baby around inside yourself for nine months. They *know* what it's like to give birth, don't they?'

'Well, not exactly,' George admitted.

'Not *at all*,' Colleen told him. 'I sometimes wish that men could have babies now an' again, then they wouldn't go round sayin' such daft things.'

George laughed. 'Maybe you're right, love.'

'Of course I'm right,' Colleen said, smiling

back at him. 'I'm a woman, aren't I?'

Philip Taylor arrived at the party a little late, and not alone. With him was a pretty young woman with black hair which hung in ringlets.

'I'd like to introduce you to Miss Ellie Dawes,' he said to Fred. 'Ellie, this is Fireman Fred Simpson, the hero of the hour, if not of the whole year.'

'I'm very pleased to meet yer,' Ellie said shyly. 'Wasn't it kind of Mr Taylor—'

'Philip!' her escort said emphatically.

Ellie reddened and looked confused. 'Oh, I've done it again. Wasn't it kind of *Philip* to bring me to yer party?' Her confusion deepened. 'I mean, it was very kind of you to 'ave a party in the first place, but Mr Tay—Philip ... was kind to ask me as well. If yer understand me ...' she said, before finally drying up.

Fred laughed. 'An' I thought *I* was good at gettin' meself tied in knots.'

Ellie joined in with his laughter. 'Oh, I'm the world champion at it,' she said. More confusion crossed her face. 'I mean, I'm not sayin' yer not very good at it yerself. I'm sure that yer've often found yerself in a situation where yer simply don't know what to say next ...'

Philip put his hand on the girl's shoulder. 'Why don't you try to relax a little?' he suggested.

'That's it,' Ellie agreed. 'That's what I should do. I should try an' relax a bit more.' She closed her eyes, put her hands together, and took a few deep breaths.

'So 'ow's the livin' picture that yer took of me gettin' on?' Fred asked Philip.

'Goin' like a house on fire,' Philip said. 'Like a *warehouse* on fire, anyway. Half the music halls in London are begging me to let them show it, and I'm already getting requests from several big entertainment palaces in the provinces.'

'That's good.'

'You're going to have to get used to being famous, Fred. You'll have to learn to take it in your stride when people stop you in the street and want to shake your hand.'

'Yer don't think that will 'appen, do yer?' Fred asked, obviously alarmed at the prospect.

'It's bound to,' Philip said. 'And I'll tell you something else. If you ever get tired of being a fireman, there's always a job for you in my living pictures.'

'Thanks very much,' Fred said, 'but I think I'll stick to what I know.'

Ellie had opened her eyes again. 'I'm feelin' much better now,' she said.

'That's good,' Philip told her, 'because I'd like you to meet my brother, George.'

'Yer brother! Yer never mentioned nuffink about yer brother bein' here.'

Philip grinned. 'I didn't, did I? I wonder why? Maybe I was worried it would scare you off coming.'

'But yer brother,' Ellie said. 'I'm not sure I'd feel comfortable meetin' yer family. I mean I'm sure 'e's a very nice bloke. I wasn't suggestin' for a minute that ...'

Philip laughed again. 'I'm glad to see your

relaxation exercises have done you some real good, Ellie.' He turned to Fred Simpson. 'If you'll excuse us?'

'O' course.'

'I don't want to seem rude to yer brother, but couldn't we just ... I mean, couldn't yer tell him I'm not really ... that I 'aven't really ...' Ellie said.

Philip took her arm and began to gently steer her to where George and Colleen were sitting. 'You'll like them,' he promised, 'and they'll like you. Who wouldn't?'

Tom Bates and Harry Roberts were standing in the corner of the room, pints of beer in their hands, talking, as usual, about life on the river.

'It's the tides that yer've always got to be careful of down Lime'ouse way,' Harry was explaining, 'because if yer've got a strong ebb tide an' yer don't watch out—'

He stopped, not because he had forgotten what he wanted to say, but because of the heavy tap—almost a poke—that he felt on his left shoulder. He turned around to find Belinda standing behind him. Tom, who had felt a simultaneous tap, also turned, and was now facing his wife.

'That's enough shop for one day,' Belinda said. 'We want to have a serious talk with you.'

'You want to 'ave a serious talk with both of us? Is that what yer mean?' Harry asked.

'No, you've got it wrong as usual, you bone-headed policeman. I want to have a serious talk with you, and Annie wants to have a serious talk with Tom.'

'I see,' Harry said, although he didn't, really.

Tom and Annie Bates made their way back to their seats on the top table.

'So what's all this serious talk business?' Tom asked, when they had sat down.

'I just thought you'd better know that soon I'm going to have to start cutting down on the hours that I put in on the business,' Annie told him.

'But I thought yer liked it.'

'I love it—Belinda makes everything so much fun—but once I begin putting on weight ...'

'Puttin' on weight? You! You eat like an 'orse, an' yer never gain an inch.'

'Once I start putting on weight,' Annie repeated firmly, 'the doctor said it would be wise for me to rest more.'

'Doctor?' Tom said, alarmed. 'There ain't anyfink wrong with yer, is there?'

Annie smiled impishly. 'Well, if you can call my condition having something wrong with you then I suppose I am ill. And it's all your fault for never leaving me alone, Tom Bates.'

'My fault?' Tom repeated. 'But I ain't ...' He had picked up a fork while they were talking, but now he dropped it again with a loud clatter. ' 'Ave I got this straight? Yer don't mean ... yer can't be tellin' me that you're ...'

'My mum'll love being a grandmother,' Annie said. 'It's very respectable to be a grandmother.'

'This serious talk that yer told me we were goin' to 'ave ...' Harry said.

'Plenty of time for that later, my dear man.' Belinda lifted an oyster to her mouth and swallowed it with great relish. 'It's remarkable, you know.'

'What's remarkable?' Harry asked. 'That oyster?'

'You are being particularly dense today, aren't you? Of course I'm not talking about the oyster. I mean it's remarkable that I am here today. Do you realise that if I hadn't met Annie at the telephone exchange, there would have been a whole area of London—and so many people—I would still have known nothing about.'

'An' are yer glad or sorry?'

'Oh, very glad. I always have the most wonderful time *sarf* of the river.'

Harry grinned. 'Yer'll never sound like a cockney, no matter 'ow 'ard yer try,' he said.

'Don't be so certain of that,' Belinda said. 'I met a chap called Shaw at a house party once. Writes plays. Said he was thinking about writing a play about a professor who tries to teach a flower girl perfect English.'

'So?'

'So maybe I could hire some kind of cockney professor to do the reverse on me.'

'Why should yer ever even *want* to learn to speak cockney?' Harry asked.

Belinda looked as if she was about to tell him, then changed her mind.

'What are yer thinkin' about now?' Harry said.

'I was thinking that it's about time you came home with me one weekend.'

'Home? Yer mean to yer flat?'

'Good heavens, no. You spend so much time there already that you're like part of the furniture. A big, ugly, part of the furniture, I might add. No, I think that you should come with me to that crumbling pile of ancestral ruins which the Benson family—with one notable exception—call home.'

'But 'ow would yer parents feel about me turnin' up out of the blue?'

'My parents will undoubtedly hate it, my dear man, but it simply has to be done.'

'No point in goin' round stirrin' up trouble unnecessarily,' Harry said.

'But it *is* necessary. They may not like the fact that I'm going to marry a common police sergeant, but I think they still have the right to meet him.'

Harry almost choked on the jellied eel he was eating. 'Are you askin' me to marry yer?' he gasped.

'Certainly not!' Belinda said emphatically. 'The very idea of me doing such a thing! You're the man—and that means it's your job to make the proposal.'

The meal had ended and the band, which would be playing them long into the night, had not yet arrived.

' 'Ow are we goin' to fill in the time till the

music starts?' Sam Clarke wondered to his wife. 'I know what we could do. We could 'ave some speeches.'

'You an' yer speeches,' Lil said. 'I remember 'ow yer embarrassed me to death at our Annie's weddin', makin' that speech of yours about waitin' for yer boat to come in.'

Sam smiled his special smile, and even after so many years of marriage Lil didn't recognise it for what it was—a signal that he was about to have some fun.

'I was readin' an interestin' article in the paper the other day,' he said. 'It seems that speeches are becomin' a very popular thing among yer respectable classes.'

Lil narrowed her eyes. 'Are yer takin' the mickey out of me, Sam Clarke?' she demanded.

'Now would I do that?' Sam asked innocently. ' 'Ave I ever in all the years we've been chained together—I mean, married—'ave I ever taken the mickey out of you?'

'There 'ave been a few times when I've 'ad me suspicions about it,' Lil said.

'Totally unfounded,' Sam assured her.

'An' it was true what yer said about speeches bein' popular with yer respectable classes?'

'As true as I'm sittin' in this pub,' Sam said, raising his backside slightly off the chair.

'Well, in that case I don't see the 'arm in us 'avin' a couple,' Lil said. 'Why don't yer suggest it?'

'If yer really sure yer want me to.'

'Only, for 'eaven's sake, Sam, don't be too obvious about it, will yer?'

'Right-oh,' Sam said.

He picked up his spoon and banged it down on the table several times. 'Speech!' he shouted. 'Come on, young Fred. This is your party. Give us a speech!'

Sam had started the ball rolling, but now nearly everyone had joined in—all of them banging the table and demanding a speech—and it was impossible for Fred to go on pretending he hadn't heard them.

There was only one thing he could do. He rose to his feet. 'I'm not very good with words,' he told the grinning faces which surrounded him, 'so I'll keep this short.'

'That's what they always say—at the beginnin',' Harry Roberts shouted.

'I'm not what yer might call widely travelled,' Fred continued, 'so I ain't got much to compare it with, but I think Lant Place is the finest street on earth.'

There were loud cheers, and Tom Bates called out, 'Not got a way with words, 'e says? I'll swear the man's nuffink less than a blinkin' orator!'

'I know the street ain't much to look at,' Fred pressed on. 'I mean, it ain't no Piccadilly or Oxford Street ...'

'Not as much 'orse muck!' Sam Clarke said.

' 'Ush! Yer embarrassin' me again,' Lil Clarke told him in a loud whisper.

'... but I can't see as 'ow yer could ever 'ope to find kinder, friendlier people anywhere in the world than yer'll meet in Lant Place,' Fred said, 'an' when me an' my Mary get married ...' more cheers from the guests '... I only 'ope that we'll be able to get ourselves an 'ouse of our own on the Place, so I'll be livin' even closer to yer than I am now.'

He sat down, blushing and breathless, to a prolonged cheer and much fork banging.

'I made a real fool of meself, standin' up there an' talking like that,' he said to Mary.

She squeezed his hand tightly. 'No yer didn't,' she said. 'Yer were wonderful.'

'Blimey! If yer think that, yer really *must* love me,' Fred told her, blushing an even deeper red.

EPILOGUE

to start a new life somewhere else, and when
the day finally came, she would go down to
the river and force herself across the bridge
one more time.

She would be . . . she did not know exactly.
She could not let herself believe for too long

She was calling herself Ginny Hope now. All day
long, she breathed in the stink of leather at the
tannery where she worked, and at night, when
she had dragged herself back to the fourpence-a-
night lodging house on Flower and Dean Street,
Spitalfields, it was to be greeted by the sickly,
oily smell of bloaters, the food of the poor.

She could not stand to be near the river any
longer. Even walking across one of the bridges
was enough to bring back to her the sudden
cold shock, the feeling of the water closing in
around her.

Sometimes, as she sat in the kitchen of the
doss house, watching ha'penny tea and sugar
mix boil up in the same pan as her eggs, she
would think back to the old days. There had
always been clean sheets then, and when she
had gone to sleep it had been in the privacy of
her own bedroom instead of in a long dormitory
where fifty other women laid their heads.

She was drinking less now, and even out of
the meagre wages the tannery paid her, she was
managing to save a little.

Patience, that was what it took, she thought. It
was her very lack of patience which had defeated
her the last time. It would not happen again.
She would wait until she had stopped drinking
altogether and had enough money behind her

to start a new life somewhere else, and when that day finally came, she would go down to the river and force herself to cross the bridge into Southwark.

She would be careful this time—very careful. She would wait for her opportunity for as long as was necessary, but when it came, she would snatch it with both hands.

It might take her a year, she thought. Perhaps even longer. But in the end, she would get her little Ellen back again.

The publishers hope that this book has given you enjoyable reading. Large Print Books are especially designed to be as easy to see and hold as possible. If you wish a complete list of our books, please ask at your local library or write directly to: Magna Large Print Books, Long Preston, North Yorkshire, BD23 4ND, England.

This Large Print Book for the Partially sighted, who cannot read normal print, is published under the auspices of

THE ULVERSCROFT FOUNDATION